I0645941

FABLE

Also by the author:
Realms of Shadowblood Trilogy
SHRILL
FABLE
FIRESTORM (coming soon)

FABLE

BOOK TWO OF REALMS OF SHADOWBLOOD

TROY M. WILLIAMS

First published in 2021 in Melbourne, Australia

Copyright © Troy M. Williams 2021

The moral rights of the author have been asserted.

All rights reserved. Except as permitted under the *Australian Copyright Act 1968*
(for example, a fair dealing for the purposes of study, research, criticism or review),
no part of this book may be reproduced, stored in a retrieval system, communicated
or transmitted in any form or by any means without prior written permission.

This publication is a work of fiction. All characters and places,
other than those clearly in the public domain, are fictitious and any
resemblance to real persons, living or dead, is purely coincidental.

Typeset by BookPOD
Edited by Dalida Boustead
Map art by Sylvie Blair
Cover art by E-Django

ISBN: 978-0-6489664-3-2 (pbk) eISBN: 978-0-6489664-4-9

NATIONAL
LIBRARY
OF AUSTRALIA

A catalogue record for this
book is available from the
National Library of Australia

For my ma, Karen, you truly are amazing.
In memory of my dad, Barry, you are missed always, mate.
With a special thank you to Sylvie and Dalida.

"Time is a game played beautifully by children."
Heraclitus

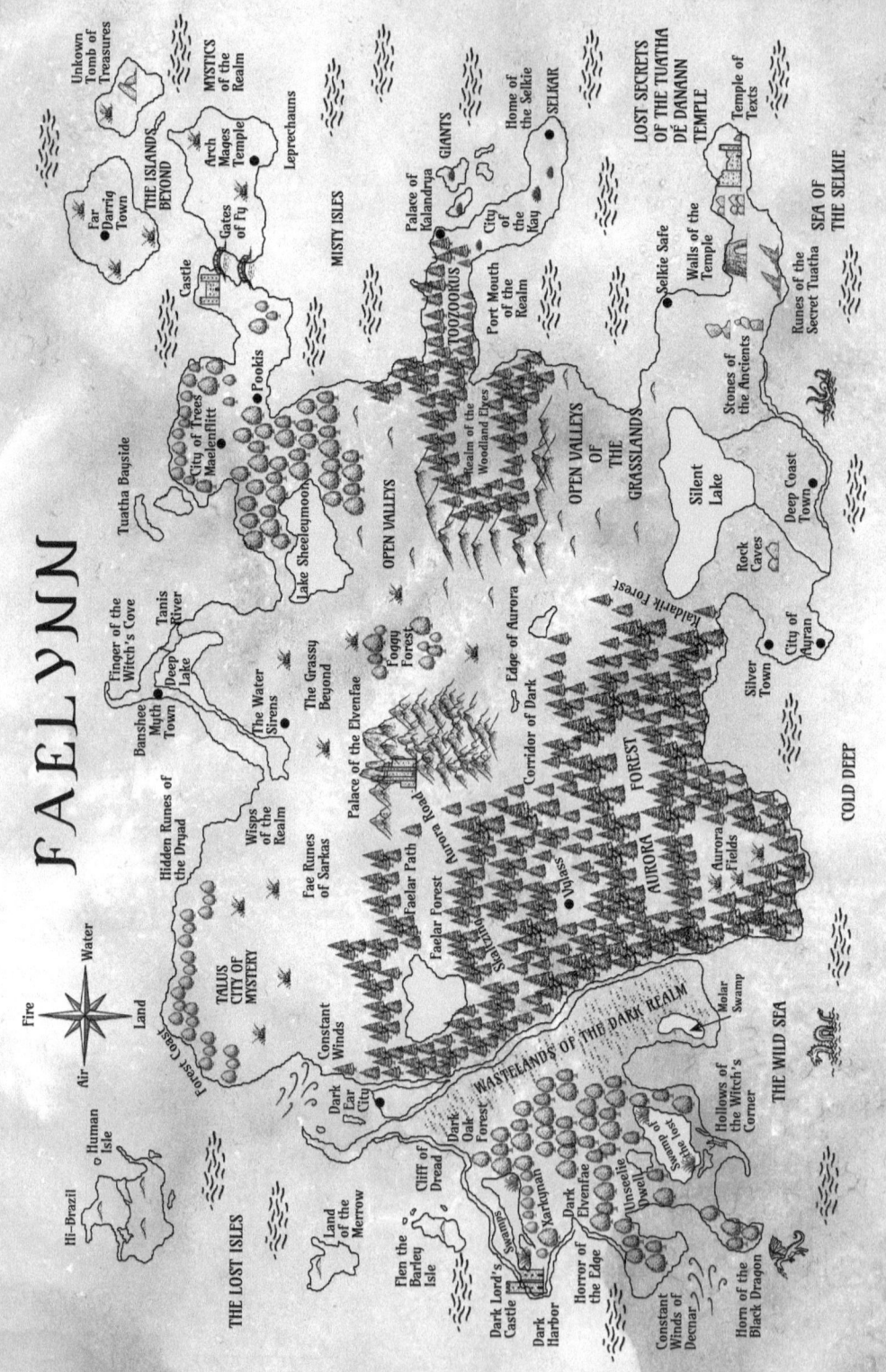

FAELYNN

Fire

Water

Air

Land

Hi-Brazil

Human Isle

THE LOST ISLES

Land of the Merrow

Flen the Barley Isle

Forest Coast

TALUS CITY OF MYSTERY

Hidden Runes of the Druad

Wisps of the Realm

Fae Runes of Sarkas

Constant Winds

Dark Far City

Cliff of Dread

Dark Lord's Castle

Dark Harbor

Xarkynan

Swamps

Dark Oak Forest

Horror of the Edge

Dark Elvenfae

Unseelie Dwell

Constant Winds of Decnar

Horn of the Black Dragon

Hollows of the Witch's Corner

Swamp of the Swamps of the lost

Molar Swamp

THE WILD SEA

WASTELANDS OF THE DARK REALM

Faelar Forest

Faelar Path

Aurora Road

Skatlithe

Vigloss

AURORA FOREST

Aurora Fields

Kialdarlk Forest

COLD DEEP

Silver Town

City of Auran

Palace of the Elvenfae

Corridor of Dark

Edge of Aurora

Foggy Forest

The Grassy Beyond

The Water Sirens

Deep Lake

Banshee Muth Town

Tanis River

Finger of the Witch's Cove

Tuatha Bayside

Lake Sheeleymoon

City of Trees Maelenflitt

Pookis

OPEN VALLEYS

Realm of the Woodland Elves

TOOZOORUS

Palace of Kialandrya

GIANTS

Port Mouth of the Realm

City of the Kau

SELKAR

Home of the Selkie

OPEN VALLEYS OF THE GRASSLANDS

Silent Lake

Rock Caves

Deep Coast Town

SEA OF THE SELKIE

Runes of the Secret Tuatha

Stones of the Ancients

Selkie Safe

Walls of the Temple

LOST SECRETS OF THE TUATHA DE DANANN TEMPLE

Temple of Texts

Castle

Gates of Fu

Arch Mages Temple

Leprechauns

MISTY ISLES

THE ISLANDS BEYOND

Far Darrig Town

MYSTICS of the Realm

Unkown Tomb of Treasures

PROLOGUE

PRE ZEYTAR CONTROL

Many cycles earlier

A RUMBLE RANG OUT OVER THE DARK LANDS as a powerful force broke the barriers and pushed through the dimensional portal, which was protected from outside intruders by the oldest magic. These were not amateurs, though. As the giant ship entered the atmosphere, cutting off the blurring blue and pink lights trailing behind it, another glow began emanating from the base of the saucer-shaped craft. It pointed directly down to the dark, barren dust below.

Three small Zeytars stepped from the blue and green lights before the ship disappeared. They set out on three different paths along the desert wastelands of what was once a lush valley of colors filling the landscape, with an abundance of life and creatures all living in harmony. That was until the dark lord Varzunnos took it and made it his barren land of destruction and evil. The forests became twisted with dark magic, and the once bustling, happy dwellers of the corner lands of Faelynn were taken, murdered, or used and changed to become part of his destructive armies, which would eventually start a war lasting an age.

After some time wandering and exploring, it was clear there was nothing there for the Zeytars. This was the first time they were scouting the realm of Faelynn, having found it by accident. They had unknowingly accessed the most barren part of the lands and decided it was nothing but a waste of time, not helpful to their agenda.

As the three approached the ship, they caught the attention of other dark creatures, those of this realm, all with a thirst for blood and in no way tricked by Zeytar mind control patterns or hallucinations. The three found out very quickly that their methods worked much better on humans and Draconians than they did on these monsters of shadows lurking at the edges of the dark, foreboding woods of Xarkynan.

They ran, barely making it to the ship before a wind swept the shadow spirits up and whirled them back into the darkness of the woods, as if they could not venture any farther. What these dark creatures were capable of was a question the Zeytars would not stick around to find out, as the blue and green lights pulled them up onto the large ship once again.

The gravity seemed stronger in this realm. It seemed to be hard to break into, and even harder to escape from. Soon the whirs of the ship finally opened another doorway out, but it took an unprecedented amount of power. This would be something the Zeytars would work on, as it would take them another century in Earth years to access this realm again. Not that the first introduction was of any benefit.

The ship burst through its portal at high speed, breaking time and space with an explosion of sound that would shatter all the glass from an entire city's buildings, and with a pink and blue blast, the giant mother ship was gone.

But something wasn't quite right. Something of the Zeytars' excursion had remained—a force that had escaped the ship to explore for itself. Without realizing the stay would be so short, the visitor had now become a permanent resident of the outer realms of Faelynn, known as Xarkynan.

The visitor appeared only as a green electric mist that blended into the shadows of the edge of the great dark elm woods. It was one of the many mind essence Zeytars that had been awaiting a body for thousands of years. Having waited for so long, it had become twisted, hoping to find a host it could inhabit while the Leader and the masters went about their agenda in Earth's realm.

This visit, though, would not be a welcome one. The entity floated through the dark elm woods, so quiet and invisible that it missed any encounters with the evil shadows that had hunted its organically clothed brethren just a little earlier. It made its way out of the most evil woods in all the realms of the Fae without even as much as a whisper, not even from the watchers of the woods, dark twisted elves that still held evil magic, awaiting the return of the dark one.

Sometime into its silent exploration, the entity suddenly became aware that the other Zeytars had left, disconnecting its link to the hive. The visitor knew that the Leader would leave it on that world forever, never to have a perfect body to inhabit when the Zeytars eventually figured out their essentially flawless cloning techniques.

It was now concentrating harder to try to re-establish a connection back to the hive and to commune with the Leader. Its green mist was becoming more prominent the harder it was thinking, as the green electrons circled around, bringing unwanted attention to the entity. Soon it gave up, reverting into shadow once more. But two dark elves had witnessed the unusual event.

Inspecting the area, the two gray-skinned beings with black hair and attired in dark, warlike forest garb looked at each other before one spoke in their native tongue, "Did you see that? It looked like the spirit of a tree dryad."

The other one slid his bent blade back into the scabbard on his shoulder, saying, "No, I thought the same, but a dryad would not survive this far into the elms without the shadows alerting us somehow, by flame or by blood."

They both nodded, agreeing, as the first dark elf also re-sheathed his stained sword into his scabbard, and both made their way back to their lookout in the twisted elms.

The bodiless Zeytar kept moving as that was taking place, gliding forward and up through the twisted trees, higher and higher, until it noticed the outer gates to an exceptionally large dwelling. It hovered over them and then made its way along the very long bridge which soon brought it to the larger main gates of an old, dark castle. The gates were ajar. In front of the huge entrance pillars, with basilisk dragons twirling down the monoliths, were the bones of many disturbing-looking creatures.

The entity floated past, not too concerned with the look of the place, as intent as it was on finding a creature it could inhabit. One of the previous elves would have been perfect, but with two of them there, and not knowing what the other might do, the visitor thought it wise to be more discreet in selecting a host.

As it flowed and billowed through large empty halls of the enormous castle, it found its way upstairs to a room with the large armor of the dark lord sitting atop his huge chair. A hooded figure stood next to the long-deceased leader, as if he were still watching over him, waiting for someone to enter and take the castle. The skin on the dark hooded watcher was old and leathery, and its eye sockets still filled, staring at nothing. Its fingers clutched a wood and bone staff, long, thin, and twisted. At the end of it was a tiny cut where a stone lay fixed in position. The entity realized at that moment that this place had a different energy, a different power to that which he was familiar with.

The Zeytars had always been a race of science, but now it seemed the game had changed. The rules were different here. It could still feel the energy around the place, from past battles and twisted, macabre events that had played out.

Looking over at the cloaked creature, the visitor noticed fresh saliva slowly dripping from the hooded figure's seemingly lifeless corpse. The creature was probably stuck in a time vortex somewhere, fully preserved, awaiting release. The larger dark creature in the chair, however, was nothing but a skeleton underneath the enormous armor of a long-forgotten leader.

The drool continued to run down the dark, scaly face of the cloaked creature and the entity felt an urge to move closer. As it did, the calling became stronger and the green mist dissipated into the eyes of the hooded watcher. Then there was a moment of silence.

With a few blinks, the watcher drew back a loud breath. It clutched its arms tight and then thrust them back, before it faced the ceiling and howled a dreadful cry, which quickly turned into dark laughter. As the creature gathered its bearings and breathed noisily, it turned to the remains of the dark lord and whispered slowly in a twisted tongue, "I have found my new home. I will use this host to bring me up to speed with this world."

Then he flopped to the ground on his knees and fell into a trance as his eyes stared into nothing, glowing purple then turning a dark red, awaiting a neuron data update from the long-forgotten host.

SINISTERS

IT WAS ANOTHER PERFECT DAY IN FAELYNN. The sun was high in the cloudless sky, shining through the trees at the edge of the realm, and illuminating an old toadstool next to a large ancient oak tree. Near it, three little forest gnomes, returning from a day's work in the thick woods, were picking berries and gathering wood for the evening's meal.

"Watch it, fool, you stepped on my foot!" the older gnome snapped, as he picked up the spilled basket which was accidentally knocked out of his thick-fingered hands.

"Sorry, Grilif, I was looking at the birds acting weird in the sky. I didn't mean it," the slightly younger, burlier gnome, Darf, retorted.

"Well, look where you're going next time," Grilif said, venting his frustration.

Grilif was an angry gnome at the best of times, and the rest of them knew it, so they tried not to upset him any more than they had to by arguing back.

"Something is strange. Have a look, Grilif, in the sky, the birds seem to be squawking and flying in all different directions," Melex said as they all looked up at the bizarre behavior.

It wasn't the first time this had happened. There were many unusual events going on in the outer part of the Faelynn realm lately. And things were about to get a lot worse.

"Help! There's something in the darkness near the giant mushroom fort," a tiny tree sprite bellowed as she flew out of the dense forest in the direction of the three gnomes who were just about to enter their small hut next to the old oak.

"What are you talking about, Stella?" Grilif said, angry again that his meal prep had been delayed.

"It's awful and scary and mean and—" Stella Rosegum exclaimed in desperation as Grilif interrupted her, saying, "Slow down, little one, there is nothing that bad in our forests. The dark ones have been gone for a thousand cycles."

While Grilif tried to calm down the fluttering tree faery, another one appeared behind her, fluttering the same way with her tiny green wings. She, too, had leafy headwear and green limbs that seemed humanoid, although they were intertwined with leaves and twigs, as if made of both skin and nature—this was their perfectly made attire that helped them blend into the forest.

"Please, you must hurry, Grilif. I think they have taken Stixx and Mella," the second sprite cried out.

They looked upon Grilif as the vigorous leader and protector of the area. Although grumpy, he was an excellent warrior and had a sense of leadership in keeping order around the place.

"Fine, fine, show me where this evil faery is, and I'll put this nonsense to bed." Grilif was not in the mood for any shenanigans. He had already fought off a spriggan who was trying to steal some of the gems attached to his satchel when he was taking a nap earlier in the day.

All five of them started making their way toward the darker part of the forest. It was usually home to the mysterious dryad Felvora, a benevolent mage of the faery oak who kept to herself most of the time. Although she reported to the other dryads every so often to help with protecting the realms, she had not been called upon for some time, so she was becoming more of a recluse these days.

"Not that way!" Stella screamed. "I've tried to find Felvora, but she won't appear for me. We must continue this way through the light of glowing shrooms. The darkness is bad—that is where they lurk," the sprite explained.

Grilif lit his lantern, which hung from the looped end of his bent tree staff. The forest had become unnaturally dark for the middle of the day, with Stella's wings now glowing to help light the way.

"Something's not right, fellas," Grilif whispered, as the forest became silently still.

Crack.

"What was that?" Stella cried out as they all turned to the location of the only sound in the woods.

"I think we need Felvora now," Grilif whispered. "Stella, try calling for her at once. Something is definitely not right. There is a dark magic here and I do not like this one bit."

Stella closed her eyes and started whispering an old poem to call the ancient dryad oak mage. Only the tree sprites could call for her, as Felvora protected them more than the others because she was a long-lost descendant of the tree Fae.

Nothing.

In the distance they could just make out a blue light as a breeze whispered through the area, until it became silent once more. Soon afterward there was another sound, then another. There was enough light around the place with the lanterns, the two tree sprites, and the glowing mushrooms to see around the area, not that it made them feel any less concerned. They were only used to the standard tricksters and thieves like spriggans, hobgoblins, the angry dwarves when they passed through, and the standard mischievous faeries, but nothing evil that would make any of the free folk scared like this, a foreboding dark presence that seemed to have a grip on them somehow.

"Where are you going, Melex? Hey, get back here," Grilif yelled as the gnome started walking to one side of a huge rock covered in rich green moss. Melex didn't even bat an eyelid as he continued over to the giant mass. He lifted his lantern and noticed something shuffling in the long, thick grass next to the rock. The lantern was illuminating a small area, letting off a yellow-orange light that flickered from the candle inside.

As he cast another glance toward the grassed area, he saw two giant black eyes looking back at him, reflecting his lantern light like a mirror.

He stood there stunned, staring at the large almond-shaped eyes as Grilif grabbed his shoulder and turned him around before saying, "Did you hear me, Melex, what are you doing?"

Grilif looked into Melex's still staring eyes, seeing only fear in them, as if he had just seen the dark lord himself. He whispered to the others, "We need to go now. It bewitches Melex."

As he spoke the last word, he too caught the glare of the dark, reflecting, almond-shaped eyes looking at him through the grass. Grilif scrambled and fell backward, which broke the gaze and the spell, as the creature made its way out of the grass and into the light of the lantern that had fallen to the ground.

"Grilif, are you OK?" Darf had rushed to Grilif's side. His lantern added to Grilif's, illuminating more of the area, and the gray creature came into full view, standing tall like an enormous giant to them.

As they all witnessed the huge creature, which was at least five feet tall, a loud rustle came from behind them and a growl that echoed throughout the entire forest. They froze in fright on seeing another monster before them, a beast that some of them would be spending a lot of time with soon.

"Stixx? Mella?" Stella screamed as she noticed several glowing faeries flying around the gigantic hairy beast's head. She flew to the top where they were hovering but realized they did not look right. There was something very wrong with them. They looked evil and gray, as if the color had drained from their body tones. They had their weapons loaded and ready to fire, and had a snarly look about them, with sharp, monstrous teeth showing, which was not normal for the peaceful nature folk.

Stella quickly zoomed out of the way, only to be struck in the middle of the air by a stun ray being held by the tall gray creature. Grilif tried to attack it by striking its feet with his staff, before grabbing the still bewitched Melex's ax and swinging widely at the sinister gray. All this was to no avail as it seemed to know his next movement, and with the blink of his eyes all three of the forest gnomes went flying into the dark of the woods.

The creature approached Stella and stared into her small eyes with its gigantic, evil black eyes, mesmerizing her and linking her up to the giant beast standing in front of her.

As this happened, Stella's features changed. She was no longer the friendly, colorful-looking sprite she had been, but an opposite version of herself, much like her kin near the beast. As she was slowly freed of the stun ray, her tiny bright wings fluttered upwards and she took up her post with the rest of the faeries controlled by the giant Sasquatch.

Milfin Dugglebox sprang out from behind the large mushroom and screamed, "No! Stella, come back! What have you done, you evil thing?"

She climbed higher and higher as quickly as she could, with her bow and arrow aimed to take out the gray sinister creature's eyes, all to no avail. Even though she had been hiding while this was all happening, the sinister gray creature knew exactly where she was. It stopped her mid-flight with a glare. Although the creature was recruiting sprites to serve its own agenda, it would not hire this one—as it intensified its stare, Milfin started screaming in pain, before she exploded into a trillion pieces. The magic of her essence dissipated into the air as the sinister creature sniffed it up like a rose's scent in the garden, leaving nothing left of the tiny sprite.

"Nooo!" Grilif cried out as the sinister walked over to the much larger hairy beast.

A howling wind started swirling up high, from the trees and down to both creatures, and then a woman dressed in green appeared before them, yelling, "Back, evil ones, I command you to release my people and go back to where you came from."

The woman in green was tall—taller than the average height of a human woman. But she was not human; she was the dryad mage of the faery oak, Felvora. She was facing both creatures, holding her scepter, made of wood with a bright crystal encased at the top, high up into the darkness, while she whispered ancient enchantments to ward off the sinisters.

Dressed by the forest, she had thick leaves covering her breasts, with flowers intertwined throughout. Felvora's midriff was bare, and she had on a small skirt made of green leaves overlapping with a pink flower vine on either side, leaving her long legs exposed and revealing her light green skin tone.

Her hands were covered up to her elbows with greenery that looked like gloves, and she had stiff pads that molded around her shoulders and hollowed around her upper arms, coming to a point next to her breasts. Her ears were extremely long and pointed, longer than a faery's or elf's, and her hair was dark, with thin iris leaves protruding from the sides into the air. Around her neck was a vine that snaked around with floral buds growing randomly, while her staff had two points either side at the top, Celtic symbols swirling down the wood, and random branches protruding from the sides. A crystal sat in a star-shaped hole underneath the top section of the staff. Covering her feet were shoes made of branches that curled up, and thick leafy socks reached up to just below her knees.

She was quite attractive as the forest folk go, but there was also a darker side to her that she didn't expose all too often. She was edging close to that now after witnessing the evil act that led to her little friend Milfin's destruction.

Felvora's rage was peaking, and as she raised her staff ever higher, her right hand began emanating a jade-colored swirl of energy. As she was about to throw the glowing green ball of essence at the sinister and its beast, a large blue light hit the creatures from above like a cylinder encasing them as well as the many sprites now belonging to the Sasquatch, and before Felvora's very eyes they disappeared into the air along with the light, leaving only silence in their place.

As she looked high into the black sky to see where the light had retracted to, Felvora noticed the darkness at the tops of the trees moving until the sun was visible again, twinkling through the leaves once more and bringing the wildlife back into a roaring natural cacophony of noise, as it was before the sinister events.

Felvora relaxed her emotions, and the green swirling light dissipated from her hand. The crystal inside her staff stopped glowing. She turned to see if the gnomes were still there or if they had fled, and when her gaze found Grilif and the other two, she was taken aback by the stony look of fear on their faces, as if the darkness had taken every shred of good and light from their very souls.

She edged forward and in a quiet tone whispered, "Little ones, little ones, are ye well?"

There was no answer from any of them, as if they were under a spell. Felvora had not seen this kind of magic before and only hoped that she could undo whatever dark enchantment had overcome them all. She kneeled to their level.

Grilif stood still like a statue. His large leaf hat drooped over his forehead. It had a feather sticking out of it, along with sticks and berries in the middle of it. His beard was white and draped to his stumpy bare feet. He was wearing brown leather pants that went three-quarters of the way down his legs, while his green long-sleeved top was met at each wrist with a jewel that wrapped around. He had a backpack on and a crossbow. A satchel draped around his right shoulder to meet his hip at the left, with a cup dangling off it along with different trinkets that he had found along his journeys. His beard had bits of sticks and bark through it, and there were random branches with leaves protruding from different parts of his attire. He was only two feet tall, but he was strong and usually greatly confident, until this time.

Melex and Darf were dressed similarly, although their beards were brown, and they didn't have as many trinkets attached to their satchels. Darf had a mushroom growing from his leafy hat instead of a feather, and he wore the mushroom with pride. Melex had a crossbow as well as the ax Grilif had used to attack the sinister with. Darf also had an ax, and all of them had lanterns and staffs as they were often deep in the forest in the dark looking for food, wood, and trinkets from passers-by who ventured too far into the woods.

Felvora asked again, and with still no response she leaned over, closed her eyes, and blew gently over the three of them. Waiting for a reaction, she opened her hand and blew another soft breath. This time a small green essence glittered over the three round faces. Grilif started moving, while the others remained silent. The look of fear in his eyes slowly reverted to Grilif's usual more mellow yet grumpy glare. Melex and Darf slowly came around too, and before long all three forest gnomes were back to normal, but still shaken up from the events that had just transpired.

"Are you all OK? I have, I hope, broken the spell, little ones," Felvora said.

Grilif looked up at her and snapped, "What's with this 'little one' talk? I might be small, but I could knock you down."

Felvora wasn't like the Elvenfae in the palace. She was not one to mess with. She loved all her free folk and protected them from harm, although she was very much one to keep to herself. Grilif knew as soon as he made the comment who he was talking to and regretted it straightaway. Felvora seemed to have taken it better than he expected, though, maybe because Grilif had a reputation in the Aurora Forest and even Felvora had heard the stories. Besides, she was more relieved that they were all alright.

"Sorry, Felvora, I'm still in a bit of shock," Grilif added as Felvora stood up and looked around the area for any more evidence of the destructive force that had just invaded her home.

"Don't worry yourself today. As long as you are all OK. Talk to me like that tomorrow and I'll change you into a slug, OK, Grilif?" She smiled, then began walking toward Stella's home.

Grilif had been through a lot today and wanted to help if he could. He was counting his lucky stars that she didn't turn him into a slug. The other two snickered when he turned his back. They were all getting over the incident more quickly than most others would in that situation.

"Can we help you, lady of the forest?" Grilif was now aware of his surroundings and much calmer after his brush with the sinister.

"If you wish. Let us go to the home of the tree sprites and see the damage. Then we must warn of this. We must seek Princess Shaylee. She will know what to do." Felvora was very concerned as she had not seen this kind of magic so close to home. The destructive power of it was scary, even for a high-level forest mage.

"What was that creature, and why was he taking the wee ones?" Grilif asked.

Felvora turned to face the gnomes, speechless for a moment before eventually answering, "I don't know. I have never seen dark power like that. Not since the times of the dark lord."

Grilif and the others just stared, thinking that whatever they had dealt with was something profoundly serious if someone like Felvora was afraid. They all continued deeper into the forest to the large tree of the sprites called Vylass, where they hoped to get some answers.

The tree was the largest in the forest. The sheer size would be impossible to describe to someone who had never witnessed it themselves, although these four had spent many a time interacting with the tree sprites over the cycles. There was a symbiosis between all the lives in the Aurora Forest that meant everyone was welcome.

Felvora stood at the base and looked up. Usually there were tiny balls of light fluttering all over the pink and blue blossoms that surrounded the tree, but this day, there were none, as if the lights had been turned off and the tree itself was asleep.

The forest mage leaned over and whispered to the gnomes at her feet, "Something is definitely amiss here. Stay together and I will see what's going on."

She transformed herself into a green mist floating with the wind to the top of Vylass where the queen of the forest sprites dwelled.

The gnomes took a seat and Darf pulled out a long length of cooked sausage along with a knife from his backpack. He started cutting small slices off and stuffing them in his mouth, then looked over at the other two sitting there staring with their mouths wide open and said, "Oh, you boys hungry?"

Grilif and Melex glanced at each other in disbelief. How could he be thinking of food at a time like this? Forest gnomes were renowned for gluttony and overindulgence, but Darf wrote the book on it.

Grilif grabbed the sausage from him and stuffed it back into Darf's backpack, and they sat and waited for Felvora to return.

"What do you think it was, Gril?" Melex whispered, still upset about losing his friends.

"I don't know, but seeing the tree dim like this for the first time in all my long life, it cannot be good. Let's wait and see if Felvora can find some answers."

Eventually, they sat back, lit a fire, and started singing old songs of their adventures to pass the time away.

Meanwhile, at the entrance to the queen's hall at the top of Vylass, Felvora was surrounded by an army of tree folk. From sprites to gnomes and hollops, along with munchkins, faeries, and sylphs, there was an array of forest folk, and Felvora knew straightaway why they were all there ... fear.

"It's OK, lovely folk, it is only I, Felvora."

Even though everyone knew her, they were still hesitant. The sinisters could plant images in their minds and trick them into thinking things were real when in fact they weren't, so it took some time for them to come around to her presence.

A guard flew up to her face and whispered softly to her, "Please, help us, I know it's you."

Felvora bent down on one knee, leaning against her staff. The hard tree mage was showing her empathy for the first time in ages. Seeing these peaceful creatures all in fear and hopelessness made her weaken until that cycle finished in her and rage poured out. "Where is your queen?" she shouted, and they all knew now that it was really Felvora.

"I am here, my lady. Please, can you help us?" The queen had been hiding just in case the sinisters returned for another round.

"Tell me everything, Queen Villara." Felvora wanted as much information as she could get to take with her to the palace of Faelynn.

The queen moved in closer. She was larger than the other tree sprites, and still made up of layers of leaves and grass stems, although her head was a lot more oval-looking from side to side. Her crown was made of tree branches with a single red gem in the middle of it that looked like a rose. There was no other clothing, the rest made by the magic of the forest.

"It started earlier today. We lost around thirty soldiers and families who had been out scouring the woods for food and playing in the toadstool caverns near Palex, you know the place?" Villara asked, and Felvora nodded back. "Piecing it together from the witnesses, they seemed only interested in the sprites, no one else; those others who tried to stop them were disintegrated by magic or stood on by the giant hairy monster. Only two escaped to tell us. That is when we called for all those needing sanctuary to come to Vylass. I am missing my daughter Stella; she was with her friends at the edge of Aurora when the attack happened. I have never seen magic like this. It is just lucky that they do not know where Vylass is. It is protected by the highest enchantment of forest magic so only natural folk can see it. If they find this place, there will be no stopping them. Felvora, please, you must help us."

As the queen finished, she was crying uncontrollably. Felvora did not have the heart to tell her about Stella, Stixx, Mella, and Milfin—especially Milfin.

"It's alright, I will help you," said Felvora. "Stay here until I get back. I am taking three gnomes and will embark on a trip to the Faelynn palace to tell the queen and princess. They may have a solution or more information about this that we can use to get back our kin. First, I will need to talk to all witnesses that encountered the incident, as the more knowledge we have, the more it may help."

Felvora then leaned in to Villara and whispered, "Take care of our people and don't trust anyone or anything from elsewhere until we get back. Open Vylass as a sanctuary to those frightened and in need of solace. I will be back before the moon is full again."

Villara smiled briefly and nodded.

Felvora spent the next little while talking to all those who had even the slightest information that could come in handy. After Felvora had finished, she nodded to the queen and disappeared into a smoky cloud of green air, which then vanished.

Felvora then appeared on the ground at the foot of Vylass, standing over three snoring gnomes who were about to get a rude awakening. Soon a huge centipede emerged from the ground, before another, and then another, crawling over the little tough guys' faces, tickling them with every stroke of a leg until Grilif opened his eyes and jumped up, shaking himself off before stamping the ground. The others followed suit, and they were all now dancing around the place like drunken fools, only to be interrupted by the forest mage herself as she cleared her throat. "Hmm. Are we quite finished dancing like fools? We have a particularly important journey. I need you all to pack some things and we will leave at first light for the great Faelynn palace."

"The palace? I'm not going there. It will take at least a quarter cycle to get there and—"

Felvora cut Grilif off before he could get her angry. "Are you quite finished running your mouth off? We will go and that's all I will say. The next protest out of your mouths will warrant a day as a slug, got it?"

As they all looked up at her like frightened children, they said in unison, "Yes, my lady."

They gathered their belongings and started making their way back home to prepare for the big journey ahead.

THE LONG ROAD

FELVORA HAD AWOKEN THE GNOMES very early in the morning after finding out a little more about the previous day's devastating encounters with the strange magic creature and its monstrous beast. She had learned some further truths. There were whispers that not more than a cycle earlier the same beings had been seen on the Skaltzing path, near the ruins of the old lookout from the dark times, only a short distance from where they were now.

Witnesses described that first encounter as seeing the day go dark, with loud howls and blue and pink lights coming from the woods, but not lasting any more than a few moments. It seemed like it may have been their first time in the area and they were just scouting.

But as Felvora thought more clearly about the recent events that had played out, she could not remember seeing her little friend Stalixus Aethelwyne, an old friend from the palace of the Elvenfae, the half-sister of Princess Shaylee Aethelwyne. She had chosen a quieter lifestyle after revelations were made about events relating to her father, who was the king, and a maid at Oakslarren the night she was conceived. This devastated Stalixus and she wanted nothing more to do with her father, although she loved the only mother she ever knew, the queen, who took her as her own after the birth mother dumped her at the palace doors one day with only a note, never to be seen again.

All this came out when it was also revealed that the king before his death had colluded with a human woman in more recent times. The council was working through it all with the queen and the king, and

Stalixus thought it best to have time away—and even more so after her father was killed in a small skirmish. It was almost as if he had planned it, so as not to put his family through any more pain, but no one would ever know that for sure.

Stalixus never hated her father. She was overwhelmed with disappointment, and she moved to be closer to her friend Felvora, hoping to share in some adventures. She felt that she could talk to her about anything. Felvora always saw her at least once a quarter cycle. Fear now flowed through her veins and entered her adrenal glands. She had to make sure that Stalixus hadn't been the first taken. If so, she would need to tell Queen Tianna and Shaylee, who were still mourning King Viltherome Aethelwyne's passing.

Felvora vanished into a jade-colored mist and left the gnomes still rubbing their eyes in a confused state, waiting for her return. Soon the dryad was standing in front of Stalixus' home. Stalixus preferred being in her small sprite form most of the time, so the front part of her home was large, for her full Elvenfae size, and the rest, which went deep into the trunk of an old oak, was tiny and was where she spent most of her time at night. The front of the dwelling comprised a veranda built by the gnomes as a favor for making some nice clothes for them when she first arrived. It was constructed onto the front of the oak, which was at least sixteen feet wide. The oaks were exceptionally large in this part of the woods, although there wouldn't be enough of them if every tall root decided to move into the area ("tall root" being the nickname the little folk gave to the changelings or larger Fae who were tall).

Felvora was getting more concerned. Stalixus' front door was wide open, and it looked like it had been that way for a while. She'd most likely been robbed by some dirty little hobgoblins or shifty spriggans. As Felvora walked inside, she saw Stalixus' belongings were strewn around the entrance to the veranda and noticed her family ring on the floor. This was a ring that entitled all offspring of the palace the right of passage anywhere in the main realms. Felvora knew her friend would not leave such a trinket unsupervised or away from her person. It was lucky that whoever robbed the place was not as eagle-eyed as she was.

It was certain then. Stalixus had been taken along with the rest, unless some other dark force had been there, but that was highly unlikely. Felvora turned to make her way out of the dwelling. She sensed some movement. Playing dumb, she continued making her way out of Stalixus' place and disappeared.

Moments later, a small, stocky yet slovenly dressed creature about the same size as a gnome exited the dwelling. But before he could even gasp, he was whisked up into the air by an unseen force. Felvora then revealed herself and with an evil glare in her dark green eyes shouted, "What do you know, scavenger of the night, under-dweller of mischief and thievery? What do you know?"

Felvora was in no mood for it, as the hobgoblin started squirming and wriggling, trying to break her strong grip. Although it was tight, hobgoblins were tricky things and he cut Felvora's fingers with a bite from his filthy, sharp teeth.

Felvora dropped him like a hot molar rock. Thinking he had got the better of her, he started running, until his steps shortened and he found himself on his stomach—running no more, but sliding instead on his belly like a giant slug. Even a milvaark would be able to catch him now.

Felvora, standing over the large slug, allowed the creature to speak, giving him a voice so she could get all the information she wanted without the trickster vanishing on her. The hobgoblin was renowned in this area of Aurora, and Felvora seemed to remember having a conversation with him many cycles ago about tricking a golloff elf out of all his earnings. Felvora had intervened and banished the dirty trickster from Aurora with the threat of being turned if he came back.

"Oh, Xack'Xax, you silly little worm, I warned you of your return and what I would do."

"Mercy, I beg ye for mercy."

The slug was making all kinds of mess at the entrance to the dwelling. But Felvora did not care for any mercy at this stage and he was about to learn a valuable lesson.

"What did you want with my friend and why were you scrounging in her house? What do you know of her disappearance?"

Felvora was in no mood to entertain a sleazy excuse for a hobgoblin. She had previously warned him, and this was about her friend, so someone was going to pay—starting with him.

"I ... I don't know who you talk of, please, mercy, I steal and scrounge, yes, but I don't hurt."

The dryad was about to unleash on the beast after that comment. "You don't hurt? You drew blood, you dark thief. You not only hurt and steal, but you also lie as well. This is going to be a permanent look for you if you do not tell me what I want to hear, starting right now."

Felvora was at her wits' end. She could see she wouldn't get any kind of intelligent response from Xack'Xax, so she tried another tack. She lifted the slug high in the air. Green and red slime was now dripping continuously from the many pores of the creature until the pain of it became too much and Xack started howling like a beast heading for slaughter.

"I'll tell, I'll tell," he said, making a promise he might not fulfill.

"Then tell, worm, what do you know about this place and the disappearance of my friend. I will spare your life if you give me what I want."

Felvora increased the grip a little more before the pain became too much and the slug squealed like a banshee.

"OK, OK, mercy! I have been living here for about half a moon cycle, I swear. Before, I was in the woods, scrounging and following your friend. My intentions were to steal her gold goblets but then the dark of the sun overtook the area. All I saw was her captured by bright lights and hairy beasts, I swear, that's all I know, after which I took her house and have dwelled here ever since. I'm sorry."

Felvora was still in no mood for mercy and squeezed harder. Xack'Xax became a dripping feature of Stalixus' front yard as she continued to drain the creature in her rage. He screamed out in pain until his life ended and he was thrown to the dirt for the worms to feast on.

Felvora put back all he had taken. Then she cast a spell on the place that would prevent anyone or anything from entering the home until either Stalixus or Felvora entered to break it. She then disappeared and returned to the gnomes.

While this was happening, Grilif had packed the entire team's lunches and backpacks and had even taken the time to cook a nice meaty breakfast before they left. He was hoping Felvora would partake of it and even be proud of his ability to take charge. Knowing she had left swiftly for a reason, he wanted to step up, and hoped she was OK.

Grilif was hard, but he had to be. His parents were taken when he was very young by a dralixx, a furious troll that had nothing but hate for any of the forest folk. One day when the baby Grilif was asleep in the haven of his home, the same one he lived in now, a troll from the dark elm woods made its way to the Aurora Forest. Brumlemd and Paargus, Grilif's parents, were finishing the new paving on some fresh land they had gained. Looking deeply into each other's eyes, they hugged. It would be their last. The dralixx picked them both up as it passed through. He threw Brumlemd at the front door as it ate Grilif's mother, Paargus, and then kept walking. Moorelton the wise had been following the dralixx for ages, and with an angry strike from his sword struck the beast down in a chaos of blood and screams, stabbing it repeatedly until the dralixx was nothing more than a mess to be cleaned up by the forest's micro-life. Moorelton didn't even stop to help the baby gnome, continuing instead with his search for the other dralixx he needed to find which had also escaped the dark elm woods.

Darf's parents took Grilif in, and they became good friends. Although Grilif moved back to his parents' abode as soon as he could, he would never forget the darkness that swept over his life at that time. He didn't trust others easily and had a hard exterior that exuded an aura of hate. But deep down he had a longing for friendship and acceptance.

Felvora suddenly appeared in front of them. As shocked as they all were, Grilif was very much relieved to see her, although he would never ever admit the fact.

"So, I made you a nice fat breakfast of lamb and pork sausages,

Felvora. Also, the camp gear is packed." Grilif knew not to provoke her with questions of why she left and other remarks, partly because he wanted to prove to her that he could be trusted to help. The other reason was that he did not want to become a slug like she had promised.

"No, thank you, guys. I am a maiden of the forest, and I will not eat meat. You should know that."

Grilif lowered his head and realized straight off that it was a stupid thing to say. "You sound upset, my lady. Are you OK? I won't ask what happened, but know we are here for you."

Grilif was really turning a new leaf, she thought. Before answering, she looked up at the sky and gripped the trinket in her hand. "Thanks, I will inform ye on the way. Now ... are we ready to journey?"

The three nodded, looking up at their protector before grabbing the camp gear and making their way to the palace path.

TWO DAYS LATER ON THE AURORA ROAD

The four had been walking nonstop for the best part of the day. They had a little hiccup the first day with Darf hurting his foot on a spike from a rosen thorn sticking up from the stony road, which stopped the urgent journey in its tracks right at the beginning. It would have been so easy to just pick them all up and disappear straight to the palace, Felvora thought, or even send a sprite, but the risk of an attack was high, and she wasn't likely to meet a sprite on the road. Everything was so raw now, but she was happy to have some very credible witnesses with her to help with her claims. Besides, Felvora had not told the group just yet about Stalixus and her disappearance.

The night was dragging on and Felvora was happy to let her ego go by saying it was time to rest; she was so used to just disappearing and appearing in another place without the exhaustion or the effort of having to take the time and toll of traveling. The gnomes had tiny legs. It would be twice the work for them to achieve any distance, and Felvora understood quickly that these tiny, strong forest people were doing it very tough, although they would not show any signs of defeat.

"Time to rest, boys," she said.

Grilif turned and looked back at Felvora. "Nah, we got a couple more hours. We need to make up for yesterday's spill."

As soon as Grilif finished speaking, Darf and Melex also responded to Felvora, in unison, "No, we are good."

Felvora smiled. Again she thought that she could easily pick them up and take them all to the palace now, in the blink of an eye, but then they would not respect her at all. The sprites in Vylass, and especially Milfin, Stixx, Mella, and Stella, were good friends of the gnomes. As important as it was to get the information to the palace quickly, the gnomes wanted to be part of the solution. Felvora knew this, so she didn't suggest the alternative way of getting there.

"Come, no arguing, ye all rest now."

Felvora had an aura about her. The dryad was awfully hard in life, hard but fair, but the gnomes were now seeing a more compassionate side. They knew that they were tired. Trying to impress a nature forest dryad with being tough was like impressing a woodland elf from the warriors' fort of Toozookus, so they just agreed from that moment on to do what the dryad forest mage asked.

Soon they were tucked into the stem of a toadstool, comparing war stories and the biggest trinkets they had ever found, all while Felvora disappeared and made sure the path ahead was safe. Then even she succumbed to the night and fell asleep inside the darkness of an open oak pit.

DAY SIX

The last few days had been exhausting, but fun and informative. On day three Felvora taught Melex how to blow a thorn onto Grilif's behind, making him swear not to say a word. And on the fourth and fifth they were in hysterics with tales about each of their abilities and lack thereof. There was a day to go and the journey was going well, but all things, even in Faelynn, can have their challenges.

"Stop, Gril, there's a shadow on the track," Darf warned him. But Grilif was so fixed on making it to their destination by the end of the day that he didn't actually see the swirling blue shadow in front of him.

Felvora had gone to ensure the path ahead was safe—as she did most days—so now, at the only time she really needed to be there with them, she was not.

Grilif turned his head and gave Melex and Darf a look of contempt, as the large sinister with gray skin and almond-shaped black eyes stepped from the light. While looking at his friends, Grilif had kept moving forward and walked right into its legs. As shocked as he was, when he looked up, extreme anger took over immediately. Grilif grabbed his knife from his satchel and started stabbing the sinister in the leg. Only two of his jabs hit before the monstrous gray creature picked Grilif up with its wiry long fingers and tossed him a good fifteen feet away into the side of a tree in the Faelar Forest.

Seeing this happen, Melex and Darf exploded with rage, pulling out their weapons and hurtling toward the mammoth creature with everything they had. The sinister turned toward the two-foot adversaries and gave a wrinkle of a smile, before bending down and picking up Melex. He lifted the gnome so its face was level with its giant bulbous eyes and created within him a mental world of torture and hate.

Darf was next. He was the bravest of all gnomes that had ever lived— that's what Grilif thought as he watched the gnome attack to defend his friends. As his ax reached high to strike, the sinister smiled. It lifted the gnome a good fifteen feet in the air with its mind, and then threw him. Grilif, in a world of pain from his impact with the tree, lowered his head, knowing an injury like that would cause great damage.

After the sinister had tossed Darf away, it crushed Melex, leaving his lifeless body in the middle of the path.

Then the road lit up in colors of blue, pink, and white, and the sinister Zeytar rose high into the clouds, disappearing into a stream of light.

Grilif sprang to his feet just as Felvora returned. He looked up at her with shattered trust and then shook his head repeatedly, not saying a word. Then he turned away.

Felvora knew immediately what had happened. The stench of the ground below her gave enough of the story. Grilif rushed to Darf, who was clinging to the end of a branch of a small tree he had grabbed hold of. He was not without injury, but alive. Grilif tried to pull him down, failed, and tried again, but only succeeded in causing Darf more pain.

Felvora was standing over the two of them by now, with great sadness in her heart. She gently picked Darf off from the branch, and laid him onto the soft grass.

Grilif, at his wits' end, gave Felvora a mouthful, knowing all the while he would most likely be turned into a dirty, sluggish caterpillar or worse. "Why? Why go? You were meant to protect us all! We never needed to know what was ahead, as we were all together. You don't care. You are just a selfish dark dryad, made to care for no one!" Grilif knew he had gone too far with his angry comments, so he looked away, waiting for his punishment.

Felvora put her hands on Darf and started to work on his injuries. She had heard what Grilif said, but the guilt of being away at such a time had crushed her spirit. However, she had to fix this and was doing her best to accomplish that.

Darf lay on the soft leaves of Faelar, moving around as the dryad mage did her work, but soon he stopped moving completely, lifeless.

Felvora turned to Grilif and shook her head slowly, before saying, "I'm so sorry, Gril." Then she disappeared into a green mist, leaving Grilif in the evening's twilight, all alone with the body of his best friend.

This journey so far was more than anything he ever thought it would be. He slumped over his friend, crying, and thinking of ways to kill the giant creature responsible for this, with no real idea how to go about it.

Grilif was now on his own. Felvora had obviously left him for the palace and her own excuses, he thought, as he laid his head on his friend's body, still sobbing.

"Hey, are you crying, Gril?" Darf whispered.

Grilif slowly raised his head from his chest. "No, what, hey." Grilif cared not for any ego or maintaining the illusion of his hard persona. His true colors came flooding through, and he hugged his best friend, letting him know he was there. "Hey, Darf, you're OK. I'm so sorry I wasn't the—"

Darf cut him off straightaway before calmly whispering, "It's OK, buddy, Felvora saved me. She has gone to find the ..." Before he could finish, Darf fell asleep, which was part of his healing before the next leg of the journey.

Grilif placed a mushroom skin blanket over him, found a mushroom for himself, and kept a lookout all night, like a guard from the palace. These dark forces would not take him. Not today.

DAY SEVEN, THE LAST DAY

Grilif had fallen asleep next to the mushroom stem. The cold of the night had not swayed his conviction, nor would it. He was the protector of his friend, and his friend knew it. Darf was now out at the edge of Faelar Forest, cooking up a storm, hoping to tease the hard-core gnome into softly begging for food.

As the light of the day struck Grilif's face, he winced and brushed his head. It wasn't until the stench of a dark blood sausage simmering on an open fire hit his nostrils, like a wave of exotic toxins, that the gnome was launched out of his coma and straight out to the fire where the enticing smell emanated from.

"Darf, you ... you're OK," were the only words Grilif could manage, caring, but eyeing the sausage as well.

"I'm fine, Gril, thanks to Felvora."

Grilif didn't care; he went straight in for a hug with his best friend and snuck a sausage behind Darf's back, burning his mouth but not saying a word.

An hour later Felvora appeared. She had given them time to connect but was still worried about how Grilif was going to react to her.

"Grilif, we need to get back to the road. The sinisters seem to be everywhere now and my understanding is that they will be back, so we need to go." Felvora was so assertive with her statement that she never expected a hug from Grilif. But he approached her and embraced her green, somewhat foresty legs. Then he looked up, and after motioning for her to bend down to him, said, "Thank you, thank you again,

I'm so ..." But before Grilif could finish, he collapsed and fell asleep, exhausted by the perilous events of the night before.

Hours later, the buzz of a gray hawk flapping right past, telling Felvora some information from Vylass, woke Grilif from his exhausted slumber.

"It's time. We are only half a day from the Faelynn palace and time has never been so important."

Felvora had already streamed ahead earlier, but she had not told or warned anyone of the unfortunate events that had been playing out in Aurora and Faelar forests, forests that were protected by the palace of Faelynn. She had only wanted to know the path was clear for her most respected friends.

They all paid their respects to Melex and continued forward. Darf was probably more excited than the others, even though he'd just been through such a great ordeal. He had never met the Elvenfae from the palace in person, and it was something he had secretly wanted to do. But most of all, he wanted to know what those gray sinister creatures were.

Felvora grabbed both their hands as they made their way from the Faelar Forest paths and onto the beautiful paths leading up into the city of Faelynn. They were immaculate. The gnomes had never seen anything so amazing. Being gnomes and aware of such a place only from stories of the past, it was extremely hard to take in. Looking behind them, Gril noticed the other paths that met up together from all different directions.

"Are you both OK? You look done. We are nearly at the palace." Felvora was trying her best to comfort the gnomes, but once the two saw the gates to the Faelynn city palace, they grabbed hold of each other and started dancing.

AWKWARD REUNION

GRILIF OPENED HIS EYES WIDER, not knowing what to expect as the gates of the enormous palace opened. It was very fortunate that Felvora had prepared them both for the arrival, although she had not given many details away.

The palace was enormous, carved high and deep into a mountain, with many levels, starting with the ground gates they were about to walk through. The Elvenfae guard at the entrance to the fortress, dressed so elegantly with his helmet of gold and armor of the Fae, demanded they stop and approached the three.

"I had word someone was coming, though we were not expecting you, dryad mage. You know you were—"

Before the guard finished, Felvora propelled her power out toward him and green electric mist hit him with full force, knocking him back. Felvora raced over and standing over him said, "Never forget what I did for you and for all of this land. Just because I had a falling out with the queen doesn't mean I should *ever* be disrespected ... Now, can you please do your actual job and tell the queen I am here as there are some quite pressing issues that need urgent attention." Felvora stepped back from the now deferential guard and waited for a response.

"Y... yes, my lady, I am sorry." The guard groaned as he ran back to the main palace entrance and announced to the head guard that there was an immediate need for the queen.

Felvora stood there, calm and passive, knowing it had been a while since she had seen her old friend Tianna. She was excited and worried at the same time as they'd had a very bitter fight that split up their friendship after the long war all that time ago. Felvora had maintained a little dignity by returning to her home and never setting foot in the city of Faelynn again. But now, this issue required the biggest council and haste of action, so the queen had to see her no matter what.

"Dryad mage, you are not welcome here. The queen has revoked your stay and you have an hour to leave the whole province before the guards take you before the council and have you stripped of all your dignity and magic. The gnomes will be taken from you, and you will be exiled to the human realm where you will live a horrid life as a tree hag. These are orders of the queen's council and guards."

As the Elvenfae speaker, in his nice gold and silver-white uniform, finished his ridiculous statement, Felvora picked up the two remaining gnomes, walked to the end of the huge entry steps and ducked off to the side of the first statue of the king. Never one to give up, she sat down and closed her eyes, contemplating the next move.

She was a strong mage and a fierce Fae, and there was no way a male Elvenfae guard or council was going to stop her from passing on the information that had to be delivered to the queen. The whole of the land was at risk and if she didn't tell Tianna what they'd seen and experienced, the dark lord may as well take the land, for this was a much more formidable force than what Felvora and Tianna fought about a thousand cycles ago.

An hour passed, and when the main Elvenfae guard approached to take Felvora into custody, Grilif was the only one there, standing at the top of the steps as if he were awaiting a fight. As the guard moved closer, Grilif lifted his arms up, a crossbow in one hand, and the other hand a fist, ready to launch. As he parried to the left for an action shot, the guard countered, thinking it was mere amateur play.

While this was going on, a green mist snuck through the main palace doors and entered the queen's guards' lower chamber. But with only three more levels to get to, Felvora fell short of her goal. She was captured by the head of the Elvenfae warrior guard as she tried to enter the main chamber with warrior Fae statues of the past.

Stexinzar Crimsonmoon, the head of the Elvenfae guard, knew Felvora very well, as they had fought together against the evil dark lord at Xarkynan. But he was bitterly disappointed that she was here right now, sensing some unfinished business was about to play out.

Stexinzar hit Felvora hard with his staff, leaving her vulnerable to mortality; his staff produced a hit of gold electric power that forced the mist into a solid form.

"Why? Why now, Felvora? You know the queen is still mourning the king and that there have been small troubles around the realms. Do you need to remind her of your lying, deceitful face once again?" Stexinzar's words had quivered when he spoke them, and he had a tear running down his cheek, showing that the events of the past were still making waves in the present.

Felvora moved forward, reaching her right hand out to calm what the head guard was saying. "Stex, I'm so sorry, you have no idea of the pain I have been in all this time. I have been haunted by her loss and I have mourned our love, but please, now is not the time. I must see her at once."

Felvora had tears running down her face, with her head pointed to the ground, resigned. As she awaited the final pull from the guards to take her out of the city, she slowly raised her head to look up. Stexinzar must have learned something in her eyes, something that gave way to truth. He knew her very well in the past and there was always a look she had that showed her true feelings.

As the guards finally reached her to take her away to the council, Stexinzar called out, "No, she comes with me today. Find her friends and bring them to me. I will summon the queen and meet her in the long hall throne room."

As soon as Stexinzar had finished his command, the lower Elvenfae guards disappeared to search for Felvora's friends.

The long hall of the palace was massive. It seemed to go on forever. Felvora had longed to see the palace again. It held so many memories of the friendships and adventures she'd had, some with her noticeably younger friend Shaylee, the daughter of the queen. But that was a long time ago and there were a lot of dark things to get over before there was any talk of friendship with her old companions again.

Leaves were dropping onto the unmarked floor of perfectly flawless marble tiles, indicating that an outsider was walking the highest of all the faeries' halls in all the lands. These were halls she grew up in and knew well. It wasn't until the end of the war in the dark lands that she returned to being a tree mage, a dryad of the forest. She was once the head mage for the queen, but her actions had caused so much pain that these halls had now long forgotten her.

"What are you doing here, dryad?" The shouted words from the immaculate throne room echoed out, the decibels the vocals had in the reverberation through the great chamber perturbing even the Elvenfae guards. "We have no time for mischief or deceit. It was only because of my daughter that I agreed to see you. Now tell me, what do you want?" Felvora and Stexinzar, who was still attached to her arm, fell to the floor, a good shout's distance away from the throne. The dryad was not in a position where she could have a decent conversation with the queen, detailing possibilities, or even coming to an agreement about anything. She felt hopelessly withdrawn. She hadn't realized that the impact of so many outer-world years would have taken such a toll. If she'd known, she would have tried a different approach, maybe gone to Markendaar, the woodland elf warrior, instead. But she was here now, and this had to be done.

The queen stood up. Her tall, slender figure inspired awe and her amazing full wings were mesmerizing. The queen was exquisite, looking no older than thirty Earth years, although thousands needed to be added to that. Her large crown, long, flowing Celtic gown, and blonde braided hair, which nearly touched the floor, reminded Felvora why she loved this place and her queen.

As Felvora stood and was about to speak, another shout distracted her attention from the east hallway as someone was running into the main chamber at full speed. "Flora, my darling, sweet Flora." Tears were streaming down the face of the princess, who was rushing toward Felvora, arms out and ready to attack.

"Sh... Shay?" Felvora knew exactly who it was. Just before they could embrace, though, a guard put his staff up to block the interaction. But the princess slammed her perfect wings along the legs of the guard, knocking him down to the floor. They finally came together in a moment of tears and emotion. Felvora pulled the princess's head back and whispered, "I so missed you, my old friend, I have missed you."

"And I you, you old, dried-up tree mage," the princess said.

Felvora gave her a stern look, as she did with all of her forest folk, and then with a smirk whispered, "I owe you, Shaylee, but please, it's Stalixus, she is ..." As Felvora tried to finish, it was as if Shaylee already knew, so she hushed her.

"Mother, I mean, Your Highness, please, Felvora has some especially important information. Dare you let her speak? If she is thrown out, Stalixus will—"

Queen Tianna stood abruptly as the name of her other daughter was spoken. "What say you of Stalixus? She is supposed to be safe under your protection in the Aurora Forest. She is your friend. What say you, leaf wench?"

Felvora's anger welled inside her, and if she were a bottle of Earthly pop she would have exploded. But she didn't. She suppressed disaster and delivered composure, as now, more than ever, she needed that anger restraint. "My queen." Felvora was now on her knees, her head bent to the floor, and every fiber inside her was fighting against centuries of defensive tactics of the forest. It had been a long time and she needed to prove to the queen she wasn't just an angry dryad tree mage from the edges of the Aurora Forest, banished for eternity for a crime she didn't commit. The anger welled in her, but she pulled it in well. This was her time.

But after she had uttered those words, "My queen," another voice rang through, a voice that made her very bones shiver in awkwardness upon hearing them.

"My lady, Queen Faery ... Elven ahh thingy, I am most impressed with this castle, although there are some things missing here, like some Oakendark beer, seasoned loaf, and thick beer bread, oh, and some—" Before the tiny creature could further his wants list, the guard who brought him in took him out again swiftly, hoping not to be chastised later for his lack of timing. He was told to find Felvora's friends, not to bring them to the throne room.

Felvora's head again lowered. "I'm so sorry, my queen, they are my friends, and they are here with me under deep duress." As soon as Felvora finished that statement she knew it had been a bad idea.

"Duress, you say. These rude little gnomes have no place being here talking of food and drink. They should be with you, back hiding in the darkness of the edges, looking out for folly. Now, guards, I have no more time for—"

"Mother, let her speak. Trouble is here by the sounds of it, and Flora is going to tell us about it," Shaylee Aethelwyne shouted at the top of her lungs. In the past she had had a long-time friendship with Felvora and her half-sister, and she would not let her mother's bitter mourning or forgotten passion stop a threat that may be upon them, even if there hadn't been a threat in a thousand cycles.

"OK, let her speak. The next interruption, though, will result in the Vaargix Drop, clear?"

Queen Tianna was not playing games—to threaten anyone with the Vaargix Drop meant she was not in the mood and she was going to lose it. The Vaargix Drop was the highest point in the palace, reaching high through the clouds, and it was where faeries first learned to fly. They would float out of the large hole in the wall, all the way down to the surface of Faelynn. The only thing was that if they didn't open their wings, they would drop to the bottom and splatter on impact ... so the ritual was stopped thousands of cycles ago.

That was not the end of it, though, as it was still used as punishment sometimes. They would attach heavy items to those who could fly, or wings were cut off. The mages would be turned to flesh by the arch mages before they hit the ground, so that flight or metamorphosis could not stop the devastating "sudden stop." So it was a decent threat by the queen.

"Thank you, my queen. What I am about to tell you is true, with every fiber of my being I promise it is true. Please place the noorion marker on my temple to prove it," Felvora said. The queen wasn't taking any chances and if this was the best way to get the truth to her without wasting time, then Felvora would do it.

The guards grabbed the intrusive headwear, wrapped it around the dryad's head, and stood back. The noorion was part of the essence of the oaks. It never lied and picked up dark impurities when worn. If truth were told, then it would only glow light blue.

"Now tell me, tree mage, dark forest dweller of deceit, tell me what you know of my Stalixus." The queen was angrier than Felvora had ever seen her before. She only ever knew her as a peaceful queen, but something had changed in her and if Felvora came through this experience unharmed, she intended to find out why.

Felvora took her staff from the guards and swirled it around several times until a tiny vortex of green and blue light wavered around the end of the crystal. As she continued to move it in a clockwise manner, a picture escaped the vortex of light, a picture from a quarter cycle earlier when Felvora first met the sinisters.

As the queen watched in horror, Shaylee lowered her head. The guards were whispering to each other and the maidens were crying. The queen and the palace had had a similar encounter when the king was killed, and although they had put it all down to dark magic, the reality of the sinisters was now coming to light.

As Felvora explained what had happened to the sprites in the forest and the disappearance of Stalixus, the queen suddenly changed her attitude. It was a full backflip to her usual persona of love and compassion—she fell to her knees and broke down. Shaylee picked her up gently and consoled her, careful with her wings as she sat her back onto her throne.

"I'm so sorry, Flora, I'm ..." Tianna couldn't finish her apology to one of her oldest friends, for not believing her. She had still not forgiven her for the past, but all this coming to light could help.

The noorion was now blue as Felvora turned and called for the two gnomes. They were very keen to be a part of the effort to stop the sinisters, although would have been much happier if they'd had a pint and some seasoned loaf first. It had been a big hike and they were still in need of solace, comfort, and care after the previous few days, days they wanted to forget but couldn't, not ever.

"My queen, here are my brave companions, Grilif and Darf. They helped me and other tree folk spook the beasts. I hope you will at least give them safe shelter and let them tell you their dark tales," Felvora said. "What will you have us all do now? This threat is real, and it is upon us. It is not since the darkness of Xarkynan that we have—"

"Don't say that name, never!" The queen turned away. She needed to speak with the council of the high order before she would decide. She leaned on Shaylee for support as two guards and her maidens escorted her to rest before the council meeting that would take place later that night.

As the queen was leaving, Darf followed, hoping he would get a high order lunch, but an Elvenfae guard hit him with his staff and flung him across the room to Felvora's feet.

"Hey, you tall, winged stiff, put your staff down and I'll—" Before Darf could finish, Felvora put her hand over his mouth to quieten his anger, laughing to herself on the inside at the might of such little creatures which she protected every day.

Felvora couldn't help being a little anxious now. She had given them all the information, but would she be invited to any further meetings? Her friend Shaylee had gone, and she was left in an empty chamber with obnoxious Elvenfae guards—pompous bastards, she usually called them. She turned around, thinking it would now be exile for her, when Stexinzar grabbed Felvora's arm gently and guided her to a tiny door on the east side of the halls. This led to the dwellings for lower-class guests, which was much more than Felvora expected or wanted.

"So, there will be a meeting in the south chamber of the Forland

Rooms tonight. I cannot say any more, Flora, and I don't want to. The queen is very distressed at the moment and even tiny gralik snails have been punished lately, so don't ask, please. You will be part of the meeting and that's it." Stexinzar was angry—not at Felvora, but more so at the way the place was slowly falling apart. The only Elvenfae that was holding things together now seemed to be Shaylee, and everyone was looking up to her. But without the queen, Faelynn would surely fall. She was the rock, the guard, and the ultimate power-keeper of the lands, so she had to be strong.

"Thank you, Stex, I gathered that."

As Stexinzar left the room, he turned and looked at Felvora. She winked. He lowered his head and smiled, then exited, leaving the gnomes to run amok and Felvora to remember the past while looking to the future, smiling hard at one stage, although not letting the ravaging party gnomes see it.

A STIR IN
XARKYNAN

WHILE THE ELVENFAE WERE HAVING their brief reunion and deciding what to do about the darkness that was taking the ones they loved the most, something was rising in another dark place, a place that had been quiet for a thousand cycles and was not spoken about.

Since the bodiless Zeytar broke the spell many cycles ago and took the body of the dark necro-mage, he had made a painful yet rewarding connection with his host. The blending of the two minds had created a formidable symbiosis. With the combination of their minds, the Zeytar was able to gain access to some of the dark necro-mage's memories. Although not all at once because it was still painful, he was starting to slowly, over time, put the pieces back together of what had happened and work out what his role could be in the future.

He liked his new home. The power he seemed to be gaining through the host was something he had never felt before. As a race of scientists, the Zeytars used technologies and their strong minds to subjugate weaker-willed races throughout their long history. But this was something totally different. This was eventually going to be real power, the mix of his mind and the abilities of the host's body. There was a strange connection to this world, and the forces that seemed to come from nature really excited the Zeytar.

Looking down at his twisted, bony fingers, the new necro-mage pulled up the sleeves of his dusty, dark cloak, then picked up a very heavy book, which he almost dropped as he was still very weak. The moon would pass over many times before he would be strong enough to explore and find his place, but in the meantime he was trying to learn as much as he could. Still battling to regain important memories from the host, he took it upon himself to do research from the books that were in his quarters.

The book was now open to a page with very unusual writing on one side and pictures of creatures on the other. He had no problem reading the very ancient text as he scoured his mind for the dialect. The Zeytar read for many moons after he awakened and had already learned a lot about the different types of dark creatures and evil that were in this realm. He could certainly use some help if he was going to eventually find a way to awaken the dark lord.

The dark necro-mage's spindly index finger flicked the page over, and ran down the next one slowly. When he thought he got close to finding some information that he could use, the finger came to a stop. He read the text closely and lifted his gray, almost skeletal face up to think.

The hood on his cloak had fallen behind his neck, revealing the necro-mage's pointed ears, long, gray, wiry hair and dark red, almost black, eyes staring off into the distance as he pondered on his newfound information. He looked down at the large, dusty page one more time before snapping the whole book shut. The echo could be heard throughout the entire level of the castle as he made his way swiftly out of the necro-mage's chambers and down the hall to where the dark lord once resided.

He had ventured around parts of the castle over time, mostly out of curiosity, although he had not yet entered the room he was heading for. He had a memory fire and knew the information he had just read led to this part of the castle. He was now most curious as to how the dark lord received his original power and if there was something that he could do to hasten his revival.

The necro-mage hobbled up to the room. The door was very large and heavy, and his spiny back and weak, thin body had to work hard to try to open it. But it was locked. The necro-mage took a deep breath. He thought to himself that if he could just leave this body for a moment, he could enter the room, find what he was looking for, and then regain his position back inside the host. However, the scientific part of the Zeytar overrode this thinking. He realized that if he were to leave this host, the body would be so weak without the spell holding it inside the vortex that it would surely perish, leaving him stranded.

At that very moment, another memory neuron fired, and the necro-mage remembered where the key was. He had it around his neck all this time, along with a green gem, and an unusual set of smaller keys. The necro-mage pulled the frayed string from around his neck. The key was quite large, but it was very light.

He peered through the keyhole and could see nothing but darkness, although upon further inspection he thought he saw something move in the dim shadows. Dismissing any kind of threat, the necro-mage placed the key inside the lock, and with an almighty push, the door slowly moved open, creaking so loud that some spiral-tailed rats scampered down the hallway. The necro-mage gave another push, and the door was now open wide enough that he could have entered the dark chamber. But he was in no rush as a crash rattled from the east side of the enormous room. He waited just outside the door, listening for any more movement that would give away the intruder's position.

He eased the creaking door a little farther, and as he pulled his bony hands back, three little goblins, only three feet tall, tried to run past the mage.

They were dark gray, wearing old, plain clothes with what appeared to be bits and pieces of a warrior's garb. Their noses were quite long and slender, pointing down at the end toward their mouths. Their ears were very long and pointed, like knives, although their actual ear cavity and lobes were rather large.

The first two got past the mage, scampering down the hall to the main foyer and out of sight, but the last one wasn't so lucky.

Encumbered with more trinkets and gold than he could obviously comfortably carry, he tripped at the necro-mage's feet.

The necro-mage bent down, his stiff spine making cracking sounds as he moved, and put his foot on the goblin's back, holding him there until he could grab the trickster. The goblin let out a high-pitched scream, still trying to gather together all his treasures while he fought feverishly to shake off the mage's hold on him. He finally succumbed to the grip of the mage's foot and then hand, and looked up into his dark red eyes.

"Let me go, creature of darkness, what does thee want from us?" The goblin was aware now that his situation was a lot more dire than he had originally thought. He knew exactly what the dark creature was, even though he had not actually laid eyes on him before. The tales of the dark necro-mage were well known in the dark realm, nearly as widespread as tales of the dark lord himself.

"What are you doing in this room?" The scratchy, hoarse voice of the necro-mage shocked even himself, as it had felt like an eternity since he had used his vocal cords. The sound was almost like that of a weak, old creature taking its last breaths.

The goblin, feeling more confident, made another attempt to struggle out of the way. As he started wriggling around again, the necro-mage's gaze became brighter and his eyes changed to a glowing red. While this happened, the green gem around his neck shone brighter. Some subconscious reflex was allowing the necro-mage's magic to appear. Stunning the goblin with his evil gaze, the mage showed his long, sharp teeth, quite crowded in his mouth, as the upper lip became more menacing. The goblin shook violently, and then passed out.

The mage's face returned to its normal scowl as he picked the limp goblin up from the floor. After locking the dark lord's door and returning the key around his neck, he carried the creature all the way back to his lair, where he waited for the thieving trickster to awaken.

He, himself, was still shocked by what had happened, but he liked this power. It was his number one mission now to gain as much of it as he could.

~

Deep in the dark elm woods, something else had made its way up close to the dark lord's dwelling, having knocked down the beasts at the edge of the woods and alerted the watchers. Behind the guards, twisted vines surrounded the beginning of steps that led all the way up through mists and over the bridge to the main entrance of the menacing-looking castle.

The cloaked intruder seemed at home in this gloomy setting, and wandered over to the dark Elvenfae guards. The watchers of the dark realm seemed to have got bored of watching, the visitor thought.

The first guard had a lot of confidence, taking every opportunity he could to humiliate anyone that came his way. "You ... What do you want? There is nothing here, only death, and I will be glad to give you that. What do you think, Daarr, do you think he came here for death?"

Daarr looked at his colleague, someone he had obviously spent a long time with over many moons, protecting with ease something that was worth protecting in their minds. It was only a matter of time, they thought, before the dark lord awoke.

"Yes, death, Fladinn, it's definitely death," the other guard spat his unwanted comment out into the world.

The hooded figure finally spoke, "Why is there light up in the dark? Why is there light where no one dares to dwell? You are supposed to be the watchers of the dark realm and all I can see is incompetents and stupidity. Now tell me everything that you have witnessed." The cloaked figure was not playing games. It was obvious that whoever this was had been here before and was likely to come back again. The guards now realized who they were talking to, and decided to be more forthcoming.

"Darkness has awoken. There have been green lights, there have been storms, shadows, and screams throughout the castle. We both have seen this, and we know it is not the dark lord. The necro-mage has awoken, and we are all under his command," the dark Elvenfae guard, obviously frightened, said.

Without a word, the dark hooded creature turned, walked back down the most dangerous path of the elm forest, and disappeared into the dense, foreboding brush.

"So, Daarr, who was that?" Fladinn said as the figure disappeared.

"I don't know, but I've seen him once before, long ago."

They knew they had screwed up, as every creature that approached the dark castle had to be taken before the necro-mage. This was the reason they were there in the first place. They lived in the bottom of the castle, about eleven of them, rotating through shifts, century after century, keeping the steps clear so no one could take ownership of the dark dwelling until the dark lord's return. They all believed that would be soon, although this was the first visitor they had encountered since the early days after the war, so they were a little taken aback.

≈

Glinoxx awoke, not calm by any means, more a mess of violent emotions and sounds that would likely wake the dead.

"Shut it, please," the necro-mage snapped, before calming his deep, dark-toned voice.

"What do you want, crazy mage—?" But before the tiny goblin could finish, the tall, ugly necro-mage was on top of him.

"If you don't want your tongue eaten by me while you watch, then I suggest you shut it!"

Glinoxx sucked his long tongue in very swiftly, sat back, and said very carefully, "Please, my master, what is it you desire of me? I will do anything."

As the goblin finished spitting his venom out into the world, one of the dark Elvenfae guards entered the room.

"You wanted us to ... tell you, sir, if something came through ... to ... um ..." The frightened guard had known many moons of darkness and fear over his lifetime, especially during and immediately after the dark war. He was now broken—broken by time and the scars of ages. But he was not defeated just yet, and that was why he was standing there, in front of the dark necro-mage.

Looking away from his goblin slave, the Zeytar in necro-mage's body turned to the guard, and whispered, "Yes, I did, didn't I. Now get me whatever it was, or whoever came through. I want to see them." He had absolutely no idea what the previous instructions were or who they were given to over the many cycles. All he knew now was that he did not want any betrayal or interruptions as he made plans for his own benefits.

The guards were very swift. They had their orders, and they went into the forest as fast as they could go. But when in the haste of their pursuit it seemed they had accidentally awoken Maliin, the rock troll, they knew they had some extra work on their hands.

The rock troll hadn't actually been asleep; they had just caught it at the wrong time. Now it swung its left arm over both guards. The land was mostly green here as they were close to the edge of the dark elm forest, however that made no difference to the troll. Bang, and again, then again. It hit one of the horses and knocked them all to the ground.

The beast stood over the two guards and lifted its mighty club up to bring it down on them. Just then a flood of flying scroot bats came from nowhere, benevolent creatures, happy to continue on with their own unknown mission. The momentary distraction was enough for both guards to leap onto Fladinn's horse, and move away from the troll toward their target.

Meanwhile, the hooded figure, who was nearly out of the dark forest by then, turned, saw the commotion in the distance, and headed back to rage at the guards for following him.

He was still covered up but wearier now. "What, why is it you would follow me, I should—" But before the hooded one could finish, the guards told him they had been instructed to take him back to speak with the necro-mage. He agreed, eager to discover what was going on in the castle.

~

Before long, the hooded one was kneeling before the Zeytar in necro-mage's body and awaiting his response.

Swiping the hood off the captured creature in front of him, the new necro-mage fired off a barrage of questions. Eventually, after the interrogation, the hood was back in its place again over the stranger's head. An understanding had been reached and a new alliance made, before the hooded stranger was escorted by dark elves back to the edge of the foreboding forest.

The creature walked out of the dark elm woods, and its disguise of grotesque features crumbled away. As he disappeared into the night, the trees folded back to their original positions.

The guards withdrew, shaking their heads, confused about what had happened. Only the necro-mage and the hooded creature were privy to the conversations that were had in the castle, and any plans or conspiracies were only known to the two of them. The guards had been sent out of the room for the duration of the talks and had to wait until they were finished. They preferred that, anyway. As long as they were fed, they didn't care; it was none of their business who this stranger was.

Turning their horses around, they took the safest way back through the forest.

≈

The dark necro-mage, the bodiless Zeytar's host, was originally a dark elven stray guard who "defected" before the war. He was nearly good enough to be one of the twelve dark warrior guards for the dark lord, however when he was denied this, he became bitter, even spiteful enough to turn against all he knew. He began practicing forbidden dark magic, learning as much as he could to earn a place inside the castle.

Eventually he became so dark and twisted that the forest feared him. The Fae feared him, and after he saved the dark lord from a flock of long-winged swamp vipers, turning them into stone, the dark lord finally saw his potential and let him rise through the ranks of mages to become the main and only dark necro-mage. He was entrusted with every secret and became the dark lord's number two over every other creature working for him, until the last day when the king, queen, and their warriors, including Felvora, overpowered them all.

They destroyed all the guards and warriors, and defeated the dark lord along with the necro-mage in a battle of magic and power with Felvora, nearly killing her before she sent his mind into a time vortex and stopped his powerful evil once and for all.

The downside to Felvora's victory was that she had had to use energy from the Fae, killing some of her own friends and guards to gain enough power to fulfill the spell. Felvora had not noticed this, as she thought the power was coming from within her, but she had become so depleted that energy tore out of two of the queen's close guards and friends. So although Felvora had saved everyone that day and put a stop to the destructive evil plaguing the realms, she was banished to the Aurora Forest, and there she had stayed since.

This memory was still very vivid inside the newly awoken necro-mage. He wanted Felvora very much, as he watched her in his mind's eye, playing out the last scenes of the war before his host succumbed to her power. He wanted her power now and would include this as part of his plan, which was slowly unfolding.

He still could not remember his name, or rather the name of his host, which would be vital in order for him to conceal his true Zeytar identity as his agenda rolled out. He wondered where he could find that information, as his mind was blank when it came to these important details.

As he pondered some more on this, he heard the goblin screaming from down the hallway. He was still smiling at the new alliance that had just been established, and the possibility of eventually awakening the dark lord to complete what he started all those cycles earlier.

The necro-mage wandered down the hall. The goblin was wailing and carrying on like a child who'd had his favorite toy stolen, hissing and scratching at his arm, trying to break free from the tight binds that held the grotesque creature on the chair.

As the necro-mage entered the room, the goblin, who thought he'd been forgotten, let out another cry. "Are you crazy, mage, what if I choked, or something came in and ate me?" Glinoxx was obviously being dramatic, although he calmed his tone very swiftly when the necro-mage's eyes started turning that same dark red color they had been earlier.

"Do I need to remind you what I can do to you, imp, or are you ready to compromise and work for me? You will be rewarded for your efforts as I try to build the castle back up and awaken the dark lord."

The goblin's face dropped. His wrinkled gray face, filled with growths as well as his permanent, sad-looking scowl, was no longer moving as he responded to the latest announcement, "You are waking the dark lord? How, why, I mean, how?" Glinoxx looked confused. Goblins were usually tricky and vile little creatures, but his whole temperament had changed into a childlike state, and he was genuinely concerned.

"Yes, and I need your help. If you tell me the truth as to why you were in his room thieving, and if you agree to be my assistant, I will set you free and give you and your friends whatever they desire once the dark one is awake. However, if you betray me, I will hunt every goblin down, skin them all, and eat their carcasses slowly while they scream, all while you watch. Do you understand me, goblin?"

Glinoxx just stared, his confidence shot, his quick vile tongue silent. He had nothing to say; he could only nod slowly up and down.

The Zeytar inside the mage had bonded well, and more of the host's personality was creeping through. Things the Zeytar would never do or say in his own body were flowing out. The hybrid of minds would eventually be a more formidable one than he could have ever expected, and these changes would continue as time went on. "Oh, I was hoping you would say no, as I was looking forward to a nice, tasty goblin feast. But anyway, good for you. Now, why were you inside that room and what were you taking?" The croaky hiss of the mage's voice was still very off-putting, although the goblin was slowly becoming used to its eerie pitch.

"Well, master, we heard that there were some dark treasures in that room. We are thieves, so we worked together to open the lock, not thinking anyone dwelled there anymore. We plundered what we could and also wanted to steal the Torc, you know, the bracelet the dark lord wore with the stone of Toozookus on it to control weaker creatures. We just wanted the stone to sell." Glinoxx looked away for a moment, and then returned the necro-mage's stare once more, awaiting a response.

"Did you find such a prize?" the necro-mage whispered as he slowly walked around the goblin, intimidating him as was usual during an interrogation.

"No, my master. We scampered when we heard you. My brothers and I only found pieces of gold and trinkets from the realm of humans, nothing of worth, my master."

The necro-mage knew he was telling the truth. The Zeytar still had that connection of mind in a small way, more intuitiveness than anything else now, but he was satisfied.

"Please, sire, will you be finished soon? I have answered your desired questions." Glinoxx was getting really agitated. Goblins could not sit long at one time as they were a hyperactive species of twisted gnome folk that needed to be constantly moving.

"One more thing before I loosen the bindings. Do you remember my name? I know you wouldn't have been born yet, but what do the histories say about my name? Tell me this and I will set you free."

Glinoxx looked very confused. Was this a trick question or was the necro-mage really having trouble remembering his own name?

The necro-mage could see this had confused the goblin, so he added, "I have been asleep for so long, and before that they always knew me as the dark necro-mage, so the cobwebs need clearing, if you will. Tell me this now."

Glinoxx seemed to understand now and without hesitation he whispered, "Viltzin'un'dandaar." He then repeated it a little louder, as the look on the mage's face was that of confusion. "Your name is Viltzin'un'dandaar. Please, you will let me out now?" Glinoxx wriggled his hands. The necro-mage stared off into the distance, until eventually his attention was broken by the erratic movements of the desperate goblin.

"Yes, I gave my word, but know this: I will also keep my other word about your kin. Find your friends and come straight back to me."

When the mage had finished untying Glinoxx, the goblin jumped up and ran for the door. But then he turned and re-entered the room. He quickly picked up his trinkets and headed straight back out. As he exited the room, he turned once again, smiled a little, and yelled back, "Yes, my master, we will return to you soon."

Glinoxx took off down the maze of halls. The mage could hear his high-pitched laughing and screaming as he continued moving away until eventually they were nothing more than distant echoes of a crazy goblin's joy at being free.

The necro-mage, feeling his strength growing, went to the room of records and magic where all the books of the histories of all the realms sat, along with all he would need for the dark magic research that would eventually assist with his plan to reanimate the dark lord.

As he entered the room of records, he fell to his knees and screamed in pain, his head on fire as the symbiotic forces were being pushed aside by the crowding of billions of voices. He was now attached to the hive again. A ship must be here harvesting, he thought. He could only listen to the hive, and could not commune with the Leader, as he had been declared a traitor and had been cut off. Why was he able to hear them, though? It must be because of the strong mind blend with the original mage. This could be a good thing, my way to get back, he thought.

He would know when they returned and eventually he could show the Leader how important this place was. By the sounds of the echoes in his mind, the Zeytars that were sent for harvesting had no idea about the magic here and how a DNA blend of these creatures could make a difference in the wars to come. "After the dark lord has risen, we could capture him, and I would be worshiped by the Leader and my peers and given redemption. Yes, once we have taken all the land, we will control all realms and all Zeytars can dwell here and on Earth," he whispered to himself, as he smiled, before the signal was completely lost and he was left with his symbiotic host once again.

"Time to start the plan. When those dirty little goblins get back, we will go for a little walk into the dark forest to recruit for our first mission, a mission to gain new soldiers and find the lost books of Varzunnos." He had received this knowledge from his earlier visitor and he now had his full plan ready to start the first stages.

"This realm is mine," he whispered.

AN INSIDIOUS
REPRISAL

THE COUNCIL HAD BEEN FULLY INFORMED of the incidents that had befallen Vylass and the folk in the Aurora Forest. Felvora's detailed accounts, along with Darf and Grilif's, were invaluable to the plans the council would now make to overcome this evil.

Felvora and the two little ones were sent back to their rooms while the queen and the council members deliberated and argued about how they were going to execute the plans. The first idea was to make sure that Xarkynan was still silent, the second was to take a small contingent of the queen's Elvenfae warriors to find the gray sinisters, and the third was to send word to the keepers of the Tuatha treasures, the four elemental stones that held in each an element. These four stones gave the realms of Faelynn their protection and magic, and if there was movement from the dark places, then the security needed to be tightened. The only issue was that the four elemental stones were separated and only accessible by the queen and a select few, so she would have to leave the palace, with much resistance from the council, to alleviate any threat that might bring down their world.

"My queen, I sincerely insist that you do not go ahead with this. Without the king now, and with you leaving, Faelynn is under threat. We have already closed off all the human portals to the Earth realm, and we have guards on every single oak portal, mound, or ring. The only ones who can now enter the Earth are the enchanted ones, including yourself and Shaylee. If something were to happen to you, the risks to our realm would not only come from here but also from the humans we have kept away from for millennia." The head of the high council, Faelondar, was wise. He was the adviser when the queen was busy visiting her people, from the little folk to the giants, in more peaceful times when there was no threat, although at the rate her people were disappearing, she would soon have no one to protect at all.

"It is unknown at this stage, Faelondar, what these creatures are after, and every attempt should be made to insure our people are safe. There has been nothing but whispers and rumors coming from the dark elm woods near Xarkynan for centuries, and besides, some turn out to be just a dark elf pretending to be the dark lord here and there. We have had peace, but I will not risk these entities finding out about our power. So I must go to Maelenflitt and make sure nothing has been disturbed."

Tianna knew where every one of the treasure stones was located. One was in the palace, one was in Aurora with Villara, one was in Maelenflitt, and the last was hidden in plain sight in Xarkynan. The Tuatha Dé Danann placed them there at the very beginning of time and there they stayed, safe, with only a very few at a time knowing where they were, each king and queen along with the protectors of the treasures.

Faelondar couldn't argue. Although he wanted to very much, he knew it would be useless. So, he went the other way, offering as many council guards and warriors as he could.

"Fine, my lady, I see we will agree to disagree. Then, I will set you up with our finest warriors along with your best palace guards to accompany you. However, Shaylee must stay. We cannot afford our last two leaders risking themselves for these creatures."

The queen nodded, stood, and made her way to the main throne room. Her wings were loose, pointing down to the floor like they were tucked away, ready for riding. The Elvenfae royal guards very rarely chose their sprite form. It was dangerous to be so vulnerable, but at times it was necessary, as they couldn't fly very well in full Elvenfae form with ceremonial armor on. So sometimes their wings would fold down, out of the way and out of sight, when they weren't needed. The warriors and standard guards were different—they were strong and could fly in all conditions.

The queen was in a hurry; she had heard enough and was losing family members fast. This threat had to be stopped. Even one of the elemental treasure stones harbored enough power to amplify most threats, so she was fixated on this. It was her fight now.

Shaylee ran into the throne hall, quite upset. "Mother, this is not a good idea. Let me go. I am the best warrior here and I know what I am doing. Besides, I want a piece of them too." Shaylee was excitable. She had not been apart from her mother often, and after hearing what they raised at the council, she was very concerned for her mother's safety.

"You know you cannot, Shaylee. Now see Felvora away for her trip to the edges of Xarkynan. There she will commune with some dark sylphs to find out anything she can and bring that information back here. I need you here, Shay. Now go do what I ask of you."

Reluctantly, Shaylee turned into a sprite and fluttered swiftly to Felvora's room to say goodbye. As she entered the room, she turned back to full size and there to greet her was Felvora.

"Hey, Flora, before you go, can you put a spell on the throne hall with an illusion of me? I am going to dress in my warrior garb, along with my bow and sword, Howling Tooth, and follow Mother to Maelenflitt."

Felvora looked at her friend for a moment, knowing it was a risky plan. But she knew she couldn't talk her out of it. Shaylee and her mother were close and this was something she needed to do.

"OK, Shay, but if I get caught, it was your spell, OK? I'm already hated enough."

Shaylee nodded and turned to change into a sprite again, but before doing so she whispered, "I will meet you back here before we both leave."

Felvora nodded. She looked like she fit in with the royals now as she had changed herself. She was wearing a jade-colored dress with large sleeves and a low neckline, with the bottom flowing to the floor. The dryad was looking quite elegant.

Just then, Darf and Grilif dropped from the ceiling with food in their mouths.

"Ha, ha, you look ridiculous, Felvora," Darf announced.

With the flick of Felvora's finger they were both sucking up crumbs from the floor as slugs for the next five minutes.

Shaylee was back in a flash, turned to full form again. She had folded her wings to point to the floor and was dressed in heavy Celtic battle attire, with bow, quiver with arrows, and a scabbard with her beloved sword. She was definitely ready for battle, although she had to be discreet. Her sprite form was that of tree folk, and they all returned to nature when they were small, which gave her a perfect disguise. She would hide inside one of the guards' satchels, and if she was caught, she would seem just like the others until it was too late to send her back.

Felvora gave her approval, and before Shaylee could turn to sprite form the dryad leaned into her, gave her a kiss on the cheek, and tied a small concoction of powder to her quiver.

"Here, this is a blend of some very strong powder for you for your journey; it is very powerful and used for healing, along with—"

Before Felvora could finish, Shaylee interrupted. "Thank you, my friend. I'm hoping I won't need it, though, but thank you. Be safe yourself and when we both return, we have much to catch up on." And as she finished talking, Shaylee turned back into a sprite and caught up with the warriors on horseback traveling with her mother as they started off on their journey. She hid inside an Elvenfae guard's satchel like she said she would and waited there.

Meanwhile, Felvora returned the mischievous gnomes back to their original forms and then cast a holographic spell onto the throne before all the maidens, guards, and other staff arrived back in the room. After she'd finished, she found herself a horse from the stables and went about her journey to the edges of Xarkynan, while the rest of the warrior Elvenfae guards took position in their ranks to go searching for the sinisters.

All contingents were in place; however, the palace was now empty. There were no Aethelwynes ruling. If this got out, it could start unrest in the palace and eventually in Faelynn. Felvora's hologram would only work for a brief time, and after that the council would have to select a temporary ruler in their stead, but they would find it hard to control the situation the longer they were away.

Night fell on the palace. Eventually the hologram dissipated and Faelondar was left standing in front of the throne, scratching his head, and hoping quietly to himself that they all return soon.

ON THE ROAD TO MAELENFLITT

The queen had been traveling very swiftly for two days; they would reach the outskirts of Aurora soon and enter the realm of the woodlands. The queen had only stopped for rests at night, getting back on the horses as soon as the sun started illuminating the trees. She had to check on the two far treasure stones. The one in Xarkynan was not accessible or protected by any guards.

They rode with haste, reaching the forest of Toozookus. Within a few short days they would reach the outer forest of Maelenflitt so they had plenty of work still ahead. Shaylee had found a nice little spot, although she felt bad that the others were doing all the work to reach the locations. She would wait until they reached the first outpost and then she would reveal herself. But something was about to change— not only her plans but also all those of the queen and the guards.

When they arrived, the sun had an hour to set before it became completely dark. The queen took two of her most trusted guards, Stexinzar and Feelik, to the forest entrance.

Enchanted by willows and large oaks, this place was a very mystical part of Maelenflitt. The sylphs took care of the forest, getting their magic from the thick willows. But it was more than that. The first of the treasure stones was somewhere here, giving the land a deep power boost, being so close. The willows seemed to be charged by its power and the flow-on effect trickled down to each of the enchanted creatures that dwelled in the area, none of which were any the wiser that the priceless artifact sat somewhere nearby.

The queen climbed from her horse, then the two guards did as well. As they approached the large willow at the entrance to the forest, several creatures started manifesting around the queen, curious why she was there. Before the guardian of the treasure stone appeared, the willow tree started shedding its white fluffy pollen as if it were fall, and the leaves began floating down even though it was not fall and there was no breeze.

Tianna knew who it was as the pollen slowly came together forming the shape of a woman. As the particles connected even more, taking their place was a beautiful woman. Her dress was pure white and flowing, and her hair was also pure white like snow, as was her face. Her legs were hidden as if she were in a cloud, but she could walk normally, moving slowly toward Tianna. White and blue sylphs were dancing around her head, singing in harmony.

As she moved another step closer, she spoke, "My queen, Tianna, oh how wonderful it is to see you again. I know why you have come." The woman's voice echoed as she talked, as if there were several of her talking all in sequence.

"It is so wonderful to see you too, my old friend. Please tell me the treasure is safe," Tianna whispered.

The sylphs who had turned into a woman with no name, for she was made of the forest and was as old as the land itself, spoke once more, "Yes, the treasure is safe, but I am afraid you are not. You must leave this place before the evil returns. They do not know about our treasure. They only want our little ones to control for their beasts. Now, you must not stay."

As she said her final words she started breaking apart into millions of white follicles, returning without a breeze to the branches they once sat on. As the light of the day was now completely gone, the illuminated willow started dimming to match all the other trees in the area.

The queen was satisfied, although disturbed by the last thing the messenger said.

"Come, we don't have a lot of time. We will rest and continue in the morning."

The guards nodded, led the queen to the camp, and rested from another long, weary day.

Hours later, there was a rumble through the trees, a huge shrill and a glowing light. One warrior woke up several others and he wandered over to the edge of the forest. As the first guard turned to his companions to indicate nothing was there, he was struck over the head with an almighty force. Along with the blunt blow came a loud growl. It was a Sasquatch.

It was obviously recruiting, but there were no gray sinisters with it and it had no sprites attached. It came closer to the rest of the guards. In response, they shot it with several arrows, piercing its enormous face and heart. The beast let out a high-pitched cry as it ran into the forest and disappeared into more glowing lights, leaving nothing more than a few drops of blood on the ground.

The queen and the other warriors were awake now. There was no discussion at all as every one of them packed up the camp and horses, and fled from the area.

Shaylee had planned to come out but had fallen asleep. She was more than awake now but couldn't get out of the satchel until the guard stopped.

A scream came from the rear of the group of riders. When they turned around they saw several gnomes, sprites, sylphs, even trees running toward them, screaming nonsensically.

The queen ordered everyone to stop and wait. As she did so, a tremendous noise came from above as the moon and stars were blocked from view before three light beams descended from the sky and disappeared soon afterward. There in front of them all were the gray sinister creatures that the other troupe were tasked to find. These creatures were everywhere, although the one out in front looked sicklier than the other five that were standing near him, thought the queen.

Ugly destructive goblins from the dark pits, she thought. As she was gaining her composure and gearing up to give orders to attack, she was struck from behind by one of their gigantic beasts. Tianna was out for a moment, and as the commotion continued, Shaylee surfaced from the satchel. Just as she was about to transform to full size, she was stunned by one of the gray goblins. Pulling her closer with one of its strange toys, he raised her above the head of another beast along with several other sprites that had been caught previously.

Shaylee fought and fought as much as she could, but to no avail. She eventually succumbed to the dark magic the creatures had over her and the rest of her people, and was now under the complete control of the beast underneath them.

Tianna had no idea that Shaylee had been captured. In fact, none of them saw it. The guards were doing everything they could to eliminate the threat, but it was no use. One by one they were hypnotically forced to change into sprites, stunned, then placed with one of the many beasts that were standing around.

Tianna stood up. She noticed one sprite had a tiara like Shaylee's, and when the realization sank in, she screamed out her name over and over, "Shaylee! They have taken my Shaylee! Help, guards, they have her."

The guards were also in strife as they tried to battle the gray goblins, but the closer they got, the quicker they were being transformed and added to the collection. The dark magical symbiosis that the sinisters had over the Fae was like nothing Tianna had ever seen before. They were unstoppable. Quick, controlling, and pure evil.

As the last of her guards were taken, three turned into sprites and dashed for the quiet of the woods without being seen, leaving Tianna there alone to face the creatures all at once. She pulled her sword from her scabbard and swung at the sickly looking one first, although upon further inspection they all looked to be changing color to a pale scaly form. They did not look well at all. As she tried a second strike, Tianna was zapped, changed, and sent among her people like her daughter had been, becoming angry and hateful, and controlled through the mind of the beasts they were now attached to. As the lights from the ships illuminated again, the unlucky Maelenflitt folk that had sought the warrior guards' help were all incinerated from the external lights, purposely turned on to burn an imprint of the visitation.

As the ships ascended quickly into the sky, the remaining gnomes, sylphs, trees, and forest pixies were left screaming in pain as they slowly burned alive from the searing heat of the sinisters' craft, a reminder of the destructive nature of such an insidious race.

The three guards had watched the last of the devastating effects unfold, turning into full Elvenfae form and rushing out to help the victims who were still alive. But by then it was too late.

Feelik looked down at a little pixie forest girl, still with her red and white socks pulled up and her dress made of flowers, half cindered, as her youthful face turned up toward him, eyes wide open in a gaze of pure fear. Feelik bent down, with tears running down his cheeks. The strong guard was obviously very upset. He picked her up and turned back toward the forest. Her body had only just finished burning so she was still very hot, but he didn't care.

The other two were Stexinzar and a trainee guard. They followed suit, picking up some innocent forest folk and putting out the other ones who were still ablaze. This all happened so quickly and there was no time to save any of them, let alone the lot. There were about thirty that would now have loved ones missing them.

Feelik laid the small pixie girl on a soft edge next to a tall dotted mushroom. This was where most of these folk lived and he just wanted to be as careful as he could. While this was happening, the ones that had not ventured out into the opening when the disaster played out were appearing from their houses, one by one finding loved ones and screaming in grief and despair for their loss. It was devastating for the guards, the protectors of the free folk and all of Faelynn, to watch as families of sylphs and gnomes took their loved ones back to their homes. This was a place that had never seen evil. It was not involved in the dark war and had nothing but love within its people.

Feelik could not take it anymore and with no orders from Stexinzar, he gathered a frightened horse that had fled, and made his way back to Faelynn with haste.

The other two were not happy that he had just left like that.

After finding horses, they too left the free folk to clean up a devastating mess they should never have had to deal with. Stexinzar looked back over his shoulder and saw some gnomes and forest people searching in desperation for them, crying and screaming. One even ran alone behind the horses until she could no longer keep up and fell to her knees as the Elvenfae disappeared out of sight.

TWO DAYS LATER

Feelik was always ahead of the other two. He himself had not rested. He would pause briefly to get water for his horse and then was on his way again. When his horse needed rest, he would pause, but not for long periods of time.

He arrived at the palace first and called for a meeting of the council immediately. He knew that Stexinzar would not be far behind so he wanted everything ready and in play before he arrived—though he respected Stexinzar as a brilliant leader and a brave warrior, he didn't fully trust him. He knew that Stexinzar was fiercely ambitious and would be the one to want control of the whole province until Shaylee or Tianna returned.

But the council did not believe Feelik, even though he was trusted by the queen. He was a lower-ranking guard and there was no one else around to corroborate his story. Feelik was arrested for making false allegations and sent to the prisons below the palace.

Three hours after Feelik's arrest, Stexinzar arrived, and without answering the council's questions went straight down to the dungeons where Feelik was being held. Stexinzar had been forewarned as he entered the gates to the palace, and upon entering the dungeon cell, he whispered to Feelik, "I know why you did it, running off like that. I know all three of us betrayed our queen, but if you ever leave me when I need you the most, I will cut your wings off, do you understand me?"

Feelik lowered his head, nodded slowly, and looked back up at

Stexinzar, whispering back, "I will never forget her face, Stex, never. I'm sorry."

Stexinzar unlocked the cell door, grabbed Feelik's shoulder. "Let's concentrate now on protecting the rest. Are you with me?" he asked.

Feelik regained his composure, nodded, and walked with Stex up the stairs and out into the fresh air again, where the heads of council were awaiting some long overdue answers.

Once everyone was seated in the meeting room, one guard closed the doors; this would be a private council because of the sensitivity of the information, and to prevent panic sparking in the land. Stexinzar stood on the high stump in front of the council. The council was a mixture of all the main heads of the city folk in Faelynn, a representative to help maintain a peaceful balance across the land. There were twenty-five council members, led by Faelondar.

Stex explained everything that had happened, the reasons they fled, and described hearing the last words of the queen, screaming for Shaylee. The council were silent. Feelik had been telling the truth and after hearing it from Stexinzar they had no other choice but to believe it.

Faelondar stood, walked over to the royal stump after Stex had left it, and spoke to the room, "If this is true, we have no leaders here, we have no one to protect us. This must not leave this room. Anyone caught whispering or spreading these truths around will be dealt with harshly. There is only one way to proceed—the council must deliberate and discuss what should happen from this day forth until either Shaylee or Queen Tianna return. The council meeting is adjourned until the petal bells ring around the palace, after which every single Fae in this room now will be required to attend this chamber immediately, not one more or one less, do we all understand?" Faelondar finished and the crowd all yelled "yes" in harmony.

Hours passed and Stex was getting agitated. He really wanted the top spot, but he would never admit it. All the councilors were excluded from taking the highest post even as a fill-in, as that was deemed corruption and would make the council unfit for decisions in the future. So one of two things was going to happen, Stex thought to himself. They would either run the palace as a collective and announce the queen and princess were on a particularly important mission that required them both. Or they would choose from the Elvenfae warriors of the queen to fill in. Giving one guard such power was dangerous, and having the council run the palace and decide without a leader would cost valuable time when a decision needed to be made straightaway, which could also be dangerous. Either way the decision was out of Stexinzar's hands.

The petal bells finally rang throughout the palace. Normally this meant the council had made some sort of decisions that required the queen's attendance, so the rest of the palace Fae went about their business as if nothing was out of the ordinary.

Stexinzar was the first of the guards in the meeting room, followed by the rest of the guards involved. The council was already seated and Faelondar was atop the stump.

As the last guard entered, Faelondar opened the record of his decision and began reading.

"As you are all aware of the situation that has played out over the last days, we the council of the queen's Fae and her lands within Faelynn, excluding the dark realms, will be under a provisional leader. It is of the utmost importance that this decision be met with positive response and that all in this room be held to account for any whispers about the events."

Stex was fidgeting. His wings, folded down and pointing to the floor, were flittering at the ends, showing his nervousness. This was a first, as he was always the strong, positive, calm Elvenfae warrior guard that was respected by everyone—why would this decision make any difference?

Faelondar went on, "This decision was not made lightly. After assessing every detail of how this could all play out, we have no other option than to assign the high warrior guard to the queen and friend to all Fae, Stexinzar Crimsonmoon, with the power to the palace. It will still be under the direction of the council, although the running of things will be left to Stex. He is the highest ranking guard, the strongest warrior. He knows all the protocols, procedures, and is the most respected and trusted by the queen. We have considered his version of events and why he wasn't protecting the queen at the time of her capture, and believe this is the best option to hold off any dark forces that try to enter Faelynn, including the sinister goblins. How do we all feel?"

Stex was now smiling. His flittering wings had stopped moving. There was a unanimous clap of approval and Stexinzar made his way up the stairs to the high stump.

"Thank you, council, my resolve is to protect these lands, destroy the sinisters, and hunt for our queen for as long as I still have breath."

As Stexinzar finished his very brief speech, Feelik noticed Stex's wings flittering for the second time, but not as if he were nervous. It seemed more like Stex was enjoying this, like he had wanted the queen away so he could rule. Feelik hated thinking that because he respected Stexinzar, but this whole situation just wasn't making sense. The times were changing fast and he did not like it one bit, so in his mind he resolved he would keep an extra eye on Stexinzar, hoping he was wrong.

ABSENCE BRINGS DARKNESS

ZEYTAR CONTROL

IN THE TIME FOLLOWING THE ATTACK in Maelenflitt, Felvora did not return from her mission to the dark elm woods with the gnomes. The Elvenfae warriors sent to find the sinisters were also not seen again, and whispers spread that either the queen had embarked on a secret journey with her daughter, or that she had been killed in battle. Either way the Fae were becoming agitated.

The sinisters returned several more times, taking whomever they desired, and incinerating the rest. They always seemed to aim for the more remote places, making it hard to track them down or work out where or when they would appear.

Stexinzar had lost many guards over this time. As much as he wanted to make a good impression on the council by finding these creatures and ridding Faelynn of them, he was always two steps behind. It wasn't until twelve moons had cycled that he received his first piece of good news.

One of the sinisters had fallen in a small outpost near the edges of Maelenflitt. A pooka named Viddiar spotted it at the edges of Lake Sheeleymoon. She was gathering some water for her family when she was grabbed on the leg by what looked like a bony goblin. She hopped up in the air with fright before realizing there was no more movement coming from the creature and she lowered her head slightly to inspect it.

Viddiar had a humanoid face with exceptionally large and wide, furry gray ears, and her arms with paws on the ends were also furry. She had the body of a rabbit, although her face was a pink skin color with brown eyes. A mischievous creature, although friendly and quite whimsical when it suited, she could also be extremely dangerous and chaotic. Renowned for their poison, pookas could blow an intoxicating dust in their immediate vicinity, incapacitating their victims or even killing them.

As Viddiar leaned in closer, she heard a crack from behind her. Turning with haste she was confronted by a sinister goblin, standing tall, looking into her blinking eyes. The gray sinister with massive dark eyes and enormous bulbous head stood there staring at her. She started receiving disturbing images coming from the creature in front of her, images of darkness and evil that would break anyone's mind. The sinister was trying to do just that, tear her down.

Zeytars had no use for most creatures, so the ones they came across that were useless they murdered with their minds or one of their technical devices. But this sinister met with the wrong Fae. As the images became more intense, Viddiar started moaning. The pain was becoming more severe, so she blew some of her dust into the eyes of the gray creature, stunning it for a moment. This was enough to break the mind lock it had over her and gave her time to reciprocate the pain.

She concentrated hard on sending images straight back into the Zeytar's mind, breaking it from the inside with puzzling and cryptic thoughts. While the poison set in, the sinister grabbed its head, screamed, and fell to the ground, shaking and convulsing before its mind finally broke and it was left limp and lifeless.

Viddiar noticed the poison must have choked the creature as it turned red upon its collapse, then its skin started turning from gray to a scaly red and white before its dark open eyes fell inside its huge skull, letting Viddiar know that whatever she did worked, and worked well.

Viddiar then snapped back to her normal jovial self and even started humming a tune while she gathered the water she originally came for. She hopped over both the Zeytar bodies and swiftly made her way back to the forest where her family were awaiting her return with the water she had promised.

As the news found its way to the palace, Stexinzar sent out a young guard to find the Fae involved in bringing down the sinister. They seemed to always be accompanied by large metal birds in the sky and monstrous beasts that stole the sprites; he wanted very much to find out what exactly happened.

The lone Elvenfae guard left for Sheeleymoon Lake where the event occurred not more than half a cycle before. Whispers had spread of a warrior tall and strong from deep in the Toozookus forests somehow finding his or her way to the lake where it happened. The truth didn't need to be revealed, as the story kept hope alive for the defenseless Fae and forest folk that needed it.

Maalik Nightingstar was an expert rider, not extremely high in the ranks of the very well trained Elvenfae. Very diligent, loyal, and a promising future warrior, he had begged Stexinzar for a special mission and had now found himself on a dangerous one. He had no idea who it was that informed Stexinzar of the fallen sinisters—only he and the council knew, to protect the individual from Toozookus. But the informer must have been convincing, Maalik thought, as they were running out of fully trained Elvenfae warriors and Stex would not have risked one for a silly quest.

Maalik ceased with his daydreaming about conspiracies and concentrated on the job at hand. He was given a certain area to look at and specific questions to ask a forest dryad named Faiay'aar. Other than that, if he turned up nothing, then he was to return to the palace immediately.

Meanwhile, at the palace, a hooded figure dressed completely in black galloped out of the entrance to the low-lit unguarded gates, slipping out of sight and into the darkness while a guard was making his way up the stairs to the tower to take up his post. The palace was so short of guards, due to the many security missions, that the shifts were becoming longer and the guards were always fatigued. They sometimes left the tower to get food if no one brought it up to them—although, if they were found out, they would be severely punished. It seemed like the dark rider knew this and timed it perfectly.

The rider was very swift. His or her horse was also black, one of very few in the palace, a descendant of the great King Viltherome Aethelwyne's dark horse Nixxin, so the steed was strong and fast. It was a well-chosen colt for a hasty journey, as the rider jumped fallen trees and wrestled with the sweeping fog. The hooded one moved on and on into the darkness and the thickness of the woods leading out of the Faelynn realm, on to a much darker place, a place that at this pace would take the rider only five or six days to ride. But the dark rider would not need that amount of time. A male voice rang out and at the same time he headed straight for an enormous old elm tree.

After reciting some strange words, a blue light began to emanate from the elm and the twisted branches unwound, making an entry point through a portal to another location. As the rider reached the blue lights and disappeared into the elm, the light went out. The branches became twisted again, returning to normal as the elm finished swallowing the horse and its rider.

At the start of the dark elm woods at the edge of Xarkynan, another elm repeated the exact sequence of the first, although this one was far bigger and more twisted, and the light was different, as a red glow replaced the blue one. Hurled through the mouth of the now fully opened tree, the dark rider with his horse hit the dirt with force, before he pulled on the reins and turned to see the last of the elm's branches curl back to their comfortable resting position.

The rider couldn't help but notice the creepy smile on the elm's trunk, as if it were alive. Recovering his composure, the dark rider flicked his cloak out, kicked his heels to the horse's side, and swiftly galloped through the entrance to the foreboding and evil dark elm woods.

≈

Maalik finally reached the outpost of Maelenflitt. He was only an hour's ride away from Sheeleymoon Lake, where he was to look around and try to find evidence of the sinisters. He was hoping very much that this would pay off for him, as he wanted to become one of the main palace guards and eventually be an Elvenfae warrior, just like his father had been before him and his grandfather before that. Being a warrior was the last stage of training. First he had to take the basic trials and build his way up to guard, then he had to study and show historical knowledge of the realms as well as of the dark times.

Becoming a guard and a member of the palace warriors was not a given. It wasn't just about fighting skills and knowledge, but also loyalty, basic magic ability with the mages, and successful tasks like this that all built up. The last stages were tests of endurance of the entire spectrum of abilities under the high council, the high mages, and the high Elvenfae warriors with the queen or leader.

Even with all the warriors and guards that had fallen or were on missions now, he still wasn't guaranteed success. The standards had not dropped; in fact, due to the absence of the queen and the princess, all promotional tests were on hold. So he thought asking for these tasks now would show potential for later when these dark sinisters were no more.

Maalik finally reached the lake. He was only told bits and pieces of where the event played out, however one key piece of information was related to the two small islands in the middle of the lake, facing the entrance to the woods, and two large pillars with traditional Tuatha Dé Danann markings on them. Around two hundred paces to the left of these pillars was where the incident had allegedly occurred.

Maalik bounced off his horse once he saw the pillars and scoured the area for any clues. He was a very smart Fae so his deductions on these matters were very thorough. As he moved farther into the area, he noticed a small hand-held device that looked very foreign to him. Something made of materials he had never seen before. He was hesitant at first to pick the item up, although it would not help him in the future if he did not bring back any evidence.

Maalik thought he had nothing left to lose so he bent down and gently lifted up the unusual-looking, bent silver device, before placing it carefully into his Kaldarik bark satchel. He scoured the area but could not find any evidence of the sinister creatures that he was sent there to find. The next part of his mission was to meet up with the dryad of the forest to see whether she had any further information.

The Elvenfae reached the entrance to the forest, where a brownie jumped onto his head and tried to pull out the silver jeweled ring attached to the point of his long ear. They were brazen little creatures who didn't care for authority or size. He was dressed in ancient brown leathers with tree sap and twigs intertwined throughout his clothing. His long nose pointed out then down at the end, and his long hat, which pointed up, was stuck very well on his head.

The little forest imp was very hairy and as Maalik went to grab the tiny mischievous creature from his head, he accidentally pinched his long beard. He pulled the brownie down in front of his eyes, while it screamed in pain using very untoward language, wriggled around, and swiped at Maalik.

"Can I help you, little one? If you would like my ear jewel, maybe next time ask. It's not polite to just take what you want." Maalik had learned a lot about the forest folk, not through spending a lot of time with them, but from his studies, so he talked to the brownie without getting upset.

"Let me down, you fool! I'll scratch your eyes out with my nails if you don't."

Maalik laughed as he answered, still holding the tiny thing by his beard, "On one condition, little one. Tell me where I can find Faiay'aar and I will let you go. Now I know you are tricksters as well, so I will hold on to you until you show me the true way, not a trap to a spriggan, hobgoblins or dark elf, do you understand?"

The brownie yelped out, "OK, OK, but when I'm loose you're going to be sorry, you hear?"

Maalik only chuckled, while he squeezed a little tighter.

"Alright, stop, I will show you."

Maalik only half believed the little trickster but gave him the benefit of the doubt. Although not letting go completely, he adjusted his position so he wasn't pulling on the beard anymore, only holding the brownie in his hand and waiting for directions.

The trickster led Maalik down a thick path when they came across a small group of pixie girls, singing and dancing in a circle, looking happy even though some very dark things had happened over the last twelve cycles. The brownie laughed at the pixies, who didn't even bat their eyelids.

Maalik moved in closer as they all darted off in different directions. They were very shy creatures, although lively and happy. But Maalik was quick and blocked the escape of one of them, and then he let go of the brownie, who darted off into the dense green shrubs swearing and carrying on. He disappeared into a hollowed-out trunk, the sound of his voice waning as he got away.

The pixie stood around three and a half feet tall. She could move swiftly, with her tiny wings fluttering as she looked up at the tall Elvenfae messenger. Her dress was green, made from leaves and grass, with colored socks, obviously stolen at a time when they could enter the human realm, before the forts were closed because of the sinisters. She also had on a blue sweater which she had stolen from a clothesline in the old world many years before. Pixies were radiant creatures, although could be quite tricksy and mischievous in the human realm.

"What is your name, little one? I am here to help you," Maalik said, very slowly and calmly. He had not laid a hand on the pixie, although his body had blocked her from running off with the others.

She answered Maalik, as she tried to get past him, "I am Alvina Whittleleaf. Please, sprite, let me pass. I want to play."

The pixie was becoming a little agitated, although seemed willing to help. Maalik had spoken to her the right way and not frightened her by grabbing her arms or legs.

"Hi, Alvina, that is a beautiful name. Could you please show me where Faiay'aar lives and I will give you a gift."

Alvina fluttered her wings even more in excitement. She would have a trinket to show her friends. "What be this gift, sir?"

Maalik was not silly. He pulled the jewel from his ear, the one that the brownie was trying to steal earlier—if he had not been such a grump and hassled Maalik, he may have received the same reward. The ear jewel was not his important one as he would always put his good one from his father away when on any kind of mission or training regime. This was his spare that he had found one day.

"Here, little one, this is a very important ear jewel from my family. If you tell me where she is, I will give it to you immediately."

Alvina jumped up and down with joy. Her wings were fluttering so fast that she floated up to Maalik's eye level. At the same time Maalik closed his hand and whispered, "You may have it after I am looking at Faiay'aar."

Alvina nodded, lowered herself back down to the ground, grabbed Maalik's hand, and started running through the woods. The light streaming in was illuminating the crystal salt in some plants, creating a green and wondrous sight as the pixie kept moving on and on, still holding Maalik's hand. Her friends were chasing them, hiding behind trees and toadstools when Maalik turned his head.

Soon enough Alvina stopped, looked up at an old willow tree, and fluttered her wings fast enough to rise up to a knot in the center of the willow. She tapped three times and lowered herself back down, as they both waited silently. The other pixies were now surrounding Alvina, whispering and talking fast, like an echo, although Maalik could not make out a single word. To him it seemed like a made-up language between them.

Soon there was a bright flash and Maalik jumped back. The pixies didn't seem to mind too much as a yellow and white mist bellowed out of the willow and down onto the ground. The mist slowly formed a young woman dressed in sparkling silver from head to toe, as if it were painted on her skin. There were leaves around her midriff, under her neck, and around her wrists and ankles. Her hair was golden and sparkling in the glittering sunlight, looking quite stunning to Maalik's eyes. The beauty of the dryad in front of him mesmerized him, causing him to stutter when he spoke. "Hello, m-my ... m-my lady."

Maalik was fluttering his wings, which were all pointing down, and embarrassingly his pale face began turning a slight reddish color.

Alvina was becoming agitated, as she had her little hand out, waving it back and forth to show she wanted her prize. Maalik broke his gaze for a moment, looked down, and realized he needed to do something. He bent down to face Alvina, opened his hand up, and watched Alvina take the jewel from him as he whispered, "Thank you, my little friend, thank you very much."

As soon as he'd finished thanking the pixie, she was off in a heartbeat with her friends, disappearing into the long grass before the path to the river.

Maalik returned his attention to the lovely dryad, who was standing there looking a little put off by the attention directed toward the pixies rather than at her, although she knew what he was there for.

"My lady, I have been sent by the current guardian of the Fae and the lands, Stexinzar, to find out some information about an attack by sinisters that ended with them being defeated. Could you help me locate this individual so we may find something that could be useful in taking these creatures out forever?"

Maalik was polite and stood tall and confident in his request. The dryads were very protective of their forest folk, and even though Maalik himself was a sprite from the Aurora Forest, he was also a city dweller and it was usual for him to be treated as such—as an outsider. But not on this day. Faiay'aar had been expecting Maalik and as soon as he finished with his request he was taken up inside a mist and into the forest dryad's dwelling in the willow before him.

Maalik awoke shortly after, inside the massive home furnished with fine woods shaped from the willow itself to make fittings for doors, shelving, bedding, chairs, and so on. Nothing was constructed of materials from outside the area. All the curtains were green and purple, made from the forest, and added only to create a comfortable, functional home to live in, not for exotic, expensive, or wasteful luxury. The dryad had a symbiosis, it seemed, with the willow and the surrounding forest. She would protect them all as best she could from those who would bring harm, and the forest reciprocated with the comforts of a peacefully decked-out abode.

Maalik had seen nothing like it. He was incredibly young when he moved from the Aurora Forest and never saw the inside of Vylass or Felvora's residence. This was obviously taught in his early learning inside the palace, but nothing compared to seeing it for himself. Besides, only a few ever made it inside the walls of a dryad's home, *very* few.

"You have a very lovely home," Maalik whispered.

In the silent interior of her abode, Faiay'aar was watching through the walls like she had a sixth sense, always monitoring for her people's welfare.

"Thank you, young one. I know why you are here. They sent an owl from the palace with news of your arrival. I am not one to give out details of such matters without the consent of those involved, although when I spoke with the pooka witness, Viddiar said she would be more than happy to talk with you. Now, in saying that, have you met many pookas before? They are exceedingly rare creatures in the lands and can be very mischievous and hard to understand, especially if they are spooked or nervous, so I suggest you only speak softly and without fluttering your wings, or any sudden movements. I only know a fraction of her story at this time as she has been waiting for someone from the palace to come. Do we understand each other?"

Maalik looked blankly at her face for a moment. The Elvenfae was a little put off by all the information and rules. He had never met a pooka before, not in the flesh. He had seen some once in a field and learned about them in his studies, but he dismissed as nonsense the warnings he received when younger about dealing with one. Maalik now knew that it certainly was not. This was going to be an arduous task.

"Of course, my lady, I will be very calm and polite to her, I promise. Is there anything you can tell me beforehand or will she be the one to give all the information?" Maalik thought getting a little head start might help in case the pooka decided that she wanted no more to do with him, or if she was ranting and going off subject.

"I'm sorry, Maalik, it's now between you and her. She is waiting down the hallway and left, in the last room. I must warn you this won't be easy."

Maalik stared at Faiay'aar for a time before he turned and quietly walked down to the room where the pooka was resting and waiting.

≈

Soon another full cycle concluded. A shadowy figure entered the rear of the palace through the secret entrance only very few knew about. Dressed in a dark cloak and trying to keep out of sight, the figure entered without detection at all. He was now without the dark horse which he had ridden out of the palace three days earlier.

The figure looked as though he had some injury, as he struggled with the last part of the climb back into the unlocked spare dungeon. He disappeared into the night's darkness while two guards called for the front gates to open as Maalik entered after a long, swift ride with very important news for Stexinzar.

"Summon the Fae council and Stex. This cannot wait another moment." Maalik sounded shaken and weary, although assertive and rushed at the same time.

The guards took his horse, led him to the council hall, and sent a maid to call for Stexinzar.

Mileana approached the stand-in leader's room. He had been leader now for so long, everyone just went along with it. He had been sick for a quarter cycle with exhaustion from the ongoing dealings with running the palace. It wasn't an easy job, not by any means, and even a strong Elvenfae warrior guard had his limitations.

The maid knocked, then quickly entered his large room. Stexinzar was sitting at the end of his bed, his fluttering wings indicating he was struggling with pain as he finished rubbing some lotion on his left leg. His clothes were off and he was completely naked.

Mileana rushed straight back out of the room, calling out, "I'm so sorry, I thought you were still asleep. I'm so very sorry."

Stexinzar was a powerful warrior, although he had the reputation of having a kind heart. She did not want him to be angry with her, though.

He spoke loudly from the end of his bed, "It's alright, my dear, come in, I have covered up. I was rubbing some grilchin oil on my skin to help ease my muscular aches from my ill health. I was not expecting anyone until morning. Now, what seems to be so important that it cannot wait until then?"

Stex was now fully clothed in his evening attire as Mileana opened the door and whispered, "Maalik has returned with some very important news, sir. They have summoned you to the council for a briefing."

Stexinzar, who seemed to be feeling a lot better, nodded to Mileana. He picked up his sword, Swirling Splinter, walked to the door and then down to the council hall.

After everyone was set up and the doors were locked, Maalik began relaying his interpretation of what the pooka Viddiar had witnessed and accomplished. He was coming to the most important part when he noticed that Stexinzar seemed to be getting agitated, moving in his seat and writhing around. Maalik stopped.

"Are you alright, sir? You look very ill," Maalik asked.

"I am fine, young one," said Stex as he sat up and began controlling himself a little better. "I have been unwell, but I am anxious to find out how we can defeat these creatures. Please enlighten us with this."

"Yes, of course, sir. Well, the pookas have a special dust they blow onto any prey or dangers," Maalik continued. "This seemed to influence the sinister's mind. She said it tried to control her, however after the dust was sprayed into its huge face, she seemed to see into its mind, reversing its effects. She was able to really get a glimpse of what they are after and why they are here, before destroying its mind completely and killing it."

Everyone in the room sat silent. Not one of them even blinked or fluttered. They were all like stone statues, before Maalik broke the tension and continued.

"It gets worse. She could interpret a part of the agenda—why they come here and why they do what they do. She said she saw flames, humans, and even some of our own kin briefly, locked away with the gigantic hairy beasts. They cannot live here in our realm or the human realm, their bodies are too frail. So they sent down some of their manufactured ones, but even they succumb to the diseases on our plane. Some stronger, bigger sinisters eventually came down. They could survive the environment for longer, finding a use for some species, syncing the minds from us to the beasts to kidnap humans without sickness."

Maalik looked around at those gathered. "That's all I have of that information, although she also said that they had enough now, and that when they take the human realm for themselves, they will be back here to destroy what they don't need and make slaves of the rest. What happens to the humans will eventually happen to us. Then she saw flames again and millions of humans in water tubes hanging in the air."

Maalik was about to finish when he reminded them all of one more thing. "Remember, this was a pooka, and she was very agitated. Although you need to know that she placed those images into my mind, so I believe her. The words she was using were not making sense, so I asked her to show me. I assure you they will not be back here until they have finished with the humans. How long that takes, we don't know."

Maalik had finished. He stepped off the high stump and made his way to a seat next to Faelondar. While he was doing this, Stexinzar finally stood and began. "Thank you, Maalik. Your mission has given us vital information that we need. By the sounds of this, we are still under threat and will need to prepare. Not knowing how long we've got means we could have time, or could be rendered vulnerable immediately. We know what they want, and what the number one rule is when it comes to the humans and the Earth realm, that what happens to them will eventually affect us, so we must prepare ourselves. Lastly, this information must not get out. I want a group of warriors to find some pookas close by and bring them to the palace. If we can somehow manufacture a potion, we may be able to use the dust as a quick defense if they decide to come back. I want another contingent of soldiers to be recruited. We will need all the help we can get. Lastly, we need to find a weapon or weapons. I will liaise with the council in the morn about such matters that do not require the audience we have now, so go—

Before Stex could finish his speech, he collapsed into a heap on the floor, turning a bluish color, which could only mean one thing. He had been poisoned.

THE WYRM

CYCLES WENT BY AND NOT ANOTHER SIGHTING of the sinisters ever came about again. Stexinzar took a long time to recover from his poisoning attack, an attack so severe and destructive that it almost took the leader's life. Investigations were commenced, and as this was going on, the council started worrying that there was a traitor in their midst. There were more stirs in the dark realms as well, and in time the dark oaks started whispering to the edges of the forests that the dark one would return.

The Fae did not care too much for those rumors as the dark oaks were renowned for making up stories to frighten the sprites, although they had been silent for a thousand cycles, so this was out of the ordinary. As were the disappearances of some forest pixies and gnomes.

All the doors to the human realm were guarded and locked, only accessible by the guards who watched over the forts in case of any returns of the Fae, good or evil. There were protections put in place by the council to make that a strict law—no one was to enter the old world and all those who came back through would need to attend the council and give feedback on where they had been and what was happening. Some brownies, spriggans, and selkies, along with gnomes, sprites, and pixies, had lived in the old world of Ireland since the war of the dark lord, returning occasionally through the portals. Now they were returning in droves, but among those coming home were never any of the taken.

The last one to come through was at the narrow end of the path from the old oak named Great Wisdom in the deep woods of Toozookus, which was the entry point to the old world, leading to what the humans called a faery fort. He had been the only one to come through this entry, an old and wise gnome that had been watching the chaos unfold in the old lands. He had let the guard know that he would be the last. There were sinisters hunting Fae-kind in the Ireland realm. He had witnessed bodies of old forest folk, even a merrow named Alvantaar who had washed up and was taken by humans in shadow clothes, as if they were working together with the sinisters. The secrets of the Fae were being told by the captured ones.

The guard closed the entry to the old oak with a long iron crossbar, stopping anything from coming through. In time, once this information was relayed to the palace, an order would come through to close all portals permanently, locking out any others and bringing the depleted trainee guards back to the palace for more training.

It seemed the Fae were still under attack. At this stage only a few of the portals were still accessible. The palace guards did not know every location, but they knew most. They were directed by the council who thought they knew them all, but in fact only the queen and princess knew the locations of each one, including ones that had been kept secret. This was a defensive tactic from when the dark lord was gaining power a long time ago, so they could come in and out if they felt in danger.

Some mystical creatures in Faelynn, like the dryads and some very ancient forest folk, had the ability to enter the old lands through magic, bypassing the portals, but nothing could be done about that.

⁓

The dark cloaked figure had made no moves for a long while, keeping very quiet to not give away their identity after the poisoning of a leader of Faelynn put everyone on high alert. But this night the shadow dweller seemed particularly agitated and in need of escaping the walls which had held him for many a cycle.

Late in the night a fire started raging inside the entrance to the guard tower. The solid white brick that had shone in the moonlight was now becoming charred and blackened. The chaos stirred the guards and they began waking up, as the shadow-cloaked betrayer scaled the very high palace gates without the slightest force of effort. Only a sprite could do that in small form, and no Elvenfae guard could scale with its wings not hidden, as the chances of being detected would be higher.

Before long, the dark hooded figure was half a mile down the path and disappearing into the edge of the woods. Soon the shadow found an exceptionally large stag standing next to some very tall pines, as if it were waiting for someone. The stag was enormous. The antlers alone reached high into the trees, making the shadowy figure look quite small in comparison, which didn't seem to worry him.

The hooded figure, with face covered completely by the shadow cloth, pulled on the back of the stag's neck and off they went, galloping fast into the night. The moon lit the way for them both as they came to the same elm the figure had been using to jump realms. Even though the portals were all supposed to be closed, the iron crossbars on this one had been melted off, leaving the entrance exposed and ready for use.

He let out a flurry of words and before long lights were again emanating from the large tree. The branches twisted and groaned outwards, leaving a hole filled with color, big enough for both the stag and the shadowed one to go through. It locked back into place after his hollers faded away and the lights became duller as the tree resumed its original position once again, until there was no evidence at all of what had transpired.

Soon, at the edges of Xarkynan, once again the dark figure appeared with a howl from the twisted elm, which spat both stag and rider yards away from the entrance. Then the elm groaned as it shifted back into its resting position once more. It seemed this activity had been going on for a long time over the cycles.

The dark figure, who had been away for some time, galloped through the dense dark woods and onto the twisted path to the old castle.

One of the two dark Elvenfae greeted the rider with a snide comment,

"He's been waiting for you. If you don't have what he wants, he will be most upset. What he did to you last time will feel like a sunny day in the flowers, I can assure you of that."

Both guards started laughing, a coarse phlegmy laugh, as the rider continued up the steep path and onward to the twisted and foreboding dark lord's castle.

The dark figure finally ascended to the heights of the entry point. There he was greeted with an array of different creatures, goblins, foul pixies, demented brownies. Standing in front of them all was a hideous dullahan, a foul, headless creature on a huge black horse, with the spine of a human as its whip, while its head sat under its arm staring all around with a massive grin on its face. It looked all melted and twisted, one of the most horrifying of all creatures ever to set foot in the realm.

The dark figure gulped as the nostrils of the dullahan's horse flared and snuffed, its red eyes piercing the stag's, making the creature lower its head in fear and turn away. The dark hooded figure pulled at the fur behind the stag's neck to keep it on track while the headless beast cracked its whip in front of them both, before taking off down the path and into the darkness of the night.

Once he composed himself, the masked, hooded figure entered the castle through the massive doors, stag and all. He met up with the necro-mage in the foyer, dismounted, and stood in front of the ever more powerful being, face to face. Viltzin'un'dandaar lifted up his right arm, creating a whirl of red and purple light in his hand, then threw a ball of energy at one of the black wolves at the entrance, sending it hurtling against the doors and knocking it out.

"I've learned some new tricks since you've been away, my friend. I have been reading a lot in my host's quarters and have refined some old methods of magic not even known by the dark lord himself. It won't be long before I can bring him back, making me the most powerful necro-mage that ever existed. Now take that stupid mask off so I can see your ugly face, then we can talk somewhere more privately about the tasks I had you complete. Let's hope for your sake they are positive acquisitions and information."

The Zeytar had full control of Viltzin'un'dandaar whose body was now completely healed through magic. He had taken his name along with everything else. The host himself was nearly all gone, giving the Zeytar all the pertinent memories and information he needed over the many cycles before fading away to the deepest, darkest part of his mind, still trapped and mind-broken.

The Zeytar could not believe how strong he had become. His powers kept growing and growing. After the takeover of Earth, the Leader would have to take a step back from being the alpha, he thought.

"I have some news and some gifts," the hooded figure said as he slowly took off his hood and mask, showing his twisted face. He followed the necro-mage up the stairs and down a long hallway, nervous and fearful of what might happen, considering he was almost killed last time by the crazy creature for not answering some simple questions.

"Come, take a seat, let's talk some more."

The necro-mage had taken him to the secret library behind the dark lord's room, where all his secrets were kept hidden from everyone, secrets of his ancestors that even the Fae would not know, about magic and the realms. But there were pages missing and many questions that the necro-mage wanted answers for. As he looked around the strange room, he noticed the green glow from behind the opposite door, pulsating on and off from time to time.

The mage snapped his concentration back to the figure before him. "Now, creature—or should I call you Wyrm, yes, Wyrm, I like that, I like that very much—now, what do you have for me, Wyrm? And please don't disappoint, it took me a long time to find a dullahan willing to come here and suck your scaly life force from you. Part of me actually wants you to fail." He let out a hoarse laugh that echoed down the hall.

Wyrm was turning white; his anxiety was peaking now, as he started trembling while taking a piece of leaf parchment out with some writing on it. In his husky voice, he begged, "Please, there is no need for that, I have it here. In the days of old the power of Faelynn was given by the first people, the Tuatha Dé Danann. Each of the four stones held an elemental—fire, water, land, and air—separated by distance and protected by high magical beings, and only known by the highest bloodlines of which the Aethelwynes are the last—"

Viltzin, frustrated with the lack of progress, interrupted Wyrm with a booming voice, "Everyone knows that, fool. What I want to know is: Where are my missing pages and how do I find these elemental stones?"

"Please, let me finish, oh dark one ..." Wyrm was really trembling now. His deformed wings were fluttering like crazy, which was calming the necro-mage. "Access to the missing pages that you seek so the dark lord can be resurrected is something I cannot help you with, but I can do one better. Any life can be brought back if there is enough of the body to start with. Using all the elementals can do this and I know how to gain access to two of the Tuatha treasures already. I'm working on the others as we speak."

Viltzin turned around with such force that his bony neck nearly snapped off. He walked over to Wyrm and slowly asked, "What did you say? You know where to find the elemental stones that run the lands here?"

The Zeytar in him was now overwhelmed with excitement. He was at first only interested in resurrecting the dark lord and gaining more power through him, not having a whole world's power source in the palm of his hand, for him to control. This new information would be enough to override the Leader and take control of multiple worlds. His mind was consumed with a gluttonous greed for power and he started watering at the mouth, messing up the floor with his acidic saliva.

"I can do one better, my master. I can gain access to one right now with your help." Wyrm was just beginning to feel more confident when he heard a scream coming from the room with the green glow.

"No!" echoed through the room and out into the castle hallways.

Viltzin smiled, showing his sharp, reptilian-looking teeth. He licked his lips and disappeared into the room where the screams were emanating from, grabbed whoever was there, and dragged them out.

Wyrm's jaw dropped when he saw who had been behind the door, someone he obviously either knew or had heard of before. "Felvora," he whispered.

Viltzin heard him and quickly asked, "What did you say, Wyrm?" When he didn't get an answer, the grotesque dark Elvenfae hybrid repeated the question, but changed his tone to one of malice.

"Isn't that Felvora, the crazy dryad from Aurora? I've heard about her, banished after she turned you into a drooling mess in a time vortex, am I right, master?" Wyrm gave an awkward smile before easing back on his seat, awaiting the mage's response.

This information was already known to Viltzin as his host had her image playing out in his mind, plotting for revenge for a thousand cycles. So, the Zeytar was well and truly aware of her, even feeling her as she entered the elms all those cycles ago. She had been captured by twisted sylphs whom she thought she could trust, only to be imprisoned by Viltzin using the dark lord's Torc bracelet, which the goblins finally found not long after Glinoxx was set free.

Viltzin found a spell strong enough in one of Varzunnos' books and changed his green gem to target forest sylphs as well, nearly killing her. It took three of the twisted sylphs in the dark elm woods to hold Felvora long enough for Viltzin to contain her with his new toy. Now he drained her life force from time to time, building himself up and slowly recovering from a thousand cycles of slow decay.

"Yes, Wyrm, this is my favorite toy at the moment. Our beloved Felvora has been assisting me over the moons to gain my strength back and I am finding her company quite pleasurable."

While Viltzin smirked, Felvora took whatever energy she had left to cringe in disgust. Her only focus was revenge. Over time, she had learned some particularly important information about this so-called necro-mage, and her essence was fighting to one day be strong enough to pass that information on to the palace and her queen, who she had no idea was still missing.

Viltzin took Felvora back to her chamber, excited to see what Wyrm would find for him.

As he left the castle, Wyrm looked back over his shoulder at one of the highest windows, and through the mist of dark clouds could just make out a faint green glow in the swirling air. He stared for a moment while moving forward on his stag with the rest of Viltzin's evil army. Then he turned around, and looked ahead, before slowly lowering his face and shoulders.

THE PRINCESS
RETURNS

DEEP INSIDE THE THICK OF THE AURORA FOREST a lonely old stone stood, three yards tall, with ancient text sprawled most of the way around it. A rumble started, but only for a moment, and then the forest returned to its natural buzz of wildlife and noise.

A short while later the stone itself began rumbling, this time faster and harder, causing chaos in its immediate vicinity. Birds took off up through the trees and the local pixies began squealing and tearing off in all directions across the woods.

Tiny little forest girls could make a very loud noise when they screamed, and this soon attracted the attention of other inquisitive and protective creatures wanting to know what was going on.

Although the tremors were gaining quite a lot of movement around the place, they didn't last long. It was all over soon when a blue, purple, and red light burst out of the center, illuminating the whole area of the forest like a Christmas tree. Then finally the rumbling stopped, the lights disappeared, and the locals were left scratching their heads, wondering what actually happened. This was an ancient stone only ever used by the ancient ones. It couldn't have been the sinisters, they thought, as an inquisitive little pixie with long black hair, buckled shoes with white socks, and a yellow dress gathered enough nerve to wander over and look. As she crept slowly over to the stone, the pixie placed her hand on the writings, then, as if she'd been shocked, pulled her hand away from the heat that was still clinging to the surface.

She placed her hand on it again, this time more carefully, feeling it cool beneath her hand before a groan coming from her right made her jump and run back behind a tree. The pixie looked over to where the sound had come from and soon another, much louder, moan echoed throughout the local environs, until the noises turned into movements. A tall female figure grabbed a log for support and slowly stood up, rubbing her eyes, and looking around at all the forest folk staring blankly at her.

The female child was very tall to the pixies, who only stood two to three feet tall. The girl reached her arm out at the pixie who had touched the stone and said calmly, "Hello, little one, my name is Serena O'Halloran. I am twelve. What is your name?"

The pixie darted off. She had not seen a human in such a long time and with everything that had been going on in Faelynn over the cycles was warned not to take chances with anyone or anything that was strange or not from there.

Serena pulled her hand back. A look of disappointment came over her, until a bright flash hit the area for a moment and a voice explained, "Don't be upset, child. Pixies are very curious creatures and very easily frightened. I am surprised they are even out this deep." Shaylee's voice was calming and friendly. Even after the ordeal with the sinisters, she still managed to stay positive for Serena.

"Oh OK, Shaylee, thank you, I think I am going to have to relearn what I have learned about your world. My eyes seem to be seeing things. Even though it's quite dark here, my eyes seem to be picking up every color in bright detail, as if I am looking through magical glasses. It is so beautiful, Shaylee."

Serena was so excited. She could never have dreamed that her day in the fields of the faery forts with her family would end up leading her to the actual place where they came from. Her mind was rushing and was overloaded to the point where her heart started racing hard and she couldn't breathe properly. Before long she fainted.

Serena was out for a few minutes. When she came around, she was looking straight into the eyes of a pooka; the creature was patting her head softly, then hard, then softly again with a damp moss square to soothe her head as he whispered to her in a soft voice, "You smell, human ugly. Shaylee, she is ugly."

Shaylee giggled as Serena jumped up and protested, "Hey, that's not very nice. Well, maybe you look like a stupid rabbit with shorts ... and clothes ..."

Serena stopped, thought about what she was saying, and sat back down on the soft mushroom lid that the inquisitive pixie Fayetta Honeyleaf had placed for her.

"Easy, Serena, this will be a lot for you to take in so just absorb all this as it comes. Trust me when I say this is another world within your world, different rules, species, environments, laws of nature, and magic. I will bring you up to speed as we go; however, I must get back to the palace. I am not sure how long I have been gone from here and what damage has been done." Shaylee's voice was now trembling as she helped Serena back to her feet.

The cheeky pooka seemed to be very taken aback with Serena, mimicking every move she was making. The males had more hair on their faces than the females and without looking twice you could mistake them for full rabbits, although they were bipedal.

Serena stayed behind Shaylee as they moved out of that part of the woods. Shaylee blew the pixies a kiss and thanked them for their help before facing forward again. But Serena kept glancing behind her, and Shaylee's wings brushed along her face every time she did. She was looking back at the naughty rabbit who now had his tongue stuck out as he poked his head from around a tree trunk, but pulled it back in when she turned again.

This went on for about five hundred yards until Shaylee whispered, "He is going to follow you all the way, my dear. Just ignore him. They are a very quirky race, our little pookas, but loyal and friendly—well, to most anyway." She giggled to herself, knowing all too well what a pooka could really do.

After walking for what seemed like forever to Serena, Shaylee stopped and whispered to her, "Look up, Serena, we are at the Edge Willows, a section of the Aurora Forest that all lines up in perfect order like a wall and keeps the entrance safe from any darkness or evil dwellers. Willows have special symbiotic relationships with tiny sprites called wisps, who are very strong warriors that glow bright, far brighter than us when we change. Although they are very strong and protective, the wisps cannot transform. I only hope the sinisters never found these hidden warriors who warn the trees to move together to connect their branches all along the line, creating a force field barrier to anything unwanted entering this section. This is the main entrance to Aurora, and a direct path to Vylass, where I cannot take you as you are human."

Shaylee was getting very weary. She had run out of the healing powder that Felvora had given her before her journey to Maelenflitt. It had saved her life at Serena's house, but her wounds needed special treatment, and she had been away from Faelynn far too long—though she would not tell Serena that.

Serena looked up at the swirling willows, with the bright lights buzzing all around the soft white, purple, orange, and green blossoms all around the branches. She had never in her life seen anything more beautiful, and stared continuously without even blinking. Some wisps even came down to inspect her. As they flew by her face, they slowed down so she could see them more clearly. Shaylee was whispering to the willows, who in turn told the wisps she was a friend and of importance, hence they let her see them.

One wisp stopped on the end of Serena's nose, wings fluttering like crazy with golden sparks flying off them. The wisps were completely gold and naked, so human-like yet not, Serena thought. Their ears were very straight and pointed, much longer than Shaylee's, and their eyebrows were more bent. They had longer faces than humans, but they still just looked like tiny people.

As Serena wrinkled her nose from the tickling of the wisp's feet, it sprang up and darted back to the trees, allowing for two more to land on her nose. This time two females greeted Serena; one curtsied and the other bowed, and then they swapped, before waving and saying, "Goodbye," in unison in the softest of voices.

The magic of the place overwhelmed Serena and she was so mesmerized that she didn't hear Shaylee calling to her, "Serena, come now." Shaylee wasn't angry at all; she was just trying to gain her attention.

Serena whispered, "Thank you, Shaylee, they are amazing. I'm sorry, what were you saying?"

Shaylee laughed as Serena didn't quite get the joke.

The entrance to the Edge Willows opened, and there in front of them was a road and a very large white horse standing in front of them. The willows also protected these creatures, and this was the last one, Shaylee's own, whom she had known since she was only a child.

Serena turned and looked at Shaylee, then back at the horse, as the last of the wisps finished grooming her and took off back to the tops of the branches. Serena could not stop staring at its beauty, especially the long single spiraled horn that pointed to the sky.

"Is ... Is she a unicorn?" Serena asked, not even turning to look at Shaylee, who until just now was the most beautiful thing Serena had ever seen.

"Yes, my dear, she is my longest and oldest friend. Her name is Vyyuna Majestixx, and she is the last of her species, the oldest, wisest, and most mystical creature that ever walked in Faelynn. I want to introduce you to her."

Serena turned, grabbed Shaylee's long-fingered hand, and whispered, "Did you say the last?"

Shaylee lowered her head, clutched Serena's hand back, and nodded, before answering, "Yes, dear, I am afraid so. She is very special to us all. She knows nothing but love and peace. Just her being here helps bond every creature to each other with compassion and caring. To not have her with us would be very harmful to the Fae, especially if the dark realm ever awakened again."

Shaylee had tears slowly moving down her lightly flushed, pale face as Serena asked, "What ... happened?"

Shaylee couldn't keep the knowledge of things about the Fae from Serena, especially knowing who she really was. So she thought she may as well know about the dark times, at least in a simplified manner, to explain this situation. Telling it all to a twelve-year-old girl would most likely scar her for life, but there was something about Serena's heart that Shaylee loved already, and she knew she could handle it.

"Long ago there was a dark lord who turned part of the realm into his fortress, growing in power, and building himself up to eventually take over the whole of Faelynn. He couldn't go to your world as he had no power there, so it was here that he tried to build an army to take us over. In doing so he found our weakness, the power of love and compassion. Through all this we knew that he had nothing on us, that his power would never be strong enough to take all of us. With the power of the original ancestors hidden safely and protected, Varzunnos, son of an original Tuatha Dé Danann, the peaceful Cernunnos, could never be that powerful. But over time he created abominations, including twisted Elvenfae sprites, dark twisted elves to do his bidding, even gaining a mage who turned dark and twisted, manipulating natural forces and creating dark magic."

Shaylee paused. Serena only stared at her face, watching all the emotions of the past come out. "But finally he found our weakness, the love of the unicorn that held our realm's people together. Varzunnos made it his mission to destroy all the unicorns and burn the Alicorns."

Serena jumped in with a question. "What's an Alicorn, Shaylee?"

Shaylee turned and looked at Vyyuna, as they were now close to her, before she continued, "The Alicorn is the horn from a unicorn. It is like an antenna, giving off its signals to the world. When the dark one found out about this, he wanted them all. What he didn't realize, and only a very few know, is that when a unicorn dies and the Alicorn is destroyed, the power from it goes to another, the closest to it. That unicorn takes its power and it builds, and so on and so forth, until now the last stands here before us with all the power from all the previous beauties that ever lived, all living inside her Alicorn, well, the essence anyway. The dark lord thought he had killed them all, but what he didn't know was that a filly was born not long before he slaughtered its mother. So the last of them is Vyyuna, whom we have protected ever since. She lives with the willows and the wisps and no one outside of the high royals knows about her Alicorn. I raised her to be strong, and she accompanies me on missions when required, although never to the darkness of Xarkynan where pure evil grows."

Shaylee hadn't realized that Serena was now shaking while crying uncontrollably. As she put her arm around her, Serena blurted out, "How could anything be so evil to hurt such a creature, or any of these beautiful lives? It's just wrong."

As Serena was trying to stop her tears from flowing and wiped her nose with her sleeve, Vyyuna trotted up to her, lowered her large, mighty head, and nudged Serena's cheek with her moist nose. Serena looked up, the tears suddenly stopped, and she felt like singing and dancing. She slowly put her hand onto Vyyuna's nose and stroked her long face very gently. She could feel the love and positivity radiating out of her the closer she was to her. She understood the magic of the unicorns now, not like in the folktale books or movies, but real magic and love.

"Come now, my child, I have told you too much for now." Shaylee lifted Serena up onto the back of Vyyuna and fluttered up slowly herself. She whispered in her ear as Vyyuna galloped off onto the palace track. Riding her, the journey would only take them hours, instead of days.

And so the pair made it to the palace gates within hours, thanks to Vyyuna. She lowered her head and shoulders, easing Serena off gently, as Shaylee leaped up and off, losing balance when she hit the well-paved silver-edged stone, which was not like her. Then Vyyuna took off again, not going all the way back in case Shaylee needed her, staying close enough but out of sight.

Shaylee hobbled up to the main entrance to the palace where two guards approached her, one even boldly saying, "Who are you and what are you doing disturbing ..." before pausing and coming to her aid as Shaylee collapsed. She had tried to hide it for as long as she could, but she had reached her limit.

"My princess," the guard called out. Serena tried to assist as the guard picked her up and took her inside the gates to the main entrance of the palace, where he shouted, "Help! Somebody help, Princess Shaylee has returned."

The guard lowered her to a comfortable position in the entrance hall, while maids and members of the council rushed over to see what all the fuss was. Stexinzar had been away on a mission and was weary from his journey, but when he heard the commotion and the guard's call, he raced out to see for himself. As he gazed down at Shaylee, a look of jealousy flashed across his face, though only for a moment, before he started shouting out orders to get some help for her.

The palace was frantic—some jumping with joy, while others worried it was a trick of someone who wanted to take over the palace and kingdom for themselves.

After they took Shaylee to get help, Serena was left sitting on a side couch in one of the palace halls. A tall figure walked over and whispered, "What are you doing here, human? Come with me."

The Elvenfae guard picked Serena up, and with his hand around her mouth so she wouldn't scream, he walked down to the closed dungeons that were no longer in use so no one would find her.

He threw her in the last cell, locked the door, and could only hear a faint scream as he made his way back up to the main chambers where the rest were scurrying around not knowing what to do with themselves.

Serena was all alone in the dark. The thickness of old stone dungeon walls blocked her screams.

SERENA LEARNS
THE TRUTH

T HE COUNCIL HAD CALLED A DIRECT MEETING while
Shaylee was being attended to. She was exhausted and would need
plenty of rest to make a full recovery. There were already rumors starting
that she was an intruder sent by the sinisters to control everyone from
the inside. Others were organizing a parade and festival to celebrate her
return, while the council itself had already had a preliminary meeting
to discuss their own issues.

Stexinzar had now been allowed to enter the council chambers,
along with some high guards and members of the Fae community
that were respected in their houses. Faelondar was the first to speak,
stepping up onto the stump, with a parchment ready to go, to discuss
the council's concerns, not only about the princess returning, but also
about whispers of dark ones near Toozookus.

"OK, so everyone is aware of the recent events that have played out.
The council will reserve the right to make a comment on the princess
until she has spoken—"

Stexinzar stood up swiftly, interrupting the council leader with a
protest. He was dressed in his warrior garb, as if he was about to go to
war, which was not typical council meeting attire. "How can you say
that? No one loves Shaylee more than I do, but we do not know who
she is. And where is the human girl that was with her? She seems to
have disappeared. It reeks of a trap, and with the oncoming threat of

war we must play this one right. The timing is all too convenient, if you ask me."

Faelondar stared directly at Stexinzar, not saying a word until he sat back down. He continued, "We will all get a say, Master Stexinzar; however, the council needs to finish. We will deal with the princess in due course. Now, this threat somewhere in between Aurora and Toozookus has been brought to our attention by the woodland elves who informed us of a growing number of dark elves, a significant number of goblins, and trolls, along with a dullahan, which can only mean one thing, and that is that there is an antagonist out there trying to stir up troubles from Xarkynan. The Fae have had some losses over the recent cycles to that dark place that can't all be put down to rock trolls, twisted faeries, or witches of the swamps. We believe something is not right there. We must go to Toozookus to find out what they are doing and eliminate the threat. We have had to deal with a lot, and we will not lie down now so some low breed evil wretch can cause panic and trouble in our lands. We will send a significant army to obliterate the lot of them."

Faelondar took a breath and finished with, "Now you may talk, Stexinzar, but ye be warned to keep it short and not about the princess."

Stexinzar nodded, took up the platform and started, "For the record, I believe this Fae to be an Unseelie witch. We have not seen the forest dryad Felvora since she was sent to Xarkynan. Also, before we pack up for battle, I want all celebrations to cease immediately, and lastly, I am putting up a reward for anyone who finds the human girl and brings her head to me."

Stexinzar was consumed by jealousy and rage. He was in danger of losing his empire and the loveable Elvenfae high guard warrior was cracking.

"I beg your pardon, Stex, what did you just say?" Shaylee had been at the entrance the whole time. The maids were supposed to warn them all if she moved or got out of bed, but they were her original maids and they were loyal to the princess. "What is all this, Faelondar and Stexinzar? Do I hear treason in my house?"

Stexinzar lowered his head, while Faelondar tried to smooth over the situation. "No, no, my princess, of course not, we were just discussing—"

Before he could finish, Shaylee, with a voice coarse from exhaustion continued, "I do not care what you all have to say. Before I go any further and take all of your heads, I want the human child back here now. Where is she?"

Shaylee was staring directly at Stexinzar. She had learned some truths from the maids and healers while she was being cared for, and one of those was that Stex had made himself caretaker of the lands and was using his power a little too much lately.

"Tell you what, if you bring her to me unharmed within the next five moments, to my chambers, I will not execute the parties involved. However, if she does not appear, unharmed, in that time, there will be a suffering you have never seen before. Finally, I am your queen, not your princess. While my mother is still under the control of the enemy, I will take up her mantle. I want the child back now. Then I want you, Faelondar and Stexinzar, in my quarters, do we all understand?"

Shaylee finished and with the help of her maidens returned to her quarters and lay down on her bed.

Stexinzar was panicking. The council was also in panic mode. How were they going to find a human child that was lost, and where would they look?

As they all dispersed, Faelondar picked up a small device and placed it in his pocket as he made his way up to the new queen's chambers. Stexinzar was taking longer, for some reason. Faelondar waited outside, but then, with a shocked look on his face, he saw Stexinzar turn the corner with the human girl child, a leather bag over her face as she kicked and screamed.

"What are you doing? Are you crazy, Stex? She will kill you for that!"

Stexinzar pulled the satchel off her head, rubbed some smelling powder over her face, and whispered some soothing charm in her ear, before Serena succumbed to the potion and complied, gazing up at her capturer with a look of surprise and angst about how she had gotten there. He had only removed a tiny amount of her immediate memory, so she knew well that she was in Faelynn still.

As they approached the doors, Serena asked, "Was I asleep or what? I can't even remember getting up those stairs. I hope you are taking me to Shaylee's room. How is she?"

Stexinzar glanced at Faelondar with nervous tension and nodded for him to agree with his mischievous secret. Faelondar knew not to get on the wrong side of Stex so just went along with it, but he would sink him like a ship if it came out.

"Yes, little one, we are here now to see her. Just open the door and she will be there," Stexinzar said.

Serena pushed the door open slowly. She saw Shaylee lying on her bed made from oaks. She burst into the room and dove onto it as if she had not seen her in ages.

"Oh my, where have you been, little one? I thought something serious happened to you."

As she rubbed her face, some residue from the potion Stexinzar had administered stuck to Shaylee's fingers. She looked up at both of them standing in the doorway, and lowered her head, producing a scowl, all while continuing to stare at them.

Serena said, "I think I fell asleep somewhere. I can't remember; I must have zonked. Anyway, this handsome guard helped me … I think?"

Stexinzar smiled a very awkward smile, sweating a little, all while Shaylee continued scowling as she rubbed Serena's face softly. She knew something was wrong, and that she had come home to some in-house troubles and conspiracies. "Well, you are here with me now, my dear, and I promise you, your time here in Faelynn will be that of wondrous joy from now on."

Shaylee seemed to mend quicker than the other two had expected. Her potion from Felvora was strong and seemed to take full effect with the help from the maiden healers. Her energy levels were rising, and her wings were fully healed. She could fly as a sprite without pain, pain she had hidden from Serena when she first turned and flew through the old oak near Serena's house earlier on. Dealing with her exhaustion would be the focus for her now and a good night's sleep would be the order of the day, after one more task. "Faelondar, I want a full council meeting with all the leaders of the houses, and I want you to organize it now, please."

Shaylee was always the adventurous warrior and friendly princess. Her mother did the heavy lifting, and father before that. She was adored by all for her generous nature and sense of humor. But now her tone was quite assertive, and she was in no way the same high Elvenfae she had once been. There had been a change, and it would come out soon, very soon.

"My lady, I mean, Your Highness, you seem to be still unwell, don't you think—"

Before Faelondar could finish Shaylee went completely gray, her eyes turned black like those of the twisted faeries in Xarkynan, and she roared an echoing displeasure which could be heard all the way down the halls of the palace, "Did I ask for your opinion? Now go!"

Serena put her hands over her ears, very frightened by what had just taken place. The other two standing at the doorway were both trembling, wings aflutter, and with sweat streaming.

Slowly Shaylee's color came back and her eyes turned blue again as she apologized softly, "I, I'm so sorry, I ... must still be affected by the sinisters' mind blend with the large beasts. I knew only darkness and evil for so long, I must still be suffering the effects of it. I am sorry, Serena, please forgive me?"

Serena rubbed her hand gently. She was a tough kid and a compassionate one, and she would not pretend that it didn't rattle her. She didn't know much of what Shaylee had experienced, and was still confused by the lack of information, but she could only hope that whatever happened to Shaylee for all those years would not affect her permanently. Serena thought that this was her reason for being there, to help Shaylee and keep her mind soothed. She could feel a calmness straightaway when she found the sprite. Whether that was the reason for Shaylee taking her to Faelynn or not, it would be her mission.

Faelondar seemed to be doing all the talking now. Stexinzar was smart and knew to keep his mouth shut at the right times. Even when he and Shaylee were little, playing together and getting into mischief, the king would tell them off and Shaylee would get in more trouble for trying to be funny, while Stexinzar just sat there and took it. He was a very skilled warrior, although cracks of cowardice appeared more and more frequently.

"My lady, sorry, Your Highness, please, before you say anything, it seems you may be still affected by the sickness of the sinisters," Faelondar said. "I have only ever seen that look and heard that shrill of a voice once before, and it was at a time when the dark lord Varzunnos was twisting good faeries and creating his dark realm, turning them into pure evil and deforming their bodies while twisting their minds. I implore you, can you please take the bloodline test. If you are not a sinister, a witch, a twisted faery, or imposter, I have a test for the bloodline that can prove it. They used this in the times of the dark one when the king was at war and Varzunnos tried to infiltrate our side with witches and shape shifters." Faelondar paused for a second before finishing his request, "It was designed by Felvora and a descendant of the Tuatha, the first people, so it cannot be faked; it is the only one in existence and has been kept by the leaders of the council for thousands of cycles." Faelondar wiped his brow, although he seemed much calmer now that Shaylee had also calmed.

She looked up at him, nodded, and gestured for him to come forward. "I have heard of this. If it appeases you all, I will give you my blood. Now, after I prove to you my worth, I will not hear any more of conspiracies of betrayal and witches, do we all understand?"

Shaylee looked over at Stexinzar, who was nodding very quickly. "Maraenor, please send for the two guards at the palace halls and return yourself, my dear. I want you with me when this happens. Then we will begin."

Maraenor was Shaylee's longest serving maiden and the most trusted. She turned hastily, ran for the door, and when no one was looking changed to a bright green sprite flying at full speed, before changing back and summoning the guards. She wanted this over as soon as possible so that Shaylee had full power back in the palace once more. Soon they returned, guards at the door with the others, while Faelondar readied the test.

"Now, Shaylee, this will only sting a little. With one prick on the finger a drop of blood will enter the vial, and with a shake of the potion inside, it will reveal a color. The bloodline you seek is blue, commoners are purple, humans red, and all other creatures will turn up green. Are you ready?"

Shaylee nodded and Faelondar steadied the device, pricked her finger, and watched as her dark crimson blood dropped once, twice, then thrice into the vial. Shaylee pulled her finger back, placed it in her mouth, and sucked the blood to soothe it, before returning her hand neatly back onto her other one as she waited.

They were all mesmerized. Stexinzar had his eyes fixated and wide, and even the guards were taking an interest. Serena had Shaylee's right arm for comfort and Maraenor had her other hand.

As time seemed to drag, the vial slowly went from a clear liquid to a purple. Stexinzar was licking his lips. He had won, he thought. The color then became softer, turning from purple to white, before eventually settling at a crystal-clear blue.

The two girls, Maraenor and Serena, jumped up in excitement, with Serena even bouncing on the soft bed of silk. Faelondar, meanwhile, glanced at Stexinzar, who seemed defeated and angry, and then turned and stormed out of the room. Shaylee was smiling as she watched her old friend leave. What was his game? she thought. Why did he hope it would fail? She snapped out of it and looked over at Faelondar before remarking with her old wit, "So, there you have it, I will hear no more of this rubbish. I want the council set up within the next hour."

Faelondar shook the device, returning it to its default clear liquid, ready to be used again in the future. He placed it at the end of the bed while he walked over to Shaylee to whisper something in her ear. The guards had followed Stexinzar out of the room and it was only the two other girls, Shaylee and Faelondar left. Why he had to whisper was beyond Shaylee, however she accepted, and gave him her ear.

"Your Highness, now that I know it is you, please forgive me. I meant no disrespect. This place has been under a lot of pressure for some time and I want to warn you about some troubles, along with—"

Before Faelondar could finish, Shaylee whispered, "Stexinzar!"

Faelondar nodded, and they were both in agreement for the first time that day, as they turned to face Maraenor and Serena.

Shaylee instantly jumped out of bed in shock, wings fluttering, as her long, elegant ears turned from off-white to a blushing red, as if she had just seen something horrific.

Faelondar was the same, although his reaction was more vocal. "What is going on here? Someone explain to me this dark magic!"

Serena was holding the device in her left hand, while her right index finger was still in place, and they all watched the now darkening liquid turn crystal-clear blue in the vial.

"Shaylee!" Serena shouted. "What is happening to me? I thought it only turned blue for your bloodline."

Shaylee moved toward the young girl, who was trembling. Faelondar snatched the device from Serena's hand and shook it to reset it, before Shaylee gave him a spray, "Please, never speak to her like that ever again, do you hear me?"

Faelondar nodded. He never meant to. But they needed some answers, and they were needed fast.

"What is it, Faelondar? Is the device broken? What could have caused this? Serena is a human girl." Shaylee had felt there was more to her, though, and that was partly the reason why she had brought her to Faelynn. Not all humans could see a faery in the wild like that, as the magic was too strong and only those that chose to reveal themselves could be seen without the proper spells or tricksters. Her poem was not the reason Serena found her. There was something deeper to this whole saga, which by the looks was only just beginning, Shaylee thought.

"This device is tamper-proof, as the magic and the potion are too strong. There are only two things it could be. The first is that you, Shaylee, must have had excess blood on the device, and when Serena touched it, the residue was enough to mix again and give another reading. The other, well, the other can mean only one thing—your young friend here is related to you."

Serena sank down on the bed, still sitting although hunched in deep thought. Shaylee had a tiny smile on the side of her mouth that no one could see as she responded to Faelondar's information, "So how do we prove this? Can we do the test again?"

"Yes, here, give me that cloth. I'll wipe the needle, shake it once more to return it to clear, and then we will watch your maiden Maraenor do the test, after which we will retest your friend." Faelondar did just that, wiping, then lining up Maraenor's finger and drawing three drops of blood. "Now, maidens are common faery folk, so hers should, like the rest of us, turn bright purple."

They all watched in anticipation, especially Maraenor who was quietly hoping she was an Aethelwyne as well. As the liquid changed, her disappointment became a reality when a bright purple color stained the vial. Faelondar wiped the needle very thoroughly again and shook the contents of the device to bring it back to a pure clear liquid.

Shaylee looked over at Maraenor, winked, and whispered, "You will always be my sister, my dear Maraenor."

The maiden blushed and smiled, as she turned her gaze to Serena who was placing her finger back into the wooden device. Three drops fell into the vial and they all moved closer as the blood turned to white first, then to red, which indicated human blood. The disappointment showed in their eyes, but the device wasn't finished yet. The red color slowly turned again, and the magic potion inside changed to a crystal-clear blue once more, and that's where it would stay yet again, for the second time. "Why did it go to red for human and then change again to blue—"

Before Serena could finish Shaylee cut her off, "Now, no one is to tell anyone about this, are we all clear? I am leaning more to you, Faelondar. We have known each other forever so please do not betray me now, especially to Stexinzar, not ... one ... word."

Shaylee had that look in her eye again, not quite twisted, but enough to shake up Faelondar who she knew would not betray her.

"Now I need to be alone with Serena please. I will be down in one hour to attend the council and there I will explain everything I know, about what I have been through and where I have been."

Faelondar and Maraenor both nodded at the same time and exited Shaylee's large quarters.

Shaylee gestured to Serena with a pat on the bed to come and sit next to her.

Serena looked very confused now, and she was desperate for some answers, which Shaylee was about to confront her with. "Did you know, Shay? Is that why you brought me here?"

Shaylee grabbed her hand and calmly answered, "I had a feeling, child, although I was not sure in what capacity until now. What I mean is that I knew you were special, with some essence from here in one form or another, although I did not believe the rumors to be true about my father, King Viltherome Aethelwyne, and his, let's say, outside love for another woman, which here in Faelynn is frowned upon and illegal from the council's perspective. I will explain."

Shaylee sounded sad and Serena was slowly coming around to understanding that she was involved in something big.

Shaylee continued, "Many, many moons ago my father had an affair with a maiden, which came out soon after when that baby was left at the palace gates with a note. She was ... no, is, my half-sister Stalixus who was one of the first to be taken by the sinisters I was telling you about at your house. Well, the king was punished, not by the council, but by the queen herself. He was sent away to battle a horde of goblins that had taken residence in an outpost near the dark lands. Kings were not supposed to leave for dangerous battles as that was for the high Elvenfae warriors to do, although my father liked to swing his ax from time to time. My mother needed time to dwell and fester, although she took one look at Stalixus and fell in love with her straightaway. My mother, Tianna, has a loving and forgiving heart. Stalixus was born after the war of the dark one and I was a child through it, so I cared for her and taught her how to fly and how to transform, along with all the other mischievous things young ones do here in the land of natural magic.

"The king returned with a few bangs and bruises, nothing that you would say was too serious. My mother took him back in. It was best for all as a fragile leadership could always bring unrest in Faelynn, so long as he promised to never stray again. Time went by, many cycles in fact, until the king had a massive falling out with Tianna and he not only broke the law by entering your realm, which we call the old world, but it came out later that he saw a beautiful woman and fell for her, posing as a handsome gentleman. He then broke another law, that by which an Elvenfae mixed breeds with a human—not just an Elvenfae, but a king of the Fae.

"He confessed on his return, as the watchers of the Sidhe, or the faery forts, as you call them, witnessed the events and warned him of the consequences if he did not tell the council. My mother was devastated, and soon a watcher of the Sidhe came and informed that the human woman was with child. The king knew he had wronged his beloved wife and queen for the last time. Tianna spent months in her quarters before the king announced there had been trouble brewing in Maelenflitt and he needed to attend with his warriors. Tianna assumed he was going as payback again like the last time. But there were consequences in Faelynn for this kind of betrayal. Mixing breeds cannot be done by a royal line, especially with the other enemy, humans. There were conspiracies that there was no battle, but a setup by the council and heads of houses that the king be taken and killed in an honorary battle. He died with his beloved ax. They cut his wings from his body and they shaved his long white beard clean. They gave him this honor instead of banishment or public execution, we think, for all his service through the great dark war. Wings were trophies to some evil creatures. They believe if they eat them, they will gain that power and shaving a warrior was a custom from the old times so this made it look like a battle."

Shaylee took a deep breath. She had tears in her eyes as Serena gripped her hand. Serena was taking it well for a twelve-year-old, Shaylee thought. She had to hear it now before whispers rang out and she found out the wrong way. Besides, Shaylee had a plan for her later that would soothe any concerns.

She continued, "After this there was much mourning. He was the first king to die in over fifteen hundred cycles, breaking the stronghold of protection over Faelynn, which the council had no concern over as the dark lord had been defeated long ago. Also, most of the outer Sidhe had been closed so interactions with men would be few, leaving no threat. But the sinisters came soon after. The timing couldn't have been worse, as normally your birth would have been picked up from a swirl of twisted winds, a black rainbow, and a flurry of green sloop birds that only left the forests of Aurora when there was a birth outside of Faelynn. See, interactions between the Fae and humans happened now and then, and they were picked up from the signs. Those born were taken from their cots and replaced with changelings, punishment for the human, and we kept the faery bloodlines here in Faelynn and brought out their abilities. What happened with you was poor timing. You should have been taken at birth also, but the sinisters arrived, the signs were missed, and you weren't picked up. See, children aren't to blame for the mixed breeding, so they are looked after. It's only humans who ..." Shaylee realized what she was saying and rephrased it, "I mean, you are very lucky to have such wonderful parents, and you will return to them. I just have some things to teach you before you go. When you found me at the Sidhe, I felt a sudden connection to you. I only heard a part of your poem. Why do you think you are who you are, strong and fearless with such a sixth sense for our people. You found me, Serena, because you are my half-sister. We have a connection. I had intuition and feelings about it and this device confirms the rumors about my father were true."

They both started crying, Shaylee grabbing her sibling tight to comfort her. This was so much to take in, and they spent the next part of that hour hugging, talking, and sharing stories.

SHAYLEE'S COUNCIL DISCLOSURE

THE COUNCIL AND ALL INVITED MEMBERS of the houses of the Fae were seated, silent, and waiting for the stand-in queen to arrive for a briefing that would bring hope.

Princess Shaylee Aethelwyne had been gone for many cycles here in Faelynn, and who knows how long on other worlds she may have been to. So the hesitant audience who had been informed of her true bloodline and that she was not an imposter were keen to find out some good news they could use against further attacks. They wanted their beloved heroine back, the only escapee and survivor of the insidious attacks on their peaceful lands. Nevertheless, everything that Shaylee said now would influence whether they trusted her or turned on her.

Shaylee entered the room, looking around at all the worried faces and stern council members, all of whom she had known well in some form or another, friends for a long time. She knew this briefing would be particularly important, especially to gain their trust for the upcoming battle at Toozookus.

Shaylee took the stand. She looked a lot paler than before, which meant she was returning to normal and was more rested. The time spent with Serena must have also helped. Not even days earlier she was in a field, in the old world, dying, and weeks before that with an insidious twisted creature under the control of the Zeytars.

She took a breath, while Serena found a place on the floor with her legs crossed, gave Shaylee a wink, and nodded in approval that she could do this. Before long Shaylee addressed the crowd. "Hello, all my beautiful people, oh how I have missed every one of you. I feel like I was here only yesterday, yet so much has changed. Baldaar, I see you have a new horn, and Faleesa, you are with child. I see all the changes in your looks and faces, and though we do not age here, I feel you all have in my eyes, as I have missed out on so much. But I am lucky, if you could call it that. I escaped the inescapable. If it wasn't for this amazing young human girl Serena here, I would have been lost forever. You owe my life to her and each one of you is in her debt, for without the information I have to pass on, all of your lives would be in danger.

"These sinister creatures, as we have so perfectly named them, are cruel, intelligent, cunning, powerful, and for the most part evil. They trapped me with the beasts in dark holding cells when they weren't using us. There was a link between us and the beasts, created by the so-called Zeytars to control us—whatever they planted in our minds, we had to fulfill. They were under the control of the hive too.

"The hive is where all the sinisters communicate with each other. The beasts were prisoners too and I felt their struggles at times. And before you say it, no, we could not transform. Our minds would not allow our bodies to do so. We became twisted and hungered for blood. The beasts could sense humans with special blood and our job was to surprise attack them and hold them at bay, until the beast appeared and took the boy, girl, man, or woman, it didn't matter."

Shaylee took a deep breath and continued, "Without the power of Faelynn, we had no magic, and we would have perished. They must have known this. Like I said, they are intelligent. They seemed to know a lot, as if they had studied us. So now and then they would enter a part of Faelynn, we would recharge, and then go back. We wanted to stay. Our bodies were trying, but our minds let us down. The control was too strong. We had free will to fly, shoot weapons, scream, and talk, but the hold was more powerful than anything I had ever imagined.

"I also saw some of our own eaten by the beasts if they looked like they were defecting or overpowering the control. This was rare, though, and none of us wanted the queen to be one of those, so we obeyed. I got glimpses of what they were doing through the minds of the beasts and some sinisters. They are here to take over all humans, create new powerful bodies for themselves, and kill the rest."

Shaylee took another deep breath and finished by sharing what was hardest for her to speak of. "We were in the old world. We spent most of our time in and out of there. The beasts would scream and we would appear. If any of us did not stay with the beast when it opened the portal back, we would have been stuck. All the Sidhe are closed. I saw a goblin trying to sneak back when we were in the middle of an attack. He looked at us and laughed, and then turned and scampered off when he couldn't get through. It wasn't until we were taking a young girl ..."

Shaylee started crying. No one had seen the princess cry, not in an exceptionally long time. She was always the pleaser and positive one in the palace. She took a moment, wiping the fast-flowing tears from her eyes.

"I'm sorry, this is hard," she eventually said. "We are a peaceful race, and the things we had to do under their control I will never forget. So, we had a little girl by the hair, arms, and legs, awaiting the beast. A couple of us were with her older companion—we always tricked them when they first saw us. We looked like friendly folk to gain their trust, after which we turned twisted again. The Zeytars had complete power over us. When I was in the presence of the older man, I was unprepared and he swatted me so hard that I hit the ground a good distance away and passed out."

Shaylee paused for a moment, casting her gaze around the room, and then continued, "When I came to, it was dark. I couldn't move. Everyone had gone, and I was all alone. I lived off the surrounding grass. I had lost some of my weapons, and my sack with healing powder was too difficult to reach due to my injuries. I was away from my world, and because of their evil grip on me, I had no protection. My powers faded, rendering me very weak. Humans scoured the area for a time. Just when I felt like I had reached my end, I heard a lovely girl giving thanks to the Fae and I felt a connection immediately. There was something about this girl, so with everything I had I called out to her, hoping she would see me. I opened myself up to her to see me and she did, with such ease, picking me up and gently placing me in her pocket where my quiver and powder sack fell from my body, lost in the darkness with my sword that she had also found. She took me to her dwelling, opening the powder sack and enabling me to heal myself enough so I could change and fly back home through a royal doorway. I owe my life to you, Serena, and so will they."

Shaylee rubbed some more tears away and finished up, "When I was flying out of Serena's window the first time, a Zeytar stopped me. He was watching over her as she had something important that they wanted. He had a hold over me, very powerful, although not controlling or evil. He was kind—well, as kind as a Zeytar/sinister could be. He explained some truths to me about the effect their plan will have on us in the future and asked me to keep Serena safe from his dark partner who was close to uncovering truths about her. He was doing his best to keep him away but he just needed a few more hours. Lastly, he told me that he was building a team for the future to help bring his kind down, and he wanted Serena to be a part of that when she grew up. He said the battle would give us an opportunity to save the queen and release our people, although we had to be patient, as time would move fast, slow, or how nature intended. He advised not to dwell on when, but just to know he will be there when the time is right."

The room was silent as they all tried to process what Shaylee was telling them. "I will have to see this Zeytar again over time for information," she said. "I will have to leave you at times in the future. Our people and our queen come first, but remember, although we are a separate realm, we are connected to the old world, and whatever happens to them, will eventually happen to us."

Shaylee looked out at the entire crowd—jaws were open, wings were fluttering from nerves, and there were tears as the silence grew. A pixie elder stood on her chair and started clapping, then another, before a forest gump, a gnome, and a wood elf joined in.

Before long, the room was filled with roaring and clapping, and shouts of "Shaylee, our queen! Shaylee, our queen! Shaylee, our queen!" She nodded, thanking them all, raising her voice to be heard above the noise, "Thank you, my people! It's only until my mother returns but thank you. In the meantime, we need to protect what we have, so let's saddle up tomorrow morning at first light and slay some imposters from Toozookus. We will build Faelynn up again, I promise." She gazed down at Serena, who was wiping away tears and looked horrified at some truths, but proud of her new friend and sister.

The crowd finished roaring, and all came up one at a time to greet Shaylee and show support. Even Stexinzar looked shocked by her dark story. He was the last to come over to her, and when his turn came, he bent down on one knee, lowered his head, and said, "Your Highness, please accept my apology. I had no idea. I am so deeply sorry I did not believe you. It must have been torture." Then he turned to Serena, stood up, and whispered, "And thank you, young one, for bringing our special Shaylee home again. We are in your debt."

Serena smiled, blushed, and lowered her head for a moment, before Shaylee answered, "I understand, Stex. Please do me one favor though."

Stexinzar look up into her watery blue eyes. "Anything. Name it."

Shaylee placed her hand into his and asked, "Would you please lead my guards and warriors for me, while staying as my number one Elvenfae guardsman?"

Stex smiled. It was like he was returning to his old self once more, as he said to Shaylee, "Of course. Try to stop me."

They both smiled and made plans for the following morning's early departure.

$\approx$

The night didn't drag; it was dawn before anyone was ready for it, everyone save one—Serena. She was very excited to see this world. She knew she would not be near any of the danger, so she was happy to be able to witness some of the lands. She had her new satchel bag that Shaylee had given her, with old Celtic writing over it. Shay had also given her some boots and clothes from some young maidens, although one maiden had a late night sewing patches in the backs—they were not used to having a wingless one among them.

Shaylee also made her protector of her famous sword Howling Tooth while she didn't need it, more to make Serena feel like she was contributing to something special than anything else. She had heard stories from the maiden before she went to sleep about how the handle was made from a tooth of one of the last dragons, the creatures which used to enter the old world and Faelynn before they moved on to other realms after the dark war.

Shaylee's sword handle was in fact from a tooth of the dark lord's dragon, slain in front of him by her father, the king. It was said that the mystical protectors of the realms departed because they had lost too many of their kind during the war. Viltherome took a tooth for luck and eventually had the smiths mold a sword for Shaylee for when she came of age. The tooth was carved for the handle, and a nice bend was added in the blade. Metal spikes at the sides would come in and out of the hilt with the flick of a button, adding damage to the enemy when she eventually used it in a fight.

The king had it made like that in preparation for future wars, to give Shaylee something vicious to fight with that would increase carnage. The smith designed the whole blade to be light and swift, and to put fear into her enemy with a howl from the swinging of the blade. When Shaylee came of age and started training with it, she eventually amended her style to incorporate moves and parries that would enhance the blade's howling. Her acrobatics and unique fighting style had some of her enemies in the past turning and running almost before they even saw her. So she appropriately named her sword Howling Tooth.

Serena held the scabbard in her hand; it was far too big for her, but she didn't care. She put on her new boots and her Celtic garb, which she adored, and had the maidens braid her long dark hair to be just like Shaylee's, in a Celtic knot. She was ready for her adventures.

Shaylee had also been awake for some time. Serena had slept next to her in the enormous bed, and when she heard Serena excitedly getting ready and whispering to herself, she turned around and looked at her with a smile before saying, "Well look at you, looking like a princess of Faelynn. The maidens did a wonderful job on your hair, my dear. How long have you been awake?" Shaylee knew she had been up for a while, but just enjoyed the excitement on her face.

"Oh, sorry, Shay, I didn't mean to wake you," Serena replied, dropping the sword from her hands in fright and looking back up at her half-sister.

"It's fine, Serena. We have to get ready as we have goblins to cast away from our beautiful lands. Besides, soon you will meet the woodland elves—they are the most skilled, handsome, and friendliest Fae in our lands. I would love to have them fight for the palace, however they are a very loyal race of elves that stay with their own, protecting all the amazing land of Toozookus. They help us on occasions and, like now, we help them when they need it."

Serena smiled. "Wow, I cannot wait to meet them, Shay."

Shaylee flew out of bed with a smile on her face and went off to her private quarters to ready herself for the battle.

Serena took all her gear and wandered down to the kitchen where the cooks were preparing a very vegan breakfast. Serena wasn't used to this lifestyle. She would give anything for a burger, but she respected the fact that everything here was protected and used only for natural purposes. There was no waste. While they sometimes made parchments and satchels from animals, this was after the animal had expired, and they hunted nothing for any higher gain or profit. That was why they disliked some human acts. Buildings, weapons, metals for swords and construction were all made from the lands, although with permission, and were replenished afterward; clothes were made from a special tree in the forest of Kaldarik, next to Aurora, which shed a fur from its bark and was harvested carefully, with permission. Serena thought that maybe they could teach humans a few things about environmental recycling.

Gnomes were different, though. They did like their meat and they would get it if they could, but were still careful of how, normally through entering the old world and stealing a row of sausages hanging in a butcher's pantry or stealing a pie from the windowsill of a mother cooling it down for her children. Nothing was wasted and everything was respected. All except those animals that hunted Fae, which were targets of the gnomes, especially the Pandaron pig, an animal with almighty tusks and an appetite for sprites and mushroom homes.

Shaylee called out for Serena a short time later. It impressed Serena how quickly she got ready. She had a particularly important question to ask her as she ran from the kitchen to greet her.

"Ahh, there you are, young one, have you had your fill?"

Serena nodded, looking up at her with wide eyes before asking, "Shay, how come when you change into a tiny faery your clothes are all natural looking with greens and purples and you aren't wearing much, and then when you change back you are in your same attire. Also, your sword shrinks and then goes back. How is this possible?"

Shaylee burst out laughing and Serena frowned, thinking she was making fun of her. "Oh, you are special. I am not laughing at you, my dear. I forget that you do not know this place and all our magic, and that's what it is. We are from the land, and even though our mother births us, we are still all part of the grass, the trees, the wind, and the flowers. From the very first ones ever born of magic, we are chosen, special beings, and when we change, we go back to the natural world, as that is where we are more magical, with the land. When we are in full form, the magic is still with us but allows us more choices, and we can wear clothes and jewels. Anything attached to our bodies shrinks and expands at our will when we change."

Serena looked confused, although content. "That is cool. Do you believe in God? We go to church every week, and sometimes my sisters and I get the giggles at the old people."

"Of course we do. Our mother is Faelynn, and she takes care of us, and then there is the Overseer, above the world, who takes care of the realm and of us. Our ancestors, the Tuatha Dé Danann, said to be from the stars, talked about the omnipotent Overseer who knows all. We know little of the history and have been taught from birth to honor the mother Faelynn. Is that who you mean by God?"

Serena looked confused again. "I guess, whatever omni... om... that word is?"

At that moment Stexinzar entered the room and informed Shaylee that everything was in place and the group was now ready to depart.

Serena loved Shaylee's special warrior attire. It was a little different to what she wore at her house. There was less armor this time, although she had a nice flowing cape from her waist, and her vambraces looked more natural. Serena loved how her scabbard and quiver sat on her shoulders while her wings were all pointing low, enhancing the cape's effect. She was such a beautiful creature and Serena loved every part, from her looks to her personality. She was her favorite person in all the worlds, she thought as she was living her own faery tale.

"Hey, are you ready, I've got a surprise."

Serena snapped back to reality and followed Shaylee out the front of the palace doors then out of the gates where the guards were all waiting for her to depart.

The council head Faelondar was put in temporary charge until they returned. Shaylee went to the head of the troupe and whistled a high-pitched whistle in a tone only she could achieve. As the echo of the sound waned, a flurry of white and pink petals appeared, flying around in the breeze. The guards looked in wonder as the petals danced around the place, before realizing they were wisps. In the distance they could all hear the pounding of fast footsteps until out of a cloud of colored wisps came Vyyuna, storming up the path to greet her friend.

The guards and warriors did not get to see her often, and each time they did, they were in awe. Some had never even seen a unicorn, let alone been near one. Vyyuna came charging up the path and stopped right before Shaylee, who had her hand out to greet her. She placed her soft hand onto the creature's perfectly long face and hummed to her for a moment. As Vyyuna settled from the audience, she lowered her head down to Serena's and gave her a little nudge with her nose, wetting the side of Serena's cheek. Serena didn't wipe it off. She just smiled as Shaylee leaned over and whispered to her, "I think she really likes you, Serena. You must be very special."

Serena did not say a word. She could only smile as she placed her right hand onto Vyyuna's head and gently rubbed her soft white hair. As she was doing this, she couldn't help but notice something moving from behind a tree a good few yards up the path. Serena only glimpsed it, making out some very shadowy features. She turned, looked up at Shaylee, and whispered, "Did you see that, Shay, there is something hiding behind that tree. Can you see it? What is it?"

Shaylee chuckled softly. "It looks like Vyyuna is not the only one that has taken a liking to you, my dear. It seems you have an admirer."

Serena looked confused and she focused a little harder. The clouds broke, allowing the early morning sun to hit the tree. There with his head looking around the side of the trunk Serena saw that cheeky rabbit poking his tongue out at her again before ducking behind the tree once more. Shaylee was laughing while Serena seemed a little concerned at being stalked by a talking rabbit.

But Shaylee eased her worries. "Come out, little one, come say hello," she said.

As the queen finished speaking, the pooka came running over, still keeping his distance, although now he was invited he felt more comfortable about showing himself. Besides, he knew exactly who was asking him to come out.

"What is your name? This is my friend Serena, do you remember? Would you like to meet her again?"

The pooka bounced closer. He was wearing a grass headband, overalls made from brown tree bark which had been softened for clothing, and had grass and flowers intertwined around him. His massive blue eyes were mesmerizing. Serena thought he looked like a cute bunny from something she might have watched when she was very little, although this one was different. He had all the characteristics of a rabbit, but he was taller. One ear was always standing high and the other draped over his back; they were very long. He seemed to be always on his back feet and could actually run, not only hop. And the most bizarre difference was the fact he talked in a child's voice and had the behavior of a three-year-old, even though he had the intelligence of an adult. Very bizarre, Serena thought.

"Come on, she won't bite," Shaylee added as he inched toward Serena, tongue poking out still.

Serena remembered now what he was doing, so played his game, and as she bent down to greet him, she whispered, "Your tongue stinks, furry feet." *Furry feet*—what was that? thought Serena, but it was the best she had under pressure. It didn't matter, though, as it seemed to do the trick.

"My tongue stinks? The only reason I'm here is because I followed your breath and it kept me awake."

Serena fell to the ground in fits of laughter as did the cheeky pooka. It seemed he was only in need of attention, and with Serena, he had an audience.

As she wiped the tears away, Serena asked, "What is your name, goblin face?"

"King of the poop, but you can call me Van Coinan."

Serena giggled once more and responded, "Van Coinan, is that your name? Sounds like a poop. Pleased to meet you, I'm Serena O'Halloran."

Serena put her hand out to greet Van Coinan. As he finished shaking her hand with his soft-fingered paw, he pulled it up to his mouth and licked it, before letting go and retorting, "Pleased to meet you, Serena of the ugly face. Now we are friends?"

Serena pulled her hand back and rubbed off the naughty pooka's moist saliva before returning fire, "If it means I'm friends with a fat-nosed rabbit, then yes, we are friends."

Van Coinan smiled and whispered, "I'm a pooka, you poo, not a rabbit, but that's OK, you look like a boy."

Serena laughed once more. Meanwhile Shaylee had just finished discussing the details of the journey with Stexinzar and the leader guards, and she turned and approached Serena saying, "Are you ready, child? I'm going to show you Toozookus. It's time to run along, Van Coinan. You can play with Serena when she gets home."

Van Coinan pulled out his wooden sword from his leafy scabbard and yelled, "I can help, I can fight, that's why I came. I can beat all your guards in five moves—here, I will show you."

As Van Coinan approached the front guards, they all looked at each other with confusion, but Serena quickly called out, "Can he come with us, Shaylee? Please, pretty please?"

Shaylee looked at Stexinzar, who shrugged, then at Van Coinan with his wooden sword, and finally at Serena. The girl was begging again, and Shaylee couldn't resist. "Now, you know this is a dangerous mission, Van Coinan. Will you be able to handle it?"

Van Coinan did a backflip, fell on his shoulder, then stood upright, swinging his sword around before answering, "No sweat, I'll eat them all alive."

And with that Shaylee nodded, and the three of them mounted Vyyuna and trotted off into the morning sun, headed for Toozookus.

THE ROAD TO
TOOZOOKUS

IT WAS A GOOD LONG RIDE TO GET TO TOOZOOKUS at their pace. They weren't in a hurry to get there as they believed the woodland elves would be strong enough to hold the intruders off until they arrived, giving Serena time to explore during their breaks.

She still could not believe the awesome beauty her eyes were showing her; it made the best of her world look like a desert. It was something she couldn't explain, and her eyes were constantly getting uploads of intense visuals that her brain was struggling to process. If she was half faery, she thought, how would any human be able to withstand the intense chaos of all the visual stimulation that she was constantly subjected to?

Van Coinan had disappeared. Flithiin, a lower-level guard, was relieved, as he needed a break from the annoying pooka. Van Coinan wasn't silly—he picked his targets, and finding Flithiin was like pulling a fish out of a puddle.

The pooka had just run off. He had been gone for a good while, but Shaylee wasn't concerned as pookas did that. Whatever they wanted, they did. Besides, any smart creatures in these parts would be wise enough not to go toe to toe with one.

Serena had veered off the path. She led Vyyuna to the edge of the small lake, and while she was drinking the crystal blue water, Serena wandered into the entrance to an arch-shaped vine tunnel at the edge of the Aurora Forest. It seemed dark inside, however she could hear voices, soft voices coming through, echoing like a soothing invitation. Vyyuna looked up and shook her head back, neighing loudly. But Serena, who seemed to be in a trance, glanced back and whispered, "It's OK, Vyyuna my dear, they won't hurt me, they just want to say hello."

Vyyuna continued her protest before turning around and heading back to camp. Serena was now fully committed to the dense arched vine that was still calling her, "Serena, over here, come with us. You will love it, Serena."

The voices were so soft and inviting, hypnotizing her to delve deeper. As she continued on, she could see tiny, winged humanoids flying everywhere and whispering as they fluttered. They were not like the sprites, Serena thought. These things were light green and others very pale blue, fully naked with long wings and pointed ears. They were smaller than sprites. It seemed Serena's eyesight was working incredibly well now, with all senses heightened.

She kept walking as the space became darker. Serena delved farther, to the point that when she looked over her shoulder, she could only see trees and darkness.

Serena was now lost, but it didn't seem to concern her at all. She was waving her hands around and letting the tiny winged faeries touch her, and she touched them. She kept walking. Deeper in she went, and as she came to the end of the long, arched vine walkway, she entered a small section of forest filled with colorful toadstools and bright trees. Serena could see her mother putting the clothes on the line while her father was cutting wood. They waved to her, and she held her hand up and waved back. Then she looked to her right and saw blossoms flying off the trees, filling the area with a continuous flow of colors.

The soft voices continued luring her deeper in. Her parents were still there in the distance, although the farther she went the stranger things became. She was still not frightened, though.

Serena lowered her head and looked at the ground. She saw a gnome gazing up at her as it kicked her foot. She became angry and stepped on its head, crushing his skull. Serena laughed and continued walking.

She could hear voices coming from behind her, very faint and off in the distance. The green and blue faeries seemed agitated and scurried up, still whispering soothingly to her. Then Serena heard the distant voices again. She noticed the faeries were all coming together to make one adult size faery, all attached and still fluttering like crazy. Each one molded to the next to give the impression that the hundreds of tiny creatures were now one large one.

The large blue and green faery fluttered its giant wings, which made all the tiny ones move in unison, like a symbiotic entity all working together. As it put its arms out to reach for her, Serena also extended her arm out, allowing herself to almost touch it. As the large faery extended farther to connect, Serena heard commotion and yelling coming from directly behind her. The spell broke and the large faery scattered into the little ones, before disappearing completely, revealing a hideous creature in its place.

Shaylee came charging in on Vyyuna, leaped off the unicorn with a flip and cut the creature's arm off. It was quite grotesque and Serena squealed. The creature had a long nose that pointed down, long pointed ears, and dark gray skin. It was dressed in leathers and wool of a dark color, and its face was twisted, showing its long-fanged teeth as it screamed in pain. It pulled its sword out, a large blade with two to three different sections, and while it tried to match Shaylee, she whirled her howling sword around. The creature opened its eyes wide in fear, realizing who it was, before the substitute queen finished her acrobatic dance and swung hard, cutting the creature's head completely from its neck.

Shaylee wiped the tar-like black blood from her sword with the creature's fur coat, as it flailed and writhed around, before finally falling to the ground, silent and still. She placed Howling Tooth back into her scabbard as Serena ran to her and hugged her very tightly, trembling with fear.

Serena slowly let go. She realized something very disturbing while looking around the place: that it was a prickly lair of vines, ugly and dark, with nothing else growing there but twisted trees—not a lovely forest with beautiful faeries and her parents. She looked up at Shaylee, blubbering. "Where am I, Shay?" she said through her tears. "What was that thing? The last thing I remember was hearing voices and seeing tiny faeries with my parents waving. It all felt so real, like a dream, but living it in real life."

Serena's crying grew hysterical. She was not letting go of Shaylee anytime soon. Shaylee knew how frightened she was, so gave her time, while she motioned with her hand to the other guards to move back and not overwhelm her too much. Soon Serena settled down and looked up at her sister again.

"Are you alright? Are you hurt?" Shaylee asked, and after Serena shook her head, she continued, "You, my lucky dear, have had a run-in with a particularly dark and twisted goblin. In fact, the highest breed of goblins, the witchin goblins. They have the power of illusion and coercion on unsuspecting minds. Vyyuna sensed it there and that is why she warned you, but then when you continued, she came and got me. They lure you in by twisting images in your mind before ..."

Shaylee paused and so Serena probed her for more information, "Before what, Shay? Tell me."

Knowing she couldn't keep it from her, Shaylee answered reluctantly, "Before eating you."

Serena began trembling again. "Can we please get out of here, Shay, please?"

Shaylee held her tight as they made their way back to the camp. Van Coinan was back, and Vyyuna stepped forward and nuzzled Serena's cheek once again before talking in her mind, saying, "I am glad you are alright, Serena. You scared me."

Serena looked up at the magnificent creature, confused. But before she could talk, Vyyuna began speaking to her mind again, "Please, Serena, do not tell anyone, not even Shaylee, that I can speak with you. I am only connecting so I can warn you better next time. This is our secret."

Serena whispered back, "Yes, Vyyuna, thank you." She was still in shock and unsure what was real and what wasn't.

Meanwhile, Shaylee was discussing the event with Stexinzar and the head guards to make sense of it. "A witchin goblin this far away from Xarkynan—that is disturbing, Stex. It must mean the troublemakers in Toozookus aren't the regular type and we might be dealing with something much darker. Always monitor Serena—it is not a request, OK. That goes for all of you. She is special and important to me, and eventually will be to others as well. I should not have brought her along. We will kick off from here, find another site, and take turns at guarding. And we have to keep Serena entertained for the rest of the journey. I don't want her broken."

When Shaylee finished, they all nodded and got back to their duties as per her request.

As the light from the perfect evening sky disappeared into the mountains, revealing the stars and all the wonders of the sky, the adventurers built a camp, far away from the edges of Aurora where Serena had encountered the dark magic. She had calmed from the event swiftly, and as Shaylee looked over at her while she was setting a bed for herself, she couldn't help but wonder who this Serena was really. She had so many strengths. Did that come from her father, her own mother, her sister Stalixus? And then it hit her hard—not that Shaylee was proud, and she was far from having an ego. She is just like me, she thought. The sentiment put a smile on her face, and as much as she was close with her half-sister Stalixus whom she missed every day, she saw so much of herself in the young Serena, and that made her happy. But there was still something she couldn't quite grasp, and she hoped over time it would eventually reveal itself.

Later that evening Van Coinan put on a show for everyone, trying some acrobatics that failed spectacularly, though in his eyes were amazing. The group was in stitches and Serena was rolling on the ground with tears of laughter flowing from her eyes. Shaylee was deep in thought. She had Howling Tooth out and was polishing her after the earlier scuffle, staring into darkness as she went over every small detail of her sword. The intricacies of the lower part of the blade which went up from the handle all the way to the tip revealed carved Celtic words and symbols of all the histories of her house name, up to her own.

The side spikes were now completely hidden inside the hilt, and the pommel was small, etched with symbols of the first Aethelwyne king's name. The magnificent handle of dragon tooth was hidden under detailed binding, wrapped in a stunning pattern with a small section next to the start of the blade with holes either side. This was where the spikes that resembled dragons' claws sprung out at the press of a button in the middle of the hilt at the top. Shaylee hit that button to clean the sharp, piercing blades which curled slightly at the end to look like claws. After the inspection satisfied her, she hit a button on the other side, and they retracted.

The edge of the blade was thinner than the middle as the metal started expanding out in width. Howling Tooth's blade went on to a slight bend and thinned again as it came to the sharp cutting end. The blade wasn't wide, but it was very elegant, and Shaylee took it everywhere she went. She was going to let Serena look after it some more, although the earlier experience revealed that the journey wasn't a friendly camping trip. She kept staring into the shadows, thinking of the day's events, coming up with plans for Serena and where she would have to be when the battle took place.

Shaylee continued to clean her blade, still lost in thought. Her mind shifted to one of her earlier loves. Deep within Toozookus was a handsome woodland elf whom she was forbidden to marry by her father. Shaylee started smiling as she tried to picture his face again and wondered what he would be doing now—if he had married, and had a family, or if he was even still around. The memories hurt, although they were also soothing. When you live an exceedingly long life, you make lots of memories, she thought to herself. Some, like these, she had not thought about in many moons.

Shaylee, now content with the perfect condition of Howling Tooth, placed her sword away and was hit suddenly with the answer to her conundrum. She would hide Serena with Malarviar, the sister of her beloved Darphanin, the prince of the woodland forest near Toozookus.

Shaylee felt she could sleep a lot better now, knowing that Serena would be safe.

The camp had finished encouraging the cheeky pooka some time ago and had settled in for the night. Shaylee walked over to Serena's camp and a tear rolled down her face. Van Coinan had succumbed to exhaustion, resting his face next to Serena's head, while Vyyuna was on the other side of Serena's back, nestled next to her. All were fast asleep. Shaylee had communed with Vyyuna and she knew what happened had upset her. She was looking out for her new friend.

Shaylee leaned down, kissed Serena on her cheek, and whispered, "You are very special to me, my dear, and I worry what that Zeytar will have you do in the future."

Suddenly a huge mental vision hit Shaylee like a volcanic force and grabbing her head she dropped to the ground. She saw Serena as an adult and sinisters all around her in darkness and with flashes of fire. Shaylee screamed out in pain and the entire camp shot up and ran to help the princess. Serena awoke with a fright and when she realized what was happening, held Shaylee and crooned to her. The song seemed to help as Shaylee's hands slowly retracted from the tight grip on her skull and hair. Serena said nothing, just kept singing. She could see it working.

Serena smiled as Shaylee looked up at her, admiring her soothing, youthful voice. Her face was an off-reddish color, far from her perfect pale tones. Whatever happened in her mind must have been terrible, Serena thought. She finished her song and gently asked Shaylee, "Are you alright, Shay, did you have a nightmare?"

Shaylee, wiping her tears away and slowly turning back to her normal color, replied, "Something like that, my dear. Flashbacks from my incarceration. Nothing for you to worry about."

Shaylee was not about to tell her she would be in danger in the future, a future she dreaded now for her sister. That sinister friend Wilkes better help her, she thought, as she slowly stood up and ushered everyone back to their camps for rest.

Stexinzar looked at her with concern. He was really seeing the toll the sinisters had taken on her and thought about what all the others must be going through at this moment.

It wasn't long before everyone finally succumbed to sleep as three guards stood watch. The rest were dreaming in no time. Well, almost everyone—Shaylee rested little that night.

≈

Dawn broke as the camp rose. Some got moving faster than others. The night air had been quite mild, Serena thought, even though it looked cold. There were so many rules broken here that science would struggle with, she thought as she rubbed her eyes. Van Coinan had been up for ages. He's silent today, though, Serena thought.

There had been no movement from Shaylee. In fact, Shaylee was not there at all. Serena was a little concerned after last night's nightmares or visions. She wandered over to Flithiin, who was having a staring contest with Van Coinan, and asked, "Excuse me, Mr. Guard, sir, have you seen Shaylee?"

As Serena finished the question, Flithiin blinked and hit the log next to him in defeat, picked a silver button from his uniform and reluctantly handed it over to Van Coinan, who was still staring at him intently. He placed his new prize into position on his overalls, still not blinking, as the guard looked up at Serena and whispered, "Thanks, I nearly had him."

Flithiin realized who had asked and remembered Shaylee's request to look after her, so he readjusted his demeanor and said in a more mellow tone, "Sorry, Serena, what was it you said?"

"I'm sorry, sir. I just wanted to know if you had seen—"

Before Serena could finish her question, two horses came charging up to the camp. On one was Shaylee, and on the other was a taller stranger dressed in green and brown clothing straight from the pages of a medieval book, Serena thought. He was very handsome, and he was only armed with a bow and arrow. She couldn't help but notice his brown eyes and long dark hair, very long, braided to one side. There were no jewels or silver, and he had a green leaf-weaved tunic on, with brown undergarments. Other than his quiver, that was all he had, although his hair had symbols shaved into it on the other side of his head as he turned to face the other way, revealing also his elegant ears that were slightly longer and more pointed than those of the Elvenfae.

Shaylee jumped off the horse and ran over to Stexinzar, whispering, "We have trouble, Stex, the woodland elves have been monitoring the situation, and they have said that the evil ones have changed direction and are now heading for Maelenflitt. We cannot let them anywhere near the area. Those who live there have been through enough. We have to stop them."

Stexinzar nodded. He rustled up the guards and warriors, and mounted the horses. The rest of the camp was being packed as this was happening, and in no time the entire group were ready to depart.

"We will head to Toozookus, Stex, and from there we will devise a plan of attack."

Stex nodded once more as Shaylee dismounted the horse and returned it to the guard. She walked up to Vyyuna, who lowered her neck and allowed her to mount. With Serena and Van Coinan already in position, Vyyuna raised her head high. Shaylee turned to Serena and whispered, "We are off to Toozookus, Serena. We are going to meet the wonderful woodland elves."

Serena smiled as Shaylee gave the orders to move on. They galloped off together, their pace now a lot faster, heading into the lower mountain forests toward Toozookus.

They were nearly at the foot of the lower mountains when the leader of the group, ahead by about two hundred yards, came off his horse. The rest stopped as Stexinzar jumped off his horse to check what had happened. Upon inspection, he found a woodland arrow in the guard's neck. He had been killed immediately.

Stexinzar yelled a warning to head for the trees at the edge of the mountains. They still had to get up through them and over the other side, before arriving at a clearing and the start of the woodlands. This was the edge of Toozookus, home to only peaceful forest folk, with wood elf guards scoping the environs and protecting their home.

The entire group galloped to a dense section of cover as more arrows flew by their heads, barely missing Stexinzar as he mounted his horse again to join them. Nimaalah, the woodland elf who was riding with the group, had his bow out, sending arrows flying into the forest, as did Shaylee and the guards. They could see movement in the direction they were aiming for and there was no hesitation—they needed to kill whatever it was. As peaceful as the Fae were, they would protect their stand-in queen at any cost.

The arrows ceased as the group took deep cover in the dense brush. Stexinzar bolted over to Nimaalah and placed his sword around the bowman's neck. What Stexinzar had not realized was that Nimaalah was quick and at the same time had placed an arrow deep inside the main vein to Stexinzar's wing stem, ready to cut a primary artery. Nimaalah dug it in a little harder to start the nerve off. As he did this, Stex realized how precarious his position was and slowly lowered his sword. Nimaalah kept the arrow in place, not being able to trust anyone now as he was on his own in the group. He slowly took the pressure off the vein so they could at least talk. Stexinzar went first as he now had his sword well and truly away from the bowman.

"Is this a trap, wood elf? That was one of your arrows that killed my guard. We are here to help, and you ambush us? Is this a trick to take the princess?"

Nimaalah started laughing, then halted, staring directly into Stexinzar's eyes with a stern look of warning. "If those were our arrows flying straight at all of you, no one would be standing. It is clearly a trap to make you think it was us. Besides, we train to shoot directly into a faery's heart not their neck—the neck is too messy." Nimaalah smiled as he pulled the arrow away from Stexinzar's back.

Shaylee had heard the argument and said, "Stex, Nimaalah is right. One of our guards found a woodland elf over behind the pine. He was without his quiver and bow, and had his throat cut."

Stexinzar looked at Nimaalah and witnessed the woodland elf lower his head in grief. "I'm sorry, Nimaalah, I knew that guard well and I snapped. Can you forgive me?"

Nimaalah looked up at Stex, then at Shaylee, completely dismissing his request. He asked her, "Can you show me his body, please?"

Shaylee nodded and galloped off with Nimaalah and the guard who had found the body. When they reached the spot, Nimaalah jumped off his horse and leaned down to see. He knew straightaway who it was. Looking around, then up at Shaylee, he said in a soft, mournful tone, "It is Japhony, a well-trained guard from a well-known family. I will need to take him with me to his family."

Nimaalah and the Elvenfae guard helped each other as they mounted the body on his horse. Upon further inspection of the ground while they were finishing tying off, Shaylee noticed a black crooked dagger next to where the body had lain. She jumped off the horse she had borrowed and picked up the blade. It was long and bent, with a crooked black handle that looked like it had been handmade from black saprock. She turned and got the attention of the other two. "Look, a dagger with a blade made from black saprock. You know what this means?"

They both looked shocked as Nimaalah answered, "Yes, they are definitely from Xarkynan. Only lower goblins carry such disgusting weapons, and black saprock is only found under the weeping oaks attached to the castle. We have been played and we'd best be on our toes. Come, we must get to the woodlands, fast."

Shaylee nodded. Nimaalah shared a horse with the Elvenfae guard, pulling the spare with Japhony tied on, as Shaylee galloped off in front to give the rest a heads-up.

After they were all debriefed and they had completed a search of the area, with no one and nothing to be found, Nimaalah took them through a secret cave under the mountain that no one could access except the woodland elves. They couldn't take the risk of going up into the forest without knowing where the goblin was.

The cave had firelights glowing all through it, giving them all plenty of light to find their way through. Nimaalah had been given the Elvenfae guard's horse that Shaylee had borrowed earlier from the fallen guard, as she had now returned to Vyyuna and Serena.

Soon they reached the end of the cave and Nimaalah hit a series of rocks on the side. The mountain wall rose, allowing them all into the fields of the clearing and away from the mountain forest. They all rode swiftly for another three miles and then they finally saw the edge of the very tall and dense entry to the woodland forest. Serena was mesmerized. She had never seen trees so tall and wide; they pointed high into the clear blue sky. Her jaw was stuck open in awe.

Shaylee smiled, as she could hear her quiet comments, and then whispered to her, "You have seen nothing yet, my child."

Serena looked at the back of Shaylee's blonde hair covering her neck, then at the forest, as Nimaalah rode off ahead to allow safe entry. Not long after, several woodland elves came out to escort them inside. They did not look happy, as Nimaalah had informed them about Japhony.

Upon entering, it felt like they had transported through a portal into an entirely different realm. Serena had never seen anything so wondrous in all her life, not even in books. Up and all around her was a city in the trees, with ladders and walkways attached from the bottom to the tops. There were holes in the middle of huge trees which connected walkways to others, with houses built up around the massive woods, like cubby houses on steroids. The connecting houses went on for miles and miles into the darkness. Not one thing was on the ground save for the stables and animals.

Serena saw a young boy about her age swing from a vine and fly up into the air, do a somersault, and land on his feet, before running along a pathway through to another house. He then looked out at the visitors through his window. She caught his eye, and he smiled, then disappeared deeper into the house.

The elders were gathering to see them all as they came to a stop directly across from the lower section of the high elf elder's house.

Serena, still looking around in awe, taking it all in, heard Shaylee whisper again, "See, Serena, I told you."

Serena smiled; this time nothing could break her concentration as she leaned over, still looking around, and whispered back, "You sure did, Shay, you sure did."

THE WOODLAND
ELVES

NOTHING WAS SAID AND THERE WAS NO welcoming party or greeting until after they had said goodbye to Japhony. The custom was to gather at the oak of the ancestors in the middle of the city. There they had Japhony still in his clothes with his bow and arrow placed neatly on his right side, as family and members of his clan made a single line, each taking turns at saying goodbye and reciting ancient prayers.

They invited the Elvenfae to witness this exceedingly rare event as guests, for helping them and keeping the peace between both parties for thousands of cycles. Serena had taken up a seat with Shaylee and Stexinzar, close enough to see, although far enough that they would not interrupt the ceremony. As the last of the family and friends said their goodbyes, the high elf stood on a tall rock. He was dressed in ancient traditional clothing which looked like the trees had wrapped him up with flowers, branches, and leaves, all intertwined around his legs, body, and arms, with a large green leaf on his head that pointed to the sky. The woodland elves were very natural, not spoiled like some in the city environs of Faelynn near the palace. They lived only for nature, and as much as the Elvenfae did too, they were spoiled with riches of high quality clothing, armor, food, and dwellings, though they still very much respected the world around them. The woodland elves did not judge them, nor did the Elvenfae mock the nature elves; in fact, all of Faelynn respected the woodland elves.

Serena was taking all of it in, soaking every bit up so she could tell all her friends when she went back, although she didn't know yet that Shaylee would not let that happen. The high elf elder raised his hands in the air, as the rest of the clans, tribes, and family were all now in a large circle. He said some words in the old language. Serena had heard bits and pieces of it before but didn't understand what it meant. She had trouble at times understanding the Elvenfae with their strong traditional accent, English, but a far stronger accent than hers.

His arms stretched all the way into the air while a light came from the surrounding trees, tiny and green, then another followed, and another, until a whole flurry of tiny green lights now circled the body of Japhony. Serena was once again mesmerized. Toozookus was wondrous so far, and she hadn't even left the woodlands yet. She continued staring intensely, watching what would happen next.

The green lights were now making a humming sound all in unison as they started moving away from the body and returning to the tall trees they came from. As Serena watched them disappear, she smiled. It was like a beautiful light show, however upon glancing at Japhony, she soon realized that he was slowly disappearing. As each light took a part of him, he was soon completely gone. This was all happening very swiftly and without mess or any macabre sight, as if he were being returned to the trees of which he had been a part since his birth.

Serena kept staring as the lights finished completing the task they were summoned for, eventually leaving nothing but the hard oak bench where Japhony's body had been not more than a few moments ago. They had even taken his clothes and weapons. The high wood elf slowly lowered his hands, gave thanks to the trees, and stepped off his altar to greet the waiting family and friends.

Serena turned to Shaylee and whispered, "Did that just happen, Shay?"

Shaylee smiled and answered, "I'm afraid so, my dear, it is a first for me too. The woodland elves are quite remarkable people. As sad as it was to lose one of their own, they will celebrate tonight knowing he is with his ancestors in the trees watching out for the rest of them. They are very special and ancient, and you have seen something no one else in Faelynn has ever seen, let alone anyone from your world."

Serena smiled. She didn't feel sadness for them now; she felt happy that at least they believed that Japhony was still there watching out for them.

After the ceremony, the woodland elves invited Shaylee along with Stexinzar and two high guards to a meeting with the elders to discuss the game plan for the next day's attack on the intruders. Serena was happy playing with some local children who were in awe of a human girl being able to live in Faelynn without becoming sick or brain-loaded. Van Coinan was chasing some younger ones, hiding behind the trees and scaring them as they ran past. The giggles echoed into the night as Serena laughed and tried to catch the pooka. Happy that she was safe and content for now, Shaylee disappeared into the meeting room high in the trees where discussions were being held.

"Welcome, Your Highness, and thank you for your attendance here today. We are humbled by your presence and welcome any help from the palace to maintain peace in our lands," said the high elf elder.

"No, it is we who thank you," Shaylee replied. "We are so sorry for your loss and are also humbled to be invited to your home, to witness such a remarkable event, and to fight alongside you like in old times. Please update us on what you know of these dark events."

Shaylee smiled as she took her place in the council room, the only woman, although not for long. The female warrior elves had been out scouting the edges of the forest and would return soon. After the ceremony they went to clean up the area and make sure no other dark creatures were lingering. This was requested by Japhony's sister and leader of her clan, Kapheeny, as she herself wanted to end the life of the putrid creature that took her younger brother.

"Well, from what we know, Your Highness—"

Shaylee interrupted immediately, "Please, call me Shaylee or Shay. We are all friends and equals here while this threat is around. We cannot afford hierarchy; we must work together."

Sarphonel, the high elf elder, nodded and continued, "Thank you, Shaylee. Word is that they are a day's ride from Maelenflitt. What they want from there, we don't know. Whether they had word of the attacks by the tall sinister goblin creatures cycles ago and thought they might be vulnerable, or whether they had other ideas, all we know is that there are many—a good hundred goblins, trolls, dark Elvenfae warriors, and at least one dullahan. Darphanin has more information as his tribe was the last to see them. Nimaalah is one of his tribe members but he was sent to greet you before this information was witnessed, so you will need to listen to what Darph has to say."

Sarphonel finished and sat back. Shaylee's ears had turned red at the tips on hearing the name Darphanin. She had not seen her first love in so long, or even heard his name. He walked through the door and apologized for his lateness, looking over at Shaylee and giving her a tiny smile. Shaylee could not believe how handsome he still was, as if he had not aged a day, more like he had become younger somehow than he was in her memory.

She smiled back and awaited his feedback on the events at hand, trying not to get distracted by his dark eyes, long brown hair in traditional braids, and his dark green and brown tunic, which was the uniform of the houses in the trees.

"Sorry I am late. I wanted to make sure everyone was safe, so after Kapheeny left with her tribe, I took a ride around the other side with mine. I have set up extra watchers for now in addition to our watchtowers near Maelenflitt and the edges of Aurora. Any information we need to know will be sent by special owls so we will start on the right foot with intelligence. Also, welcome, Your Highness, I am sure we will get plenty of time to reminisce, as your group will travel with my tribe. Kapheeny will head straight to Maelenflitt and I am placing Nimaalah as leader of Japhony's tribe. You are more than ready, my friend. You will take up the far flanks as we rush through the middle, head-on to the dark ones.

"The last two tribes will stay here and maintain a stronghold over the edges of Toozookus and our city here, in case it is a decoy for us to leave so they can attack. I cannot give you all any more than that, other than that there are more than a hundred at last count. We witnessed another group of warriors meet the horde right before we returned. We will leave the festivities for now, and upon returning after our victory, we will show the Elvenfae how we celebrate. So rest up, and we ride before dawn. Thank you all."

After everyone had left the council room, Darphanin winked at Shaylee, who stood up and hit him in the arm, then hugged him tightly, whispering, "That's for not coming to see me after my father banned you. I am glad you are here with us."

Darphanin grabbed his arm and rubbed it gently, then put his arms around her, replying softly, "I see you haven't lost your strength, Shay. I am so sorry for not returning. Your father made it quite clear that I would see the Vaargix Drop if I was to return, so valuing life I decided not to, not that I didn't have spies check on you now and then." As he finished his quip, he started laughing, and Shaylee hit him again, forcing him back. As she did so, she started laughing too.

Shaylee and Darphanin spent the next hour reminiscing, while Serena talked to the boy who was showing off earlier in the afternoon. She had met him while Van Coinan had her on the ground, with his ears hitting her face softly. She was laughing so hard that the boy thought the pooka was hurting her, and he came running over to save her, but quickly realized she was laughing and that she wasn't under attack.

Van Coinan had looked up and called out, "Do you want a go, do you?"

The boy, confused why someone would want to play with a pooka, just stood there, about to turn and run off, before Serena added, "Do it. It's so much fun. His ear is soft and doesn't hurt; in fact, it tickles." She continued laughing.

The boy was quite conservative and did not understand human customs or emotions, but there was something about Serena that intrigued him, and he wanted to know more about her. So he lay down next to her while Van Coinan used his other ear and started gently slapping both their faces, which eventually led to a cacophony of laughter from them both. Soon they were playing other games with the cheeky pooka. In time Van Coinan tired and fell asleep under a tall toadstool, while Serena and the boy sat and threw tiny rocks at his feet, watching him kick every time while still sleeping and snoring.

Serena eventually lay back, looked up at the sky, and asked, "So, what is your name?"

The boy lay back too and answered, "Chaxinn, but everyone calls me Chax."

Serena repeated what Chaxinn had just said, "Chax, cool name. I'm Serena and that pooka is my friend Van Coinan. He's the funniest bunny, I mean pooka, I've ever seen. He makes me cry laughing all the time, but he gets tired and just sleeps wherever he falls, usually from exhaustion because he doesn't stop."

They both chuckled for a moment as Serena looked back up, trying to see some stars. "I cannot believe how beautiful your home is, Chax. The trees are so tall, and everyone is so friendly. I think I can just make out the full moon shining through the tops, can you see?"

Chax turned, looked at Serena, and grabbed her hand before jumping up in a hurry and saying excitedly, "Hey, I want to show you something, come with me. I promise it will be worth it. Come on, your pooka will be asleep for ages by the sounds of it."

Serena jumped up with a smile on her face. There was something about this place that just made her feel safe, not like when she was near the edges of Aurora earlier on. This place was magical. She held on to Chaxinn's hand and he led them to the ladder of an abandoned tree house. There was no light emanating from it, but he seemed to know what he was doing so Serena followed him to the inclined ladder that soon formed a walkway. This then led them higher into the trees where the high paths led from one building to another.

Chaxinn, still holding her hand, deviated from the main path and onto a smaller one. This inclined very quickly as the path became steps, and she was now running behind Chax. She looked down and realized they were ascending extremely high into the trees. No longer could she see any woodland elves or tops of houses. Chaxinn turned and noticed

Serena had stopped and was becoming afraid, so he doubled back, grabbed her hand again, and whispered, "We are nearly there. Trust me, it will be worth it. There is nothing to fear here. I won't let you fall."

Serena was a brave and inquisitive girl at the best of times, so she would not let her fear of heights take hold of her, although that fear would soon disappear forever. They had reached a large lookout at the top of the wooden stairs which was designed and placed to see far and wide across Toozookus.

Serena walked gently on the large expanse of flooring which had rails at the end to stop anyone falling off. She was unsure how the trees were holding it up, but soon stopped questioning anything in this land. She walked to the railing and could see the moon full in the sky, disappearing now and then when some gray clouds masked its glow, which didn't happen often this night. Serena could see some stars, although the light from the moon made it hard to see them all.

The best part was the view across the land. She was able to see very far with her new incredible eyesight and she could make out the town of Toozookus from one side of the lookout, then the lower mountains from the other side. And if she really concentrated hard, she could see the hills far away beyond which was Maelenflitt, although she didn't know that, as she could only see so far.

At a strain she could make out a glowing orange light just before the hills. Dismissing it as just campers, she continued her investigation of the land, before lying down on her back and looking up at the undisturbed sky.

"See, I told you to trust me," Chaxinn whispered as he too lay down and looked up. "I come here sometimes when my father is out on a journey or when I just want to be alone. I'm going to be a warrior one day like my father, so I like to watch them all out in the open practicing their moves with the horses. I have quiet competitions in my head trying to guess who can fire their arrows the farthest. My father always wins. He is the best archer in the lands, and I think he even teaches some Elvenfae warriors from time to time."

Chaxinn continued telling Serena all about his life and the adventures he would like to go on one day when he came of age. They spent a good part of the early evening discussing their lives and comparing their different worlds, until a horn sounded and Chaxinn jumped up. "Oh dear, I didn't realize we were up here so late. We have to go now."

Serena jumped up and started following Chaxinn, but then stopped, asking, "What was that horn noise? What's the rush?"

Chaxinn turned and explained, "It's an alarm to call all the children in to get ready for sleep. If we don't come when the first horn is blown, then we get punished on the second."

Chaxinn sounded scared, trying to pull Serena's hand, but she stayed solidly in her position, asking another question, "What happens? What is your punishment?"

Chaxinn looked her in the eyes and answered, "We have to brush the horses' hair and pick up their droppings."

Serena looked at him for a moment, then burst out into laughter. Chaxinn felt uncomfortable for a moment before he realized what he had just said and joined her in a chorus of belly laughter. Serena was trying to talk, but it took a few moments for her to calm down. She quipped, "Well, we better get a move on. I would hate to have to brush those horses."

As she started laughing once more, she realized something as she made fun of him. She could see that the task itself wasn't much of a punishment. It was more about the disappointment of letting his elders down by not adhering to the rules and the laws, the discipline. So, she finished up with a snort, grabbed his hand, and started running down the stair path, back to the homes in the trees. On the way down she turned and said, "Thanks for tonight, it was amazing. I hope you don't get into any trouble."

Chaxinn responded as they entered the main buildings' pathways, "No, we are close now. I am glad to have met you, Serena. I hope to see you again sometime."

As he led her to the Elvenfae guards, he then darted off to his own home, showing off and doing acrobatics while in Serena's line of sight.

The guard led Serena to another house where Shaylee was waiting for her inside. She walked in and straightaway Shaylee whispered, "Well, it looks like someone has had some fun tonight. May I ask who that young elf is?"

Serena was smiling from ear to ear and in a hurry answered, "His name is Chaxinn, and he showed me the tops of the trees and he wants to be a warrior like his father and—"

Shaylee interrupted her, "OK, OK, slow down. I am glad you have met some friends, because you are staying here with my friends tomorrow when we go off to battle the enemy."

Serena's face went from excitement to disappointment as she protested, "What? Why, Shay? I can fight. I have Vyyuna and Van Coinan, I can help."

Shaylee knew this was going to happen. She didn't want to use potions to put her to sleep, so she just calmly explained, "Vyyuna and Van Coinan are both staying here, Serena. I have strict instructions that no children will be going."

Serena kicked off again, and Shaylee knew she had messed up this time. "Oh, so I'm a child again now, is that it? Fine, then, this child is going to bed. Goodnight, Shaylee."

Serena stormed off to another bedroom as Shaylee sat back thinking to herself that it went better than she expected. She smiled as she laid out her own bedding, then blew out the candle, and fell asleep for the night.

Early in the morning, before dawn, Shaylee awoke hearing the stomping of horses. She looked down beside her as Serena had come and lain next to her through the night. She smiled, kissed her forehead, and gently got up. She changed quickly into a sprite and then back again, and her sleeping clothes were now her warrior attire. She picked up Howling Tooth and her bow from the table, pulled her purple hood over her head, and started making her way outside where the tribes had all gathered and were ready to depart.

Shaylee leaped from the wooden path up in the trees and dropped several yards onto the ground. Darphanin had her horse set and ready, and she did a flip and lightly fluttered down onto the horse's back so as not to hurt the mare. She then retracted her wings out of the way so they wouldn't flutter in the wind.

Darphanin handed her some berries and a small bread loaf before he whistled and they all took off in their planned directions. The elven women had left a little earlier to get a head start to Maelenflitt while the others left at the same time, splitting off as they began the journey.

Shaylee had a bad feeling about why they were going to a peaceful place like Maelenflitt, although she didn't want to bring it up just yet in case it was wrong. If their enemies got their hands on even one of the four treasures, then that would give whoever was plotting these attacks from Xarkynan a healthy advantage. And the fact Felvora never returned from the dark lands all those moons ago meant something was seriously amiss.

It would take a day and a half of riding at a good pace to reach the dark horde. According to the last message from the owls the previous night when Shaylee was talking with Darphanin, the enemy had only encroached a little farther. This meant that at their pace Shaylee and Darphanin's group would reach Maelenflitt at around the same time that Kapheeny's group would get there, so it was imperative that they keep a good pace. There was no need to go any earlier, as they wanted the advantage of the forest to help with their battle. The Maelenflitt willows had a mind of their own and did not like outsiders. Kapheeny's group would hopefully be there to wake them and get them ready for the attack.

Meanwhile, back at the woodlands, Serena had woken up at the same time that Shaylee had, but she waited until the entire group had left. She didn't want to stay with Shaylee's friends; she wanted to help her fight the dark creatures. She felt safe with Vyyuna and knew the unicorn wouldn't let anything harm her.

However, what Serena didn't realize was that after the attack the day before by the dark goblin that killed the Elvenfae guard, Shaylee had resolved not to place Vyyuna in harm's way, because if the dark ones were after power, there was nothing quite like the power of the last Alicorn, fresh from a unicorn's head. The wisps would also not allow her to be placed in such danger. If they found out, there would be consequences.

Serena knew none of this. Her pure and fierce heart wanted only to help her friends and to be there for Shaylee. She worried that without her she would succumb to the awful visions of her time with the sinisters.

Serena snuck outside and over to Van Coinan, who was still in the same position he was in when she left him the previous night. She gave him a little tap on his foot with hers, watching him twitch and talk to himself. Serena waited for a moment, then tried it again, this time giving it a little more force. Suddenly, he jumped up in the air, fluffy hands in fists as he looked around waving them around the place, saying, "I'll bash ya, come on, let's have a go."

When he noticed Serena standing there giggling, he put them down and yelled, "What was that for? You know you never wake a pooka up like that! You were lucky I didn't spray your face with dust."

Serena's giggle turned to worry as she whispered in an assertive tone, "Keep it down, would you, we don't want to wake anyone up yet. As you can see, the sun is coming up and we have a very serious journey to save Shaylee. It's very dangerous. On second thoughts, I don't think it's for you."

Serena turned her back on him and stood there waiting for his response.

"Please, Serena, I can help, honest. I'll be good, I promise."

Serena loved his high-pitched, childlike voice. He was so tough, but sounded so small. She also enjoyed playing with his mind.

"Well, OK, as long as you listen to me the entire time, alright? Do you have your wooden sword with you?"

Van Coinan jumped up with joy, pulled his wooden sword from his scabbard, and started thrashing it around.

Serena continued, "Good, now be quiet. We have to find Vyyuna, so we can start our journey."

Van Coinan stopped and waited.

Serena turned and in an agitated state said, "Come on, Van, we have to go!"

Van Coinan, still standing firm, said to Serena in the most mature and adult tone, "I'm sorry, Serena, Vyyuna cannot go with us. Shaylee does not want her in danger."

Serena looked at him and whispered, "She will be alright, I promise. I can't say why, but you have to trust me."

Van Coinan went straight back to his cheeky tone and said, "Well, I tried, can't do any more than that. Come on, she is over here under the willows."

Serena turned and followed Van Coinan. Vyyuna was already awake and standing there as if she were waiting for the two of them to approach her.

Serena went over and placed her head on Vyyuna's long face and whispered, "Vyyuna, we have to go. I have a feeling deep in my heart that Shaylee is in danger. I feel she needs us. I'm not being insensitive or wanting adventures, I actually feel she is in danger."

Vyyuna rubbed her face across Serena's, pulled her head back, and Serena took in the sight of the magnificent horn in between her eyes and just above. It spiraled from a very thick bone at the base, all the way to a point at the top, with winding lines that twisted along the horn. She never thought one would be as large as this, however there it was, right in front of her.

Vyyuna spoke into Serena's mind, "I have felt the same, Serena, we must go. I also believe she is in trouble."

Whether it was Serena's own intuition or closeness to her sister, or whether she had bonded with Vyyuna somehow and she felt what she felt, one thing remained, which was that they needed to help their princess-queen.

Vyyuna lowered her neck to allow both Serena and Van Coinan to access her back. She then turned and started galloping toward the front entry to the woodlands at a pace that would match any racehorse, before heading out onto the tracks toward their beloved Shay.

SHAYLEE FIGHTS FOR FAELYNN

THE RIDE WAS ARDUOUS AND SERENA'S BOTTOM was becoming very sore. They had been riding for hours without a break, and she thought it would never end. Vyyuna could feel her becoming uncomfortable, so she slowed her swift pace to more of a gallop, then to a trot, before stopping completely and lowering the two companions onto the flat green grass.

"Why are we stopping, Vyyuna? We have so much farther to go." Serena was glad but did not want to show weakness.

Van Coinan skipped and jumped, happy to show his genuine feelings of joy at having even a tiny rest before he questioned Vyyuna, "So why did we stop?" Van Coinan had a feeling there was more to Vyyuna and Serena's relationship, although didn't want to ruin any secret they had.

"Well, I think Vyyuna needs a rest." As Serena finished her response to Van Coinan, Vyyuna spoke into her mind, "Are you alright, young Serena? I could feel your pain for the last several miles and knew that you were uncomfortable."

Serena answered wearily through thought. She was becoming used to the novel way of communicating with her new friend, and she felt it easier than talking. "Yes, Vyyuna, I am fine, a little sore, although I do not want this rest to become a delay in meeting up with the rest of the groups."

Vyyuna replied, "No, it won't. We have made very good time and

I believe they are about to set up camp for the night about ten miles away. If we ride for another five or six, we will catch them before they meet up with the dark horde early in the morning. Are you ready for more?"

Serena nodded before running over to where Van Coinan was chasing a multhrai moth. She grabbed his arm and whispered, "Come, Van Coinan, we have more riding to do. When we stop for the night, I will play with you, OK?"

Van Coinan seemed to think that was a good trade-off. Pookas were easily distracted, but they were also easily bargained with. Vyyuna lowered her head, and they both climbed onto her back once more. She had raised her mane to suit Serena, so she had more cushioning underneath her, not that it mattered now as Serena's backside was aching far too much for any kind of comfort. But she thanked her for the gesture as Vyyuna let out a huge neigh before galloping off again to reach the next checkpoint.

≈

Shaylee and the rest of the teams had set up camp for themselves. They had been riding nonstop since dawn and needed much rest before continuing in the early morning.

Darphanin had helped a few of the riders with him who were worried about the upcoming meeting with the dark ones. He soothed their minds, gathering them all around the fire to discuss plans, and to relay to the younger warriors stories of ancestors' successes in the fields of battle with minor losses from times of old. He did not mention the losses of the dark times during the war of Xarkynan; it was agreed upon that the history of the great war would never be discussed with the new generations of woodland elves.

Shaylee prepared the horses with some elder woodland elves, looking over her shoulder and smiling at Darphanin as he told great tales of battles won. She was a part of some of them and she didn't realize how skilled a storyteller her old beau was, finding herself immersed in some of his telling of old tales.

Eventually, she handed the reins of the last horse to the warrior stewards, then placed herself in a comfortable position near the fire to find out what happened next to Darphanin's ancestors.

It wasn't long before Shaylee succumbed to the long day and fell asleep from exhaustion. Darphanin saw this and after he finished with his wonderful tales, having lightened the mood for the younger warriors, he wandered over to her, placed a rug over her exposed body, and sat staring at her for the longest of moments. He was remembering some good times they had spent together all those cycles ago.

Eventually he stood up, went to the fire, and put it out for the night. The air was quite warm, and he did not want any unwanted attention through the night from the dark horde that could be anywhere around them. He placed five watchers and an owl as lookouts. If anything were to ambush, they would know about it well in advance.

Darphanin took up a position near Shaylee, lowered his head on the soft rug he had laid out, and closed his eyes for some much-needed rest.

Morning rolled around very quickly, and a little before the sun came up an elder sounded the horn. Everyone awoke in haste and they were all on their feet with weapons in hand in the blink of an eye.

Darphanin bolted over to the elder, who was distressed. "What is it, Pharnanin? Tell me what you know."

The elder Pharnanin held up the owl with an arrow through its heart. He then pointed to the ground at the five guards who were lifeless.

Darphanin's face dropped. He had never felt so vulnerable in all his life. This had never happened in his time as a warrior. He fell to his knees, looking around in all directions to see if any of the dark horde were around, killed by the watchers. The warrior found nothing. It was as if they had just drifted through the camps and took the watchers and the owl before disappearing once more. It was terrifying.

Darphanin rose to his feet and yelled out to the main warrior leaders in his tribe. "I want a head count. Have they taken anyone or killed

159

more of us? Send out a sparrow to the other tribes. No one is to go anywhere alone. Move it."

Darphanin then ran over to where Shaylee had been sleeping to make sure she was OK. If they had gotten to the warriors, they could have easily gotten to her. When he arrived at the spot, Shaylee was nowhere to be seen. Darphanin shouted out her name several times, but there was no answer.

A warrior ran over to Darphanin. "Darph, I saw the princess—sorry, queen—riding off not more than a few moments ago. She was heading forward to where the hordes may be."

Darph patted the warrior on his back, ran to his horse, and mounted it, before galloping off in pursuit of Shaylee, as the others quickly packed up and began heading off in the same direction. Pharnanin was an elder and had chosen five warrior elves to stay with him and help take the bodies back to Toozookus. They could not be left there.

In a matter of minutes, the rest of the woodland elf tribe was well on the heels of Darphanin and Shaylee, riding into a danger none of them were ready to contemplate. They all just knew they had to get their fast.

Darphanin soon reached Shaylee's horse, abandoned and panicked. He quickly jumped off his and ran over to the large creature to try to calm it down. He had handled horses all his life and had dealt many times with horses in distress. Shaylee's horse seemed more wound up than any he had encountered before. It was tied to a tree at the edges of the foggy forest, a dense wooded area about five miles from the beginning of Maelenflitt. Many had not used that path in the past, and Darphanin was questioning why Shaylee would deviate off the main road to this place.

"Shaylee, Shaylee, where are you?" He repeated his call for the next few moments. There seemed to be an eerie silence coming from the trees, as if all the creatures were too frightened to make any noise.

Before long, the rest of the tribe had all caught up. Darphanin directed them to make a line along the edge of the trees so they could all enter together. If she was hiding there out of fear, they would discover where she was. "Come on, tie your horses and spread out. If Shaylee is here, we will find her."

As the entire tribe, now reaching out several hundred yards, entered the misty woods, they heard a scream from the end of the line, then another and another before there was silence again. Darphanin stopped and so did the rest, flowing on down the line. They all stood there not making a sound, trying to determine if this could be something dark and elusive.

The silence was deafening and as Darphanin started moving on again, there were more screams, this time on his right side. He couldn't even tell whether they were his men or something else. Darphanin stopped once more. As the silence took hold, he heard something incredibly soft flutter behind his neck, before he felt the soft sensation of something small now standing on his shoulder.

Before he could turn or say anything, he heard a whisper in his right ear, "Do not move, Darph, please do not move at all. It is a dullahan, and it knows we are here. We have to move out of the woods slowly and carefully."

Shaylee then flew off very swiftly back to a hiding place high in the trees.

Darphanin knew it was her and did exactly what she said. He slowly backed up, one foot behind the other, very carefully. At the same time, he gestured without a sound to the others next to him on either side to pass it up the line.

Slowly and very steadily, without a whisper, they all kept in step with each other to escape the harshness of the woods. All the horses were agitated, and it was each elf's responsibility to keep theirs under control.

Shaylee had returned to Darphanin's shoulder, whispering again, "We need to leave. They are after me, Darph, that is why I had to change. They know I am here, but they cannot see me, so you will need to bring my horse."

Shaylee was shaken up. She still hadn't explained why she left without them earlier, and there was no time for explanations now. It was time to go.

All of the tribe were now on their horses and galloping away toward the main track to Maelenflitt. As the last of the warriors looked over their shoulders, they could see the horrendous dullahan protruding through the trees with its whip of bones high in the air and several victims attached to the ends of its sword and whip.

The woodland elves could not gallop fast enough, moving ahead of the pack, as the last ones did the same when they saw the destructive chaos behind them. Most of the woodland elves had never seen a dullahan, especially not this close to home, and if that was only one creature called to wreak destruction, what else was awaiting them?

Eventually they got away far enough to feel clear of the dark creature, only to find themselves heading into the path of another danger. There were now several dark goblins in front of them, shooting arrows directly into the middle of the group. There was no cover, and it looked like the dark horde had expected that, and so planned an ambush at different intervals. Darphanin only hoped that the other two tribes were OK, and that they were more prepared.

Arrows kept buzzing by, hitting a target now and then, so the entire tribe slid off their horses, and positioned themselves in the thick green grass. Darph could see smoke coming from the outskirts of Maelenflitt as the dark goblins encroached farther into the safe zone of the woodland elves' cover.

More arrows whizzed past the closer they got to them all. It confused Darphanin why they were missing at such a short range, as if they were missing on purpose. Then it hit him hard—the arrows were intended to hold them up for the dullahan, which could now be heard screeching only a few hundred yards away behind them.

Darphanin was at a loss. How was he going to save his tribe, Shaylee, or even himself. The goblins had full advantage now, because if anyone stood up, they would be a prime target for the arrows, while the dullahan moved ever closer. Darphanin closed his eyes, pulled out his blade, and stood up, ready to run at them. As he did that, an arrow struck him deep in the shoulder. He kept going as three more warriors stood up and did the same. The goblins were not expecting heroes on that day as they scampered to pick up arrows and aim them. Then an arrow hit Zeexalin in his throat, immediately putting him out of action.

Darph was now only yards away from the first of the dark goblins. He lifted his blade to strike at one, while the goblin, with its bow and arrow, pulled back hard. Darph, in plenty of pain, stood still, waiting for the arrow to find a place in his skull as he closed his eyes in anticipation of what was coming. He heard the whizzing go straight past his head.

He looked up to see the dark goblin fall where it had stood. He turned at the sound of several galloping horses, and saw Nimaalah leading the pack. The goblins fell one by one as Darphanin just stood and watched it all unfold. Shaylee even turned back into her Elvenfae form to cut the head off the last of that goblin pack before racing over to Darphanin and assisting him and his wounded shoulder.

"Are you OK, my love? You are the bravest yet most stupid wood elf I have ever met."

Darph fell to his knees, then onto his back as Shaylee tended to the arrow with some healing potions. The dullahan had disappeared, which gave the tribe a small amount of time to gather their thoughts and make plans for the next onslaught.

A short amount of time later, after the tribes had rested and Darphanin was healed to the point where he could go on to the next battle, a fireball exploded in the sky, piercing through the clouds, from the direction of Maelenflitt. The battle had obviously taken a turn for the worse, as the last of the tribes were holding off the enemy at the edges of the forest.

Darphanin jumped to his knees, turned to the tribes before him, and yelled, "This could be it, my friends, my people. Can we hold them off, I don't know, but we have come this far, and we need to protect our sisters who are amid battle right now. Those who are frightened, I will not say one word if you pack up and go. Those who are with me to the end, follow me and let's stop this horde from destroying our homes and killing our sisters."

The crowd shouted in unison, "Yes, yes, yes. Darph, Darph, Darph."

Witnessing the brave acts that Darphanin had just performed solidified in all their minds that they would do anything for their leader and anything for their sisters who were in trouble in Maelenflitt. "Then we ride!" Darph shouted as they all galloped off over the hills and in the fiery direction of Maelenflitt.

~

Serena could hear some commotion coming from miles away. She could also see the smoke rising high into the clear blue sky. Shaylee wasn't far, she thought. Van Coinan was asleep in Serena's lap as they rode. He was still exhausted from all the hiding and seeking the pair of them got up to the previous night. Serena was the opposite, wide awake; she was worried about Shaylee and wanted more than anything to get to her and make sure she was alright.

Closer and closer they came to the noises of war and the screams. Vyyuna was moving twice as fast as any horse now, as even her anxious thoughts were hitting her hard. On and on they rode until they came to the edges of the original battle with the dark goblins that had played out earlier in the day.

"Stop, Vyyuna, please," Serena shouted in a desperate voice. Vyyuna did not need to be told twice. The relationship of these two seemed to be symbiotic.

Vyyuna let them both down as Serena scanned the location. She saw the head of a dark goblin and started to retch. The blood was a dark blue to black, something she thought she would never witness in all her life.

Serena finished throwing up, and then with a slightly queasy feeling ran back to Vyyuna and begged for them to keep following the tracks to Shaylee. Serena was quite worried now as the noises were growing, and the screams were becoming more prominent. Vyyuna sped off, keeping her wits and senses about her in case of any surprise attacks.

Serena had tears in her eyes. She knew something wasn't quite right. She had a feeling of dread, whether it was the emotions of all the screams or of the unicorn she had bonded with who felt far more than she did.

Vyyuna was deep in the grassy tracks ready to climb a small hill, which would be followed by the descent to the foothills and a clearing before the forests of Maelenflitt began. Vyyuna raced as they started passing woodland elf and goblin bodies. She then reached the peak of the small hill in record time, giving Serena and Van Coinan a view of the devastation below them all. Serena scoured with her perfect vision for any sign of Shaylee, as did Vyyuna, while Van Coinan grew more and more angry at the sight of so many homes of peaceful people obliterated and at witnessing creatures he knew scattered around the place, lying still.

The burning of some forest folk led to some oaken nochkz running out of the dense brush and out to the edges of the Sheeleymoon Lake. There the dark Elvenfae, trolls, and goblins awaited them, tearing at their long limbs and setting them on fire, thus creating clearings inside the Maelenflitt Forest.

The devastation was severe. Not since the dark times over a thousand cycles ago had such destruction taken place. Vyyuna sped down the hill. Warnings from the wisps started echoing into her mind as she continued downward. Van Coinan already had his wooden sword out as they reached the bottom of the foothills. He dove from the back of Vyyuna and straight into a cluster of goblins. Serena turned back and shouted his name, as she continued to search for Shaylee.

Vyyuna was now in the midst of the chaos, with tall trolls eyeing her off, as were greedy dark goblins and dark Elvenfae. They all knew the prize that awaited them if they could get to her.

Vyyuna was smart, tough, and quick. She had finally found a connection to Shaylee and kicked into gear, galloping fast. She knocked down any creature in her way, and tore them apart with her powerful horn. Moments before she reached Shaylee, a large hand grabbed at her ankle. She managed to shake it off, but not without injuring it. She could no longer gallop at full speed.

Serena let out a scream as she dove off the unicorn and into the dense mix of warriors and grotesque creatures, spotting Shaylee who had Howling Tooth working full time. She called out to her, but Shaylee did not hear it.

Serena was very agile and nimble. She could move closer to her half-sister but not close enough, as a dark Elvenfae warrior hit Shaylee hard across the face with a punch, knocking her to the ground. Serena screamed her name and pushed through some injured goblins in the grass.

She was just about to reach Shaylee when a goblin, like the one she saw in the forest days earlier, with pointed ears and long bent nose but without the lower half of its body, grabbed her leg, pulling her closer to it. She let out a scream, as she turned her gaze away from Shaylee, who was out cold on the ground. Serena punched the half goblin as it tried to pull her to its mouth, shouting at the top of its lungs, "You will make a delicious last meal, human girl!"

Serena screamed for Shaylee once more as she writhed around, trying to break free from the goblin's grip, but getting caught up in the dark mess of blood which seemed to be pouring out of the ugly creature. Serena's attacks on the goblin made its grip tighter. It did not seem concerned that it was losing blood quickly. The young halfling Fae was now nearly unrecognizable, covered as she was from head to toe in tar-like blood.

As the goblin neared its sharp teeth to her exposed calf, Serena knew she was losing the fight. Nearby, the dark Elvenfae warrior was pulling at his scabbard to expose his knife, ready to finish the queen. Serena's hope was fading as the goblin had her leg and was about to bite. But she continued screaming. She was down low, below the rest of the able bodies fighting around her, and before the goblin could sink its teeth into her tender skin, she saw Howling Tooth right next to her.

Serena snatched the sword up. It was far too large for her to wield, but she had seen Shaylee use it enough. Serena then turned just as the goblin bit into her leg. She let out a bloodcurdling cry as she drove the sword deep into the goblin's throat, pulled it out, then did it again until the goblin lay spurting blood from its throat and through its mouth.

Her grip on the sword loosened slightly for a moment as she rubbed her leg where she'd been bitten, but then quickly, without thinking, she drove the blade into the dark Elvenfae guard's heart, watching his reaction as his wings fluttered and bright blood came gushing from the wound. She took the sword out once more, this time driving it deep into the twisted-looking dark elven neck, watching him writhe in pain, all while he screamed and tried to stab at Serena. Eventually he succumbed to his vicious wounds and fell on Shaylee, covering her also with the thick, fiery blood from his fresh wounds.

Shaylee seemed OK for the time being so, knowing none of them were safe just yet, Serena started hacking at the legs of all the dark Elvenfae and goblins. The trolls were overwhelmed by three to four oaken nochkz at once, who ripped them apart and drove their sharp thick trunks into their torsos for setting them all on fire. The tables were turning.

Pixies, sprites, sylphs, gnomes, a dryad, mushroom folk, and pookas were all coming out of the safety of their dwellings to help protect their homes from the destructive forces of the dark creatures.

Stexinzar had returned from the deep of the forest where he had followed three goblins to earlier on and was the only one who galloped out. The dullahan had succumbed to Faiay'aar, the forest dryad, as she put a spell on it, rendering it smoke and unable to take physical form; it retreated away from the woods and dissipated into thin air.

Van Coinan had swapped his wooden sword for a couple of goblin knives, and with one in each hand he was slicing them up as quickly as he could. His wooden sword was packed back into his scabbard for next time. The day was violent and full of death. Neither side could escape that.

Serena continued to cut down as many goblins as she could. She didn't see a dark Elvenfae coming up behind her with sword ready to attack. As she turned to strike the leg of a troll, Vyyuna raced into the danger zone and stabbed the dark elf right through his heart with her long sharp horn. The creatures that were eyeing her off before she entered the battle ran over and began tearing at her body, pulling her down and attacking her. Serena shouted out her name, as the last of the unicorns was being pulled apart. There was nothing anyone could do.

The wisps started to turn her into tiny sprites so she could fly away and escape. But while she was breaking up into thousands of tiny faeries the spell was broken when a dark Elvenfae warrior cut Vyyuna's throat with his sharp knife. The fluttering stopped as the parts of her that had turned into tiny wisps and sprites went gray and fell to the ground, while the rest of Vyyuna that was unicorn continued to be attacked, creatures pulling out vital organs and eating them on the spot.

To eat the flesh from such an animal would give them power, they all thought. The dark goblins fought over kidneys, liver, intestines which were being unwound and pulled, to the mouthwatering heart that three goblins stabbed each other for. A dark Elvenfae warrior took his time drinking from the once beautiful creature's throat, making a crimson mess over his dark, twisted uniform. Serena stared in horror as the rest of the horde stopped what they were doing to get a taste of it.

Shaylee was now standing upright, like Serena, watching the events unfold in horror. Vyyuna had whispered into Shaylee's mind before she died, which added to the emotion for the queen. Serena was crying so hard, she passed out from shock.

Shaylee screamed to the woodland elves, "The horn, we must save the Alicorn!"

The events had startled the rest of the tribes and forest folk too, yet there was still a job to be done. Darphanin ran to Vyyuna's remaining carcass and slaughtered several goblins, as did Shaylee and Nimaalah, clearing the way to the sight of a once beautiful creature decimated. There was nothing left but some of her beautiful white coat, some back leg bones, and part of the top of her snout.

The Alicorn had been ripped off, stem and root, and was now in the hands of one of the leader goblins, who was retreating from the battle, back to the safety of its trolls. While it escaped, Shaylee took back her sword from Serena, and demanded a warrior stay with her sister, before she turned into a sprite and disappeared into the sky. The woodland elves were in hot pursuit of the goblin, but it was still far from their reach when two trolls came between them and started stamping their feet, trying to crush them.

The goblin seemed pleased as it moved closer to a safe zone. All had heard the leader of the dark Elvenfae warriors blow a horn to retreat, so there was chaos, with stampedes everywhere. The focus for a small group was the Alicorn. If any dark creature were to possess such a thing and wielded it with the knowledge of its worth, they would have unstoppable power.

The goblin stopped, thinking it was out of danger. It was still on its own and took a moment to look at its new prize, thinking what it would mean to the necro-mage—that's if it gave it to him. It cackled a dark, wailing laugh as it held the Alicorn high up in the air. As the goblin lowered it back down to hide it, it felt an almighty blow to the back of its head. The creature fell to the ground as the Alicorn was flung out of his scaly fingered hand. Looking up, he saw Shaylee in full form ready for another strike.

The goblin reached for its sword, rising to its feet and clashing metal on metal. Shaylee parried, swinging Howling Tooth hard, strike after strike. The goblin was no hack; it seemed well versed in the art as they both continued. Sparks flew from the impact of the blows, Shaylee slicing her wings at the beast as she flipped and attacked some more.

The goblin would not lose its prize, and as they continued for an exhausting while, the goblin struck Shaylee's shoulder slightly with the blade. She didn't even blink as she flipped once more, swung her wings in a spin, and at the same time with her right hand moved across and sliced the dark beast in two.

Its body writhed as the two pieces convulsed and twitched. The scream was like that of three goblins screeching at once, horrendous to the ears. The creature continued to cough and splutter, and the last words that came out of its mouth would resonate with Shaylee for some time to come.

"Dark is coming, fall you will,
safe, you think, but dread will fill.
Look for the moon, high and red,
Varzunnos rises as ye be dead!"

As it finished its last words, the exhale ceased, and it was left in a motionless mess of tar-colored blood.

Shaylee didn't have time right then to reflect on the goblin's words. She raced over and picked up the last piece of her old friend. The Alicorn was placed into her satchel as she gathered her bearings and went to get Serena. There seemed to be only a few dark elves and goblins still fighting at the battle scene. The rest had absconded or disappeared up the hills.

Darphanin finally reached Shaylee. "Are you alright? You gave me such a scare. Your shoulder ... You are injured."

Shaylee didn't even care. She was so puzzled by what had just taken place. Looking across the bloodied fields, she noticed Serena with Van Coinan, sitting, looking very distraught.

"What have I done?" Shaylee whispered.

"You have saved all of us, that is what you have done," Darphanin responded. He put his arms around her as Nimaalah gathered the remaining warriors and helped the forest folk with the injured. It was going to be a long day.

Three parties went in search of the whereabouts of the dark hordes, including Stexinzar, while the heroes spent the rest of the day healing wounded, preparing the dead, and counting the high toll.

GHOSTS AND VISIONS

A FULL CYCLE PASSED SINCE THE BLOODY DAY in Maelenflitt. The toll had been high and there were no celebrations to be had with the woodland elves. The dryad had disappeared after the dark events, and there were multiple casualties from all groups on the day.

Serena had taken it hard for the first half cycle, slowly coming around as the fill-in queen spoiled and reassured her it was not her fault what had happened to Vyyuna. She couldn't tell her at that stage what the unicorn had said before the end, as she was not ready for that. But she could tell her some other truths.

"A unicorn has free will and a love that is matched by no other. She would do anything for those she trusted. Saving you was worth it. She saw something in you, Serena. I know she mind-blended with you; that is why she did what she did. She saw your future. I cannot say any more than that right now," Shaylee said to ease Serena's mind.

The pain would be there for a good while and as much as Shaylee wanted to take Serena back to her home, she needed to fulfill some faery training with her first. The more she learned now, the easier it would be if she ever came back and for her own future. Shaylee had given her time away from her world to stay, although she wouldn't be able to push it for a long period. Time did not work the same in the two realms, but eventually it caught up with everyone.

Two cycles after the dark day, Shaylee was lying in her bed. She was asleep and dreaming, tossing and turning as her wings fluttered and sweat started beading down her face. Before long she awoke in a fright to be greeted by a misty white humanoid figure dressed completely in white staring at her.

The image of a ghostly pale woman who had a large dark scar on her forehead haunted Shaylee as she rubbed her eyes and realized she wasn't dreaming any longer. Shaylee gradually moved out of bed and toward the specter. There was a strange familiarity that was drawing her closer. Shaylee reached the ghostly woman in white, seeing through her body, while the dress she was wearing seemed to move with a breeze that wasn't there.

Shaylee could only stare before she finally gained the courage to talk to her. "Who ... no, what are you? I feel I know you, yet I have never seen you before. Are you a dryad or a ghost from the old world?"

Shaylee felt silly asking, but the truths would soon reveal themselves as the specter spoke, "You do not recognize me, my love, but I have not been gone that long."

The ghostly woman's dress was still moving in slow motion, while she was as still as a stone. Shaylee walked all around her before returning to the same place she was at when the conversation started.

"I am sorry, how do you know me?" she said to the misty being.

Shaylee felt silly. She had no idea who this apparition was. The clue that was staring her in the face had not made an impression yet, so the woman continued, "Shaylee, close your eyes and hear my voice." So she did. Shaylee felt she could trust her at this stage.

The apparition continued, "Look after Serena for me, she is very special as I know you know. Keep her well and—"

Before the ghost could finish, Shaylee opened her eyes and quickly said, "Vyyuna? Is that really you?"

Shaylee was shaking as the woman in white replied, "Yes, my dear, I have come to help you both. Something dark is heading our way soon. Faelynn is in grave danger and I have returned from my rest to help you as much as I can. You need to hide the Alicorn, for a start. Hide it close to Serena but do not tell her about it, not just yet. She saved your life, Shay, right before they attacked me. She slayed a dark Elvenfae with your sword."

Shaylee was in shock. For one, she was still trying to come to grips with the news that Vyyuna was there; second, that Serena risked her life to save hers; and last, that they were not out of danger from the dark ones.

"Serena did that? I knew she was strong. I have just the idea for how I will hide the Alicorn near her, and it will serve as part of her training. What more can you tell me of the dark ones?"

Vyyuna's spirit was fading as she finished her conversation, "I cannot say too much at this stage. Keep in mind the four treasures and make sure you protect them well. I will appear again when I can, but I cannot interfere. The nature spirits will only allow me to help three times and I have used up one. Goodbye, my love, I will see you again."

As soon as Vyyuna finished speaking, she dissipated into the dark of the night, leaving Shaylee wondering what had just happened. For the rest of the night her sleep was restless as she contemplated it all, wondering by morning whether it was all a dream.

A crack of lightning pierced the sky. There had not been a thunderstorm in a long time. Shaylee awoke with a start. Looking over to the end of the bed where she had last witnessed the rare spirit of a unicorn, she now saw a worried Serena. She was just standing there, staring past Shaylee as if she were in a trance.

The queen composed herself, putting aside thoughts of her hard night, and spoke to her half-sister, "What is it, my dear? You look terrified."

Serena just continued to stand there, not moving or looking at Shaylee. She still seemed to be in a trance that she could not snap out of. Beads of sweat were rushing down her youthful face as her large brown eyes just stared past Shaylee at the dark red patterns on her bedhead.

Shaylee fluttered up out of bed, her perfect wings folding straight down into place like a human moving a limb, easily and without thought. She rushed over to Serena, put her hands on her sister's shoulders, and with a slight shiver repeated, "What is it, Serena? Please tell me."

Serena snapped back to reality. Her eyes blinked as she composed herself, then they seemed to focus and pierced Shaylee's beautiful blue eyes before she answered, "They will come, and they will destroy, Shay."

As soon as she'd finished her comment, Serena passed out onto the soft throw rug next to the bed. Shaylee swiftly kneeled down and clutched Serena, wiping her face of sweat and tears while gently fanning her with her wings to give her some air.

Serena opened her eyes slowly, gained her composure. She jumped out of Shaylee's arms and stood in front of her crouching sister for a moment before she spoke, "How did I get here, Shay? The last thing I remember is that I was having the most horrendous dreams about a dark warlord with huge horns like that of a stag tearing through the city and reaching for me. As it tried, it told me they are coming, all with mists of green flurrying around the monster."

Serena fell to her knees. The vision was all too real for her, and after the recent events, Shaylee realized that it had all affected her more than she expected. What Serena just relayed to her, though, was quite disturbing, as without prior knowledge of the appearance of the dark lord, Shaylee could only put it down to a vision of the future. A council meeting would need to be called for the Seelie Court as soon as possible.

Shaylee did not want to upset Serena with any news of dark times ahead, evident from Vyyuna's prophecy and now this. The thunder was a sign something was not quite right in the magic realms.

Serena was sobbing quietly as Shaylee tickled her chin with her wing, hugging the young child. "Do not dwell on such things, child. It was merely a dream, most likely from the trauma you felt at the battle. Worry yourself not. Now tomorrow we are having a ceremony and you are the guest of honor, so run along down to my silk maiden and she will fix you a beautiful gown to wear. Go now."

Serena smiled, wiping the tears away and forgetting the awful images in her mind's eye for a moment as she scampered out of Shaylee's room and down the stairs to the silk maiden.

Shaylee stood up, and rang the Seelie Court blue bell, which had not rung in a thousand cycles. Then she transformed into a sprite and zoomed out of the room. She went straight to the council elders to inform them why the bell had been rung and why a Seelie Court was required.

Shaylee wished her mother, or father, was still around for this. She had always been a princess of the Fae as well as a warrior, so the big decisions were always left to the queen, especially when the king was out fighting the wars in the past. She had no idea who would be summoned to the Seelie Court.

All she knew about such things was that if there was ever a serious threat to Faelynn from Xarkynan, they would summon all representatives from all over the realms of good and peace to prepare themselves for the upcoming events. Unlike the council, whose representatives were all palace city Fae, the Seelie Court had as representatives oaken nochkz, woodland elves, dryads, pixies, gnomes, benevolent pookas, wisps, queens of the sprites and small folk, far darrigs, sylphs, along with other benevolent creatures of the bright realms. The Unseelie would already be planning attacks, being of the evil folk from Xarkynan and other stray creatures that had made their homes in hiding throughout the realms of Faelynn.

Shaylee stood before the council leaders and explained what she had been witness to, without giving away anything about Vyyuna. She concentrated on Serena's vision and added some of what she was told by the ethereal white visitor, keeping to herself the secret of the Alicorn and the fact that a unicorn had appeared in humanoid form.

The council leaders looked frightened. They couldn't debate or deny the information for it had been told that if evil were to lift its ugly head it would start with skirmishes of goblins, thunderstorms that lasted half cycles, and altered magic that might fade from the realms or show in greater power at certain places. So they were not angry that the Seelie Court blue bell had been rung, and the processes to gather as many representatives to the Seelie Court as possible in a couple of days were in place. The council knew it to be the right course of action.

Elvenfae guards scurried on horseback, tearing off in all different directions. The leaders of smaller Fae groups in the council sent sparrows, owls, and ravens to message as many as they could. The palace was in a commotion as Shaylee went on a search for Stexinzar, whom she had not seen for a quarter cycle. She needed him more than ever now, as he was the leader of the warrior Fae and the Elvenfae warrior guards. After an exhaustive amount of searching, Shaylee gave up. She went to find Serena, who had missed out on all the meetings and commotions. She was with the silk maiden who was working on the last stages of her brand-new gown that she was promised to wear the next day.

Shaylee entered the silk maiden's room where Serena was standing with her back to the doorway as the maiden placed some pins into the bottom of the long garment. It was dark red with tinges of gothic black flowing through the outer fabrics, giving it a very olden Celtic look. Shaylee slowed right down and forgot about the chaos for a moment. A couple of tears fell from her eyes as she took in the innocence of her sister's happiness. It was all worth it, she thought as she entered the room.

"Oh my, who is the loveliest, most elegant half blood in all of Faelynn, then?"

Shaylee smiled as Serena turned ever so slowly to face her, trying not to upset the silk maiden. Shaylee had informed her most trusted maidens of Serena's secret, including her silk maiden.

"Now, are you trying to upstage the queen of Faelynn, young one, as your beauty is by far the greatest I have seen in the land."

Serena blushed, lowered her head for a moment, and then looked up at Shaylee to respond, "Isn't it the most beautiful gown you have ever seen, Shay? I absolutely love it, thank you so much."

Shaylee was glad to see her smile. She continued, "You are welcome, my dear, but it is Miss Jestica Hornmyst you must thank, as she is making it and she is the best in the land. Only royals get to have gowns made by her."

Jestica nodded but didn't say a word while she continued working on the bottom stitching to the dress. Serena looked down and thanked her, and the silk maiden stood up, saying, "It is my pleasure, Your Highness. Now I need the gown to finish it in time for tomorrow, if that pleases you?" Jestica curtsied to Shaylee and respectfully lowered her head.

"Of course, my dear. Serena, carefully get changed and meet me outside. I would like to go over some protocols for tomorrow."

Serena smiled excitedly as Shaylee walked out, helping Jestica remove the half-finished gown. She put on her training garb, which she had thrown on for her morning session with the master Elvenfae instructor but had missed because of her visions. After she dressed, she ran outside to meet with Shaylee, and they went somewhere quiet to talk.

After a small discussion about protocols with Serena, Shaylee asked if she had seen Stexinzar while she had been training with the master instructor. Upon receiving a reply in the negative, Shaylee left Serena in a happy state of excitement to attend a private meeting with her particularly good friend, the blacksmith Darlygah Frostdrop.

There was no rest for the new queen and the stress was showing on her. Her experiences with the Zeytars, even though that was many moons ago, still lingered. She was feeling the strain of loss, the absence of her mother's support, and anxiety that she would not be able to protect her people from an enormous threat if something evil from Xarkynan were to rise. There had been recruitment of guards and warriors since the attacks by the Zeytars, but would she have enough to fight a plague of the dark ones all at once? She hoped the Seelie Court would fulfill a commitment to her as this threat would affect their lands as well.

Shaylee shook off those feelings for the moment. She needed to fulfill another promise, and the Seelie Court would not begin until the day after tomorrow. Shaylee made her way down to the lower sections of the palace, not normally set aside for royal visits. But she hadn't always been a royal of the highest order, and she spent a lot of time with the masters, Elvenfae guards, warriors, and trainers in her youth. She had trained more than any other princess ever had. She never trained for potential threats; it was more the love of the recreational side of keeping her skills up, and she loved her sword Howling Tooth. And besides, she'd use any excuse she could to get out of regal duties.

Shaylee entered the dark, hot workshop of the master blacksmith, looked around, and before she could turn again, there was a knife at her throat.

"You are getting slow, my princess, maybe you need to get down and train some mor—"

Before the deep-voiced owner of the blade could finish, Shaylee had disarmed, flipped, and put to the ground the strong Elvenfae blacksmith. She was holding the knife to his throat and Howling Tooth to his limp lower wings. "You were saying, old Fae? And I am your queen, not your princess."

Shaylee fluttered up off the larger than normal Fae, stood over him, and offered her left hand, as she dropped the blade and slid her beloved sword back into her scabbard.

"OK, OK, just testing you. Go easy on an old Fae, would you, my queen?"

Shaylee finished helping him up and they both laughed. Shaylee needed the distraction from everything, and she always felt better when she could talk to her old and wise friends, one of which, Stexinzar, was not around, so Darlygah would be the next best thing. He was one of her most trusted friends of all the lands of Faelynn.

"What brings you down here, Your Highness?" Darlygah had a slight smile on his face.

"You know there are no titles with us. I was joking before. Don't make me use my sword." Shaylee reciprocated the smile and continued, "Darlygah, I have something incredibly special to ask you and of the utmost importance and secrecy. I need a favor from you that will require immediate work and it's a secret that will last all your days. Are you up for the challenge?"

Shaylee knew that as soon as she threw in the word "challenge," Darlygah would not just consider the task but would jump at it without even thinking.

"Of course, Shay, you know that I will. Tell me what you need."

Shaylee opened a long satchel. As she began pulling the item out, she became quite paranoid, a feeling she only experienced since the dark ones started showing up more frequently. She turned, walked to the old oak door, and locked it behind her. Darlygah looked confused. She was the queen—what could she have that would be so important and secretive?

Shaylee returned to where the blacksmith was standing and continued to extract the delicate item. As Shaylee pulled out the artifact, Darlygah dropped to the floor and onto his knees.

The hardened old blacksmith spoke with a quiver in his deep tone, "How did you come to have this in your Fae hands, Shay? There have been no unicorns since the dark times."

Darlygah had not been briefed on Vyyuna, her death, or the fact the horn had been taken. He knew of old magic and through tales from the old ones while growing up learned that an Alicorn was the most sought after and powerful thing in all the lands besides the four treasures of the Tuatha Dé Danann. Only Shaylee knew of its existence. The others assumed it had been destroyed when Vyyuna was killed or that the wisps took it back. Some even wondered whether the goblins took it for themselves. Shaylee would address those assumptions later with a deception. It was something she did not want to do but needed to for the protection of the Alicorn and Serena.

Darlygah would be the only other who knew. If there were any leaks from their meeting, she would know they came from him. But Shaylee was confident of his loyalty. He was, after all, her departed father's best friend and most trusted adviser in the past before he longed for a more peaceful life after the war.

"What will you have me do with it, Shaylee? A powerful object like this should be hidden in safe quarters under constant guard or even given back to the wisps for protection. Having this will cause divisions in the palace and even attacks on the city if the dark ones learn of its existence."

Darlygah was now on his feet again. He wasn't worshiping the powerful relic; he was more shocked and in awe of its presence.

"That is why I locked the door and came to you. I have been given information, from where I cannot say at this stage, and the outcome of that information is the best outcome and is as follows." Shaylee took a deep breath and continued, "Tomorrow there will be a ceremony for Serena, she is a halfling Fae child I have been caring for and training. You may have seen her lately with the master. I need a special sword made for her, strong in steel and light. She saved my life at the recent battle and this will be her reward."

The smith nodded; he was wondering when he was going to have to make a sword for her. He had seen her with the master, and all the weapons were much too heavy for a young teen child to maneuver.

Shaylee continued, "After which I need our ancient family crest, lineage, and code carved into the top half of the blade, including this piece at the end, carved in ancient magic fire."

Shaylee handed the smith a note in the old Celtic scribe. As he read the print, his eyes shot up at Shaylee, very wide and in a state of shock, before he replied, "If this be true, Shay, why hide it?"

Shaylee looked sternly at Darlygah before answering, "All of this is for her protection; no one at all is to know just yet, not until I can rescue my mother or until we take out the dark ones. Be of mind that it will be written, so must be believed. Should anything happen to me, I give you permission to use magic fire under the authority of the palace and the reign of the Aethelwyne house."

Darlygah understood now. He had not been given all the information, but he knew he was tasked to do something never done before and questioned it no more.

Shaylee continued, "Last, I want the crest on the pommel and the Alicorn as the handle to the sword wrapped in the twining of the Aethelwyne colors. I need adjustments made for the Alicorn to blend with the sword itself, hiding the tip with more magic fire and creating a shortening of the horn without cutting it. This will create a hidden series of roots and veins that will journey through the metal from the hilt to the tip, leaving the larger stem of the Alicorn for the handle. Here is the spell and the magic fire along with the ingredients from several items to make this old magic work. I cannot stay, but I need it by first light."

The blacksmith stared at Shaylee for a good while, and Shaylee stared back, giving him time to process before he questioned it all. But he never did. Agree or disagree, it didn't matter—if Shaylee wanted this done then he would do it more than better than she had asked.

Darlygah nodded, took the items, and after Shaylee left, he locked the door and windows, and settled in for what would be a stressfully long day and most likely night for the seasoned blacksmith.

LONG LEAF

SERENA COULD NOT SLEEP FOR THE FIRST part of the night. She was far too excited about the ceremony taking place in the late morning of the next day. She closed her eyes and kept thinking about what was going to happen. Serena had visions of her gown and wondered if some of her new friends would be there for the event. She was becoming lost in the lifestyle of Faelynn. Serena thought at times she was dreaming, but upon awakening every morning she was still there.

So much had happened since she arrived and it would take ages to process it all, but at this moment in time, she was not thinking of her actual home in County Clare or the darkness she had encountered two cycles ago; she was only concerned with the ceremony.

Eventually Serena succumbed to the night and her eyes became too heavy as she drifted off into a deep sleep, a sleep that would only last a few hours, as she was eventually taken into a dark place in her mind.

Her eyes were closed, but the dream was very much real to her. Serena looked around the dark room and tried to adjust her eyes to see anything at all. Soon she could see outlines of dark figures, silhouettes of tall, strange creatures. She tried to yell but was mute. The silence was oppressive. Panicking as the tall gangly creatures moved forward, she tried to run but was locked to that position somehow.

Serena's eyes were still closed as she lay in bed tossing and turning while sweating profusely from the dream she was having. Inside her mind she was now hoping for the faintest of lights so she could get a glimpse of the creatures. She moved her head to the left, then right, and before long a flash of light hit the room with a burst, illuminating the whole place at once, allowing Serena to see better.

After adjusting her eyes, she focused. She could see green mist flowing through the well-lit room, and then she locked eyes with the creature. A tall, gray, skinny being with a huge oval head and dark soulless eyes, it had no nose and only two fingers with opposable thumbs. There were wrinkles on its face and it looked very aged.

As it moved closer, the creature changed into a grotesque scaly monster with red eyes, a dark hooded cloak, and long sharp teeth. It seemed to hiss at Serena, but then a female voice rang out and screamed, breaking the silence, "Please, young one, you must tell Shaylee I am here, please, I am trapped, tell her it's Fel—" Before the female voice could finish, the creature hissed once more while waving his hand, and crushed the link between all of them.

Serena woke up calling out for Shaylee, crying and trembling with fear. Shaylee's room was close to hers and she was with her in only a few moments. She held Serena tightly, knowing she'd had another vision. Shaylee would not press her for information. She would wait for Serena to tell her. But the frightened girl opened straight up and relayed every part of the dream to her half-sister, leaving Shaylee on edge.

Shaylee could not show Serena any kind of stress in her face, voice, or eyes. She comforted her with an old song after reassuring Serena that after all her experiences it was just her body's way of sorting it all out. But Shaylee knew better, and she now had more to tell the Seelie Court.

Serena finally drifted off to sleep and Shaylee returned to her room. She lay in her bed and whispered, "Mother, I need you. I can't do this without you."

She had a tear welling, but it didn't fall. Instead, a thought hit her hard and she sat upright with haste, reviewing in her mind what Serena had just told her. She was trying to put all the puzzle together, from the cryptic visions to the ethereal unicorn to what the dark goblin said as it lay fighting for air after she had cut it in half.

Shaylee couldn't get past the thought that the sinisters were involved somehow. She remembered what Serena had said about the description of the creature in her dream, which was identical to that of a Zeytar. Shaylee spent more than enough time with them to know exactly what they looked like; in fact, she would never forget. And then there was the constant green mist and the changing of the Zeytar to a deformed creature. Could it be one in disguise reaching out for her? Then she answered herself: No it couldn't be, there was a female voice as well as a warning for Serena to pass on to me; and what does "fell" mean?

Shaylee was struggling. She wanted answers but wasn't getting them all. She knew that she had to keep Serena with her for longer as there were definitely Zeytars involved in the whole thing. She needed to see Wilkes but could not do so until she took Serena back, as that was the only place she knew he would be at that time.

Shaylee let it go for now, concentrating wholly on making Serena's day a worriless event. She closed her eyes but would not get much sleep this night.

Morning hit hard and Shaylee must have either convinced Serena that it was all just a terrible nightmare, or she had given her mind-wiping dust, because when Serena opened her eyes, she was a buzz of excitement and joy. She bounced from her bed and straight into the strange washroom off to the side of her bedroom—strange because the setup was all for Elvenfae with wings to freshen up in, and the facilities for washing were therefore all designed for Fae with wings. Serena had adjusted, and after she finished, she darted straight down to the silk maiden's room where her gown was hanging up, finished, and awaiting the last fitting.

Jestica was already awake and awaiting Serena's arrival. She knew she had to make any adjustments for the last fitting early, just in case. There were only hours until the celebrations, so it would be cutting it fine if there were major issues. Not that she was expecting any.

She helped Serena, who was glowing with excitement, fit into the gown. The maiden looked all over the marvelous crafting and felt quite happy with what she had completed in such a short amount of time.

She told Serena to go have a look in the mirror behind the fitting room door and come back with any issues.

Serena was gone for a while and Jestica was becoming concerned. She walked over to the fitting mirror and saw Serena just staring and smiling. The grin was from ear to ear, which made the maiden smile as well. Serena had a positivity about her that made people feel good when she was happy herself, and this day was no different.

"How is it, Serena? Does it fit OK? Ride up or scratch anywhere?" Jestica said, a little concerned but confident at the same time.

Serena responded, "No, my lady, it is amazing! I absolutely love it, thank you so much. I can't stop looking at myself." Serena felt so alive at that moment, important, not at all like when she was getting teased at school. Here she felt like she belonged.

Jestica smiled and helped her out of the gown. Serena changed and was sent straight to other maidens of Shaylee's who would now fix her hair and face before she returned to Jestica who was preparing the gown for the final reveal.

Serena skipped breakfast. She was far too excited, and she wanted to make sure she would fit back into her gown.

The hours rolled on as Shaylee had everyone working like a well-oiled machine for the final reveal of the halfling Fae who saved her life. The main hall started to fill. Some Seelie Court representatives had already arrived and were invited to be on the guest list. Shaylee had extra guards stationed at all sensitive posts, dressed in ceremonial attire so as not to alert the guests of a threat that may not be there. Shaylee was becoming more protective the more she learned. There were whispers of paranoia, but they dared not let that get back to her. Her time with Zeytars had changed her somewhat and it showed in times of stress.

Stexinzar had returned early in the night from a small skirmish that needed immediate attention. He had not met with the queen to gain approval prior to going, as there was no time. Shaylee was only glad to see him and did not chastise him for not letting her know. There were more pressing issues at hand, and he would be briefed on all in time.

Shaylee had kept Serena with the maidens until she was ready to call for her. Even though Serena knew about the ceremony, Shaylee wanted to make it as much of a surprise as she could. Soon a bell rang, and Serena looked up in haste. The maidens never said a word, just gestured at the door.

Serena turned to the mirror one last time. She felt like a princess and now looked like one. Her hair was long and dark, twisted in old braids from Celtic and Gaelic traditions. Her gown fit perfectly, a dark blood red with black trails and tails, also designed by the old ways. Her feet were fitted with sparkling black shoes, not quite high heels, but enough to give her height a boost and show her profile. She was a young teenager, or at least in the first stages. But she was dressed like an adult and felt more grown up. Shaylee had loaned her the palace jewels, including her ceremonial tiara with the family bloodstone crest in the middle jewel.

Serena finally made her way to the door, excited for Shay to see her and even more excited to see some friends. Serena opened the door and to her surprise was greeted by Chaxinn—the woodland elf she had only cycles ago lain under the stars and played chase with.

She smiled as he held out an arm and whispered, "Wow, Serena, you are exquisite today." The boy paused and blushed before continuing, "I mean, you always look—"

Serena interrupted Chax. "It's alright, Chaxinn, I know what you mean. Thank you for being my date today."

Chaxinn wasn't too accustomed to all the pomp and ceremony and didn't really understand the concept of a date, but he smiled and knew enough protocols, which his father had taught him, to get through the event.

They walked arm in arm down the stairs as Serena tried not to trip on her gown or fall in her shoes. They made it to the long hallway where they would be introduced by the maidens at the top of the stairs to the great hall.

"And now, introducing the guest of the day, Serena O'Halloran."

Serena could hear a chorus of clapping, fluttering wings, and stamping of feet, which gnomes often did to make up for their hands being busy with food and drink. She walked out from behind the velvet barrier and could see hundreds of Fae folk, some she knew, most she did not, cheering and clapping for her.

Word had got around fast that a halfling Fae child saved their princess, now queen. And they were happy for it. Shaylee had leaked the halfling part, but kept her ancestry close to her chest. Some of the Fae had started asking questions on how a human could last this long in the realms so she told a few, who in turn told others.

Serena just stood, her normally pale face slightly blushing as her hands became clammy. She felt overwhelmed and was becoming slightly dizzy from the excitement, but then she felt a swift kick in the back of her right ankle—not enough to make her fall but enough to sway her from her overwhelmed state.

Serena let out a groan. "Hey, who did tha—?"

Before she could finish, Van Coinan jumped up to the balustrade, interrupting the guest of honor, "Snap out of it, girly, before you fall down the stairs. Oh and another thing ..." Van Coinan gestured with his furry paws for Serena to lower her head to him, before whispering in her ear, "You look mighty ugly, especially for a stupid girl."

Serena snorted as she laughed and watched Van Coinan bounce away. She was thankful for his help, which had saved her from passing out. Chaxinn looked at her for a moment as Serena covered her mouth, stifling the last of the giggling brought on by her furry friend. She turned, realized Chaxinn was watching her, and said, "Don't worry, I wasn't laughing at you."

Chaxinn knew very well it was Van Coinan. He had spent enough time with the cheeky pooka to know he was strangely hilarious.

They continued to the bottom of the stairs where they were met by Shaylee, who was not to be outclassed with evening wear. Serena had wing envy. She loved the Elvenfaes' long, powerful wings and their pointed ears, along with the grace with which they carried themselves, and the shape-shifting. But it was short-lived; this was her day, and Shaylee was a queen after all.

"Look at you, my beautiful ... friend." Shaylee had to be careful not to say "sister." "You look absolutely amazing; I am so jealous of your long black hair—it looks stunning in those braids." Shaylee winked at Serena, which made her feel so much better, knowing she had something the queen was envious of.

She began greeting her friends and invited guests. The overwhelming feelings kept trying to take a hold of Serena—after all, she was only a child, a child who had spent much time already in such an enchanted place and who had experienced so much in such a short amount of time. A child she may be. But a mature young woman was rising from the depths—more than she would ever know at the time. Her fate had a major part to play and, in her innocence, she would not understand the extent of her importance until much later.

Serena was talking with some woodland elves and was deep in conversation with a ranger who had been on the journey with them, a young ranger but a handsome and well-spoken one at that, when Shaylee rang the ever-annoying bells to seek attention from all who were in the main hall.

The loud barrage of cackles and conversation ceased immediately as Shaylee stood on the fifth rung of the majestic staircase. Her wings fluttered slightly in a nervous gesture as two Elvenfae guards stood next to her.

Their bright silver armor glittered with gold edgings and an almost blinding shine came from the body of the silver encasing. The guards' wings had bindings and what looked like a metal casing around the ends of their wings to showcase the beauty and strength of the Elvenfae, although they could not move their wings because of this restricting covering of steel. But they were the best in the palace and would have no trouble finding a target, destroying it, and moving on to the next without even one nervous flutter of their disabled majestic wings. The helmets were a rarity. Such pomp of the Elvenfae guards' attire was not often seen, but Queen Tianna had insisted on it for certain occasions after the inauguration of her king and husband over thousands of cycles before.

So they stood, silver and gold, looking positively glamorous as

Shaylee turned and requested an item from the guard. She took the longish metal thing, raised it into the air and spoke, "My people, my queen's people, I am so honored to have you all here with us inside our central home for all the Fae. I thank the Seelie Court members for their prompt arrival and look forward to our meeting in the morn. My friends, we have had many cycles of torment and anguish come from the most unlikely and faraway source with the sinisters, I ..."

Shaylee lowered her head. The flashbacks of where she had been and what she had done to innocent humans haunted her nights, and although she struggled to remember a lot of it, she remembered enough, and sometimes she still felt the pull and connection to the Zeytars as if they were only around the corner. But she had overcome so much and learned a lot that could be used.

She wiped away the tears and raised her head proudly before beginning the next part of her speech, the one she was most looking forward to. "The sinisters were—sorry, are—evil. They are damaging the human realm as we speak, therefore we have cut it completely off. But we have our own problems here and now. The darkness is rising again over the Fae and we have had firsthand encounters with them.

"At the battle in Maelenflitt they knocked me down, and a creature was about to take my life when a very brave young halfling Fae girl, showing great courage even though she was afraid, picked up my sword and struck the creature until it was dead. This act not only saved me, but also saved many others, as the dark goblins were getting away, and because of that act I was able to smite the leader and the biggest threat."

The guests were all in awe of the story. Nothing like that ever happened in Faelynn, at least not on that scale, and to have an outsider now known as one of their own save their most beloved was admirable. Shaylee finished her heartfelt speech, shedding more tears as she did, "So, what I am trying to say is, Serena, for your brave acts against the darkness, saving the life of a queen of the Elvenfae, and having a pure heart of love, I give you this gift from the palace unto you, a sword molded from the palace steel and designed for you, to finish your training."

Shaylee met Serena at the bottom of the stairs. Serena had no idea she was getting such a gift or a speech; in fact, she thought it was just a ball or a formal dinner in her honor. Shaylee unsheathed the long but light sword from its scabbard, placed it on Serena's head, and closed her eyes, whispering in the old tongue before snapping her eyes open and saying, "Serena O'Halloran, half Fae and half human, you have saved me, the princess and acting queen of Faelynn, along with many other lives. I hereby give you this sword as a gift and anoint you Member of the Queen's Fae."

The honor of that title was in the past only ever given by the queen, for the most important deeds, and only to Fae beings. The fact that she was half human could have started a war, as the Fae mostly despised humans. But no one in the great main hall objected as the silence indicated acceptance. Soon every Fae cheered and danced, all trying at once to get a look at the newly anointed queen's Fae.

It overwhelmed Serena. The guests were respectful enough to allow the young one to have her space, all the while staring and cheering for her until Shaylee raised her right arm high, sword in hand, the signal in the palace for absolute silence as an important message was about to be delivered to the people. Shaylee was bending the rules to her advantage while her mother was away and only did it so Serena could speak, a worthwhile reason, she thought in her head.

"Come, Serena, please say something. What will you call your new sword and what do you plan for your role while you are here in the palace?"

Shaylee smirked from ear to ear. She loved that Serena was feeling special and that the secret of their kinship was magically written onto the sword if something befell her.

Serena cleared her dry throat with a quiet cough, stood on the third rung of the great stairs, and began with a nervous quiver in her voice, "Th... Thank you, Shaylee, and everyone ... I don't know what to say, I am so overwhelmed with excitement and emotions. This gift means the world to me, and I thank every one of you who is here tonight. I did what I did in that place with the dark ones because I saw a beautiful light just about to fade when that monster was over Shaylee. I am human, well, half now."

Serena chuckled to herself as the crowd of guests hung on to every word she was saying. She continued after clearing her throat once more, "What I mean to say is that even humans have compassion. We aren't all bad, not like those dark things near Maelenflitt who killed many of our friends ... Sorry, I mean, saving the one person in my life that has given not only me but all of you some hope against the sinisters and the dark ones was easy. And for her, who had endured so much torment and loss herself, to come out and smile with you all ... Well, I'm no expert, but that's a queen and a leader to me. Thank you, Shaylee, so very much for this honor and I hope to make you proud."

Shaylee had a small tear flowing down her right cheek. She didn't want the guests, especially the Seelie Court members who knew little of Serena, to find out they were too close. Shaylee's perfect hair in long blonde braids swung gently as she raised her head, and the crowd stared deeply into her immaculate blue eyes. She spoke softly but loud enough for all to hear because of the silence, "Thank you, Serena, you are most welcome here and are now fully a part of the Fae. No human has gained this honor at the age or with the actions you have, never. There have been halflings over time, but we Fae have mocked humans and tricked them for being so cruel, so to have one in our midst at the time of the shadow cloud encroaching is special. We all welcome you, my young Serena."

As soon as Shaylee finished, with more tears, the entire room erupted in gleeful cheering and celebration. Serena was feeling very overwhelmed as the petal band started playing and the guests started dancing.

Shaylee tapped her on the shoulder, pulling her from the mesmerizing trance she'd been sucked into. Shaylee whispered into Serena's ear, softly but gleefully, "Hey, sister, what are you going to call her?"

Serena was confused. She turned her head slightly, cleared her throat, and responded, "What do you mean, Shay, name who?" Serena wasn't even thinking of the precious item in her left hand. As Shaylee tugged at the pommel of her sword, Serena soon realized what she meant. "Oh, like Howling Tooth? Do all swords get a name, Shay?" Serena asked inquisitively.

Shaylee leaned closer and whispered, "Only the great ones, my dear, only the great ones. So who will she be?"

Shaylee was smiling as she awaited her sister's response, taking in the excitement on Serena's face, and noting how much she was like a battle warrior now.

"Long Leaf. I'm going to call her Long Leaf, as she is shaped like the long leaf grass in the flowing fields of Maelenflitt. Is that a good enough name, Shay?"

Shaylee lowered her face, so her cheek was against Serena's, and said softly, "That's perfect, my dear, perfect."

Serena smiled and had the guards look after Long Leaf while she taught her friends some not so coordinated dance moves from her hometown. As Shaylee looked over at her half-sister having the time of her life, she felt a sense of pride, before the anxiety set in about what the next day would entail.

THE SEELIE COURT

THE NEXT MORNING ROLLED AROUND SWIFTLY. Shaylee had been preparing for the last arrivals of her allies in the Seelie Court and could not wait to get some answers. The previous day had been a huge one and Serena was still fast asleep, which was a good thing as Shaylee did not want her anywhere near the meeting. There was a guard posted outside her room to distract her with some training once she eventually awoke.

The large meeting hall was much bigger than that of the council's Forland Rooms. It was at the rear of the palace, through the entrance to the cliff face, on the mountain side of the enormous dwelling, far enough away so that dark eyes and ears could not learn anything.

Each of the members was screened as they walked, fluttered, hobbled, or slid into the long torch-lit hallway. Stexinzar and his best Elvenfae guards were the ones screening, and the process seemed to go smoothly as each member was known to the queen and to the chief guards. If any Fae of the Unseelie appeared, the crystal of the palace would light up from an old spell cast in the days of the dark war.

Most of the Fae were benevolent creatures. Some weren't even friends with the palace or the queen, but they had an understanding after the destruction of the dark war and the recent events that took place in Maelenflitt. One such Fae was Gaelenthark Quartermoon, a leader among his tribes, a cunning warrior and stubborn as they come.

He was of the far darrig clan, Fae who were dangerous and mischievous. They were benevolent to Faelynn, but sinister to humans, and were known for kidnapping them and creating horrific sounds to torment them with. They would even take human babies and replace them with changelings. This hadn't happened for a while as the realm doors were closed after the sinisters arrived, but they had stopped their mischievous behavior long ago anyway after a compromise had been reached with the queen to leave the human realm alone. Now they hunted more for treasures and made gold for the leprechauns who dwelled in the far lands near Maelenflitt.

Gaelenthark's short stature never concerned him until he stood next to an Elvenfae, when he would always quip about them being inbred with humans at the dawn of time and that's why they were so ugly. But the Elvenfae were not. They were the direct ancestors of the Tuatha Dé Danann, the first of the Fae, mixed with the original magic in Faelynn. He knew all the legends but loved to stir the Elvenfae up anyway.

As he moved closer to Stexinzar, his short red cape flowing, he adjusted his large red cap and scratched his gray beard. His people were a little taller than a gnome, but far trickier. Hitching his sword hilt up and lighting his pipe, Gaelenthark stood under Stexinzar's shadow looking up as the torch-lit room created somewhat of a half-light in the hallway.

Stexinzar knew he was there but tried to ignore him. It was never wise to make the first quip to a red cap and Stex knew this all too well. It just wasn't worth the trouble, and he did not want to get offside with Shaylee as she was under enough stress. Gathering all these different Fae species into the one area was always a mission for her mother and father in the past, as some did not get along with others.

Gaelenthark lightly tapped Stex on his foot, which was covered in metal armor, to gain his attention, and in doing so Stexinzar looked down and kindly whispered, "My old friend Gaelenthark, the human lover."

Stex knew that quip would not sit well with the red cap, but he couldn't help himself. In anticipation of a retort, Stexinzar leaned down to hear what Gaelenthark would say back to him.

"I see the human side to ya is still reekin, do ya need ta wash your shit-ridden mouth out every time ya speak? Oh and I see ya not gettin' smaller, it still blows me mind how y'all can stack cow shite that high."

Stexinzar just stared at the far darrig for a moment, taking his comments in, while the red cap lit his pipe again and blew some smoke up, waiting for a response.

Stexinzar straightened and burst out laughing. Gaelenthark was shocked; he was expecting a to and fro for a while. But when he saw Stexinzar's response, he too burst into roaring laughter which echoed down the long hall and into the Seelie Court meeting room, gaining glares and unwanted attention from Shaylee and some other Fae guests.

Stexinzar leaned back down and whispered, "It's good to see you, my old friend. Thank you for the laugh. It has been a very stressful time lately and I needed that."

Gaelenthark mumbled to himself, and walked past the tall Elvenfae guard, quietly smiling once he had moved beyond him. Clearly, there would be no trouble this day as everyone there was concerned with what was threatening their lands if it wasn't the sinisters.

It took a good while to have all the Fae comfortably seated or positioned inside the great room. The oaken nochkz stood inside along the far edges with the giants from the farther reaches of Toozookus. The enormity of the room became apparent as it filled. The larger creatures had to come down through a massive shaft from the top of the mountain cliff that held the palace, the secret entrance only known to very few as it was a weak spot if an invasion occurred.

In the early morning Shaylee had briefed Faelondar before they all arrived, and he himself was concerned with the very cryptic information, hoping someone in the court could help.

Shaylee took up position, and once there was silence in the room, she began.

≈

Serena woke up not long after the Seelie Court had begun. She knew something was going on but what the details were she did not know. She had slept with her new sword, hugging it tightly all night long. It was an amazing gift, and she would treasure it forever. The only concern she had, though, was that Long Leaf had to stay in Faelynn. She didn't know why, but that was the rule that Shaylee gave her upon receiving the gift. Serena didn't know how much longer she would be in Faelynn for and she knew her time must be coming up so she wanted to get as much training done as she could before she left. She had heard Shaylee discuss things with her best friends and maidens, things she wasn't supposed to know, not that she understood much of it. Only Shaylee's most trusted maidens who were her best friends knew.

Serena freshened up and put her training attire on, loose gray clothing. Her dark hair, still in half braids from the previous night, was now in a ponytail as she grabbed her sword and opened her door to leave for some solo training. Out in the hallway, she was met with the tallest of the Elvenfae guards. She had not come across him before, and Serena sprang back and nearly fell from fright upon seeing him.

"I am sorry, my lady, my name is Marlifyn Strongholm. The queen has tasked me to train you with your new sword. I am a master of all blades and she thought it best while the others are busy that I help you with your training."

Serena couldn't believe it. She not only had her own sword, which was so light she could actually wield it, but she also had her very own Elvenfae warrior to train her, one that was quite handsome at that.

Marlifyn escorted Serena downstairs and out into the forbidden section where only guards and warriors trained. She had been given special clearance two cycles ago to train there with the other warriors who had been extremely helpful and accommodating because of her small build and lack of skill. There were no egos within the warriors and guards—if you were Elvenfae, male or female, and could fight or wanted to learn, then you were welcome, which was unlike the sexist rules back home, Serena thought.

Marlifyn was enormous for an Elvenfae and Serena was looking him up and down in awe as they walked, from his long neck where his immaculate silver helmet finished, to his quite large torso, protruding from the nearly blinding silver of his armor, which connected to his long legs. From head to toe he was quite a striking-looking Fae. His wings were enormous, twice the size of Shaylee's, and even Stexinzar's didn't come close, as they fluttered on and off like a muscle twitch.

Serena wished she had wings so beautiful. She didn't even care if she couldn't change into a sprite, but just to show off with such incredible features would be enough. She was also learning that unlike in all the faery tales she grew up on, the wings on these Fae seemed to expand, shrink, slice and cut, or change shape to suit the surroundings and task at hand.

She looked down at the ground when Marlifyn caught her staring at him; he looked back up and smiled. He was hard though feminine-looking like all the Elvenfae, but he was the most masculine out of all the males. His short brown hair that Serena could just make out underneath the gaps in his helmet most likely helped, as all the Elvenfae men and women had long hair. It was the custom and the tradition. Marlifyn had kept his short after Princess Shaylee and Queen Tianna were taken all those cycles before and had not been chastised by Shaylee on her return because of the stresses of being the substitute queen.

They finally reached the training area and seemed to have it to themselves. Marlifyn was an outstanding teacher, although he wasn't officially one in the eyes of the palace. He was particularly good at explaining things to beginners, along with enforcing discipline and respect, which all went hand in hand with being a warrior. Serena was about to find out how hard it would be. She was in for a tough day.

~

Shaylee was quite nervous. She had not had to deal with this sort of thing before as her mother and father were the ones that had met with the Seelie Court. As this was the first one since then, she wanted to make sure that it was done in the best way possible.

She cleared her dry throat, approached the makeshift stone lectern, fluttered the tops of her wings nervously, and began, "Hello, all my special guests and friends. Those that could attend last night, I thank you for your support. It made our young one Serena feel incredibly special."

As Shaylee finished with her introduction, Gaelenthark jumped up onto his seat and yelled out at the top of his voice, "Aye, we've heard about this halfling here, how could ya let a human inta the palace, let alone the realm of the pure Fae, it's a crime, I tell ya, a crime."

The red cap sat back down after a series of glares from the guards. Shaylee, and most of the court before her, continued pretending to ignore his ridiculous comments.

"As I was saying, thank you. Serena is far more than a halfling Fae. She saved my life and the lives of many other special Fae. If we had found her as a young child, she would have blended in and gained the magic through her Fae blood, but the sinisters came and took that chance away, along with many of our friends and family. It has been too long since the first attacks and now I fear we are under another." Shaylee did her best not to give her true ancestral history away.

"We have not seen the sinisters since some perished near the shores of Sheeleymoon from a pooka's dust; we gained some very precious knowledge that day to use against them if they were to return, but they never did. Now the threat seems to be coming from Xarkynan." As she said those words, the audience in the court all gasped in unison. They knew something dark was around, but from Xarkynan, well, that was something entirely made of nightmares.

Shaylee continued, "Yes, I am sorry but the information we have received over time leads us to believe that something is definitely stirring in that dark place. The creatures we fought against near Maelenflitt were of the dark realm and they seemed to know what they were looking for. It has come to my attention that Faiay'aar and many cycles before that Felvora have both disappeared. Felvora who was banished but saved us all in the dark war was en route to the edges of the dark forest when she disappeared, and Faiay'aar was not seen again after our recent battle. It seems there is a connection." And the realization came to her as soon as she'd spoken her last comment. She nearly hit herself across her face for not seeing it straightaway.

Shaylee had just figured out what had been bothering her the most since Serena told her about her last vision with the sinister gray creatures, the green mist, and the voice that said "fell." She took a moment to reflect on the new revelation as the audience of the court waited in anticipation of what would come next.

Shaylee looked up, and with a horrified look on her face, she explained. "I'm sorry, it ... it has just come to light that the dryads are in Xarkynan."

As she explained about the dream Serena had had and the revelation that Viltzin'un'dandaar had awoken and was raising the dark ones, the realization hit hard that the next stage would be the dark lord himself.

"What do you mean, my queen? Felvora destroyed the dark mage with powerful magic to hold him for eternity, and many witnessed the bones of the dark lord as she destroyed him. No magic could bring any of them back," the last dryad of Faelynn, Kalandrya, called out.

"Ahh, but there *is* magic that powerful: the Tuatha Dé Danann treasures. They have the power, and the two dryads have the knowledge," Faelondar said, as he pushed in next to Shaylee to explain. It was funny a dryad did not know that, he thought.

Kalandrya replied in a harsher tone. "The Tuatha treasures are our power source protected by ..." She stopped as she suddenly understood everything. She lowered her head and sat back down with a thud.

Shaylee was at Faelondar's side as he went on to explain, "Felvora's original mission was to check on the edges of the dark forest for the treasure there and Faiay'aar helped the sylphs protect the treasure in Maelenflitt, which means the attack on Maelenflitt was a diversion to gain the treasure not to ..." Faelondar lowered his head as well. They seemed to all be working it out together, but was it too late? Had they not done enough to protect the treasures? Faelondar continued, "Only a very few of the queen's trusted know of the exact whereabouts of all the treasures. I believe we have a spy in our midst."

It sounded like everyone in the room had gasped. Shaylee had her feelings about such a person but did not want to cast any doubts or highlight trust issues just yet. It could be detrimental to finding the truth. "We don't know for sure. I trust everyone in my palace and all who are here, but we need to be careful. If this is the case and they have two of the treasure pieces, then we are in trouble. Kalandrya, what could two pieces of the Tuatha treasures in the hands of the dark ones mean?"

Kalandrya stood and moved closer to the front of the room. Her long red gown sparkled with intertwining jewels of gold and silver. She was the keeper of the Toozookus palace at the edges of Faelynn past the woodland forest. She had her own small army of half elves from the far lands through the everlasting Misty Isles that she called upon when needed, but she had not been affected by the sinisters. She was also a dryad mage and had a good knowledge of the natural magic that Faelynn offered.

She cleared her throat and gave her knowledge of what she knew of the treasures. "Well, everybody here, especially those closer to Maelenflitt, have been experiencing more storms, wind, lightning, am I correct?" she asked as most of the court nodded. "I thought it was just a coincidence, but knowing that now tells me at least two treasures are missing. Having two would mean the enchanted ones would have increased and decreased magical abilities along with quakes and more severe storms. Three, with the help of the dark mage and a dryad using the treasures, could raise the dark lord, without the dark lord's power. And four ..." Kalandrya took a deep breath before continuing, "Four would mean the dark lord could change good Fae into creatures of the dark, could resurrect dust and bones, bringing back armies of the dead, and could turn the whole of Faelynn into a dry, barren, lifeless desert with one swift directive."

Some of the court started crying, others were getting angry, and the rest just sat staring blankly as if they had lost all hope. Shaylee even felt sick as she nodded to Kalandrya and faced the court.

"OK, here is what I need from you all. We have to stop this before it gets worse. I need all of your best, mediocre, and amateur warriors. We will build shelters for them here and we will train them all, thousands upon thousands if we can get them. Put a call out to the islands in the mists, off the ports of Sheeleymoon, to the great river folk and all forest dwellers who can wield a sword. I will not state the day of attack. It will be with me and only me, and on that day we will attack Xarkynan and regain our treasures and dryad friends, before we burn it to the ground.

"In the meantime, protecting the remaining two will be paramount and a priority. I will meet with another, who is amid battle, soon to gain some more insight. Then, when I return, I will inform the leaders of the court of the imminent attack. Are there any objections?"

There was only silence, with no one budging. Shaylee felt betrayed and way out of her league, until the entire court shook the room with bellows of cheering and screams of support, shaking the entire palace in an eruption of hope. Shaylee wiped away some sneaky tears and yelled, "Now go, we need to start this immediately!"

When she'd finished, the court began leaving and the start of the next phase was now in place. They had answers and a plan. It was more than anyone had had when they awoke that morning.

≈

Serena had been training with Marlifyn for several full cycles. Her skills had come so far in such a short time that there were whispers she could eventually join the Elvenfae guards. Marlifyn was a fantastic teacher, hard but fair, and saw the potential from the start. But this would be an incredibly sad day for the much-loved halfling Fae. No more would she wield her beloved Long Leaf or train with her mentor. This day she would have to say goodbye to Faelynn.

Shaylee was not in a good mood. The ever-buzzing and positive Elvenfae queen had something on her mind and she was dreading going through with what it was. She had to tell Serena that she was going back home. She paced up and down the hallway, reciting in her mind just how she would inform her younger half-sister that she could no longer stay. Eventually she decided that there was no simple way to do it and that she just needed to get it done.

Shaylee went into Serena's room and had a look around but could not find her. Shaylee remembered there was only one place that she could be, and that was with Marlifyn. As she descended the stairs and entered the courtyard, making her way to the private training section of the palace, Shaylee's heart was racing. A faery's heart beats faster than a human's normally anyway, because of their light bones and blood composition, but this day hers was beating dangerously high. She took a couple of long breaths, closed her eyes, and walked into the training yard where Serena yelled out in excitement, "Shay, check this move out, I've been practicing all week."

Shaylee put on a forced smile as she watched Serena do a full backflip, pull her sword out of its scabbard, run up to the wall and then a couple of steps along the vertical bricks, to flip again into a parry of thrusts and moves with her sword.

"What do you think, Shay?"

Shaylee was quite impressed. That move usually only worked for those with wings as a few flutters helped, and they could run along the sides of buildings more easily and for longer. Even the flip was hard, and yet Serena could do all that without wings.

"Very impressive, Serena. You have come such a long way in such a short time. I can see you becoming a very able warrior in the future, but for now we need to finish up your training as I have something very important to say."

Serena looked concerned. Her smile slowly faded into more of a worried look; she knew Shaylee well now, and her tone was not of excitement. She turned and bowed to Marlifyn, sheathed Long Leaf into her scabbard, and walked over to Shaylee while wiping the sweat from her face with a small towel. Shaylee held her hand as they walked from the training yard to a private little room nearby where they could be alone. Shaylee sat opposite Serena, still holding her hand, and began the inevitable conversation.

"Serena, my child, I have loved having you here with me. You have helped me through the ordeal with the Zeytars and saved my life a second time fighting dark goblins. You mean so much to all of us here in the palace and as much as I would like you to stay forever, I need you to understand that Faelynn's magic is shifting. We are losing some control of it through the loss of the Tuatha treasures that give us our magic. What I'm saying is that if I don't take you back home soon, I am afraid you will be stuck here forever if we lose our power. The other thing is that I can only hold time back for you for so long. If you stay, by the time you get home all of your family will be old. Lastly, there is turmoil coming and I cannot risk your life."

Serena was crying. There were no words as she had known this time was coming eventually. Shaylee was waiting for one of her strong objections, but there were none.

Shaylee went on as she wiped her own tears away, "You will have a friend in the future to help with the Zeytars and after we find a way to save my—no, our—people from them, I have set in motion plans for you to return, if we defeat the threats here. Your training has been for a reason."

Serena looked up at Shaylee's watery blue eyes, still sobbing as she awaited the last of her devastating speech.

"I'm sorry, Serena, but I will need you to give me back Long Leaf—"

Before Shaylee could finish, Serena shouted out, "No! Please, Shay, not her, please not her."

Serena, crying uncontrollably, now had both hands over her face, as Shaylee finished, "If they find out who you are, Serena, the Zeytars will kill you. Besides, I have your birthright etched in magic fire on the blade and pommel, so whenever you return it shows you are an Aethelwyne."

Serena was still crying but slowing down as she looked up at Shaylee again.

"Here, my dear, drink this potion. It will make you feel better."

Shaylee pulled out a small see-through cylinder filled with orange-colored liquid. Serena didn't argue as she swallowed the whole amount down in a single gulp. Shaylee had her hand over her head, whispering some words that Serena couldn't quite hear and the young girl started feeling better.

"Can I say goodbye to my friends, Shay?" Serena whispered in a very childlike tone.

"No, I'm afraid not. With a spy in our midst, I want to keep your departure quiet."

Serena scowled before chiding, "Not even Van Coinan?"

Shaylee smiled. "OK, Van Coinan can know. Now hand me Long Leaf. She will be looked after, I promise. I will check on you from time to time, but when we get home, I will have to block your mind until you return. It is far too dangerous knowledge to have on your world."

Serena didn't argue. This was going easier than Shaylee expected but was still hard. She was losing her sister, and what her sister would have to endure later in life would be tough. Shaylee talked with Wilkes in depth of the upcoming battle in her future and that she was now being watched by the only Zeytar that was good. "Now get your backpack. I have also placed some clothes in the bottom drawer. Then meet me at the entrance. I will have Van Coinan ready."

Serena reluctantly handed over the sword. She had no idea that the handle was of Vyyuna's horn and had such power. She also didn't know that the orange liquid she had just consumed would eventually erase her memories of her birthright.

Eventually Serena made it to the front entrance of the palace. Van Coinan was there and she bent down to hug the cheeky soft pooka tightly, with tears hitting his matted fur.

"Hey, stop dripping snot on me, girly," Van Coinan muttered.

Serena gave a tiny snort of laughter before standing up and saying, "I'm going to miss you, dirty face. Don't forget me."

Van Coinan didn't speak. In fact, for the first time he showed some emotion. With tears in his blue bulging eyes, he grabbed Serena's leg tightly, before whispering, "I never will, Serena, I never will."

Van Coinan let go as he watched Shaylee and Serena walk down the path away from the palace. Serena looked behind her and saw the pooka staring still, waving, before he lowered his head.

Serena turned back and whispered, "This hurts too much."

Shaylee caught Serena's words and said quickly, "It will be all over soon, my dear, and you will be back, happy, with your friends and family."

Serena hoped she was right.

They soon reached the outpost where the stables for the extra horses were. Shaylee hopped onto a small but fast horse, brown with gray tips on her mane, and then reached down and grabbed Serena. They took off in a whirl of dust to the Aurora Forest where the secret portal awaited. It would take a few days on horseback, so they tried to make up as much time as they could.

Camping under the stars, Serena and Shaylee shared stories and plans, spending some quality time together, but by the second night Serena was forgetting key facts and Shaylee was careful not to re-educate her with the lost information. By the time they made it to the Aurora Forest, Serena was not aware at all that she was half Fae or that she was the half-sister to a queen. She could only remember some of her adventures.

As they entered the forest, Serena turned to make sure the horse had been fastened properly, giving it one last check. To her horror, a group of goblins had started tearing at it, and one made eye contact with Serena. She shouted, "Shaylee, run!"

Shaylee grabbed Serena's hand, and they made a mad dash for the depths of the forest. One goblin was making headway toward the two, gaining distance quickly. Shaylee stopped and waited for it, and cut its head clean off with a surprise attack from Howling Tooth. The goblin let out a shrill cry before convulsing and writhing on the ground. Serena hated the noise they made when they were cut down. She was missing Long Leaf at that moment.

The pair kept running. A few branches caught Serena on her face, so her skin was stinging, and some black tar-like blood had splashed her clothing. She would not be going home in the same condition as when she had first arrived all that time ago.

The two kept up the pace. They could hear yelling from where they left the goblin mess moments before.

They were nearly at the portal when another goblin burst out in front of the pair. Shaylee fluttered up a few feet into the air, startled at first but ready and waiting to strike hard. Down came Howling Tooth, slicing the goblin's head in two.

By then the other four had caught up and one grabbed Serena with a blade to her throat, yelling with a gurgled cry, "Throw your sword down or I'll cut her from ear to ear."

Shaylee did not move. She looked at Serena and nodded ever so slightly. Serena knew exactly what she meant and used a flurry of self-defense moves against the goblin, rendering the creature helpless in only seconds. As she did that, Shaylee had already removed two more heads from the other goblins. Serena struck the creature in the back with its own blade several times. The remaining goblin tried to run away so Shaylee threw Howling Tooth at it, hitting it in the back of the neck. As this last one fell, so too did Serena and Shaylee, exhausted from the ambush and the mad dash.

They held each other and gathered their strength. As they stood in front of the portal, Shaylee whispered some ancient words, turned into a sprite and they both disappeared into swirling lights. Serena was finally back home, hours after leaving.

Before too long, Shaylee returned through the portal. She looked down at the cassette tape she was holding, then fell to the ground, sobbing uncontrollably as her loss became all too overwhelming.

THE RISE OF
XARKYNAN

THE DARK CASTLE WAS NOT SO QUIET ANYMORE. Guards, goblins, mercenaries, and creatures of all kinds of evil were now dwelling in the massive structure.

The negative energy that surrounded this hive of evil was giving Xarkynan power. But there was some help—the two Tuatha treasures and now two dryads. Viltzin'un'dandaar was becoming immensely powerful. He kept questioning whether he should raise the long-lost dark lord or keep the power for himself, only to quash the thought as he reminded himself he would need the dark lord to finish his plans.

The dark necro-mage held the two large stones, one in each of his hands, and placed them both in front of the dryads who were chained up with magical bindings to keep them from transforming.

He calmly asked in a scratchy tone, "Now you see our last little adventure to trick the faeries worked and we now have two Tuatha treasures. But in order to use the power, I will need you both to unlock them for me as I have no spells to break them. I know the four treasures are the elementals fire, air, water, and land, but for them to be used I need them open."

Faiay'aar and Felvora both kept silent. They would stop at nothing to keep the secrets of the treasures. They had agreed to give their lives for the secrets to stay safe. Felvora had tried to warn Shaylee through

Serena's dreams. Even though they had never met, Serena seemed to be the only one she could connect with.

The silence of the two annoyed the dark necro-mage. He decided to question them one more time before using some other strategies. He knew it would not be a simple task to get them to share their knowledge, so he had some leverage as backup.

"I will ask you both one more time nicely—how do I unlock the stones?"

Viltzin was becoming agitated. He was still a Zeytar, after all, and Zeytars were known for their cruelty. As the silence from the two indicated they were remaining defiant, Viltzin called out to his goblin assistant, "Glinoxx, fetch me the two guests from the lower dungeons, please, and oh, give them the elixir before you open the door. I don't want them getting loose inside our enormous building."

Glinoxx smiled and then laughed all the way down the hall, out into the open chamber, and down the stairs. It gave the dark necro-mage pleasure listening to the goblin's echoes of laughter.

Soon Glinoxx returned. He held in his large, clawed hand two birds that seemed to be asleep and limp. Viltzin took the birds from him and sent the goblin on his way. As he placed the two birds down onto a table next to the elemental stones, he looked at Felvora, whose eyes were beginning to well. She knew exactly who they were, but had no idea how they could have been caught.

Viltzin gave her a moment before speaking, "Now, green tree witch, I have some of your friends here. Would you like me to snap their necks, or would you like me to release them? You know what I want."

Felvora felt sick when she heard the dark mage's request. "I changed them—they were safe. How did you even find them, let alone catch the two?"

Viltzin smiled, showing his yellow needle-like teeth. "I have spies everywhere now. It was lucky one of them witnessed you changing them and followed the two. I paid the mercenary well and he went on his way, quite simple. Now do we have an agreement?"

Felvora couldn't use any of her powers. The magical bindings saw to that. Viltzin knew how powerful dryads were, and he couldn't take that risk.

She lowered her head and nodded before saying, "OK, I will show you, but you need to do something first. Let me change them back, and release them both afterward."

Viltzin nodded. "Agreed, but try nothing foolish or I will crush them both in front of you, and then I will kill you, slowly."

"Are you crazy, Felvora? You cannot risk the entire lands over two creatures, you just cannot do it!" Faiay'aar snapped, but so Viltzin couldn't hear.

Felvora closed her eyes and said quietly, "They have been through enough and I know what I am doing. He cannot use the power of the treasures even if they are unlocked. The power has to be released and only we can do that with him, so he will try unsuccessfully, which will give us time to plan an escape. I will set in motion a spell when I am released; this will hopefully make it to the palace."

Faiay'aar didn't like it, but she knew Felvora was right. She had to trust she was doing the right thing.

Viltzin yelled at them when he heard them whispering to each other, "What are you conspiring about? This better not be a trick."

Felvora turned and answered the crazy mage, "No, it's not a trick. I will try nothing if you release one of my bindings."

Viltzin loosened the bindings that held her arms up to the wall. While Viltzin walked back to the two lifeless looking birds, Felvora whispered some incantations as she dropped some leaves from her headwear onto the floor. As he turned around, Felvora had just finished her spell and looked up at the dark mage. "OK, I'm ready."

Viltzin held the two birds high and Felvora reversed the changeling spell, turning them back into their original forms. Grilif and Darf were too heavy for the mage so he dropped them onto the floor. They woke up instantly, scratching their heads. Grilif gave a groan and ran to Felvora. She hugged him, and then Darf joined in. A leaf she had dropped grew some burrs and clung to Grilif's leg, and then she whispered, "You must go straight to the palace."

Grilif nodded. He had been aware throughout the entire ordeal who they were and what had happened to them both but seeing Felvora looking aged and weary next to some loose bindings, along with Faiay'aar still attached to the wall, made him feel very uneasy.

"Now, tree witch, show me how to unlock the treasures."

Felvora nodded. With a wave of her arms and some incantations under her breath the two stones started glowing from white to red, then transitioning into an invisible vortex, glowing in all kinds of color. The stones started unwinding from the tops as though they had lids which then molded into the sides of the stones. They eventually found their new form with one showing a storm throughout the translucent shape and the other was like it was on fire, with flames climbing all around it.

Viltzin looked in amazement as she finished unlocking them both. He thought he could use that power now but would not find out for some time that he still needed the dryads to help. Felvora was getting anxious. She knew how cruel the dark mage was and wanted her friends to get out, but when she looked for them, she realized the two gnomes had disappeared. They had left when the dark mage became distracted with his new toys.

Felvora was going to escape but stopped short when she felt a chain link on her ankle. She had forgotten about that one, and she was too weak to transform. Besides, she would have to help Faiay'aar as he would certainly kill her if she escaped and left her there.

Viltzin snapped out of his trance as a thunderstorm rolled into Faelynn and Xarkynan. He looked up at Felvora standing there. He wandered over, replaced the bindings, and whispered, "I knew you would come in handy someday. Now, where are your little friends? I would like to pay you back by helping them home."

As he uttered his sarcastic statement, he drooled over Felvora's face, hitting her with it across the cheek. She shook her head viciously as the dark necro-mage kept his smiling gaze, thinking awful thoughts of what he wanted to do to her. He then leaned over and with his scaly forked tongue licked Felvora's face from the bottom of her chin, past her closed lips, over her nose, and up to her forehead. When he finished tasting the dryad's skin, he laughed his hideous gurgling cackle and turned around. He picked up the elemental stones and whispered, "You taste like wood sap, but I can live with that."

He walked out of the room, leaving Felvora fighting back sickness from the scaly feel of his tongue and the sickly stench of his rotting breath.

Viltzin had established quite a large garrison. The word had got out, and all kinds of dark creatures found their way to the castle to be a part of whatever destruction he was planning to unleash. The dark mage had been receiving information for a long time from his spy in the palace, Wyrm. But he did not like that he had been quiet for some time. Ever since the skirmish at Maelenflitt, Wyrm had been keeping a low profile, so Viltzin was not aware of the Seelie Court and the plans they had been putting together.

The dark necro-mage had two of the Tuatha treasures and a massive contingent of goblins, soldiers, and twisted Fae, so he wasn't too worried about what the queen would do. All he knew was they would eventually come, and he would be ready. In the meantime, all he could think about was using the new power he had just uncovered.

Viltzin had looked through countless spell books, history both dark and light, to uncover the Tuatha. He knew that it would take three to raise the dark lord and all four to turn the lands into a barren waste like Xarkynan. With two, he could at least raise the castle's defenses and provide an unlimited power source to fight back the Elvenfae.

Hours and hours, spell after spell, and the necro-mage could not even budge the two stones that were now alive and writhing all around the large containers. Light could be seen miles away coming from the dark windows of the top floor, flashes of red, green, and yellow sparking throughout the night until the lights stopped and there seemed to be a peace in the dark night.

Viltzin was furious. He stormed into the cells where the two exhausted dryads were trying to rest and cut Felvora across the face with a long whip. She awoke immediately and gave out a nasty cry, mostly of anger, although it did hurt her.

"Ah, I see you've tried, evil creature, and you cannot use the treasures, can you?" Felvora said. She was bleeding from her cheek but laughing softly.

The necro-mage was in no mood for the dryad's games and went to pick up his long staff. It acted both as a staff and a weapon. The metal point at the end was quite sharp, with two prongs on either side.

Viltzin moved in swiftly and was about to plunge the blade into Felvora's neck when Faiay'aar screamed out in desperation, "No, please, don't kill my sister!"

Both Felvora and the necro-mage turned, staring at the white dryad.

"Sister?" Felvora asked. "But that cannot be, how?"

Before the white dryad could answer, Viltzin interrupted, "Excellent, simply perfect. I don't care about why or how, I just want to know how to gain the power, so if one of you doesn't start talking soon, I will kill the weakest first while the other watches. Now who is going to tell me what I want to know?"

Felvora was still looking across at Faiay'aar as she whispered, "OK, I will help you."

Felvora winked at Faiay'aar and then rattled her bindings to show she needed to use her power for it to work. As assistant keepers of the Tuatha treasures, they were the only ones besides the Aethelwynes and the sylphs who could unlock the power source because of the direct bloodline of the original Tuatha Dé Danann arch mages.

"But you will need two of us as I am too weak to do both on my own." Felvora had been through such an ordeal since they captured her at the edges of the dark forest all that time ago, trying to protect the treasure. She was caught and held in the castle. She was still immensely powerful regardless, more so than her sister, as she had seen much more war over time and could tolerate it, but she knew Faiay'aar could not.

Viltzin looked at them both. The staff was still awfully close to Felvora, but he now seemed a little calmer. He moved toward Felvora and undid her bindings slowly. He wasn't stupid and had his best guards always close by if needed. The dark mage then moved toward Faiay'aar and undid her bindings. They both knew that they would never be released. As they were two of only three dryads left in all Faelynn, he would need them to open the other two stones if Shaylee could not stop him from getting his hands on them.

Felvora walked over to the elemental stones and placed her hands just above one, while Faiay'aar did the same on the other, and while reciting an old verse from the book of Tuatha, they unleashed a barrage of green and white light which pulsated over the two stones.

Viltzin watched in awe, trying hard to learn something new but happy he was now achieving what he had been wanting to from the start of his campaign.

Felvora eventually fell to the floor exhausted as Faiay'aar was sent hurtling backward once both the elemental stones had opened and were active, pulsating and swirling.

Viltzin moved in closer. He could now add his own touch to command the power, and at this stage wanted the rest of Xarkynan to behold the force he now controlled. He carefully took a stone at a time and placed each one inside a cavity with a chute that was made for power sources when the dark lord reigned. The chutes were hollow all the way to the roof of the castle and once turned on would send out a barrage of force.

Viltzin closed his eyes. He didn't notice Felvora picking up Faiay'aar. His sole purpose was to activate his new powers. He had learned his incantations well as he was waiting for a long time to use them. He began reciting the words with his hands held open, pointing to the cavities with the stones in them. The noise and atmosphere changed.

Felvora was trying to sneak her sister out. But it was short-lived when her ankle chain pulled her back. She forced her hand hard toward the chain and with a gust of green mist she broke free. She moved her hand over Faiay'aar's chain and broke that as well. The guards were too busy looking at the fire and winds swirling all through the room to worry about the dryads.

Faiay'aar grabbed Felvora's arm, whispering, "Come on, we have to go now!"

They were keeping out of sight of the enemies. Felvora shook her head and whispered, "No, I have to finish this. Go to Shaylee and Kalandrya. Protect the other treasure stones. Now close your eyes."

Before Faiay'aar could protest, Felvora had turned her into a giant eagle with white wings. Not wasting the opportunity, she went for the open window, fighting against the wind in the room but managing to fly out before it became too overwhelming. Felvora followed her to the window and watched as she flew higher and higher into the air. Faiay'aar was free.

Just as she climbed far enough away, an explosion of fire and wind burst through two sections of the roof of the castle and the two elements became intertwined. Fire mixed with the air, slowly forming what looked like a shield around the entire castle.

Viltzin opened his eyes as he fell from exhaustion, like Felvora had before. Never had he tampered with that much power at once. Before he could use it to his advantage and test what limits he had with it, he would need to rest. He raised his scaly but sweaty face. His eyes seemed to glow red as he looked directly at Felvora, who was finishing off the last of his guards with a changeling spell, turning them into bugs and stepping on them.

Viltzin laughed, although the look on his face showed that he was not happy at all. He moved closer to Felvora and with the wave of his right hand he commanded some fire from its new home in the cavity. The fire swirled inside his hand for a moment, and as Felvora attempted to change the necro-mage into a bug as well, she was knocked to the floor with the blast of energy, rendering her motionless.

Viltzin moved closer to reattach her to her original bindings, asking the barely lucid and not moving Felvora a question, "Where is she? She won't get far, I promise."

Felvora couldn't talk at that moment but was more concerned that the necro-mage had grown in size, and his voice was even deeper and coarser than it had been previously. He seemed to feed off the elements and was now fully back to health after activating the castle's shield.

Felvora lost consciousness as Viltzin secured the last of the dryad's bindings. He had an idea and wanted to test it out but first summoned Glinoxx to the room.

Glinoxx was there momentarily, ready to please his master. "Yesss, master, how can I assist you this day?"

Viltzin leaned down. He was taller now and Glinoxx noticed it immediately, shifting back ever so slightly when his master moved in. "Glinoxx, send out the small dark faeries to follow that dryad. She must have flown out of the window."

Glinoxx nodded and backed away slowly so as not to upset his master, then turned and ran down to the dungeons where the tiny dark faery sprites were chained up awaiting their orders.

Glinoxx got to the dungeons in record time, as he knew the request was urgent, and quickly unlocked the smaller cages. Chained to the inside were three tiny sprites who were quick and fluttered with great speed. They were turned a long time ago from normal Fae to dark faeries, now twisted and mean. They were caged for their own safety as they would not last in Xarkynan without protection, but over time they were forgotten about. It was Glinoxx who found them stuck in a larger cell, feeding off bugs and moss.

Just before he let them go, he whispered to them. The promise of a decent meal was the reward for completing the job and returning home, so they did not hesitate to fulfill his request. Vaelenflixx was the youngest and fastest of the group. He had a mind of his own and often had to be brought into line by the other two when he was going off his path. But they picked on him and he had not forgotten. As the cage door opened, the two fluttered out faster than Glinoxx could see, while Vaelenflixx zoomed off to the side out of Glinoxx's line of sight. As far as the goblin was concerned, all three had fluttered out that quickly. Glinoxx then left the cage open and would await their return.

Meanwhile, in the dark lord's quarters, Viltzin had a plan. He may not be able to resurrect him completely yet. But there was a spell he had been working on that, with the help of at least two treasures, would see the first stages of his return.

Viltzin spent the next few hours preparing spells, with the dark lord's remains closer to the elemental stones. He had a perfect unobstructed path along which to suck the power out and transfer it over to his would-be master's body.

The necro-mage closed his eyes and started pulling power from his right and left hands, facing away from the stones but toward the dark lord. He started his incantations with the book of darkness in front of him. As he opened his eyes, he repeated the chant and forced all the power from both of his hands directly onto the remains, fire and wind picking up the dusty bones, and swirling them all about into a mini-storm.

The noise in the room woke Felvora, who was now staring wide-eyed and writhing all about, trying to break free. The lights were orange and red with a barrage of explosions and noise emanating from the storm in the center of the room until the dark lord's body was assembled in the air. All his bones were structurally placed as if he were being built from scratch. Viltzin's hands were still pulling power like a conduit and throwing it at the storm.

Finally, there was silence. The winds ceased, the fire waned, and the power that was being pulled from Viltzin was now seeping away, back into the power cavity. Viltzin dropped to the ground, exhausted once more, but he garnered enough strength to look up to see if it had worked.

The smoke was dissipating as some movement began where the body was. Viltzin heard a groan and a loud metal crash as the last of the smoke parted and left a silhouette of a skeletal warrior standing, slightly wobbly, in full armor, holding a sword. Viltzin smiled, gulped the last of his saliva, and listened as the figure spoke, "What ... Is ... Happening? Why ... Am ... I ...?"

Before he could finish, he lost his footing and fell back onto Viltzin's large chair, his red eyes piercing the necro-mage's own red eyes. The enormous creature was something to behold, even though he was only bone and some skin at this stage.

Felvora was crying. She couldn't even scream. Then she heard some fluttering next to her head and turned. A leafy looking sprite with twisted wings was standing on her shoulder. He had three sections of a tiny chain still attached to one of his feet. The dark faery leaned in and whispered into her ear, "Methinks it's time to go."

SHAYLEE LEAVES/ DARKNESS FALLS

WITH ALL THE DESTRUCTION HAPPENING in the lands, as skirmishes of goblins and dark mercenaries caused chaos in peaceful places while they searched for the remaining elemental treasure stones, Shaylee needed to remember Serena.

Time moved on since she had left, and the young one would be an adult in the blink of an Earth time eye, so she needed to watch her. She caught up regularly with Agent Wilkes to find out when she would be able to finally contact Serena again. Wilkes was the only one with knowledge of where her family would be. So Shaylee left from time to time to meet Wilkes, but only for brief moments. She couldn't be in two places at once and had relied more on Stexinzar and her woodland elf friends to help her out.

The Seelie Court had made huge headway with gathering and training Fae warriors to take on the dark ones. But many times they were caught up in their own lands, trying to defend them, rather than being able to spare too many to join the main contingent of warriors that would eventually take on the dark of Xarkynan.

It was like the evil ones planned it that way so that the queen could not build big enough armies. Her people were still prisoners of the Zeytars, and it had been far too long since she had returned from her ordeal with the gray sinisters. She seemed to be torn between two worlds now. But nothing was more important than protecting what they had in Faelynn to make possible the eventual return of her people along with Serena.

Time ...

It was causing the most pain for her. In the blink of an eye Serena was grown, but with the way things were taking shape in Faelynn, time seemed to have completely stopped or at least slowed. The magical essence of the world had changed and there were whispers coming from the dark forest that something evil was taking place inside the castle.

The more power they used from the treasure stones, the more chaos they unleashed in the peaceful realms. Sometimes it could be torrents of rain and storms, other times it could be as simple as a potion failing or a Fae's wings not working properly. It was all becoming too much for Shaylee and she wanted the nightmare over.

She went to her room to change. She had been informed by Wilkes the last time she saw him that the time when things would happen was getting awfully close and she was promised she could help fight the Zeytars alongside Serena. Wilkes had no idea she was planning her own rescue of her people. She needed Serena's help and to concentrate entirely on her plan. The palace was in expert hands and she wouldn't be gone too long. This trip was to meet with Serena and prepare her, giving some, not all, of her memories back. As an adult, she may not take all the news at once too well.

Only a select few knew of the planned attempt to rescue all the Fae captives from the Zeytars so as not to let the dark necro-mage know the palace was without Shaylee's protection and to not give false hope in case the rescue failed.

Faelondar, Stexinzar, and some close maidens and council knew of it. As Stexinzar was head of the warriors, he would hand over control of Faelynn to Faelondar until Shaylee, and hopefully Queen Tianna, returned.

Shaylee was ready to take the journey to the only portal left in Aurora, when she realized she needed a backup plan to get home if they were caught away from the portal entrances on Earth. Shaylee sat on the end of her bed, her hands over her face, taking all the stresses of the two worlds in her mind once more, when a wind swept through her room. She looked up in fright, thinking it was something more serious, as a woman dressed in white appeared in front of her.

"Vyyuna, oh how I need you right now, please help me."

Vyyuna looked disturbed. She had lost some of her aura since the last time, as if she were fading somewhat. She answered immediately, "Shaylee, you must take my horn and hide it from here, I sense danger in the palace and a power struggle. Take it with you and give it to Serena. She will take care of it."

Shaylee nodded as she asked, "Who is entering the palace? Should I stay and fight? Tell me what to do." Shaylee sounded desperate. Her world was falling apart and there were too many decisions and directions to take at once.

"No, it was a vision from the wisps. I cannot be certain, but you still need to rescue our queen and bring Serena back to help us."

Shaylee was at least satisfied that she had a directive she needed to take. She swallowed hard before asking, "I need you to help me with the Tuatha treasure stone here in the palace. It's the only thing I can use to get back here if I am stuck on a Zeytar world. I only need a tiny amount to fill the portal crystal."

Vyyuna nodded. "Meet me in the Tuatha vault immediately. I have little time left."

Shaylee grabbed the crystal from her side table and the cassette from her top drawer, and then changed into a sprite. She headed down a cascade of halls and tunnels before finally reaching the hidden vault door. Attached to the end of the castle was a continuation of mountain rock her ancestors carved the palace from. When she was a child Shaylee had seen her mother use the secret handprint to unlock the smooth, thick door made of rock to descend the stairs into darkness. She never ventured down herself as a child, but always remembered her mother's actions. Shaylee was told never to play in that area of the palace.

Shaylee smoothed her hands over the section she remembered and felt her hand fall into the stone, swallowed by it. She then felt a prick on her index finger. As she let out a yelp, the wall disappeared and her hand came loose, leaving a small pinprick on her finger. In front of her was a dark staircase leading to somewhere she had never been before.

Shaylee quickly descended, and as she raced down the dark twisting stairs, torches would light themselves on the walls right before her, giving her perfect lighting. Upon making it to the bottom, she looked back up, realizing it was a lot farther down than she had expected. Vyyuna was waiting for her, standing right in front of a marble table with ancient Tuatha writing all over it, with a large perfectly smooth stone sitting on top.

"We have little time. Place your hands onto the stone and repeat after me."

Shaylee repeated the incantation perfectly as Vyyuna closed her eyes. Shaylee watched the stone unlock. Old enchantments created Vyyuna, and she knew exactly how to open the stone for the task. But she had become very translucent.

"Now place your crystal inside the opening and repeat the incantation again after me."

Shaylee did as she was directed, then spoke the ancient words. She noticed the swirling and colors of water splashing around as it turned blue then red like blood, mixing into the crystal. When she had finished, Vyyuna instructed Shaylee to carefully take the crystal out and close the stone by rubbing her finger around the top. With her eyes closed she imagined the stone closing and when she could no longer hear the swirls and waves of the elemental treasure, she opened her eyes, satisfied it was shut.

She turned to thank Vyyuna but she had faded away. Shaylee could barely hear her say, "I will return once more. Be careful, dear, darkness is here." Once the sound of the last words of Vyyuna's warning faded away, Shaylee darted upstairs, each section with a torch returning to darkness after she ran past, until she reached the top and looked down into a completely black void.

Shaylee was in too much of a hurry to notice someone had been watching the whole time from behind an ancient pillar. The figure remained tucked away in the shadows as Shaylee closed the door, changed into a sprite, and fluttered away to her potion room where she would cast the portal spell on the crystal.

The dark silhouette emerged from the shadows, moving toward the section of wall where Shaylee had been to open the door. The hooded figure raised his hand and imitated Shaylee's actions.

Meanwhile, Shaylee had finished with the incantation on the crystal. She grabbed her satchel and raced to the throne room, where Serena's sword was hanging high above the queen's throne. She fluttered up and took it before changing into a sprite and heading out of the palace, onto the Aurora path. Little did she realize that a pooka would be waiting for her when she reached the stables.

Shaylee turned to full form. She leaned down and looked at Van Coinan, dressed up nicely with a grass headband and brown leather overalls covered in leaves and grass. His signature ears were still one pointing up and one flapping back. He didn't say a word, but Shaylee knew he had found out about seeing Serena again.

"Hey, Van Coinan, I know what you want. Meet me near the semi-open area where the under folk live. There is an old table there. I am not sure how long I will be, but Serena will be there with me soon, OK?"

Van Coinan was very smart. He was trustworthy and Shaylee could count on him, but he was mischievous also. If he wanted to know something, he would find out. As smart as he was, he was simple as well. The little things in his life gave him pleasure, and he missed his old friend Serena very much.

He hugged Shaylee's legs and darted off down the path before changing into a racehorse and disappearing out of sight. Shaylee had not seen a pooka change from an original form in such a long time that it looked very strange. She shrugged it off and climbed onto a horse herself. She didn't have to go far now as she had a portal in her hand; she just wanted to get out of sight in case the spy caught her leaving. Little did she know, the spy was already busy.

Shaylee made it to a dense clearing at the edge of the Aurora Forest, looked around, and whispered, "Agent Wilkes," and soon after, in the blink of an eye, she was gone.

Meanwhile, at the under folk mushroom tree, Van Coinan was playing with some pixies. It was a perfect part of Aurora. The sun was shining through the trees as he kept leaping up onto the old oak table where Shaylee had asked him to meet her.

An hour before the sun would reach its peak in the sky Van Coinan and the pixies were scared off by a big gust of wind. They scurried away from the table where things were changing. They could see strange metal walls and flickering lighting before it flashed away, and there at the table was Shaylee, like she said, and a strange lady sitting opposite her. Van Coinan was curious, so he moved in closer to hear them talk. He soon learned that the lady was not a lady but Serena, his old friend. She had turned into an old person, he thought, before studying her face further.

No, not an old person. She was beautiful, just in a taller body, he thought. Getting closer, not too worried about what they were saying, he scampered up to Shaylee's dress and slowly poked his head around so that Serena could see him, then without warning jumped up onto the table and said, "Did you miss me, ugly?"

Serena looked sternly at Van Coinan, who was holding her gaze also. Her frown slowly turned into a smile before she exploded into laughter. She picked the pooka up, hugging him lightly, and answered, "Are you kidding me, snotty face, seeing your head makes me want to puke."

Van Coinan smiled as he said, "OK, OK, put me down, stinky breath, I missed you too."

Serena lowered him down onto the table, still amazed at seeing him again, with his little brown leather overalls covered in leaves and grass.

"Come along, Van Coinan, you can catch up soon enough," Shaylee said before Van Coinan kissed Serena on the cheek with his soft face and wet nose.

"I missed you, kid," he whispered, before bouncing off the table and disappearing into the thick green grass.

Soon the entire forest went quiet. Van Coinan missed the part when Shaylee turned and told them all to go about their business, so he whispered to Glabbish, a gnome who lived in the area, "What happened?"

Glabbish said, "Serena doesn't know she is one of us, she must have forgotten about us when she left."

"She knows," said Van Coinan. "She just needs reminding."

They all kept their ears peeled as Shaylee continued explaining who Serena was, but she was leaving far too much out, they all thought. Soon the reunion was over as Shaylee handed over a sword, a square thing, and a crystal, and then Serena disappeared, leaving Shaylee sitting on her own at the table.

Van Coinan and a few of the concerned folk approached Shaylee, whose head was low as she was deep in thought.

She looked up and calmly said, "I'm sorry, my lovely people, I had to block some memories from her when she was young. I couldn't tell her the whole truth now either, as we have to keep her head clear to save our people. I gave her enough so that when she returns, she will know all those she has met." Shaylee didn't tell them she would be leaving to join her in the fight against the sinisters.

Shaylee stood up, looked over at Van Coinan and yelled, "Now, my friendly little pooka, how about giving me a ride back to the palace?"

Van Coinan's eyes lit up. He knew he shouldn't have transformed in front of her, but she did do him a favor by letting him see his old friend. Shaylee had let her horse go back to the palace earlier knowing she could test the pooka's loyalty.

Without hesitation he changed into a gray charger once more. Shaylee fluttered up to his back and he raced off out of the forest and clearing only a few miles away from the palace.

When she arrived home, Shaylee knew she would not have much

time to prepare once she was on Wilkes' ship. He reminded her that Zero Time on Earth was happening, and the flow-on effects would eventually catch up with Faelynn, as it was in a close dimensional realm.

Shaylee raced into the palace, stormed upstairs, and called for her maiden Maraenor straightaway. She went to freshen up first before she dressed in her ceremonial warrior's garb. Then she had the maidens braid her hair in the traditional ways, after which she strapped the baldric with Howling Tooth onto her shoulder, then fastened her quiver of arrows and bow on the opposite side, before turning to Maraenor, whispering, "Mar, I'm leaving very soon. Keep your eyes open, and help when you can. I want you to fill me in on everything when I return, do you understand?"

Maraenor curtsied, without saying a word, winked to Shaylee upon standing back up, and turned to walk out of the room with the other maidens. Shaylee trusted her with her life.

The maidens were just leaving the room when Shaylee heard her name being called; it was Serena. She closed her eyes and thought of her sister before disappearing in a flash of blue and red. Maraenor was closing the door when she witnessed the disappearance, making her the only one in all Faelynn who knew that the stand-in queen was away on the most important mission of her life.

≈

At the edges of the long hall to the forbidden section, a guard on patrol noticed a light flickering from the depths. Darkness was the only thing anyone should see upon opening the door and looking down to the eerie section of the palace. Stories had been told to all Fae that it was a place of evil and if anyone ventured down there, they would be taken by dark goblin spirits to feed on their souls. Of course, it wasn't true, as the stories were created to ward off anyone going near the elemental stone treasure.

The guard was confused; he had never encountered anyone down there in his entire time as a guard. He figured it was important, so began the long trek to find out who was authorized, or not, to be there. As he moved closer to the light source, his wings fluttered in a nervous twitch, as if he instinctively knew that something wasn't quite right. As he went to pull his sword from his scabbard, a blade cut deep into his throat, slicing a quarter of his head from his body. Blood soaked the hooded intruder who had heard the footsteps coming toward him, giving him time to act. The guard fell to the ground as his wings fluttered and twitched only a few times more before his life drained away along with his fast-flowing blood.

The hooded intruder picked up his large satchel with the heavy object inside. He creeped around the corner and out of the hallway before descending another staircase into the dark of the dungeon cells. There he would wait until an alarm was raised before slipping out of the secret exit he had used many times. Wyrm was getting good at this, but he had not seen Viltzin in such a long time. He hoped this surprise would be payment enough.

Wyrm waited a good hour. He wanted them to find the body, so he left the torch lit and the entry door open before he left. As the alarms rang out, he waited until all the guards left the danger zone, and then he stole a horse and escaped from the palace; he didn't use the large stag anymore and couldn't use portals, so this was the only way he could travel.

At the same time as the alarms started ringing, an eagle slammed into a tree outside the palace gates. As the bird fluttered its wings around, it began changing into a woman. Faiay'aar had managed to make it back, though she'd been lost for ages, trying to find home. She was not without injuries and exhausted, and the journey had taken a huge toll on her mental state. It was lucky that a passing guard who was sent straight out from the throne hall to look after the main gates saw her, lying in blood, her white gown now tattered. As the guard moved closer, he recognized the woman, calling her name before he shouted for help.

"Faiay'aar, is that you? Are you alright?"

Obviously, she wasn't, but he was in a state of shock himself seeing a powerful dryad mage like that, accompanied by the constant ringing of the alarms which only ever rang when there was an attack on the palace itself.

Faiay'aar looked up at the guard, her face covered in blood. He saw she had binding marks on her wrists. She whispered something the guard couldn't hear before she laid her head down once more.

The guard kneeled, lifted up her head, and whispered, "It's me, it's Maalik Nightingstar."

Faiay'aar opened her eyes, placed two fingers on his face as he held her, and smiled before passing out. Maalik picked her up and took her inside for immediate medical help.

～

The dark lord's resurrection seemed to have failed. The skeletal remains of the large creature had come together and, in fact, he moved and tried speaking at times. But it was not nearly enough to get any kind of cognitive functioning out of him. Viltzin was frustrated, but he knew that it had been a big gamble to even try such a thing.

He needed another elemental treasure stone but had no idea where the last two were. He was relying on the Wyrm to feed his knowledge, but he hadn't shown up back here since taking the white dryad from Maelenflitt.

The necro-mage was becoming frustrated. The dark faeries had failed to return since going after Faiay'aar, and Felvora was not giving up any more information. He couldn't kill her now as he had no leverage. She also knew that he would need her again in the future if he was successful in obtaining another stone.

Felvora only hoped that her two friends Grilif and Darf had got through the harsh and densely populated dark forest, and that they and Faiay'aar had reached safety. She was in luck, though, as the little dark faery that escaped from Glinoxx's cage seemed to have a fascination with the tree mage, hiding when others entered the room but keeping her company when she was alone. He gave up valuable secrets of the makeup of the castle and where Viltzin would go when he left the room, as well as listening to conversations of all kinds of dark creatures and relaying information back to Felvora.

Vaelenflixx had also started cutting the bindings attached to Felvora's wrists and ankle. Being small made the task nearly impossible, but he worked on it every chance he had. He was a peculiar little sprite, made from the Aurora Forest but twisted into darkness when the dark lord was around all that time ago. He couldn't remember anything about his home. But there was something familiar about Felvora. He talked in riddles and was very jerky with his flight, but what Felvora admired the most about the tiny creature was his hatred for the dark ones now. He had been through far too much over time to ever trust or like any of them.

Felvora promised him he could live with her if they got out of the current situation, which he was most excited about. He had had a terrible life, and she thought he could use some help and positive company.

Meanwhile, in his library of dark books and potions, Viltzin was studying intensely, trying to find alternative ways to bring the dark lord fully back. But book after book, page after page disappointed him. He worked through the night, then again the next one. He tried to commune with the dark lord Varzunnos to gain some extra insight, but his memory was just not there. He needed the firing neurons of his brain to get that information.

Several more days passed. Felvora was becoming too weak. If she didn't get out of that place soon, she would not make it. Vaelenflixx was working like a soldier when the coast was clear cutting away at her bindings.

Though she drifted in and out of consciousness, Felvora opened her eyes briefly and glimpsed a large hat with a leaf sticking out of it. She blinked a few times and realized that Grilif and Darf had helped Vaelenflixx finally cut through all the bindings. Felvora was now free, but far too weak to change. She would have to get away on foot. Grilif had just finished covering her wounds with a special remedy he kept in his satchel, and as she had just collapsed to the floor, he gave her a strong herb called "fight." It was from Aurora and came from a rare tree near Vylass, given to those who needed an adrenaline boost to fight when injured or to run from danger.

The necro-mage was still in his quarters rummaging through books when Felvora in a weakened tone spoke, "We cannot escape this place. There are creatures everywhere."

Grilif smiled and whispered, "We are gnomes. We find the impossible and that's exactly what we have done. I cannot explain any more than that. Now, that 'fight' should kick in any moment and when it does, turn into something small."

Felvora thought she was dreaming and when the "fight" kicked in she was ready to go. Before they ran off, Felvora whispered, "I can't sustain a mist but if I turned into a rat would that be better for our escape?"

Grilif nodded and responded gruffly, "Just hurry, we have a small window of time."

In that moment Felvora swirled into a small mist and landed next to Grilif and Darf, with Vaelenflixx hovering above. Grilif gestured for them to move, as they began going into small hallways and pipes, passing other rats and mice, dropping, level by level, staying out of sight, moving fast in tight places even for them, before coming to an enormous drop.

Felvora looked down. With her whiskers vibrating like crazy and her eyes bulging, she shook her rat head. Grilif tried to reassure her, but she kept shaking it, and then in a squeaky voice said, "Are you both crazy? That drop will kill us all."

Now Grilif shook his head and asked straightaway, "Do you trust us, Felvora? If you do, you need to take the leap with us now." And as soon as he finished speaking, he slid down the large pipe as if on a crazy slide, going left and right, up and down, water flowing alongside him, until he finally reached the end, and with a small drop fell onto a soft bag of flour.

Next Darf followed, and then Vaelenflixx. As they waited in

anticipation for Felvora, they soon heard a screech coming from the rat as she dropped next to the others.

Felvora changed back into her full dryad form, looked around, and whispered, "How did we get onto a flour boat, and what is one of these doing so close to Xarkynan?"

As she looked up from where they came, she could tell they were at the other end of the castle and directly underneath.

"When we escaped, we tried to smuggle on board one of these vessels but couldn't get past the creatures at the ports picking up the food from the barley islands past the mists of Faelynn. We looked around to this side where a special boat was always kept. It must be for repairs. We watched it for days and it didn't move so we thought if we can get to the island Flen, we have a better chance than going through the dark forest where everyone would be looking for us."

Felvora stared for a moment at Grilif, taking in what he had just said, then with the last of the "fight" left in her she picked him up and kissed his forehead. Grilif only groaned for a moment, and then as she placed him down, she moved back into rescue mode. "Now, who is going to row us?"

Grilif laughed, knowing no one could, and as he looked at Felvora it was like she could read his mind.

"I think I have enough puff left in me to get us started," she said. And with that a wind picked up and slowly led them out to sea, taking a quieter route than the other two boats on the water. As they hit the mist, Felvora remembered something from legend. The second island was where the ancient merrow dwelled.

THE DARK LORD AWAKENS

SOON AFTER FELVORA'S ESCAPE, Viltzin entered the room to attempt another resurrection. His thoughts were that she must have had enough time to recover from her ordeals by now, as she was a strong mage.

There were still those parts of the original mind of Viltzin that filtered through, and always close to the surface was the hate at how he was trapped for all that time. But those thoughts and feelings of the original mind were coming through less frequently.

Viltzin discovered Felvora had gone and started tearing the place apart in rage. There were books and potions there as well as the cells. He used that room for multiple things while constantly monitoring the two dryad mages. But his obsession with raising Varzunnos had led to his lack of supervision.

The necro-mage continued his tantrum, tipping over tall storage units and pushing over tables. It wasn't until he hit the skeletal remains of the dark lord, sitting there lifeless, that he calmed down. He went to the large war horn at the opposite end of the hallway and blew it three times, alerting the castle that there was an escapee.

Glinoxx was the first to attend the necro-mage's request as he was the only one on that level after Felvora had made a mess of the guards. He chose his words carefully as he saw the look on his master's face, "Who has escaped, my master? Find them I will."

Viltzin leaned down and calmly, though assertively, whispered, "Take every single creature in this castle and do not return until you have found her."

Glinoxx knew immediately who Viltzin had meant. The only females in the castle at the time were the dryads. There were female guards and warriors, but they were all out on missions or seconded to the dark dungeons where they were used for birthing more guards. Even Glinoxx had trouble comprehending the vile and evil necro-mage's actions at times.

On he went, running down the stairs and out into the main corridor to the throne room, when a hooded rider stormed into the enormous section of the castle where in the past many feasts of blood and corpses were had. The hooded figure leaped off his horse, pulled his hood away and demanded Glinoxx take him to see Viltzin.

"It's not a good idea, Wyrm, he's not in a good mood at the moment."

Wyrm didn't care, he knew he would be rewarded after this; in fact, his excitement was that of a young Fae after first learning to fly. "I don't care, grub, lead me to him now."

Glinoxx shook his head, and said under his breath, "It's your life, idiot."

Wyrm and Glinoxx started to ascend the stairs that the grotesque, spitting goblin had just come from.

"What was that, ugly gnome?" Wyrm said.

Glinoxx wanted to eat his throat just for saying that and would keep it in the back of his mind for later, but whatever Wyrm had to show his master must be worth it, so he decided not to react.

They reached the peak of the staircase and Glinoxx pointed reluctantly over to where the necro-mage was standing. He had his hood on and was staring out of the window, hoping to get a glimpse of the escapee. The castle was extremely high, and he could see nearly all the dark forest of Xarkynan, but if she was out there, she would be deep in the woods. Any form she took would soon be carved up into tiny bits by creatures he had taken as his "people."

Wyrm slowly approached the necro-mage as Glinoxx descended the stairs once more to inform all those who could search for the escapee.

Viltzin felt someone behind him and used a trick he had learned in his necro-magical studies. When Wyrm was only five or six steps behind him, he whispered in his ear, "Why do you disturb me, traitor?"

Wyrm swung around in fright to see who was there, but it was just a dark and empty hall. He immediately turned back around and realized Viltzin had a sharp dagger connected to his throat, drawing a little blood straightaway. His eyes were always a glowing fiery red and the snarl on his scaly face would make anyone or anything drop on the spot in fear as he whispered to the visitor once more, "What do you want, traitor?"

Wyrm garnered all the strength and courage he could find just to answer that one question. He had to be quick and say the right words or the blade would find its way deep inside his neck. "I have it, master, I have a Tuatha treasure."

Wyrm could see slight changes in Viltzin's face as the blade dug a little deeper into his throat. He tried to swallow but couldn't. Viltzin looked down into Wyrm's left hand and saw a satchel, and then he slowly looked back up as the snarl showing his yellow needle teeth became more of a grin. The blade eased back until it was out of Wyrm's skin and moving ever so slowly away from him.

Viltzin licked the dagger quickly with his forked tongue and placed it back into the scabbard on his hip, before switching his temperament completely. "Come, Wyrm, sit with me. I apologize for all that, but it has not been a very productive time lately and your disappearance has only made me paranoid. Now, what do you have in that bag of yours?"

Viltzin was drooling. It wasn't for food but for power; the dark power corrupted the Zeytar's mind even more lately.

Wyrm sat back on a side stool near the great horn and handed the bag to Viltzin, saying, "I am sorry, master. I am no traitor, but my cover would have given me up if I were to visit earlier. It seems the queen will leave soon for the Earth realm to save her people from the sinisters. I followed her one night and I found what only the royals knew. There was still some fresh blood on the device allowing entry into the tomb which is what I used to unlock the door; it was pure luck. The security on it was almost impossible to crack as I found out that if you aren't an Aethelwyne, you don't get in. Witnessing the queen led me to try it, otherwise it would never have been found."

This impressed Viltzin. He shifted his gaze away from Wyrm and opened the bag. "We will see now, won't we?"

Wyrm swallowed hard. He was in a very precarious situation. If the necro-mage was happy, he still might kill him. If he was not, he would surely kill him. The unnerving feeling he always got from the unpredictable necro-mage was nauseating to the point that his paranoia told him he may even be able to read minds. So he constantly gave his master the truth and what he wanted. Better to face a blade from the Aethelwynes than from this creature.

Viltzin pulled the stone from the satchel. The smile on his face was just as horrifying as his snarl. He forgot Wyrm was there and raced into the room where he had kept the dryads and the skeleton of Varzunnos. He figured he didn't need the dryads anymore, not now anyway, as there would be more than enough power to complete the resurrection on his own.

Viltzin placed the third elemental treasure on the large table in the middle of the two cavities. It was the only piece of furniture that he hadn't disrupted in his fit of rage.

Once the stone was in position he cleared an area around it to make it accessible. With the dark lord's body there too, he began pulling power and copying the words the dryads had spoken upon the opening of the first two stones, hauling and drawing from the working elementals. The room was becoming engulfed in wind and fire once more.

Wyrm wasn't going to wait around and made a dash for it in case it didn't work.

More and more power was drawn, with incantations of the Celtic Tuatha language before the stone started swirling and humming. Water was now encasing the stone, molding and coursing all around while the top twisted, creating an opening like in the others. It was translucent like the other two as well, not just a black smooth stone.

Viltzin was now laughing which could be heard echoing throughout Xarkynan. As his power increased, the water elemental started rising and joined the other two, creating a vortex of power. The elements turned from their existing power to now a light show of mists, lightning, and force shooting out from Viltzin's hands, as he pulled more and more. He began the original incantation for resurrecting Varzunnos. He wasn't weakening at all; on the contrary, he was becoming more energetic and in control. The colors in the room were like lasers and lightning, reds and blues, purples, and greens, cycling through, as Viltzin continued pointing at the dark lord.

Soon the bones were in the air once more, as the land underneath the castle broke away, lifting the whole structure higher into the air. The bones were becoming harder to see as the mists set in, encompassing him, as if the power stones were rebuilding him from scratch. Blue flashes, then red, flames climbed higher as the noise broke windows in the lower sections of the castle.

Viltzin held as best he could, shouting out over the noise the last of his incantations and holding on, before wailing as he collapsed into a heap when the power slowed to a trickle. It dissipated from his hands and went back into the cavities of exposed stone. The mists were still very thick as they swirled the last few times, still sparking with electricity.

Viltzin closed his eyes and passed out for a moment, until a thunderous roar awoke him. Looking up to see what it was, he was met with a sight that even he feared.

Varzunnos was standing where the mist had been, naked and angry. His face was partially animal, and he had a multitude of horns on his head. Two came from the sides, pointing out and down. Two tiny horns were at the front on either side of his forehead, and two larger ones were like antlers or like branches of a tree, reaching high and outward. His teeth were razour-sharp, and he had four ears on the sides of his head, two that were tiny and two ears that pointed higher than an Elvenfae's. His animal-like face had fur over it with stag features, but formed the complexities of a humanoid face without a snout. His body down to his waist was humanoid, but the remaining part, which Viltzin was staggered to see, was that of an enormous stag with hoofed feet, with dark brown fur covering every inch of his legs.

The gigantic creature let out another horrendous cry that bellowed out into the world. The castle had stopped climbing but was hovering at least a hundred feet over the land.

Varzunnos took a step. His red eyes were enormous, and his snarl made Viltzin's look like a pixie's. He took another step, then fell on one knee; the crash echoed through the hall. Viltzin stood up and rushed over to his new master, comforting him from his ordeal, but the necro-mage was about to learn a valuable lesson that day. He did not know Varzunnos as well as he thought he did. It was like the real Viltzin inside him was laughing when the dark lord picked the dark mage up by the throat, stood back up, and raised him high into the air until he was six feet off the ground, staring into the hideous creature's face. The glare would have made anyone's heart stop. But before Viltzin's air ran out, the dark lord spoke in a deep tone, "Who are you, intruder, and where is Viltzin, my necro-mage?"

Viltzin tried to speak but couldn't. He gestured to the Tuatha treasures and kept repeating, "Tuatha ... Tuatha."

Varzunnos clutched a little tighter. His claws, even though he had humanoid hands, were digging deeper into Viltzin's neck as he retorted, "What are you talking about? I am Tuatha Dé Danann!"

Viltzin froze, staring into his eyes. He was not expecting to hear that. In all the books he had read about Varzunnos, never once did it mention he was from the Tuatha.

Viltzin was nearly losing consciousness, so he desperately pointed to his mouth, hoping the creature would release his grip for him to speak. As he gestured, Varzunnos let him go, dropping him hard onto the floor.

He would never kill him, but he wanted to let the necro-mage know that he was in charge. Viltzin grabbed his veiny, scaled throat. He had been the leader and the feared one for so long now that he didn't know what it felt like to be at the mercy of another creature. He was regretting his decision immediately and knew he had to speak the dark lord's language if he wanted to survive.

Varzunnos stepped back and waited for the necro-mage to gain his composure. Viltzin spat out some blood onto the floor, then gradually picked himself up. He stared at Varzunnos as the dark lord stomped away, out of the room and into the hallway, before he turned and gestured for him to follow. Viltzin would not disobey him, so he dragged his feet along and followed him to his throne where his armor and sword were sitting, having waited for him for a thousand moons.

After Varzunnos had fixed his armor, he seemed even larger. His helmet was black, covering his horns and his face. There was an opening for his eyes that cascaded down and surrounded his mouth. His body armor was also black, as was the armor covering his bipedal lower half. There were glints of blue and silver in a certain light, but it was his glowing eyes underneath the darkness of his helmet shining out that disturbed Viltzin the most.

Varzunnos picked up his enormous broadsword called Severed Wing, perfectly named for maiming Elvenfae in the last war. He had a section of armor where the baldrick went across his waist with a large scabbard to his right, but it was like he missed his sword, and he was holding on to it in case he was without it once more.

Viltzin went to speak, and when the first words came through, Varzunnos interrupted him with a roaring deep voice, "Bring me food, faery or bark, I don't care, just give me something now."

Viltzin nodded and nearly tripped over Glinoxx, who was listening outside. The necro-mage yelled at the goblin in a whisper, "What are you doing, fool, you will get us both killed."

Glinoxx didn't care. He was too nosy to care. Like all goblins, he did not have the sharpest of minds. Viltzin gathered his wits about him and calmed himself before asking Glinoxx his next question.

"Glinoxx, my friend, I need you to bring some meat up. I don't care what it is or where it comes from, but if you do this, I will reward you."

Glinoxx laughed, then turned and ran away, shouting, "You aren't my master anymore, he is, ha ha ha."

Viltzin hoped he would come through with the food. If he wasn't back shortly, he would get it himself, and blame the goblin for its lateness.

Viltzin wandered back into the dark lord's quarters. He slowly approached but remained a safe distance away as he said, "My lord, I have my best goblin working on it now."

Varzunnos sat forward and answered, "I like goblin, why didn't you just bring that in for me?"

Viltzin was out of his league. He needed to be smarter and try to stay ahead of him. As he moved inches closer, he answered, "Sorry, my lord, but he will bring something far more appetizing for your hunger."

Varzunnos sat back, slamming the end of his sword into the floor, and then realizing it needed sharpening. He enjoyed toying with Viltzin, or the imposter inside him. "So, who are you?" he said. "You are not Viltzin'un'dandaar. I can see your brain pattern, and it looks different. Also, you speak differently. So who are you, intruder?"

Viltzin had to come clean and began telling him everything of the Zeytars' attack, the war on Earth, and how he had plans to take the whole of Faelynn for the dark lord.

Varzunnos sat and contemplated his story. He liked the idea of ruling three races now, not just one. "After I take Faelynn, I will take Earth, and then I will take your Leader."

Viltzin nearly laughed but stove it off for now. It would be hard enough to defeat the Fae, let alone humans after the Zeytars had control, he thought to himself then, before it hit him. Let Varzunnos do all the heavy lifting, he thought, and when he's ready to take on the Leader I will betray him, and the Leader will make me number one and with the power I now have I will be the one to take over the three. His thoughts were exciting him as his plan was coming together, but would almost definitely betray him if he kept thinking on it.

Viltzin composed himself and replied to Varzunnos, "That sounds like a splendid plan and I will help you, my master, if you would let me."

Varzunnos didn't care whether it was really his necro-mage or a new one. He just wanted to rule and have a powerful mage to assist with his magic needs.

"Done. Now, what were you saying about Tuatha Dé Danann? They were my people until they banished me here for using magic against our own. They stripped me of my ancestral rights and sent me to the farthest reaches of the lands until I made it on my own, stealing enchantments and building myself back up. Now the descendants of my people are the Elvenfae. I am the only true Tuatha left."

Viltzin nearly fell over. It was true, he thought. That must have been on the missing pages.

He moved closer and calmly mentioned, as though thinking nothing of it, "We have three of the Tuatha elemental treasure stones here and working."

Varzunnos flew out of his chair, picked his sword up, then thrust it down to the ground right in front of Viltzin, smashing some parts of the stone floor. He then bent down to Viltzin, who was shaking, not knowing what he had done wrong. Varzunnos shouted at the necro-mage, "You have three Tuatha treasures here? My ancestral treasures and the power of all of Faelynn?"

Viltzin knew his time was up as he watched the dark lord slowly stand back, shoulders moving slightly in rhythm as he started making a horrendous noise. Viltzin soon realized he was laughing as the roars continued for the longest while. The dark lord laughed hard, a deep, dark bellow of belly laughter that echoed throughout the hallways, as Glinoxx entered with a huge fat pig to satisfy his new master.

≈

Felvora and the other three had been drifting for hours as the late afternoon started creeping in. They hadn't been able to see the castle since they hit the mists, but Felvora was confident that her instincts were guiding her in the right direction. Grilif was teaching Vaelenflixx how to tie ropes, and the sprite practiced on one of Grilif's coarse beard hairs. He was just about to show the gnome his work when they all jumped up in fright; the noise seemed to come from the castle, but was loud enough to reach them as far away as they were.

Felvora looked at Grilif and Darf as the eerie noises turned into dark bellows bouncing off the water. Then the dryad put her head in her hands and started shaking.

Grilif moved closer to see if she was OK. She was still very weak and he put his arm around her. Looking up at him, Felvora grabbed the little gnome by his shoulders and whispered, "I know that laugh."

Felvora was still shaking but was now teary as well. Grilif didn't know what to do, so he asked the obvious question, "Who is it, a loud troll or heap of banshees on the rocks? Tell me."

Felvora tightened her grip on him and whispered, "Varzunnos. It's the dark lord Varzunnos."

Felvora let go as Grilif turned and looked at Darf and Vaelenflixx, who had also started shaking. When Grilif glanced back at Felvora, he saw she was out cold. Most likely from shock, he thought.

～

The boat continued onwards while they all sat around the dryad mage. Then a storm hit the ocean, with lightning and winds that knocked the small vessel from side to side. With crash after crash the water kept rising as if it were in attack mode. The wind was relentless to the point that the boat couldn't maintain a balanced grip on the water and eventually was thrown high into the air, smashing them all into the ocean.

The waves swallowed them. Even Vaelenflixx, whose wings were fluttering harder than ever, couldn't fight such a torrent of winds and water, eventually succumbing with the rest of his new friends to the dark deep of the sea.

They were sinking faster into the depths, not knowing which way was up or down, fighting for the last of the air they wouldn't receive that day until they passed out.

At that moment, from the depths of the foreboding ocean, three swift shadows glided along the bodies as they sank farther into the void. One stopped and clutched Vaelenflixx in his hand, while grabbing Grilif with his other one. Soon another creature, a little larger than the first one, was holding Felvora, and the third already had Darf in its grip. They darted up to the surface of the raging sea for the shipwrecked escapees to take their first desperate breath, and then glided along at immense speed, far away from their sinking boat and the cries of laughter they had heard.

Grilif was the first to wake. He threw up a small lake of water from his lungs before rolling over and staring up at the shining afternoon sun. This was a vast contrast to when his eyes were last open. As he rubbed his eyes and focused hard, he noticed three unusual creatures standing over him. They were humanoid but had scales all over their light bluish-green bodies. Their hands were scaly and webbed but had the same number of digits as most, only awfully long claws at the ends. The faces looked like fish, with gills on the sides of their necks and large lips with hollow black eyes, but also humanoid in shape. The last thing he noticed before passing out was their long pointed ears and the mesmerizing shine of their scales.

"Grilif, hey, Grilif, wake up, you will not believe where we are!"

Grilif rolled over. This time he wasn't lying on sand and didn't need to bring up water. He was lying in a hammock, with Darf standing next to him. Darf kept talking, but Grilif was trying to get his bearings once more and was tuning in and out of what Darf was saying.

He sat up and tried to stay focused now on Darf as he whispered to his friend, "Darf, I had the strangest dreams. I dreamed I was on an ocean and ..."

Grilif didn't need to finish his retelling of his dream as he was now looking directly at the three humanoid fish people that were in it. He turned to Darf and stared before his friend responded, "That's what

I've been trying to tell you, Gril, the legendary merrow of the Lost Isles saved us. Isn't that amazing?"

Grilif jumped off the hammock and sauntered over to where the fish people were standing. He looked up at the gigantic creatures and whispered, "Is it true, did you save us from the storm?"

The younger female merrow bent down to him and with a gurgling voice whispered back, "Yes, we did. You were lucky, as we rarely get that close to the castle. We have lost some of our family over the cycles to that place and to other places, so we stick to our home mostly now. Are you feeling better?"

Grilif nodded and said, "Yes, and thank you, thank you all. Is Felvora alright?"

The younger merrow nodded and started walking, indicating for the other three to follow her. As they entered the small forest, they could see several cabins, all connected. The merrow entered through a doorway and the others followed her in.

Inside, they witnessed something they had never seen before, nor even heard of in stories. The cabin inside comprised pools and land sections. There was bedding underneath the water and on top, indicating they catered for both. Felvora was on a hammock on the other side of the floor pools.

The young merrow explained, "We need to keep hydrated and we can only stay on land for so many days before we get sick. Sometimes we prefer to stay in the water, while other times we prefer to talk with our mouths instead of using sonar telepathy. There is an opening under this pool that takes us straight to the main ocean."

The two gnomes had their mouths wide open while Vaelenflixx was fluttering all over the place chasing tiny bugs he had never encountered before. They moved nearer to Felvora who was still quite weak but awake. Grilif got in close and held her hand as Felvora leaned over and whispered, "I told you we were going to meet my old friends."

THE RETURN OF SERENA

POST ZEYTAR CONTROL

QUEEN TIANNA FLEW THROUGH HER OWN secret portal, the same one that Shaylee had used to take Serena back home, oblivious of all the other portal closures during her time with the Zeytars. Tianna wished she could have had a full debrief from Shaylee before returning to her kingdom. As the flurry of her Fae sparked into their home world, longing to be with family, the horrific reality of the tormented captivity that they'd endured hit the queen hard. She watched her people coming through the doorway she held open, and couldn't help but feel like she had betrayed her Fae. While captured and under the Zeytar and beasts' control, she had no idea of the great numbers of Fae that had been taken.

Tianna's tears were turning to anger as the last of the sprites flew through the portal. She hoped her daughter would finish those gray sinisters for good. The anger was more prominent in the new batch of escapees, as they had been taken for such a long time and had done horrendous things to humans, along with constantly being in aggressive states, something the Fae were not known for.

Tianna needed rest and so too did all her Fae. As they scattered all over the place looking for homes and loved ones, she also turned into sprite form and headed straight to Vylass to rest, oblivious to the chaos that was unfolding in her unprotected lands.

Stella was zooming behind her, as were Mella and Stixx. It was like they were racing to see who could get to Vylass first. As exhausted as they were, they were simply happy that they had found each other again after the ordeals they had all been through. The Elvenfae guards and warriors were all in a V-like formation ahead of the queen, making sure she made it through the forest with no interruptions.

Tianna was oblivious to it. The guards seemed to have picked up where they left off even though so much time had passed, especially such a difficult time in other realms. It now seemed as if they'd only been gone for a short time, although some dark memories would come back and haunt them every so often, much like they did Shaylee when she returned.

Tianna had visions of Shaylee and a woman freeing them all and still couldn't grasp how they did it or what they had to go through and sacrifice to free her and her Fae. She was immensely proud of her daughter, who looked somewhat different when she spoke with her briefly. She hoped very much to see her again but couldn't think of it for now.

Vylass was now upon them as they zoomed toward the entry to the large tree of the sprites. The guards pulled back and waited outside, allowing Tianna to be the first to enter to greet Villara, queen of the sprites, with the rest of the sprites following soon after.

As Queen Tianna, who was now in Elvenfae form, entered, Villara fluttered from her oak throne and rose to meet with her face to face. "Never in my wildest dreams, my queen, did I think I would see you again," Villara said as she panned around the room that was filling fast with freed Fae, but not seeing the one she was hoping to find.

Tianna answered kindly, "Thank you, Villara. It must have been such an ordeal for you too, my dear, losing friends and loved ones."

As Tianna finished, Stixx flew over her shoulder and headed straight for her family, who were looking around for their long-lost daughter, as were other families, reuniting for the first time in an eternity.

Villara was panicked as she was desperate to know if her daughter was with them, but she didn't want to be rude to the queen. As time moved on, she started losing hope, but then Stella flew out from the shadows and straight into her mother's arms. Both sets of wings fluttered madly while they embraced and cried together for a short while.

Stella pulled away and whispered to her mother, "I am so sorry, Mother, I didn't mean to wait so long, but I saw you talking with the queen of Faelynn and didn't want to disturb you."

Villara embraced her daughter again and without words held her tightly. Both were crying, and Tianna also wiped away her tears, thinking of her own daughter battling the sinister Zeytars.

As all those who had come back found their way home to their families, the devasting realization hit the remaining families that their loved ones had not returned. There were many casualties from their ordeal and the fallout was revealing itself as Tianna just realized that she had not seen her stepdaughter Stalixus since she had arrived home. Hopefully she flew straight to her own house for a rest, she thought.

Villara interrupted her daydreaming, and said, "I am sorry, my queen—"

Tianna stopped her mid-sentence. "Please, Villara, you are queen of your people and I am in your home. I should call you queen, so it's just Tianna."

Villara continued with a smile, "Oh, sorry, Tianna, I don't mean to be rude, but after everything that has happened here in Faelynn since you have been gone, I thought you would have returned immediately to the palace without stopping."

Tianna's mood changed swiftly as she responded to Villara's cryptic comment, "What do you mean, Villara? What has happened since I have left? Did the sinisters do it?"

Villara lowered her head as she answered, "No, Your Highness, the sinisters have been gone for a long, long time, but ..." She paused for a moment, knowing now that the queen of the Fae knew nothing about what had happened in her absence. She continued carefully, "There are whispers that the dark lord Varzunnos is awake."

As soon as those final few words were spoken by her old friend and ally, Tianna changed back to a sprite and without a word zoomed out of the great tree and past the warriors waiting for her outside. They struggled to catch up with their queen, and not knowing what was wrong, they just followed her. Faster and faster, she flew, with the guards and all her people who were returning to the palace following her. The strong warrior guards couldn't believe that she could move so fast, especially after the ordeal she had been through.

Eventually she made it to an old lone oak in the middle of the dense forest. Not even the guards knew where they were at this stage. Tianna changed into full form and stood at the base of the twisted tree. She grabbed a piece of bark from the main trunk around the side of it, and as she pulled, a small round door opened. She turned to all those who were returning to the palace and whispered, "Stay in sprite form, my people, we will be home soon."

She held the old oak door open for all the hundreds of sprites to enter. As the last of them went through, Tianna closed the door behind them all, leaving no visual evidence that a doorway had even been there in the first place. They were all learning that the queen was far more enchanted than they gave her credit for. Not even Shaylee knew about the secret passages all over Faelynn like she did, but they were for emergencies only or else they could be found and used by the wrong Fae, or worse.

They flew through a misty circular hallway with damp moss covering most of the areas for a short while before coming to a stop. Tianna opened another door to another oak right near the palace. She was the only one to override the restricted portals in the lands. As they flew out, she closed the oak door and zoomed home to her palace, where she would learn some very dark truths about exactly what had been happening while she was gone.

⚬

The queen had been back for over two cycles and although Serena and Shaylee were only hours behind them in Earth time, time seemed to have become sluggish from the dimensional changes. It was not like when Shaylee slowed it for Serena to get back to her time; this was different. With most of the elemental stones in one place, all magic across Faelynn was being affected.

Once Shaylee and Serena were sent back to Earth from the war against the Zeytars on the Leader's ship, Shaylee used the crystal she had given to Serena, thinking of her mother as it thrust them into the portal before the chaotic aftereffects of the Zeytars' destruction. This chaos was avoided in Faelynn but for how long would be anyone's guess.

Shaylee entered first and Serena followed immediately after, still dressed in the gray Zeytar uniform she wore as a disguise in the battle, not thinking anything of it before she burst through time and space to get to Faelynn. As they arrived near Tianna, they found themselves in the middle of a war.

Shaylee had to duck swiftly as a dark goblin swung its rusty blade across the space where her neck would have been. She parried forward with several harsh blows, sparking blades with the horrific-looking creature, as she moved down into the middle of a pack of them. Shaylee's sword started howling as she swung it around and took three heads, after which she carved through another goblin's skull and dropped an arm and a leg from two other unfortunate creatures.

Meanwhile Serena had fallen headfirst onto her face, but recovered immediately by twirling onto her back and flipping up onto her feet. How she did that, she did not know. She felt a lot lighter here and her eyes were adjusting again to the vibrant colors of the world. She had no time to stop there, though, as the ax of a large troll hit right in front of her, forcing her back as she jumped into the air with a flip. When she landed, she spun around, as she knew there was a goblin behind her. Without even looking, she thrust Long Leaf into the center of its chest. She pulled out her blade, which carved the monster up even further, and then she stuck it forward into the belly of the troll.

Serena looked into its eyes and gave him a tiny wry smile, before she jumped onto Long Leaf, firmly attached to the larger than normal beast, and then stood on the troll's shoulders. Before it could stretch its arms up to grab Serena, she placed her legs around the troll's neck, reached down, and grabbed Long Leaf. Then with a mighty thrust from her legs she pushed off its shoulders, turned in the air, and cut the troll's large head completely off with a swipe from the hilt to the tip of the sword.

Serena landed, caught her breath, and was now back-to-back with Shaylee. They kept guard over each other as the Elvenfae warriors fought hard to protect their queen. Shaylee had a split second where she noticed Darphanin and some other Fae from the Seelie Court with their soldiers fighting as well.

An arrow skimmed past, bouncing off Shaylee's silver shoulder armor, and she caught from the corner of her eye another arrow lined up ready to launch. This time she was prepared, and as the arrow left the bow, Shaylee was in the air slicing it in half and fluttering hard over to the creature who had shot it. She came down hard, cutting the odd-looking dwarf in half. Flying was never advised in war, as it made one a prime target for daggers, arrows, and other throwing weapons. A fluttering backflip or a quick dash was normally fine, though.

Serena was still working hard. She could no longer see Shaylee. But she realized what she was wearing, and didn't want to be classed as the enemy, so she took her gray cap off and let her long dark hair flow. She had enough dark blood on her Zeytar hybrid uniform now that she was blending in, but she had to be on guard. She would be a lot safer if she was closer to Shaylee.

As arrows flew and swords clashed, the battle was waning. Most of the goblins had already decamped. Only the brave ones or the other creatures were left, and they found themselves exposed without protection, as the Elvenfae mowed them all down as quickly as they could. It seemed the guards that had been taken by the Zeytars were fighting the hardest, as if they wanted to take their frustrations out on something, and it seemed to work as the last of the trolls were cut down. The large contingent of Fae helping the queen was now looking for wounded or dead, never the easy part of any war, especially for such a peaceful race of beings.

Serena was remembering that she mentioned the Toozookus adventures to Shaylee when she first saw her again, but she had only remembered the nice parts. She was being hit hard now by the memories of the war of Maelenflitt all those years ago.

It seemed also that the longer she was back in her old home away from home, the more she was remembering. Only one part would elude her for now and that would be addressed sooner rather than later.

Shaylee was upon Serena shortly after, before they both attended to as many wounded Fae as they could. With Shaylee's potions and some help medically through Serena's nursing skills they kept as many as they could comfortable until they could get them back home. The Elvenfae warriors had the ghastly task of picking up all the deceased and taking them back to the palace.

Shaylee wiped her brow with a bloody hand. Her beautiful long blonde hair was now more purple and black with the blood of all the dark ones. As she picked up Howling Tooth from the ground next to her and wiped the blood from it to put it away, she caught sight of her mother, Tianna. Not thinking of anything else, Shaylee was on her feet and running over to her, shouting her name. As Tianna turned to see who was calling her, their eyes met. Her daughter fell straight into her arms, and they embraced and cried.

Serena stood up, looking over at the two. She thought of Stacey and Eric, and now Shaylee and her mother, two reunions she longed for. Her thoughts then turned to her own family and how she longed to make sure they were safe, even though Wilkes had promised they were. She missed them.

Serena picked up her sword Long Leaf, and as she wiped the rest of the blood from her, Elvenfae warriors were on her in an instant, with at least seven blades inches from her neck. She dropped her beloved sword, which a guard picked up, and without saying a word, she slowly put her hands in the air.

Shaylee and Tianna had finished hugging, and were deep in conversation, though still crying a little, when they were interrupted by a guard who informed them of the prisoner. Shaylee turned, wiping tears from her eyes to look at the disgusting creature they had captured. She realized it was Serena.

She pushed the guard hard and ran to the others who surrounded the prisoner. Shaylee then jumped high into the air, and pulling Howling Tooth out, she landed in front of Serena with the blade to the leader guard's neck. As she inched it closer, she informed them, "Let her go now. She is a hero of this realm and the human realm, and you need to kneel to her, not cut her. Now, the last one to drop their blade will feel mine."

The guards knew Shaylee very well; although none of them were Zeytar captured guards, they were the ones who had been helping her after she returned from her original capture. The blades dropped together with a single clang.

Serena looked up with a smile and softly said, "It's OK, Shay, they were only doing their job protecting your mother."

Shaylee wasn't having that and continued to glare at the guards with a scowl.

Suddenly Serena dropped to the ground in immense pain, screaming, and holding her stomach. Shaylee pushed the guards and warriors out of the way and went to Serena's aid, whispering, "What is it, Serena, have you been hit or attacked?"

Serena shook her head, unable to talk at all, almost crying with the amount of pain she was in. Shaylee didn't know what to do, so she gave her some muttlebark from her satchel which knocked Serena out, and she turned to her mother in desperation. "Mother, this is Serena. She is a good friend, and we have to help her."

Tianna looked at the strange woman. She had seen her on the ship with the others but only thought of her as another human.

"Mother!" screamed out Shaylee.

Tianna finally responded, still staring at the woman, "I am grateful, my dear, but she is a human and no human will ever set foot inside the palace. I'm sorry, I forbid it."

Shaylee was getting angry, as she very quickly educated her mother and queen, "Mother, she is not human, she is a half-blood Fae, half

Elvenfae and half human. I promise I will explain everything, but please, we need to save her now."

As the crowd of Fae gasped, Tianna stared for a moment before raising her hand and nodding for the guards to come and care for her along with the other injured. Shaylee raised her head as tears flowed, then whispered, "Thank you, Mother."

$$\approx$$

Shaylee and Tianna were in the queen's quarters immediately after they returned to the palace while the rest of the warriors summoned the healers to take care of the injured. Tianna was not sure why it needed to be private, but she also had heard whispers of a traitor upon her return.

"Mother, what happened today? Why were we at the edges of Aurora, so close to the palace, battling goblins and dark creatures?"

Tianna did not want to talk about the wars at that moment but would give her daughter a little to satisfy her. Besides, she had been reluctantly put in her place since Shaylee returned. "I will inform you soon, but as far as we are aware, the dark lord Varzunnos is awake and searching for the last Tuatha stone."

Shaylee dropped to her knees. She couldn't get a break from the darkness that life was throwing at her. The once peaceful and playful princess was maturing far too quickly for what she considered normal. She missed her days of training with her friends and being pampered by her maidens, along with escaping palace life and exploring the forests with all the magical creatures.

Shaylee looked up at her mother and asked with a quiver in her voice, "He ... He is awake? If he has three, which one does he need?"

Shaylee was shaking. She wanted so badly for the last to be the palace stone. She was more worried not that the dark lord was awake, but for the safety of the last one, which she thought was theirs.

Her mother responded sternly, "He needs the land stone."

Shaylee was now crying, while the tops of her wings were vibrating at an incredible rate, which must have soon become painful for her. "I have failed, mother. I tried so hard when I returned to protect everyone and now it seems I have let everyone down. I locked the Tuatha tomb after I left, I know I did."

Tianna kneeled and assisted her daughter up and over to a velvet covered red chair. She sat her down and explained, "You have done an exceptional job. Your father would have been proud and so am I. Without you, our Fae, including myself, would not have been saved. You reunited the Seelie Court, and our armies are building as we speak. With Faiay'aar's accounts of her capture we know that Felvora is alive. We now have a chance, as we have moved the last of the Tuatha to the far reaches of Toozookus near the palace of Kalandrya where those sylphs followed and have built a secret location in some willows there. Only you and I know this, but we have sent out false whispers that the stone is in the palace here so that we have the advantage of reprisal and we can fight them off before they get closer. It's dangerous but we have to find the traitor, and I have placed guards and spies everywhere."

Shaylee felt a little better as Tianna continued, "Now, I will fill you in on the rest once you tell me about your friend and why she is here."

Shaylee slowly calmed down. She had never felt emotions like that, ever, which must have still been the residual effects from the Zeytar capture which she thought she was over. But it was not that at all. It was because of the highest amount of stress any sentient being with a heart could deal with, and she had dealt with it astoundingly.

Shaylee looked up, much more level-headed now, and answered her mother, "Alright, Mother, only Faelondar, Maraenor, Jestica, Darlygah, and now you know this, and I would like to keep it that way until we have found the traitor. When Serena was a little girl, she found me near a Sidhe on Ireland realm after I was struck by a human and left out of the portal, far from the beast's control. But I was injured. Serena found me, took me home, and helped heal me. That's when I first learned she must be special. A Zeytar defector motivated me to send her away for a few hours of Earth time, but soon we learned the truth that she was half Elvenfae."

Shaylee paused. She didn't know whether her mother could deal with talk of her husband's betrayals again, but she went on anyway, "She isn't only half Elvenfae, Mother, she is half Aethelwyne. She is Father's daughter."

Tianna didn't bat an eyelid. She had only just learned that Stalixus had perished in the war with the Zeytars, news Shaylee was yet to receive, but this information was huge. A half-blood Fae princess of Aethelwyne's rule. Not only would these details be of enormous value to the traitor, but they would also have a huge impact on her people, who would have to deal with the fact that they had a princess who was half human.

Shaylee continued, "It was Faelondar's blood device that found the truth. Remember that Fae born on Ireland realm? Well, it was her and we couldn't bring her here because the Zeytars had begun their sinister plot."

Tianna was still quiet, holding on to every word Shaylee was saying. "Once I found out, I kept her here longer so I could train her, and eventually she saved my life once more in an earlier battle in Maelenflitt, taking Howling Tooth and killing a dark Elvenfae ready to end me. She became a little hero in Faelynn and everyone adored her. They all knew she was of half Fae, but when I took her back to the Earth realm, I couldn't let anyone know she was of royal blood. So on the off chance something happened to me or you, I had Darlygah build her a sword and with magic fire place the Aethelwyne crest on the pommel, along with the history of Serena's birthright and my markings."

Shaylee was now holding Tianna's hands as she finished, "I'm sorry, Mother, but it gets worse for everyone here. You must have heard that Vyyuna had been slain at Maelenflitt by the goblins?"

Tianna nodded, a sad expression now replacing the more inquisitive one that had covered her face not a moment earlier.

Shaylee kept going, "Well, it was told that a goblin took the Alicorn and lost it somewhere, but ... and please don't be mad with me, but the Alicorn is the handle to Serena's sword Long Leaf."

Tianna stood up in a semi-rage. "What did you say? The Alicorn is attached to a sword? If that got into the wrong hands, the dark lord would have all he needed to destroy Faelynn and turn it to dust without the last treasure."

Shaylee quickly motioned for her mother to sit down as she kept explaining quickly, "Mother, Vyyuna told me to do this to protect it. She has had visions and looking back predicted this. She appeared to me in a ghostly form and helped me with the Tuatha treasure to get a portal to rescue you and she has one more visit before she is returned to the wisps forever."

Tianna had heard about unicorn magic, but not to that extent. She only knew that the power was extraordinarily strong and resided inside the horn. She stood up and replied to everything Shaylee had just explained, "Well ... Firstly, it looks like you have another strong Aethelwyne sister and a trusting one at that if Vyyuna told you to make her keeper of the Alicorn. I will invite her and treat her like I did your other sister. I knew the king, and his infidelities were his weakness. I don't condone any one of them, but he was a great king and father."

Shaylee caught a key word when Tianna was talking about her half-sister Stalixus. "Sorry, Mother, you said 'did' instead of 'do' for my other sister. What do you mean?"

Nothing ever got past Shaylee. She was as sharp as a dagger at times and her mother knew she had to tell her now. "I'm so sorry, Shaylee, she never came home. She must have been killed during a Zeytar mission, and I am so sorry, my dear."

Shaylee's mind started working overtime as she responded to the bad news. "She must have still been on the ship. I must have missed one of the cells where she was kept. I failed her too, Mother."

Shaylee's tears were flowing fast as her mother sat with her, comforting her with wise words, "No, you did not, my precious Shaylee. No, you did not. All who came back were kept in the one cell toward the end, not scattered. They were getting ready to kill all of us and when we all escaped that awful cell, Stalixus was not with us. I even have flashes from time to time seeing the faces of all my Fae, and I cannot remember seeing her for a long time. She is not in my dreams or scattered memories. I am so sorry, Shay."

They embraced for a moment, but soon returned to discussing every gap they needed to fill to bring them both up to date with what had happened in their lives. Then they would devise a plan to bring an end to the dark lord before he ramped his power up even further.

WISDOM

S HAYLEE HAD NOT YET SEEN SERENA. She had spent most of the previous night catching up with her mother, Queen Tianna. She had briefly glimpsed Darphanin, who was a guest at the palace while the skirmishes were taking place. It was a priority to catch up with him, but as soon as she woke very early that next morning she went straight over to the healers.

Shaylee had tried to see Serena late the night before, but they would not let her. Faiay'aar had been summoned without Shaylee's knowledge to Serena's room and it was at her request that the princess was still kept at bay until they had a clearer idea about her condition. Shaylee didn't like it, and she paced up and down the hallway in front of her sister's room for a few hours.

Finally, Faiay'aar opened the door and Shaylee rushed through the doorway, straight over to Serena, who was very groggy.

"Hey, you, how are you feeling?"

Serena tried to talk, but her voice sounded very croaky and weak, "I'm good, Shay."

Before Shaylee could respond, Faiay'aar whispered into Shaylee's ear, "My princess, I am sorry about all of this, but may I have a word outside?"

Shaylee was a little concerned, so without hesitation she followed the wise dryad out into the hallway for what she hoped was good news.

"Shay, I'm not sure what to say here, but the first part is that Serena is pregnant. She is at least three months by our healers' estimates."

Shaylee smiled with a shocked look on her face, thinking, I'm going to be an aunt, before snapping back to reality as Faiay'aar continued, "Now, as good as this news is, we are concerned that the child is developing at an alarming rate. That is why she is in so much pain. Her body, too, seems to be developing more Fae attributes as the child grows—her ears are a little longer and her face seems to be decreasing in age. But the rest of her is struggling to cope with the stretching and growth of the child inside her. I'm afraid that if it continues to grow like this, she may not make it to full term."

Shaylee's excitement was replaced with concern as she asked the mage, "What can we do? How long before she gives birth?"

Faiay'aar answered, "Serena had a time of lucid calmness last night before the pain kicked in again and she mentioned she was with her partner only two or three rotations ago, three Earth days. The bursting into our world and her half blood must have accelerated it, like when we give birth, which is only half a cycle from the time of conception to the birth. But our bodies are designed for that. What I am more scared of is that her human side might not cope with it and the child will eventually kill her."

Shaylee shook her head in response, saying, "No ... No, there must be something we can do. Is there no magic or potion in the mage's room to fix this?"

Faiay'aar lowered her head and responded softly, "I am sorry, Shaylee, this is something that we have not seen before. If Serena had been here from birth, she would have had the enchantment of the Fae, but because of her human side, she just doesn't have enough Fae in her to overcome it. But for you, my princess, I will pull from the archive all relevant information I can find and will stay up night and day if I have to."

Shaylee was too upset. She moved out of Faiay'aar's way and back into the room where Serena was tossing and turning, sweating profusely. Shaylee held a soft towel on her head to comfort her. Eventually, Shaylee fell asleep in an uncomfortable position. She lay there for hours as the other healers attended to more of the wounded, leaving both her and Serena alone and asleep.

Shaylee stirred as she felt she was being pushed from side to side by a slight rocking. As she opened her eyes, she noticed Serena leaning over her and gently nudging Shaylee to gain her attention. She awoke and jumped up. Her wings flew out as if she were going to fly, but it was excitement.

"Shaylee, wake up. Wake up, Shay, and look at me. I'm going to have a baby."

Serena was sitting on her bed, almost bouncing, looking healthy and a little younger. Even her hair had grown a little more, Shaylee thought, as she looked her sister over for injuries. But all she could see was a pregnant woman with a blue silk gown on, excited and happy.

"What is going on, Serena? You were on death's door earlier today and now you are fighting fit and healthy."

Serena was smiling from ear to ear. She soon calmed down and sat quietly though still thrilled as she whispered to Shaylee, "I can't explain it, my body is in its early forties, but I feel like I'm eighteen. The pain is gone, and the baby has slowed down, I can feel it."

Shaylee was confused and weary, so she took Serena's hand and said, "We should see Faiay'aar now, sweetie, just in case."

Serena didn't mind. She was happy to go anywhere, reeling from the realization that she and Eric were going to have a baby. Then it hit her. She was supposed to return to the woods to meet up with Eric straight after taking Shaylee back home. Was he even alive? He was one of the last ones to take on the Leader. Serena's excitement turned into a feeling of devastation at having betrayed him. She needed to get back home immediately.

"Shay, I have to go home. I forgot about Eric! We were meant to be meeting after I escorted you home."

Shaylee wasn't having any of it at that moment. Her health was more important, and Eric would just have to wait. "No, Serena, we must see the mage first. Please, for me."

Serena tried to argue. Her emotions were on another level now. "No! We have to go back. I don't even know if he made it out, Shay."

Shaylee grabbed Serena's hand, knowing she desperately needed to see Faiay'aar, and compromised, "Alright, if you see Faiay'aar, I will send you straight home afterward, deal?"

Serena nodded and squeezed Shaylee's hand.

When they arrived at the mage's chambers soon afterward, Shaylee knocked on the door and entered first to inform her of what was going on. Before long, Faiay'aar was at the door and she led Serena inside.

"OK, Serena, I see you are feeling much better. Why don't you lie here on this table and I will have a look at you."

Serena agreed, and after a thorough examination Faiay'aar gave her diagnosis as best as she could understand it herself. "Well, Serena, you are all good from this end. I believe that your previous visits must have helped your Fae growth when you were young. Your body is transforming more and more into an Elvenfae as your baby grows, to protect you throughout your pregnancy. Now, I cannot say how much you will change or if it will be permanent, but at this stage you are being protected by your child as its blood will help also. The only downfall may be your emotional state, as you will be dealing with both human and Fae hormones, so be mindful about how you are feeling and rest when you need to."

Serena only had one question, and Shaylee was waiting for it. "I am OK to go back home to my world now, aren't I? My partner is waiting for me and I have to get back."

The look on Faiay'aar's face said it all. Serena put her head in her hands and cried uncontrollably while Shaylee comforted her.

"I am sorry, my dear," Faiay'aar said gently, "if you were to leave now, there is no telling if your child would survive, or if you would revert to a more human state, risking your own life. It is better to be safe than sorry."

Shaylee was rubbing her sister's back when she felt some nodules. She lifted up Serena's nightgown and saw four lumps where wings would be on a faery. They hadn't pushed through yet, but it was enough to bring to the mage's attention.

"Like I said to both of you, I do not know to what extent your Fae enchantment will develop. Now get some more rest, Serena, and I will check up on you later in the evening."

They moved swiftly. Serena made it back to her bed and Shaylee comforted her until she went to sleep, after which she left Maraenor to sit with her. Shaylee needed to attend to some other business that involved the upcoming war, as well as organizing something to cheer Serena up with.

≈

Serena was in a deep dream state. She had not had one of her visions since she was a child all those Earth years ago. She started tossing and turning and grumbling in her sleep. Maraenor had gone to her own quarters hours earlier as it was late in the night. Serena was now deep inside her mind. The realistic vision had her lying in pain, screaming. She was giving birth with strange-looking hooded figures surrounding her.

As she stared at the dark hooded creatures, a gray Zeytar appeared, ready to pull the baby from her. As she tried to get away from him, she found she couldn't move at all. The gray turned into the same necro-mage she saw when she was a child. This time there was no help from a female force, and the baby ended up in the arms of the snarling creature.

Serena was tossing and turning hard in bed as her dark visions continued. She managed to get free and snatched her baby from the necro-mage as a white light filled the room and turned all the creatures into dust. Serena looked at her baby who seemed to have heterochromia, one blue eye and one brown eye. She also noticed a birthmark on his left hand in the shape of three directional horns pointing from the center outwards. As she went to give the child a hug, she was thrust back into reality, sitting upright in bed holding her stomach and trying to put together the pieces of what had just happened.

Serena was breathing heavily, enough to wake Shaylee, who had fallen asleep on the floor next to her bed.

"Is everything alright, Serena? You look like you've seen the dark lord himself."

Serena turned to Shaylee. "Close enough, Shay. I think I saw my baby and a Zeytar exactly like Wilkes before it turned into the necro-mage."

They both looked at each other for a moment as Shaylee recounted one of Serena's visions from when she was a child about the gray-looking creature. Then it hit Serena.

"Shay, I remember that vision, and after everything we know about the Zeytars or sinisters, could it be possible that one of the bodiless spirits took the necro-mage as a host? I'm not sure how much you know about them from your time with them as you don't speak about it, but when Wilkes disclosed to us their agenda and history, it was told that the hybrids were built for all the bodiless Zeytar minds. There was a Zeytar in both my visions. I never understood it as a kid because I didn't have the knowledge. Could it have been them from the very start doing all of this?"

Shaylee's eyes were wide open. She started trembling as the thought of those creatures still being here in Faelynn scared her more than anything the dark lord could ever do.

Serena saw her face but continued, "Also, I saw my son. He was born in the dark one's castle and he had a blue eye and a brown one, with a birthmark showing three horns facing outwards. Do you know what this means, Shay ... Shay?"

Shaylee was at first fixated on the Zeytar comment. But when she heard her sister talk about her son being born with heterochromia, Shaylee became very upset. She turned to Serena and whispered, "I think we should get some sleep. We will talk about it in the morning."

With that, Shaylee kissed Serena on the forehead and made her way to her own room. Serena could see she was uncomfortable with that knowledge but would not let it upset her. She was way too weary, anyway, so she lay back down and drifted off to sleep.

Meanwhile, Shaylee was in her own bed. Her eyes were open wide, considering what Serena had just told her. She contemplated getting advice from Faiay'aar in the morning. Also on her mind was Serena's official re-inauguration to the queen's Fae.

Shaylee awoke early. She raced down to the dryad mage's quarters and began bashing the door. Although this was loud, others wouldn't be disturbed, as Faiay'aar's rooms were positioned away from those of the rest of the palace staff. Shortly the door opened.

Faiay'aar looked as though she was expecting Shaylee. She was dressed and ready for the day, with a knowing look on her face. Shaylee shook it off. She didn't understand dryads most of the time, and even though Felvora was one of her best friends, she never questioned their quirky habits or intuitions.

Shaylee stormed inside the room and sat down. Without saying a word, she stared at the floor with her head in her left hand, as her wings fluttered relentlessly as if she were about to have a panic attack. Faiay'aar knew straightaway that something was wrong. Elvenfae usually showed calm under pressure and she had never really seen Shaylee act like this until Serena became pregnant and started having health problems.

"What is it, my princess? I see you are distracted at the moment, and as you are here at such an early time of the day, I can only assume you have something very important to tell me."

Shaylee remained in a trance-like state, thinking hard. She had slept little the previous night and couldn't stop contemplating the harsh reality that the Zeytar sinisters may still be involved. Had Eric not destroyed the ships? And if so, what role did the sinister have on Faelynn?

Faiay'aar tried again, a little sterner in her tone to break Shaylee's concentration but subtle at the same time so as not to upset the Fae princess even more, "Shay, what is the matter, my dear?"

Faiay'aar had her hand on Shaylee's right shoulder and squeezed just a touch, breaking her out of her concentration and into reality to face some truths.

"I'm sorry, Faiay'aar, I need you to help me answer something very troubling to me. Serena has visions when she is in Faelynn. We don't know why she is so sensitive here but she seems more open and connected. One vision she had was when she was a child and it came to pass that it was true—Felvora was trying to reach out from the castle, and when you escaped and confirmed that, it was enough in my mind to believe Serena. There have been others, but the one she had last night has terrified me and I believe it is a sign of things to come."

Faiay'aar sat next to Shaylee as she explained everything about Serena's vision, and related experiences of her captivity with the Zeytars and the tie-in with the bodiless ones. But the part that really struck Faiay'aar the most was the vision of Serena's child with the birthmark shaped like three horns on the boy's hand and the heterochromia.

"This is something else, Shaylee. If what you say is true and this gets out, there will be trouble for her and her son. I have an old book of the Tuatha, handed down to my ancestors from the grand arch mage of old and eventually given to me. I had looked over it quickly when I was a lot younger and in training. The book mostly details the histories of our Tuatha ancestors and how the enchantment was given through symbiosis of the natural life of Faelynn with the treasures, which contribute their essence to the magic of the place. But there were also some prophetic texts in there. The book was written in the old language so it may take me a little while to find anything. Are you happy to wait with me?"

Shaylee nodded as Faiay'aar went and boiled some water. She splashed some flittinberry into a cup and gave it to Shaylee to help her nerves, before hovering up to the highest shelf of the palace library in a room close by. All the important books of Faelynn were kept there, and all the dryads would come to the palace to research or study. Faiay'aar owned several but kept them safe in the library so others could learn the histories as well, but it was a no-go zone for everyday Fae, who were taught potions and the basic magic from other books. Only the learned enchanted ones could study them, the ones with the Tuatha gifts like the dryads, sylphs, and other mages. This was to protect the knowledge and to keep them safe from breaking down. There were no secrets to gaining power or to find the treasures held within them, just details of spells and potions, as well as history.

That was about to change with the book that Faiay'aar had just pulled out from the second shelf of the top tier. She blew hundreds of cycles of dust from the top as she whispered to herself, "Ah, there you are, my oldest friend. It has been a while since I delved into your knowledge."

Faiay'aar floated back down to the ground, and went back to Shaylee, who had calmed down nearly completely. The dryads really knew their stuff, Shaylee thought, as Faiay'aar gave her a little wink and smile.

"Now, let me look at this," the dryad said.

She opened the book on her large table. The pages were ancient and made of the oldest tree parchments. She hovered over sections of the enormous book, flipping through page after page, sliding her long-nailed finger down each section. For a good hour she pored over the text, until she finally found the prophetic section, slowing down as she started to read through it carefully.

Shaylee had fallen asleep after a time. The exhaustion of the previous night had taken hold, along with the drink she'd had, which Faiay'aar hoped it would do.

Another hour rolled by and Shaylee awoke. She slowly stretched her arms and top wings as high as she could, rubbed her eyes, and looked over at the dryad.

Faiay'aar was stone-faced, staring into the space in front of her, with tears on both cheeks. A small smile crept through.

"What is it, Faiay'aar, did you find something?"

The dryad mage didn't even blink. She did not even twitch as the question was asked, but replied swiftly, "Have a guard summon the queen immediately. This cannot wait at all. Then meet me back here as soon as you can with only you and your mother. Tell no one, not even the council about this meeting, do you understand?"

Shaylee was quite shocked by the response, and before she could answer, the dryad broke from her trance and turned her head to face Shaylee, repeating with haste, "Do you understand?"

Shaylee nodded. She had never seen Faiay'aar like that before. She wasn't like Felvora, she was more soft and caring, but there was something in her voice that showed she meant business. So Shaylee bounced to her feet, ran to a guard, and requested the queen's immediate attendance for a private matter. She didn't give away anything as she knew nothing as yet, but it was important not to bring unwanted attention to it. So Shaylee added it was to do with the care of a patient who was wounded in battle.

The guard took off down the hall and over to the other side of the palace where the queen had just finished freshening up to begin her day.

The queen arrived not long after she got the message. Not a word was spoken between Shaylee and Faiay'aar in that time, as Shaylee knew enough about protocols to realize that if the queen was being summoned, it was not for something trivial, and all would be explained.

When the queen entered with two guards and a maiden, Faiay'aar was quick to dismiss the others. "Please, Your Highness, may we talk alone just for a moment. It's about one of the patients and I would like to respect her privacy."

Tianna waved her hand, and the entourage left immediately. As the door closed behind them, Faiay'aar raced over and reopened it, checking down the halls in both directions. She saw the last of the maiden's gown disappear around the corner of the hallway of heavy stone.

She swiftly re-entered the room and closed the door, locking it behind her. "I am so sorry, Your Highness, but Shaylee and I have discovered something of the utmost importance, and it cannot wait, not one more second, for your attention."

Tianna sat, quite puzzled but interested at the same time. She replied to the dryad's strange comment, "Please, Faiay'aar, call me Tianna. You know that when there is no one around formalities go out the door. Now, we have been friends and allies for a very long time, and I have never seen you like this, so please enlighten me. By the look on both your and Shaylee's faces it must be very important indeed."

Faiay'aar couldn't even smile for her old friend, not until she gave

Shaylee some bad news first. So she sat them together in a comfortable position so they could comfort each other, and then she herself sat back on the chair in front of her large Tuatha Dé Danann book. She had some good and not so good news to tell her queen.

"Before I start, I want to warn you, especially you, Shaylee, that the content I am about to discuss may be quite disturbing. It is also of the utmost secrecy and this book must be protected at all times. If there is a traitor here, then we cannot let it get into their hands as it would counteract any kind of chance we have to save our people, are we clear?"

Faiay'aar had never spoken to the queen in such a tone, nor Shaylee, but she knew her worth in the palace and that if she said it was important, they would also think it was. But after hearing what she had to say there would be no debate on the subject anyway.

"OK, Faiay'aar, you are scaring me a little," said Shaylee, quivering. She swallowed hard and breathed a little heavier than before.

"Shay, it's OK, I just need you to explain to your mother the visions that Serena has had and everything you told me about this morning."

Shaylee nodded, and as hard as it was to go there again, she knew it would all be worth it if Faiay'aar had some good news for them. So she explained the lot up to the part when the dryad started researching the old book. The look on Tianna's face was blank. She was now in a trance, with flashbacks of her time with the destructive Zeytars. The thought of it was still very raw for her as she had spent far more time with them than Shaylee had and she had only recently been saved. As her face turned a pale white, Shaylee noticed something in her mother that she had never seen before, and that was anxiety. Her wings fluttered at the tops ever so slightly, enough to give her feelings away but not enough to show pure fear; at least not yet.

Faiay'aar had pre-empted her reaction so had made some more of her special flittinberry tea for the queen and another for Shaylee, this time without the sleepy additive she gave her beforehand. She handed the tea to them both and sat back at her table with the book opened to the exact page so she could read it out perfectly with no confusion about interpretation.

"Remember, this is ancient original Tuatha Dé Danann text, so my translation may seem wrong, but it will be as it's intended.

"To thee our dream, in sequence we scream.
The dark one awakens; a child will be taken.
With marks on thy hand, three Alicorn will stand.
Of human in blood, of Tuatha in blood
Two eyes look apart, two colors they start.
With the wisps' horn to powder, with the blood mixed in prouder.
With this spell you call, the dark one will fall.
The dust of the dark will rejuvenate the bark."

Shaylee and Tianna looked at each other, then back at the mage with a very puzzled expression on both of their faces. Faiay'aar knew they would be confused, so she broke it down for them both, "This is ancient and from the early Tuatha Dé Danann prophets, when some of our kind had not yet been born, so with the visions of Serena and the translation to modern Fae times I will explain it as best I can. First, we see 'to thee our dream, in sequence we scream,' meaning more than one had the visions and this was before the dark one, so it would have been quite shocking. The second one speaks for itself but, Shaylee, the child is Serena's unborn son. The three horns are that of the Alicorn; half human, half Tuatha Dé Danann, which are our ancestors. Two different eye colors and the wisps created the unicorn, so with the powder of an Alicorn, mixed with her son's blood, and finally the old spell written here in Tuatha Dé Danann we can bring down the dark lord and all his armies, as the last part mentions a rejuvenation after the dust of the dark has settled."

Shaylee knew what had to be done, but she was not happy about it. Knowing Serena had to go to the dark lord's castle was just too much for her to deal with at that stage. She knew Serena was very strong; she had known that since the day she met her, so that was not the issue. The problem in her mind was how she would fare after her son was born—would she have the strength to make the journey so soon after giving birth—and her vulnerability, as she would be the main target of all the dark ones.

Shaylee took it better than Faiay'aar had expected, while Tianna had a smile on her face. She did not have the connection to Serena that Shaylee did. Obviously, she did not want to put her stepdaughter in danger but was happy there was finally some good news to plan for.

"You are right, my old friend, we must let no one else know this, especially Serena. We will start making plans for after the baby is born to travel to Xarkynan with our entire army of Fae, including those from the Seelie Court, the far lands, the Misty Isles and the islands beyond. I will put out the call. When do you foresee Serena giving birth?"

Faiay'aar responded swiftly, as if she'd been awaiting the question, "I expect her to give birth in the next quarter to half a cycle. But, my queen, we have yet one thing that goes against everything in this prophecy. The last unicorn was Vyyuna, and she has been gone for a long time. We lost the Alicorn in the battle of Maelenflitt and we need it to fulfill the prophecy."

Tianna did not like to give too much away with her expressions; it made for an effective leader to keep people guessing. But she had a tiny smile on her face as she replied to the dryad's question, "Leave that to me, Faiay'aar. I will take care of that part. Now I must leave you all to prepare. Shaylee, watch out for your ... I meant, watch out for Serena. The festivities will be this afternoon. Hide that book, Faiay'aar."

And just like that, Queen Tianna took all her new knowledge and swiftly exited the room, leaving Shaylee a little shaken but better than she was earlier that day. She still didn't want to have to deal with any more Zeytars, but Serena was her number one priority from that point on. She hugged the mage and thanked her before walking out the door, leaving Faiay'aar on her own with the book. The dryad hadn't read any further, thinking that was all she needed, and she slammed it shut and wandered out of her room to check on some injured Fae.

Minutes later a shadow swept across the dimly lit hallway, revealing a dark hooded figure entering it. Hunched over, he made his way to Faiay'aar's door, trying the handle with a rattle and finding it locked.

The figure pulled out a large key and turned it gently. He made his way into the room, took the heavy book, and then disappeared into the shadows once more, leaving the door wide open.

A LEAK OF
TRUST

SERENA HAD NO IDEA ABOUT THE CEREMONY. She clearly remembered her special function all those cycles ago where she received Long Leaf. She had felt very welcomed by all those who attended and was overly excited to see the friends she had ventured with to Toozookus and Maelenflitt.

As she was getting into a gown that fit her pregnant frame, she reminisced about those days in her mind, smiling at the memory of Van Coinan performing his usual antics and the thought of the elf boy from the woodlands. What was his name again? she pondered. Ah, Chaxinn, that's right. I wonder what he is up to now and what he looks like? she thought. The memories kept flooding in.

Her pain had now completely subsided. She felt like she could run on the walls and swing off the ceiling, but that was not a good idea and she knew it.

As the maidens finished with her hair, they began snickering behind her back. Serena was feeling a little awkward, so turned around and retorted with a gruff, "Is there something on my person that amuses the both of you?"

Serena usually had Maraenor or Jestica help her on such occasions, but they were busy attending to the queen and to Shaylee. Serena looked at them sternly, awaiting a response before one of them quipped, "I'm sorry, but you look ridiculous as half a faery, nubs for wings, and low pointed ears that look like those of the forest elves. We don't mean any disrespect, but half-blood Fae don't belong here and never will."

The ignorance of the maidens, who were incredibly young and had been picked to help from the lower township, shocked Serena. Was that what they were all saying? Was she an aberration? Like one of Anders' lab creations? Thoughts kept coming fast. She knew her people, humans, were mean and intolerant, but she had only ever felt love and acceptance in Faelynn, not a feeling of hate or stereotyping like in her world.

Serena's anger grew as the maidens continued their prejudiced attacks on her. She rose high into the air of the room, with four amazingly colored wings that had shot out of her back, tearing holes in the freshly sewn up gown altered for her. She fluttered in place, without really being aware what she was doing, too fixated on the ones mocking her, as she snapped, "Do I not look like a Fae to you? I have been trained by the best here in your lands. I have ridden the last of the unicorns, slain goblins next to your warriors, and spilled my blood, sweat, and tears saving your people. You owe your lives to me for saving your queen and your world from the destruction of the sinisters and you stand before me laughing and mocking me? You are no better than the foul creatures that spawn from the depths of Xarkynan. Now go, before I do something I will regret."

The two young maidens stood in shock for a moment before running out of Serena's room in tears. Serena lowered herself down. Her wings were enormous, many inches longer than Shaylee's, and the colors seemed to come in and out with different lighting and mood. She looked in the mirror and noticed her ears had grown to full Elvenfae size. There was nothing about her that would differ from any other Fae now.

Shaylee stormed into the room, alerted by all the commotion, and was instantly mesmerized by Serena's wings, which she caught sight of for a few moments before they retracted into her sister's back, concealed and out of sight.

"What was that, Serena? Did I just see wings on you?" Shaylee seemed to be more excited than Serena as she continued with the questioning. "What just happened? I heard screaming and crying ...?" Before Shaylee finished her barrage of questions, it hit her hard like a troll's punch. "Serena, where are your wings now?"

Serena looked behind her on both sides, and then with a single thought from her they shot out from her back, waving in the air again. Shaylee fell to her knees. She knew something that Serena obviously did not. "Shay, they were being so mean to me, calling me a fake Fae and that I did not belong here. I have never felt so unwanted in all my life, and in a fit of anger I was in the air with my wings out and giving them a spray of my Fae history. That's when they ran out. Is that what everyone thinks of me? Do they all hate me so much because of my human side?"

Shaylee wanted to get to some key questions she needed answers to, but she had to ease Serena's mind first. "Oh no, Serena, not at all. Humans and half-blood Fae are looked upon as outsiders, especially humans. No one knows who you are. They all think you got caught up in the fight so whispers have been floating around that that's the reason we are having this ceremony. Those young ones are just as afraid of you as you are of them. Please, we all love you and once they all find out, they will all remember you and accept you."

Serena sat on the end of the bed. With a face towel she dabbed her eyes where some tears were about to form. Not wanting to mess up her freshly painted makeup, she fought hard to hold them off, as she continued to explain, "Shay, I have never reacted like that, ever. It was like this confidence and anger came through to let them have it. You know me; I am usually the passive, clear-headed one that defuses situations. Do you think it's my child again, protecting me?"

Shaylee stood back up, moved over to the bed, and sat next to Serena. "I think you still have a lot to learn about faeries, especially Elvenfae. We are a fierce race of creatures. Passionate, loving, but fierce and brave at the same time, so when something comes along that threatens that, we react as our genetically perfect, enchanted selves. Your child must already know this and is helping bring all your Fae side out."

Serena smiled. She felt much better after talking to Shaylee, as she always did. Shay had a way about her much like her own compassionate self. A sharp flash hit her then, a foggy memory of her and Shaylee talking, but only a few words came through before it vanished, with another flash coming into her mind—the words were Aethelwyne, sister and father.

"Are you alright, Serena?" Shaylee whispered as Serena came to.

"Yes ... I think so. Since my return, I feel like there is still a piece missing, and that there is some information I am yet to learn."

Shaylee knew exactly what she was trying to say and quickly passed it off. "I am sure it's nothing, Serena. You will experience more and more the longer you are here. Now, getting back to your wings, which are quite mighty and elegant—but do you know what it means to have retractable wings?"

Serena shook her head. Of course I don't, she thought, and I only just got them.

"It means you are the direct bloodline ..." Shaylee stopped herself. If she had continued, she would have given away the only secret she was trying to keep from her at that moment, so she redirected it swiftly. "Sorry, I meant the blood from your Fae child must be strong."

Serena glanced at Shaylee. She knew she was holding back, with that look in the pools of her blue eyes, with their long dark lashes blinking excessively. Serena let it go for now; she knew she could catch up later. She felt better anyway, so she put on her nice shoes and followed Shaylee out the door, her wings folded down and showing, to cover up the gaping holes in the back of her purple and red gown.

≈

The ceremony began without a hitch. Serena saw many familiar faces, but she couldn't quite make some out. As she entered the main ballroom, she was gently grabbed on her left arm by a hand which then pulled her backward ever so slightly. Serena turned to thump the rude person in the face and as her fist came up in reaction, the offender counteracted and held her fist in his large hand. She was met with a cheeky smile when she looked up at him.

"That old move. You're so predictable, Serena," he said.

As the attacker finished his quip, Serena had the large Elvenfae warrior twisted in three moves and on the floor with her knee on his jugular. "Did you predict that? Hey?" she said.

Serena took her knee from his neck. The room was in gasps and whispers as she helped the very tall Elvenfae up and hugged him, exclaiming at the same time, "Marlifyn, oh I have missed you! You look old...er."

Serena smirked as her former trainer responded, "Hey, I only started aging when I began training you."

They both laughed and reminisced as the crowd slowly began settling back to normal. It wasn't a regular sight at a ceremony to see sparring or physical violence, but they were all aware that she was a special guest.

Soon it became known throughout the ceremony through whispers that it was Serena, little Serena from long ago. She hadn't even made it to the center of the room to catch up with Shaylee and the queen when she became inundated with old friends she had not seen since she was a child. Guards, warriors, sprites, and gnomes, woodland elves, old and young, and other faces she recognized but couldn't put names to.

Shaylee was smiling as she watched her sister being happy and content for a moment, a moment she knew would not last when the baby was born—but she would not let that dampen her fun this day.

Time went on and Serena was dancing with some Fae children. As she looked up, a hand was awaiting her for the next dance. Confused a little, she looked deep in the woodland elf's eyes and realized without saying a word it was Chaxinn. She took his hand and stared into his eyes, reminiscing about the times she was with him, observing the stars. He was a young adult now and very handsome. They talked for ages about the old times and how they had both found love and were each starting families. Chaxinn had two young elf boys who were already on their way to becoming warriors like their father and grandfather Darphanin.

Serena continued catching up with all those she had missed and new ones she was meeting. None of them gave any sign of hate or resentment in their minds, as Serena's name was quite revered after she left as a child, and the stories had grown over time of a young half-blood Fae warrior. Serena was just about to spend the rest of the night with Shaylee and Queen Tianna when the two young maidens approached her, curtsied, and in unison apologized to her for the way they had acted earlier on that day. They had gone home and asked their parents about what she had said, and the parents explained that if what the two young sisters were describing was correct, then they had just upset the great Serena, so they were made to apologize.

Serena leaned down and whispered that they were forgiven but to be mindful of how they treated those different from them or who were from other places. The girls smiled, and they took off to their table where their parents were seated.

As Serena was about to move to her seat, after hearing the first warning bell that indicated dinner would be served shortly, something jumped up and grabbed her around the neck. She could feel claws digging gently into her skin as the offender spoke, "Your hair is putrid. Do you ever put mud or dirt in it to clean it?"

Serena reached around, felt the fur on her palm, and started crying. "That's the most awful thing anyone has ever said to me. What kind of creature would do that to a pregnant woman?"

As she finished, the creature jumped down from her shoulders and stood in front of her. As she continued to sob, she opened one eye to see where he was, before sobbing harder, as the creature replied, "Oh, Serena, I'm so sorry. I didn't mean to upset—"

Before he could finish, Serena stood up, pointed her finger straight at him, and said, "Ah-ha, I can still get you, Van Coinan, snotty nose and stinky breath, I can still get you."

Van Coinan looked shocked for a moment. He was out of the game for a while, as it hit him who he was talking too. He jumped up into the air, and Serena grabbed him and hugged him hard, before whispering, "I missed you the most, but not your butt, smelly tail."

Van Coinan and Serena laughed as she slowly made her way to her seat near Shaylee. Van Coinan ran off while she sat down and awaited the queen's speech.

The second bell echoed down the halls, indicating to everyone to be seated. There were many from the Seelie Court invited this day as well, as many were at the battle and were helping with the armies. Queen Tianna stood up and started her opening speech. This was also the start of the second great war—the first was when King Viltherome and his armies, along with the dryads, took down the dark lord and his dragon long ago—this being the second to save not only their lives but the magic of Faelynn itself.

"I am here today proud and happy because of two people, one of them being an exceptional player in this whole war. This young woman sitting before us, half in blood of human and of Fae, saved my Shaylee twice, once from the destructive Zeytars, or sinisters as you still call them, and once again on the battlefield near Maelenflitt. The two then formed plans and although Shaylee was here defending Faelynn, she was also looking for ways to free all our people. Over time they both risked everything to save many of us from the dark clutches of the sinister Zeytars.

"Serena is and always will be one of us. We will continue to write of her in our histories, and she will be welcome forever more. With the selfless acts you have performed for both your people, human and Fae, and in recognition of this, I have your beloved sword to return to you."

The guests clapped and stood, cheering as she received her polished up, beloved Long Leaf back. Smiling from ear to ear, the queen held her hands up as Serena stood before her. "Now, I ask one more thing of you. Will you help us fight the dark ones before you return to your other home?"

Shaylee was a little shocked at the question, especially putting her sister on the spot in front of hundreds of guests. But Serena's face said it all. She was not worried about picking up a sword and helping if her baby was safe. "Of course, my queen, it would honor me."

The crowd cheered again as Serena made her way back to her seat. She noticed from the corner of her eye that Stexinzar was yelling at one of the warrior guards, but she couldn't quite get the reason for it. Not thinking anything more about it, she sat back down. Then she saw Shaylee's now worried face. Am I missing something? she thought.

As the luncheon was in full swing, many Fae danced, flying in unison, gnomes drank heavily and practiced how hard they could punch each other before drinking again, and even the not so merry ones line-danced to the band's ancient-style music.

Serena sat back and smiled, closing her eyes and clearing her mind. It would be the last clear moment she would have in a long time.

Suddenly Faiay'aar stormed into the ballroom. She had been out of her quarters since she locked the door earlier in the day, helping the injured be ready to sit back and enjoy some festivities. When she returned to find some more potions and noticed the door open and the book gone, she immediately came to see the queen.

"My queen, we need to talk. We need to talk right now."

Shaylee saw Faiay'aar's face and direct contact with Tianna so moved in to hear what was going on.

Meanwhile, Serena was busy pulling lettuce leaves from Van Coinan's whiskers and stuffing them behind his ears.

"Come, this way," said Tianna. "We will go to my dressmaker's quarters behind us. It is private, and you can tell me there."

Faiay'aar and Shaylee followed the queen, and they weren't even noticed as they quickly exited the ballroom.

In the meantime, Serena was feeling drained, the exhaustion slowly hitting her as her mind started getting foggy and all she wanted to do was sleep. Van Coinan was off playing with some gnome children now and she decided to go back to her bedroom to get some rest, thinking such a big day was all too much for her and the baby.

While Serena disappeared around the corner heading to her

quarters, Shaylee was asking Faiay'aar what was happening, "What is it, Faiay'aar?"

Shaylee seemed more concerned than the queen, but that would be short-lived. "The book is gone. I locked the door when I left my quarters and upon arrival not long ago to retrieve some potions, I found the door wide open, and the book was gone."

The queen's wings turned red, and so did her face, but she was still calm enough to get the rest of the story before blowing her top. "You hid the book, did you not?"

Faiay'aar shook her head slowly before answering, "No, my queen, I shut the door and left it on the table. I figured it would be safe there. I am so sorry."

Tianna stared for a moment. Her wing color started becoming lighter as she was lost in thought for a moment. Then with a spark of ideas, she said to the dryad mage, "I saw Felvora once look up an event through a time spell—extremely hard to do and only possible from the recent energy that had been there, but it was clear enough to see for a moment. Do you have the ability to do this?"

Faiay'aar thought for a few seconds before nodding. "Yes, I believe I can do this, but we must be quick. As the energy fades, so too does the vision."

The three of them left the room through a back hallway and made it to the other side of the palace where the dryad mage's quarters were. They entered the room, and Faiay'aar began putting together some odds and ends into a small bowl. She boiled some water and pulled a round crystal out from beneath her bottom drawer; the crystal was clear but had an opening on the top. She mixed the ingredients, poured the water in with them, and mashed it all into a watery red paste.

Tianna and Shaylee knew not to disturb a dryad while they performed stronger spells, so they stood back but close enough to watch. Faiay'aar poured the liquid into the small opening at the top of the crystal and as she waved her hands around, she began speaking an enchantment that not even the two royals could understand.

Before long the red liquid paste began swirling inside the crystal. As she continued to say the words and fold her fingers around it, images started flashing bright then dull, the red turned to gray, and as the liquid turned, the images become stronger. Shaylee yelled out in excitement, "Look, Mother, it's us from this morning."

The two moved closer as the dryad mage continued with her enchantment spell, before a last flash, and then she stopped. They were now watching the earlier moments of the day getting up to when the queen and Shaylee left. They continued watching, as the scene showed Faiay'aar closing the book and walking out, locking the door. Moments later a hooded figure entered. It walked over to the book, picked it up, and looked up for a few seconds, giving this new audience a glimpse of its twisted, blurry face, before walking back to the door. Just before it exited, Shaylee screamed out, "Stop! Look right there, it's an Elvenfae sword at the side. I recognize the hilt, and there on the feet ... Only a guard leader warrior wears that kind of sword and that kind of armor."

Shaylee fell to the floor in shock. She was quivering and moaning over and over, "No, not him ... Not him."

Shaylee kept repeating it as Tianna lowered herself down to her level, looked her in the eyes, and whispered, "Who? Tell me, Shaylee, you must, who?"

Shaylee turned to her mother and returned her gaze. Still quivering, she whispered, "Stexinzar. The traitor is Stexinzar."

As the revelation hit them both, Shaylee jumped to her feet and shouted, "Serena!"

With her sword in hand, Shaylee tore out of the room and along the halls to the other end of the palace where the ceremony was still in full swing. Before she could reach the entrance to the ballroom, she was stopped by a sight that would shake her to the bone. Near the doorway to the ballroom was another door that led downstairs to a courtyard where the cooks and maidens would have breaks from the business of the festivities. It wasn't used often, but as Shaylee looked upon a torn section of purple fabric, she knew it had been used recently.

The color matched Serena's dress, which made Shaylee's concern turn to anger as she opened the door. As the small section of Serena's ballgown fell to the floor, Shaylee noticed Long Leaf, half unsheathed and lying mid-way down the stairwell. She fluttered swiftly down the semi-lit stairs, picked up Serena's beloved sword, and continued out into the courtyard. Once there, she took in the full view of her surroundings with her sister nowhere in sight, and shouted at the top of her voice, "Serena!" Over and over she yelled, until she fell onto her knees, sobbing as she clutched her sister's Long Leaf.

Tianna had seen the open door and descended the stairs to meet her daughter. Clutching her tight, she whispered, "We will find her, my dear, I promise."

Shaylee looked up at Tianna and answered in anger, "I want Stexinzar's head and that of any other Fae who helped him. This is war."

The queen nodded, helping Shaylee up off the ground, and ascending back to the top of the staircase. As they entered the ballroom, the guests could see the distress in both of their faces. Tianna approached the lectern to inform everyone of the latest deceits.

"My people and special Seelie Court members, I have some disturbing news that cannot wait for the council's notification. One of our own trusted members of the palace and guard has been deceiving us. Stexinzar Crimsonmoon is the traitor we have been looking for. He has taken some particularly important information from us, along with our beloved Serena. I am taking this time to let each one of you know that we are all in extreme danger and to put a call out to all of your able Fae warriors, as we are officially now at war and will leave for Xarkynan in the next few days to finish off the dark lord before the dark ones finish us."

She paused and cast her gaze around the room at all the faces turned toward her.

"There will be two contingents. The first will be the able warriors, guards, fighters, and the brave which will leave with me as soon as we can gather an army. Then there will be the second contingent which will be for the ones who need time to travel to join us. I will inform Faiay'aar to commune with Kalandrya and to try to find Felvora if she is still alive. I will send birds to each section of Faelynn to call upon the second contingent. I hope this will save time."

As gasps, cries and moans came from the guests and workers alike, Tianna finished her speech, "I repeat, everyone, Faelynn is officially at war with Xarkynan for the first time in a thousand cycles. Now go and prepare."

DARK PROPHECY

SERENA WOKE UP DAYS LATER. THE SEDATIVE the warrior guard had given her had been strong enough to knock her out for the entire journey. She looked around and tried to gather her whereabouts. Still groggy, she rubbed her engorged belly to feel if her baby was still OK. After a kick and some movement she felt somewhat relieved. But she was having trouble remembering anything about what had happened and why she was in a dark, wet prison cell.

The last thing Serena remembered was receiving Long Leaf from the queen and entertaining Van Coinan. She had no idea that Stexinzar was responsible for drugging her and bringing her to the dark lord's castle. It was the last place in the world that she would want to be when her baby was born, but that information was yet to be delivered to Serena. At this stage she thought she had fallen asleep from exhaustion in a cell of the palace. I don't drink that much, and I certainly haven't since I found out I was pregnant, Serena kept thinking to herself.

She hobbled to her feet and walked over to the thick black bars that were holding her inside. She gave a tug on the cell door. Suddenly a dark goblin dressed in rusted armor whacked her fingers with the pommel of his sword while shouting, "Oi, get away from there! You ain't gettin outta here so sit back down."

Serena yelled out in pain as she fell back onto the thick grass hay. She rubbed her hand and stood up once more, and then advanced to the cell door. "Where am I and what have you done with my friends?"

Serena was becoming very frightened. She tried not to show it at all, as she knew now that she was somewhere far from the palace of Faelynn.

The dark goblin answered, "You are far from your friends here, my pretty one. Now, if you don't get back, I'm gonna come in there and teach you some respect." As the goblin finished spitting out his sentence, he struck the metal cell bars harder this time with the blade, leaving a spark to light a tiny part of the cell for just a moment.

Serena slowly shifted back. She kept her eyes on the dark goblin guard, moving away ever so slowly until she hit the end of the cell. She leaned back as far away from the goblin as she could. Serena then felt a cold, clammy hand reach through the bars and grab her legs. Jumping in fright, Serena screamed out, "Who are you, what do you want from me?"

The owner of the clammy hand answered, "You are in Xarkynan, my pretty one, and you will be meat for our meal before too long."

Serena tried to get a fix on the other creature. It was far too dark for her to see but she could sense that it was something ugly and horrendous. Its voice was coarse and deep, making Serena shift back toward the cell door. At least she knew what goblins looked like up close.

She sat and pondered the creature's words for the next little while, wondering how she could have wound up in Xarkynan. Eventually Serena cried herself to sleep from the aftereffects of the drug she had been given all those days ago.

≈

Wyrm had given the dark mage the book he had stolen from Faiay'aar. He could turn back to an Elvenfae form if he wanted to, but did not trust the necro-mage's appetite. Viltzin'un'dandaar had a taste for faeries—not dark Elvenfae but fresh Fae from the bright lands. He had told Wyrm that frequently, and Stexinzar did not want to risk it, so he kept his changeling appearance, at least for now.

"You have done extremely well, Wyrm. You have proven yourself to me and to the dark lord many times now, and you will be rewarded."

Stexinzar wanted a part of Faelynn to rule for himself, that's all he ever wanted, and if he could get just a small place to rule, even just goblins, as long as he was in charge, he would be thrilled. But he was always too frightened to ask. With the new information that he had just relayed to Viltzin, he thought now would be the best time to do so.

"My master, considering what I have done for you and considering the information you now have, along with the woman and her child, would it be too much to ask for a small piece of Faelynn to rule when the bright Fae have been destroyed? I only want to rule a small kingdom, nothing too lavish."

Viltzin looked down his nose past the book he had been handed and stared into Wyrm's eyes. He then brought his eyes down to the book once more and continued reading as if he had not been interrupted at all.

Wyrm spoke once more, "Please, master, I—"

Before Wyrm could finish, Viltzin snapped the book shut and leaned over the trembling changeling, dribbling dark fluid over Wyrm's face. The dark mage had a snarling expression on his face as he whispered, "I will make you the king of sewage drains if you interrupt me one more time."

Wyrm was shaking. He knew it was not a good time as he started moving backward and out of the room, with the dark mage still staring at him with frightening red eyes and the snarl on his face until he was completely out of sight. Wyrm turned and ran along the hallway and down the stairs.

Viltzin reopened the book once more. He studied the part where a child would restore the world and rid it of darkness multiple times, but he had learned after waking the dark lord not to give him news that was not constructive to his cause. Having the child and the book meant that the queen could not use them on the dark lord. But he would not give up on an alternative.

The dark mage spent the next hour reading, but it wasn't until he turned the page past the original section he was studying—something Faiay'aar had missed doing—that he stumbled on something which made his dark red eyes glow and the green amulet on his chest sparkle. He snapped the book shut and headed for Varzunnos' throne room to discuss something of utmost importance.

Viltzin lowered his head as he slowly entered the dark lord's chambers. He was excited but was always wary of his master's moods. If the ideas and plans did not suit him, then he would unleash his fury, which was not pretty. Viltzin had been surprised a few times before, but deep down he knew this information would prove to be what was needed to finish the whole war and destroy the Fae along with their perfect way of life, all while Viltzin planned his own takeover.

"What have you found for me? It better be good after the failed attempt on the palace recently. Do you have more goblins and dark beasts from the forest to build back some forces lost?"

The dark lord had punished Viltzin, though not to the extent of some of the warriors that made it back from the Fae defeat. There were a few still hanging upside down, with metal nails through their ankles to swing from, in the dungeons. Viltzin did not want to be the next casualty of Varzunnos' bad temper, so continued to find solutions and tread very carefully.

"My lord, I have something even better, which will finish Faelynn for good. You will walk into the crumbling Elvenfae palace as it falls and take the last of the Tuatha treasures for yourself."

Varzunnos didn't even blink. He knew he had enough power behind him to take it anyway but wanted to make them all suffer slowly and painfully. His next attack would come soon, and once he had replenished his army some more, he was going to storm the palace and take it himself. He was just hesitant about the dryads and that's why he needed more troops—to distract them while he entered the palace. But for now he was happy to wait and see what his sniveling necro-mage could come up with.

"Enlighten me with this newfound knowledge you have unearthed; keep in mind I am in no mood for time wasters."

Viltzin lowered his head as the hood from his unwashed cloak fell forward, covering most of his face. Flicking it back behind his neck with haste, he placed the comprehensive book down onto an oak table in front of the dark lord. Viltzin made eye contact for a moment, noticing Varzunnos' face change from anger to a more inquisitive look.

"What is this you have before me? It looks like it's Tuatha Dé Danann."

Varzunnos stood up and made his way closer to the table, as Viltzin opened the book to the pages of the prophecy and explained what Wyrm had told him. He started rereading the passages and interpreting them before realizing that Varzunnos was of Tuatha Dé Danann and could read perfectly himself.

As the dark lord took the book and processed what the Elvenfae were up to, he burst into laughter and pushed the book away, leaving Viltzin with a desperate wince of confusion.

"What is it, my lord, have I not shown you—"

Varzunnos interrupted the necro-mage as he wound down his laughter to a snicker. "You bring me nothing here—prophecy from the start of our kind, nothing more than a vision from an old bored Tuatha mage. Besides, there are no more Alicorns or unicorns, so how were they going to fulfill such a foolish idea."

Varzunnos turned and started making his way back to his throne as Viltzin pulled the book back toward him and continued, "But, master, you need to let me finish."

Varzunnos turned and howled down at his necro-mage, spit and drool hanging from his teeth and lips, "I told you not to waste my time! If you are still here when I turn around, I will have you hanging with the wretched warriors in the dungeons."

Viltzin was shaking. He needed to explain the rest of the prophecy but didn't want to upset the already edgy dark lord. He knew he wouldn't get another chance, so took a massive risk and raised his voice along with illuminating his amulet before continuing, "My lord, hear me out now, this is your last chance to understand me before the Fae take control."

Viltzin knew the Fae would retaliate, so bravely blurting that out made Varzunnos take notice. Before his master could react, Viltzin had the next page open and started reading, slowing the dark lord down until Viltzin had his undivided attention, "My lord, from the interpretation and from my sources it is said that under a blood moon, in the presence of three powerful mages or enchanted ones, a child born of two-colored eyes will be sacrificed. Taking his blood along with his mother's while laying a flayed Fae wing over the Tuatha treasure stones, a spell must be spoken as the blade of old-world steel is driven deep into his heart. All this must happen when the moon reaches its apex. This will turn all light into darkness, creating a world of twisted creatures and barren wastelands."

The dark lord sat up. "Where would we find such a child and how could we get them here before the blood moon you speak of ascends into the sky?"

Viltzin smiled, he knew he had him now and the knowledge he was about to share would seal his fate. "My lord, we have her, here and now, in your dungeon. One of my Elvenfae spies has been sharing secrets and took her and the book before anyone noticed."

Varzunnos stood up and with a bellow that emanated throughout the halls of the castle demanded her presence immediately. Viltzin rubbed his long, pointed ears. He had never heard such a loud voice before. He bolted out of the dark lord's quarters and out into the hallway where he was met by two goblins.

"Quickly, bring the woman with child from the lower dungeons here to me now. Do not harm her or I will cut off your heads and hang them out the highest windows for the crows to feed off, do you understand me?"

And with that the two scurried along the hallway and deep down into the belly of the castle, descending to the darkness of the dungeons.

Viltzin returned to the dark lord's throne room. He was seated and staring at the doorway, waiting in anticipation of his new guest. The necro-mage approached Varzunnos as they waited for the goblins to return.

Varzunnos had one question for his dark mage, and that was enough to wipe the smile off the once more nervous creature, "So, do you have everything in place? I have read the prophecy myself and it states that everything must be used in succession for the spell to work. Now, enlighten me with your plan."

Viltzin swallowed hard. His throat was dry as he tried to speak. The nerves took hold, and he croaked the first few words before relaxing a little into his eventual response. "My lord, we have the key ingredient. If the prophecy is true, the child will be born with heterochromia along with the birthmark. We know them to be half-blood Fae from Wyrm, my spy. There is a blood moon in five days' time, so if the child is not born, we will rip it out. We are two of power, and I will hunt down a dark witch from the forest to assist if need be. The only two ingredients we need are an Elvenfae wing and steel from the old world to fulfill the prophecy. We have three Tuatha and it doesn't stipulate how many, it just states Tuatha treasures, so we nearly have a complete fulfillment."

Varzunnos sat there, silent for a moment, taking in what his necro-mage had just explained, before he stood up, lifted his sword and thrust it down hard within inches from Viltzin. The necro-mage looked up, shaking uncontrollably, as Varzunnos continued, "Severed Wing is made from steel of the old world, handcrafted in Faelynn by the best blacksmiths and handed to me as a tribute when I came to adulthood. As far as your Elvenfae wing goes, I am sure you will not find this task too hard. Now start the arrangements. If this fails, I will skin you alive and every time you die I will keep bringing you back until I have had my fill of your pain. Do you understand me, dark mage?"

Viltzin nodded, hissing quietly. He thought about the twisted comparisons between his Zeytar Leader and his new master as he scurried out of the throne room and into his quarters.

Meanwhile, in the dungeons, Serena was awoken by strange howls and cries coming from deeper in the dungeon cells. She was far too scared to ask the goblin guard about it, and even more frightened of the thing in the other cell. She wished she could change into a sprite like all the other Elvenfae, but her enchantment seemed to have stopped where it was, and she would not place her unborn child at risk by attempting an escape. As she sat up, she put her fingers in her ears to shut out the high-pitched shrill that was hard to ignore.

Two goblins holding torches of fire approached the cell door. Serena stood up immediately. She knew they were going to take her somewhere, so she was on guard, ready for anything. She wished she had her beloved Long Leaf with her but little good it would do her with so many guards and monsters around.

The first of the goblins opened the door and entered, as did the next one, spitting and sniffing at the sight of such a lovely creature in front of them. The first one turned to the other and whispered as he licked his lips, "Oh, Valixx, how sweet would she taste? Her blood would be like milk."

Valixx, too, was drooling at the thought of gently piercing her white flesh with his sharp fangs and suckling her pure blood until it drained her. "I agree, Moxxil," he said. "I hear she is half human. I've never tasted a human before."

Serena heard every word they were saying and took the opportunity, while they were slightly distracted, to pull a torch from Moxxil and burn his face, before tripping Valixx, stealing his blade, and running out into the halls of the dungeon, slicing goblin guards as they approached her.

Serena was weak. She hadn't eaten in days and was feeling the effects of her late stage of pregnancy. She did the best she could but wasn't like she had been a couple of cycles ago. It was only through sheer luck that the goblins were in the next room feasting on a fresh bull they had slain, so security was sparse. As the last of the guards fell, Serena threw the torch away and kept to the shadows, ascending to the top of the dungeon stairs and out into the halls. She found a dark cloak in an abandoned room and put it on swiftly, just before she heard some dark Elvenfae guards marching to their posts. She ducked down and out of sight but one stopped and looked around, sniffing the air. The leader turned and demanded, "What is it, soldier?"

The soldier stopped smelling the air and answered, "Nothing. I thought I smelled something, must be getting hungry."

The soldiers continued and Serena took a deep breath, trying to slow her accelerated heart. She got to her feet and continued on.

The castle was like nothing she had ever seen before; it had a constant smell of rot and so many rooms and cavities. It was like the palace but twisted, dark, and evil, worse than anything she had ever felt before, with a constant feeling that something was looming, making her feel somewhat depressed. Serena thought that the castle may be alive itself, leading her through halls she did not want to be in, but that would have been absurd.

Serena continued through the castle, looking for exits. When she finally came to a small window to the side of a dark hallway, she looked out, but then fell to her knees, wiping tears from her face. She had just realized the castle was floating in the air and she wasn't actually heading for any exits, as she was now on the top floor. She still believed the castle must be alive and taunting her with a small vision of freedom that she could not get.

Serena got to her feet. She ran to the end of the long, silent hallway where she could hear some talking coming from a room. She crept over lightly and when she peered inside was met with a ghastly sight, that of the dark mage from her dreams speaking to a goblin. Serena's sight was so vivid in Faelynn, she could probably see better than any of the Fae because of her half-blood abilities. Ever since she was a child she could see so very clearly, and how she saw the dark mage now was no exception. She could see Viltzin's outer skin and body, but Serena could also just make out the inner aura of the Zeytar itself, causing her to fall to her knees once more. Sprawled on all fours, she tried to get to her feet and not scream from fright. She was crying in terrified shock and her mind was blank of everything, focused only on escaping the monster she had hoped was not real. She didn't care now about noise or capture, only escape.

Soon she found her feet, running as hard as she could for a heavily pregnant woman, although it felt like slow motion to her. She saw a huge opening to a large room and her instincts took over, like when she used to play hide and seek with her cousins when she was a child. As she entered the room she was suddenly stopped by an enormous beast standing in the middle of the space. She barely missed the creature before she turned to run back out, but tripped and fell onto the floor. She picked herself up quickly and tried to take off again, but the creature reached out and grabbed Serena by the arm.

"Ah, you must be my guest. Please, don't leave so soon," he said in a deep, gruff voice.

Serena struggled but had no chance of escaping such a strong grip—her arm was tiny in his clutch—but it never stopped her trying. As she pulled and struggled, she was staring at the doorway, when the dark necro-mage entered the room, smiling and drooling. Serena knew that was the end of it and succumbed to the clutches of the dark lord Varzunnos before passing out from exhaustion.

Serena awoke minutes later. She'd had water doused onto her face. Looking up she locked eyes with the dark lord himself. His humanoid mix of stag features didn't seem so frightening to Serena now; in fact, she was quite intrigued by his strange look—that was until she looked down at his bottom half where she saw his hoofed feet coming through the bottom of his armor. She scampered back, but didn't get far as Viltzin held her down. As frightening as Varzunnos was to most, Serena was far more terrified of Viltzin. She could now only see him as a Zeytar, and although Wilkes was her friend, the race itself terrified her to the core. Viltzin's grip was tight, and Serena gained enough courage to call the necro-mage out, "Let me go, Zeytar freak."

Viltzin was shocked by her words, letting go immediately and trying to contemplate just how this half-breed could know his true form. Is she more gifted than I had previously thought or has she knowledge that could bring me down? he thought. Either way it was now Viltzin who was frightened.

Varzunnos disciplined the dark necro-mage, saying, "It seems that we are not the only ones who know your dirty secret. Do not touch her again or you will have me to deal with. Now go and leave us."

As the dark lord noticed the claw marks from Viltzin's grip fading, he bent forward and gently brought her to her feet, whispering, "Come. Take a seat where we can talk."

Serena followed and sat on an old oak chair. The dark lord took her arm and, with his finger, wiped the blood from one of her earlier falls. He placed the finger in his mouth and sucked every drop. Serena wanted to be sick, but she didn't want to upset the powerful creature. He still intrigued her. It was becoming more and more obvious that Varzunnos had the same interest in the half-blood Fae sitting before him. "Tell me, pretty one, how did you know my necro-mage's secret? Only I have that knowledge."

Serena explained carefully the Zeytars' plans and destructive nature of the agenda on Earth. She had the dark lord's full undivided attention, not giving away anything about her past, plans with the Fae to defeat the dark ones, or whether Earth survived the devastation or not. Serena finished with the last opinion she had of Viltzin. "You know he will try to overturn you. It's in their nature to take control and destroy. I know deep down that's what he will do to you eventually. They are the dirt of the universe and all realms, making you look like an Elvenfae princess."

Varzunnos stood up, his mood changing into a different, angrier one. He lowered his head to Serena's level, face to face, and whispered deeply to her, "I eat Elvenfae for breakfast. In five days I will taste your child's blood and all you know will be destroyed, after which I will take Viltzin and cut him into a million pieces before I hunt every Zeytar in every realm and spit out their bones, do you hear me, pretty one? Don't test my power."

Serena could see she had upset him, but she knew her only hope was to create friction between the two. She also knew from his calm nature when they were talking and his soft touch that she would be safe at least until the ceremony she had just learned of, so she would keep working on the tension and pray that Shaylee and the Elvenfae were on their way to save her.

WAR OF WINGS
AND SHADOWS

A DARK RIDER CHARGED THROUGH THE TWISTED forests of Xarkynan, swerving and maneuvering between the dense trees faster than anyone would dare to travel in those parts of the lands. This rider had been here before, many times. The swiftness of the ride made it hard for anything to stop him, and the dark horse he was upon had the same knowledge of those paths.

As he came closer to the dark castle, he slowed down, lined his horse up with the stairs, and ascended as quickly as possible until he made it to the highest point where the horse could go no farther. The rider was now in flight, heading to the floating fortress. When he looked back at his horse, he saw it shake its head, turn, and disappear into the darkness of the forest where it would wait to be called upon again.

The dark Elvenfae's wings were black, twisted, and partly translucent, with veins pumping black blood through his body. His face did not look Elvenfae at all, as it was much grayer and darker, with black eyes, sharp teeth, and ears that climbed higher than those of the palace kind. The dark Elvenfae had dropped his cloak mid-flight and had his sword in hand. His full black armor looked like it was molded from the dark oak of the forest. Nothing was going to stop his quest to reach the dark lord.

Glancing below, he could see that the goblins had found ways of climbing up and down to the castle using entwined swamp vines, strong enough to hold a dozen at a time. They made ladders and ropes as they were not fortunate enough to have wings to fly up and down whenever it suited. Closer and closer he got before finally reaching the lowest point of entry to the castle at the main double doors.

The left door was slightly open, enough for him to slip through. He did not want to fly straight to the top in case the dark lord was busy with other important business. The number one rule was never to interrupt him unless it was his dark mage. This was to stop any creature flying to the top levels of the castle, which Varzunnos hated.

The dark Elvenfae warrior ran upstairs, past the goblin dwellings which the dark elves hated, and upwards, until he reached the halls of the dark necro-mage and the dark lord's quarters. He ran as fast as his weary body could manage until he thought he made it to Viltzin's room, when suddenly Varzunnos walked out at the very same time, knocking the dark Elvenfae to the ground and stunning the worn-out creature for a few moments.

Varzunnos was about to bend down and pick him up to end his life when Viltzin walked out behind him, saw who it was, and stopped Varzunnos from making a mistake.

"Please, master, don't. This is my personal outlander spy. I have Wyrm for the palace and I have Neiphlax for the outer regions. If he is here, then he may have some news."

Varzunnos straightened up while Viltzin returned his constantly drooling tongue back into his overfilled mouth.

"Stand. Tell me what you saw," the dark lord said.

Neiphlax crawled backward several paces before he got to his feet. His armor was getting extremely hot underneath, as the winged ones expelled a lot of energy flying in full form. But the dark Elvenfae lost their ability to change to sprites when the dark lord first created them before the first war, so they didn't fly too much at all. He wiped the sweat from his pointed brows and ripped off the front panel of the twisted-looking metal, dropping it to the ground, as he swiftly answered, "Sorry, my lord, I came as fast as I could as they are approaching fast."

"Who is approaching? And where?"

Varzunnos' tone was not of anger but desperation. He knew exactly who was coming, and he thought they would be too weak to fight their way through the dark forests, but he was remembering very quickly that the bright ones never gave up. He still had flashbacks of his previous defeat. But they were without their king now and what good could some female queen and princess do. He was forgetting that a woman bested him the last time, Felvora, a face he dreaded to see again.

"My lord, I was twenty miles from the edges of Xarkynan and at first I thought they were rain clouds moving fast. But as they approached, the dust started swirling as well, until I could just make out thousands of Elvenfae and flying Fae in the air. Thousands more were galloping and running on the ground." Neiphlax lowered his head and continued, "My lord, I think every single Fae from Faelynn is heading right toward us and they don't look happy. I got here a day ahead as I know the terrain, but we have little time."

Varzunnos was getting edgy. Not known for his compassion, he acknowledged Neiphlax, "You work directly for me now. I want you to lead my dark Elvenfae into attack and hit them head-on with as much force as possible. Now go, blow the horn, and start planning your attack. Viltzin, come with me, I have something I want you to do for me before you prepare the ground troops for attack."

Both Viltzin and Neiphlax nodded, one departing swiftly while the other followed Varzunnos to the Tuatha treasures.

Varzunnos entered the treasure room where the power was flowing constantly from the three treasures. He walked up to the window which looked out over one side of the dark forest. He turned and explained his plan to Viltzin, "I have a spell which I couldn't fully use when I fought the king, but with these treasures we will fulfill it. I want you to concentrate power over the whole area, blocking any window entrances with dark magic. This will also stop them changing to sprite form while in the area, making it nearly impossible to enter the castle. Meanwhile, I will transform the darkness of the trees into oaken goblins to fight the land attackers."

Viltzin knew exactly what to do. He found a spell a long time ago that would stop a Fae from changing and now he was going to use it. Varzunnos was already pulling power from the treasures, reciting words from the ancient ones as he pointed and shouted them out over the forest. His eyes were closed as he concentrated the power. Greens, reds, and purple colors were scorching out of his hands and scouring the darkness of the woods. Viltzin, now at the other window of the room, did the same, only the spell was different to his master's, with more greens, reds, and purples also scorching out of his hands. The darkness of Xarkynan was being lit up with an array of bright lights and explosions, as the clouds kept the evening sun at bay and the storms picked up. It looked like a war had already begun without an arrow fired or a sword swung.

On and on the barrage of power flooded out of the window and could be seen by the oncoming Fae. Varzunnos finally finished his spell and watched, while the light from Viltzin's power continued. He could see the tops of trees swaying and moving as he smiled slightly.

Looking deeper down, he could make out the shapes and shadows of creatures lurking, screaming, as the power spawned them into new life.

Meanwhile, down in the forest, the oaks and elms swayed like they were in pain, twisting branches, leaves, and bark as humanoid creatures formed from the belly of each trunk. Hundreds of brown and black things were reaching out. First one arm, then another, and then a head would force its way out, and finally the legs, as they dropped onto the ground and screamed their way into the world.

Each one was different, made from wood save for most of their insides which were composed of the black tar of Xarkynan. They continued to sprout fingers of wood, veins of the same, and hideous heads with humanoid faces, of intertwined branches, sticks, and bark. They looked up at the lights in the castle from where their master watched on, then they spread out and began moving toward the oncoming onslaught of the Fae.

Viltzin had finished. He fell to the ground from exhaustion as Varzunnos reminded him of his task to assemble the ground force.

"There is no time for that! You can rest when it's over or if you are dead, but now I need you functioning." Varzunnos had not forgotten what Serena had said about Viltzin and he used him when he could but gave him mundane tasks to occupy him as well. "Once you are done, return to me, as the moon will rise this night and we will begin the sacrifice."

Viltzin stood up, slithered backward, and replied, "Yes, my master, I will be back soon with the dark witch and your wing after those pathetic goblins suit up and march out. Would you like the dullahan summoned as well?"

Varzunnos looked at him, his eyes twitching angrily. What part of "get all the ground creatures ready" did that fool not understand, he thought, and without a word, as if Viltzin was supposed to have read his mind, he took off out into the halls and toward his awaiting pit of creatures.

≈

Shaylee was leading the charge. She had done very well in such a short amount of time to get so many, with more on the way over the next day or so, as they would need their backup. There was no exact plan for what they were running into and the queen had been quite vocal in letting her feelings known about such a risky attack, but she was with her daughter and would fight with her until the end.

As they reached the outer sections of the dark forest, they all slowed down. Shaylee would now outline the plan of action to them all. They had covered that much distance in such a short amount of time because of the last of the treasures, which they had retrieved and brought with them. Having what the dark lord was looking for was extremely dangerous, and they knew that, but without it they would not stand a chance of defeating him and his dark armies.

Shaylee had filled the crystal up before they left as a backup to protect Serena and was relying on all three dryad mages to take the Tuatha treasure and defeat the dark lord. But there had been no word from Felvora, and Kalandrya was a way off still so there was no detailed plan, just some encouraging words from their princess.

"Everyone, thank you all. Every race has sent representatives to fight, and even some mystical sylphs and pixies have joined us. We have no other choice, and if we want to save our land, we must save Serena. Her son is the key, so we must sacrifice much to do this. Many of you won't be coming home."

Shaylee turned and cleared her throat, while wiping her eyes, before turning back and continuing without giving away her genuine feelings, "I know most of you. Those I don't, I trust in you. Having the Seelie Court fighting against the Unseelie will be very tough, but those dark creatures who hate humans so much now hate us even more, so you will find them in the forests and take them out. The rest I take to the castle, in the air and on the ground. Now let's spread our wings, lift our swords, and take down this evil once and for all."

As Shaylee finished, she held Howling Tooth high in the air while everyone cheered on in chorus, lifting their weapons of choice and chanting, "Shay-lee, Shay-lee."

On and on they yelled, the shouts dwindling slowly as they entered the dark forest. The Seelie Court members split off; they knew where the dark Unseelie dwelled and they weren't about to let the dark lord conjure them up to defend the castle. As they left, some nochkz started moving, swiping down horses as they galloped through. They had uprooted from the edges of the forest and started attacking with their long branches.

Faiay'aar lifted the treasure and turned the remaining ones into stone, as the last moving tree advanced on Shaylee. The nochkz were the protectors of the outer sections of the forest and Shaylee could feel it behind her as she flew just above the treetops. Its branches grew swiftly to knock her down, but her quick thinking led to her showing Faiay'aar where it was in time for the dryad to turn it to stone along with the rest.

It was the only entrance into Xarkynan that they could go through, and she knew it was protected, but they had no other choice. They wouldn't have much time before more would awaken, so they continued swiftly but remaining cautious. Shaylee had told all the flying Fae to change to sprites but only until they got to the forest, as being a sprite would make them easy targets for wraiths and for the dread collectors. Those creatures all used the power of a sprite to create dark magical powder out of their dried bones for witches and dark mages to use.

Deeper they delved, as the flying Fae observed from above and looked out for danger, alerting the grounded folk, while checking ahead for danger to themselves. They cut down any dark creature that approached them. Peaceful pixies were taking out smaller hobgoblins while gnomes were taking on goblins. Even Van Coinan was in his element. It was a sight that left Shaylee feeling proud but sad that her peaceful people had been pushed to that level of desperation. The Zeytars started it and Varzunnos thinks he will finish it, but my people are strong and desperate, she thought.

Shaylee was looking out for some Elvenfae warriors leading the charge on the ground when an arrow missed her right wing by an inch. She and the others attempted to change to sprites for the rest of the flight until they reached the castle, but the magic of the dark ones had reached the outer limits of the dark forest and they could not transform.

Desperate, Shaylee called out to all the winged ones flying, "Follow me, my people, we must soar higher. Their arrows cannot reach us above the clouds. It means our defenses on the ground will be weaker, but we have no choice."

Moving ever so close to the edge of the outer castle realm, Shaylee had to hope that her people on the ground would be safe with her mother and the other half of the Elvenfae guards that were leading them through.

Higher and higher they flew, into the clouds, as the sun hid behind the horizon, revealing the beginning of the largest moon Faelynn had witnessed in many cycles. It was light orange in appearance, and Shaylee had a feeling this would be the night when the dark lord would try to use everything he had to wipe them all out.

As they continued to ascend, they were suddenly met with a full onslaught from the dark Elvenfae. The dark ones had planned to lead them up into the air, separating the ground and the air warriors so they could hit the two with full force.

Shaylee, desperate to save as many as she could, knew they were outnumbered three to one. She screamed at the top of her lungs, "Bring as many down as you can! Fight, but we descend, it's time."

As she finished her desperate cry, Shaylee clanged the first sword in front of her, followed by the sounds of two, then three until every single one of her people was fighting in mid-flight, trying to descend but watching their back along with their fellow Fae. Howling Tooth was getting a workout but none of them could sustain it for long as Shaylee's Fae were tiring from being in the air so long.

Over and over, clang and spark, as Elvenfae and the dark ones began falling from the sky. Wings were sliced and heads were falling. The grounded ones could see the sparks and dodged fallen friends and enemies, all while fighting goblins and tree tarnaaks. Shaylee was feeling the effects already. While the guards were trying to protect her, she came up with an idea that could help the weary ones. "All you tired ones flee to the surface, and trade with the warriors on the ground. Do it in twenties, now go."

There was no arguing. Those who heard the call or could escape for a moment did. Shaylee with a huge group tried a deflective arrow formation, giving some a chance to descend. In no time a new bunch had surfaced and twenty more descended, on and on, as they all slowly made it down and hovered in the dark clouds away from the arrows, off the ground but invisible enough to glide through the mist and get a rest for a moment out of sight.

The sky soon lit up as Varzunnos increased his power. The clouds were illuminated with lightning, far too dangerous and constant to stay in, and too bright. Shaylee took a dive as she descended from the clouds completely. Three dark Elvenfae met her, and she took the closest one's head off as she zoomed to the side, slicing two wings of another, watching it scream as it fell to the ground as the last approached. Shaylee swung Howling Tooth enough to mesmerize the creature before slicing it in half.

Catching her breath for a moment, she heard a groan from behind her. Spinning around she was met with another one, though this one had a blade poking out of its neck. As the blade retracted and the body fell to the ground, twitching and screeching, Shaylee saw her savior, Marlifyn Strongholm, smiling slightly before he continued on, to fight others.

Shaylee pulled out her whistle and blew it. Only the bright Fae could hear it. As they continued fighting, they all understood what it meant—follow the sound.

The darkness had given them some respite but now the ever-increasing lightning storms illuminated the area through the power of the elemental treasures in the castle which was not far away. They didn't have long.

Shaylee had no choice but to take it to the ground and try to recoup. They descended as swiftly as possible but had no time for recovery as the tarnaaks and goblins were everywhere. The only light in the dense woods was sporadic, which the dark goblins took advantage of, as they were born in darkness and dwelled in it. Shaylee could see their horrific reflective stares as they glowed through the lightning strikes.

She had her army with her on the ground now, attacking sword strike after strike, cutting and slicing. She was fatiguing, as were most of her warriors, but they would not let that defeat them. Faiay'aar had the treasure and was trying not to use it. She would be a target if they found it. So instead, she used her potions and enchanted amulet to look after the weaker ones. She wished her beloved sister Felvora and friend Kalandrya were with her, as the power of three dryads was extraordinarily strong. She knew Kalandrya was on her way, but as for Felvora ... Well, she could not find her anywhere. She hoped she was alive.

Shaylee had slain yet another goblin. Her skill was second to none, and was enhanced by the coordinated help from her old teacher Marlifyn. But it wasn't enough. Soon four horns rang out from the ranks of dark goblins. They had a massive area surrounded and were closing in. The tarnaaks, born of the oak, were elusive, able to look like trees before coming to life in humanoid form and attacking.

Shaylee's army was outnumbered and outclassed, so the blades stopped clanging, the arrows stopped flying, and the sounds of despair and cries of defeat echoed throughout the groups. Shaylee could hear more horns deeper in the woods, then others, repeating throughout Xarkynan. It was over.

A large dark goblin was standing over her with its sticky black blade at her throat. She dropped her sword, which began a domino effect through the trees as other Elvenfae too dropped theirs.

"You've lost, Princess. You will make a fine meal."

Shaylee was nearly sick as the creature slid its scaly black tongue along the bottom of her pale, mostly blood-soaked face. As its tongue climbed higher up her cheek, she could feel every bump of the vile meaty thing. By the time it reached her eye, she could barely stop herself from punching the creature deep in the throat and ripping its tongue out, but she endured it for Serena and her people.

In anger she spat out, "Get your vile thing off my face. I will have your tongue hanging from my dungeon wall before this is through."

The goblin was shocked at her response for a moment, before its eyes widened, and it let out an enormous low bellow of laughter that seemed like it was coming from several creatures. Its head went back as it continued, as if this was the funniest thing it had ever heard.

Shaylee so desperately wanted to end the vile creature right there and then, and it was taking every fiber of her being not to try. But as the goblin continued its horrific laugh, which echoed into the deep of the woods, a huge red light appeared behind them, along with the noise of thousands of roars and cries.

The goblin stopped and looked, as did everyone else, to find Kalandrya with her staff high in the air, polluting the darkness with her light. She took out as many of the horrendous creatures as she could with a light enchantment that she had prepared and thrust out into the night with her staff. One after the other the goblins fell, being stunned as the magic took hold.

Shaylee quickly picked up her sword, thrust it into the belly of the oversharing goblin, and at the same time with her other hand cut its throat and ripped its tongue out as it cried out.

Seeing it fall to the ground gave Shaylee some slight satisfaction and she watched its shocked eyes slowly dim as its life faded away. She was not going to keep the tongue, so she threw it in the face of another before slicing down some more of the creatures.

The brief respite from battle gave them all a little rest and some energy back to fight as the new group and the old continued the barrage of slaughtering as many as they could before they entered the castle. Kalandrya's timing had been impeccable. Shaylee didn't know how she could have got there so fast, but she wasn't going to dwell on it.

"Where is your mother, Shay? I need her with me, and with you, together. These creatures that have just fallen are only stunned by my light spell. They will not stay fallen for long and it will take far too long to slice them all as they sleep."

Shaylee hadn't seen her mother for a while. She was leading the ground assault and was at another location. She hoped she was OK.

"I am not sure, Kalandrya, she should be here somewhere."

Shaylee remembered she had her crystal, so she could locate her with a thought. Looking through the blue and red rock she waited and thought hard, and as she did, an image appeared above it, showing some dark Elvenfae in mid-flight with her in the middle being held on either side by their arms. Her head slumped down before the crystal's vision vanished back to the red and blue color it was before.

"I am sorry, Shay. We will get her back for you. I need to ask: how did you get such an enchanted crystal?"

Shaylee answered, but with a quiver in her tone, "It is powered by a Tuatha treasure to locate anyone and then to appear where they are."

Kalandrya was impressed. She knew exactly what to do with it if she could convince Shaylee. "We could use it to find Felvora and appear at your mother's location to save her."

There was so much Shaylee couldn't explain to Kalandrya—that she was keeping it charged as much as she could to save Serena and send her and her child home, and if it was used too much, she may not get that chance. Even though there was a treasure with them, it may not be accessible when it came time to recharge.

"I am sorry, Kalandrya, it is unpredictable and the more it's used the more the power drains. If we all end up in cells in the castle with Mother, then that would be a disaster. Besides, I have it as a backup which I'll keep to myself for now."

Shaylee didn't want to lie, but she didn't want Kalandrya knowing she was saving it for her sister's rescue and not for her mother the queen's, which would be an executable offense in the eyes of the council.

Shaylee continued, "I can, however, have a look and see where Flora is and if she is alive."

As Kalandrya nodded and prepared for the viewing Shaylee was about to show, an almighty roar echoed out from the castle above them. They looked straight up into the sky and witnessed a never-ending beam of red and blue lights cascading through the roof of the castle, followed by a purple mist slowly creeping over the dwelling like a force field. They had no time to waste as they wouldn't be able to enter the castle if the mist engulfed the whole place.

Shaylee placed her crystal in her satchel, put her sword away, and they all continued as fast as they could to the entry of the castle where they would be facing another problem—the Elvenfae would have to carry the flightless ones up.

As they continued to cut down the tarnaaks and the goblins, moving toward the bottom stairs of the hovering castle, a huge explosion erupted past the dark forest in the direction of Faelynn, swirling in a circle of blue light with sparks of green and red shooting out, like an enormous vortex swirling in the sky. It kept them all mesmerized, dark ones and the light, until the burgeoning swirls of light disappeared into a cascading flash of lightning, leaving all who witnessed it stunned for a few moments, before they continued with the affray.

Kalandrya lit the way again and all of them, together with Faiay'aar, who had just met up with the others, took out as many archers and dark Elvenfae as they could to make a quick ascent to the castle. Shaylee had just taken off with Faiay'aar in her arms when she whispered, "I have a bad feeling we are not alone, Fay."

SOME UNLIKELY
GUESTS

FIRE HAD SURROUNDED THE SMALL SECTION of trees at the edges of the Aurora Forest. The beast must have unloaded as it fell from the sky, an occurrence all too familiar to the pair of travelers who were both at this moment unconscious.

The much smaller of the two visitors started stirring. He was once again saved by his quick-thinking companion as they entered yet another realm. He slid from the back of the enormous beast, onto the ground where he jumped to his feet immediately, jolted from his sleep and ready to fight.

He was taller than the Elvenfae, with three very thin horns on his forehead. One started in the middle, halfway from both his eyes and hairline, pointing several inches above his head. The other two were either side, although a little higher than the middle one, but finishing at the same level above his head. The bones of the horns were not perfect, with slight twists in them, and his ears were pointed like an Elvenfae's but a little thicker and longer. His face wasn't as long as those of the Elvenfae but was gaunt and elegant with attractive features. He was grayer looking with pure white, long hair, stronger, with larger muscles and a dense physique, but not burly or fat. His clothing was not of the Faelynn or human realm—he had leather bindings around his arms, a velvet sectioned tunic that covered his torso, dark leather pants, and a strange-looking belt with different objects hanging from it.

As the fires slowed to a soft roar, there was enough light to see the colors of his clothes were maroon and black. He had a scabbard with many carvings on it, but no sword to unsheathe, only a torn quiver with three arrows and a long bow made from a strange material—quite different to Shaylee's and much more complex in its design. His left leg had a dagger sheathed in a small scabbard, with the handle curved and marked with more strange carvings. His eyes seemed to be dark in the light but changed from brown to blue.

As the stranger calmed after his sudden awakening, he looked down at the fading glow emanating from the middle of his chest. There was a large purple crystal shard attached to a casing that was held with two leather straps either side of his chest and two over his shoulders underneath his weapons. The stranger continued watching the purple light slowly fade from what was a blinding vision not more than a few moments beforehand.

Once it had dimmed entirely, he waited, investigated the sky, then continued adjusting his clothing after this recent thrust into a new world.

After the stranger had taken a quick look around at his surroundings, he wiped some fresh blood from a wound underneath his throat. He seemed agitated but gradually got his bearings and realized he wasn't in any direct danger.

Feeling calmer, he wandered over to his fellow traveler, the enormous beast that had helped him land. He met with its humongous, long face, standing at the same level as the gums of its sharp, protruding bottom teeth as it breathed. The stranger placed his right hand high at the end of its long snout, near where a large nostril was sucking in air and loudly exhaling it. He whispered in a language unheard before in any of the lands there on Faelynn or in the human realm, *"Wake up, Vax, we are safe for now."*

The enormous creature didn't budge, seemingly in need of an extensive rest from exhaustion. It flickered one yellow and black eye open for just a second, then closed it once more with a slight exhale.

The stranger knew he was tired, but also that he was semi-conscious.

"Vaximardruusz, wake up now, there is an enormous Gloffen in the fields."

Before the stranger could move out of the way, the creature's massive, long head lifted and two enormous wings spread out—they would have covered half a small football field on Earth. The beast had four large horns on its head, two at the sides curving back and slightly inward, with the other two on the back of its head pointing back and slightly inward as well. The creature had two hind legs that were exceptionally large, and the body of the beast was quite long, at least the length of two jumbo jets.

It didn't seem to have any arms but had claws attached to its wings, which when folded in allowed it to walk on all fours. Its body was covered in leathery scales and was quite light underneath but a darker red on top, the color gradually deepening from the stomach to the back of the beast. It had thousands of spikes all along the ridge, like hair follicles that became longer as they ventured closer to its long neck.

Its tail was exceedingly long and fierce, with four horns, two on either side, curving outwards from an oval section at the end. The strength of it would bring down a small mountain if it were put to the test. As it scoured around with its constant smiling snarl, it turned its rounded chin and reptilian eyes down at the very tiny looking stranger, opened its mouth wide revealing its long sharp teeth, and let out an enormous roar.

The stranger covered his ears and stepped back, before pointing to the amulet shard on his chest. The beast looked down, and stopped roaring immediately, before lowering its head to the stranger standing in front of him.

"I'm sorry, Vax, I needed you awake. We will find food, but we always arrive at a destination with severe memory loss, an unnatural anger, and fatigue. I ... can't remember where we just came from or if Szelidus followed, so we must be on our toes."

The beast took a deep breath and exhaled, then without moving its mouth at all whispered into his mind, *"I can't remember too much either, but it was a dark place of evil. The Sorcerer Szelidus did not come through this time, so we are safe, at least for now, Rasarlin."*

Rasarlin replied with a slight sigh of relief in his voice, *"Thank goodness. You have always been right about when he follows and when he doesn't. I'm lucky to have such a great dragon as my friend."*

Rasarlin turned away. He had a slight smile on his face as he waited for the response. He could feel Vaximardruusz raise his head, so he turned back to him again so the beast could see the smirk on his face. *"Wyvern, Rasarlin, wyvern. I'm much faster and stronger than a dragon and you know it. Why do you tease me?"*

Rasarlin responded immediately, *"Sorry, Vax, it's just to lighten the mood. I know I shouldn't tease you, but that's what friends do."*

Vaximardruusz shook his head slowly, turned to Rasarlin and whispered into his mind, *"You'll keep, you're not the alpha creature here."*

As he finished his quip, he gave a snarling smile. Spreading his wings, he began flapping slowly while taking a run-up of several paces, and then climbed into the air. He glided over Rasarlin's head, barely missing him, and then extinguished the remaining sections of fire with his tornado breath.

"That dragon is so touchy," Rasarlin commented.

Turning around, he faced his large companion heading straight toward him. As the wyvern flew even lower past his head, Rasarlin could hear the beast whisper, *"I heard that."*

Vaximardruusz climbed high into the air to get a view of his surroundings, and noticed a light in the far distance high above the trees. It was only visible from the air, as the clouds were now very dark and foreboding. Next to them he could just make out the dark blood color of the moon. The wyvern immediately descended back to the safety of the ground to tell his companion.

≈

Meanwhile, inside the castle, only a handful were able to sneak in before the force field mist engulfed the whole place. While the elemental treasures' power was unleashed, that mist would continue to hold it secure.

Shaylee, along with Faiay'aar, Kalandrya, Marlifyn, Darphanin, and Van Coinan had snuck in, cloaked by a brief enchantment from Kalandrya. It would not last long, so they needed to find a safe place to gather themselves and form a plan.

Fortunately, the entire castle was lacking protection from the inside. Most of the warriors, guards, and other disgusting creatures were out in the woods fighting with the rest. Shaylee knew the Seelie Court must have been holding off the Unseelie as there had been no signs of banshees, wraiths, dark merrow, sirens, hobgoblins, selkies, and other human-hating tricksters that could cause unnecessary additional havoc to make it more difficult for them. It was hard enough, and they had already taken so many of their kin.

Marlifyn had quietly run ahead, keeping to the shadows. He returned swiftly and pointed for them all to follow. They kept to the same dark places as they followed him one by one until they reached a dark, quiet room, out of the way from the main hallways. They carefully snuck inside. The room had an awful smell, much like the rest of the castle, with bones on the floor and some soiled sheeting. It was obviously where one of the higher goblins dwelled, as most stayed down near the dungeons.

Shaylee sat down. Looking at each of them one by one, she whispered, "The blood moon is rising tonight and for the next two nights. This war won't last until then, so we must assume that the dark lord will take on some sort of ritual himself tonight. We have to stop him."

She pulled out a long item wrapped in a green sheath. Having gained the attention of all, she slowly placed it on the ground, then unwrapped it, revealing Serena's sword, Long Leaf. Shaylee then pulled the sword from the scabbard, held her hand on the handle, and recited an enchantment that had been given to her by Vyyuna.

The two dryads were very impressed with the recent high enchantments that Shaylee had been performing, and they looked at each other in secret agreement that maybe Shaylee's new role after all of this was to train to be a mystic or even a lower mage. She couldn't be a dryad mage as that role was chosen at birth, but she definitely had the talent for some more detailed arts.

As Shaylee continued, a small light emanated from the handle, white veins seemed to lock the handle to the hilt, and the blade illuminated, breaking from the rest of the sword until what remained in Shaylee's hand made everyone in the low-lit room gasp.

Shaylee was now holding the Alicorn, and with no interruption she continued chanting her spell while scraping tiny fragments of the bone into a small vial. The spell was so the power of the Alicorn would allow itself to be broken apart, as it was far too powerful to snap or break, even to get the smallest amount that Shaylee needed, just enough to fulfill the Tuatha Dé Danann prophecy.

Once satisfied, she reattached the Alicorn to the pommel, hilt, and blade, reciting another spell, as the horn launched more white stems that brought everything back together and disappeared into place underneath the binding as if it wasn't there at all, protected and hidden as Vyyuna and Shaylee wanted it.

The others did not say a word. Shaylee was doing well and Faiay'aar smiled at her. Only a few rotations ago she was but a mess, and now was back to being the leader she was always born to be. Her love for Serena was strong, Faiay'aar thought, as was that for her mother, whom she had not forgotten about.

After Shaylee had everything back to normal, she whispered, "We need to split up. I will search for Serena with Marlifyn and Faiay'aar. Kalandrya, you take Darphanin and Van Coinan to find my mother. Here, take this. It's a whistle of Faelynn, only light enchanted ones can hear it. Call it if you are in trouble, and I will call mine for the same reason. But if we both succeed, wait for my long call—that way you can all come to me and we can begin the next part of the plan."

Each group member individually hugged the members of the other before taking off, not knowing if they would see each other again. Kalandrya placed one final cloaking spell on them all. Not all would be fooled by it, especially not Viltzin or the dark lord Varzunnos, but it may allow them to pass by some less magical creatures undetected.

Shaylee's group took off to the left. She wanted to have a sneaky look into her crystal but knew the dark lord would sense it as he was now connected to the treasures. So she used her instincts, running through the halls and higher into the castle, at times passing goblins. The cloaks they found in the previous room smelled terrible, but they were dark, and although they were semi-cloaked by a spell, they would help when it wore off, which could be anytime.

As they made it to the second last level, Shaylee was first to ascend to the top of the stairs, where she bumped straight into a hideously deformed Elvenfae. Wyrm fell to the ground, and as he picked himself up, he could see through the spell and noticed it was Shaylee.

Wyrm knew his time would be short after the war with Viltzin and the dark lord, so he tried to "worm" his way back with Shaylee, changing from his twisted form to Stexinzar Crimsonmoon. Shaylee witnessed the transformation, and her eyes widened with rage as the traitor started explaining, "Shay, it's me, Stex. I am so glad to see you, my dear friend, I have so—"

Before Stexinzar could finish, Shaylee had Howling Tooth sliding down his throat, tears forming in her eyes as the flashback of friendship turned to betrayal overtook her emotions. She whispered in her former friend's ear as he started losing consciousness, "You have betrayed me for far too long. Now look me in the eye, coward, as you fade away."

As Shaylee finished so was Stexinzar. She pulled her sword from his throat and watched him fall into a heap on the ground. With tears in her eyes, she lifted Howling Tooth to her mouth and in an act that shocked the other companions to their core, Shaylee licked the blood from her sword and spat at his lifeless face.

Faiay'aar came up, put her arm around Shaylee's shoulder, and whispered, "Come, Shay, we must go."

Shaylee blinked away some tears and snapped back to reality. She turned to Faiay'aar, smiling slightly, and responded, "Yes, Fay, I'm sorry. Let's go."

On they went, up to the next level. Shaylee, who had now pulled herself back together, couldn't believe how unguarded it was. Suddenly they heard screams coming from a room above the opposite staircase. They could see some dark Elvenfae guards on that side, so they needed to stay low and quiet.

Another scream bellowed out. "Serena!" Shaylee exclaimed.

The others grabbed her, pulling her back, as the screaming continued over and over. They could tell Serena was giving birth.

The timing of it all was unnatural. Serena wasn't due for just over a quarter cycle, Shaylee thought. What influence did the dark magic have over her? Or was it her unborn child protecting her?

What Shaylee did know was that it would all be over soon.

Suddenly three dark Elvenfae carrying a prisoner emerged from the top of the far left staircase where the room being guarded was situated. As they approached, the dark lord appeared from the connecting hall. While the three heroes watched on, they could just make out what was being said.

"As you requested, my lord, the Fae queen."

Shaylee stood up. They could all clearly hear what was said next as the dark lord's voice echoed throughout the castle, "Ah, my queen, finally I have you right where I want you, on your knees and bleeding for me. It's a pity your king isn't here to witness it."

Tianna replied swiftly after spitting blood onto the dark lord's armor-covered chest, "This isn't over. As we speak there are millions of Fae about to enter these halls with magic you couldn't imagine."

Varzunnos chuckled, not deeply, but enough to insult the queen as he scraped the blood she had delivered from his chest and into his mouth. "Hmm, sweet like honey milk, I will enjoy this. Besides, I have the power of Faelynn and the outer realms here with me. Do you think one treasure will stop me? And where is your insurrection you so confidently speak of? When I have sucked your life dry, I will do the same to your daughter."

As he finished boasting angrily, he bent down farther, picked her up by the wings, and dug his sharp needle-like teeth into Tianna's neck.

He watched her writhe in pain as the blood drained from her body like a torrent of waves into the large creature's mouth until she was more pale than the blossoms of a hawthorn tree in spring. Kicking her last twitch, she exhaled her last breath. As the light faded from her eyes, the last thing she would feel was the pain and the humiliation of all four wings being torn from her body as if she were a fly being played with.

Shaylee was trembling. The screams were still echoing from the room as she watched her mother succumb to the most degrading end a queen of the peaceful realm could have had. It took both Marlifyn and Faiay'aar to hold her back, his firm hand over her mouth as they both tried to control their own emotions. Their only saving grace was Serena's screaming as the sounds of Shaylee's agony and despair continued to come, only somewhat suppressed by the hand blocking them, until she fell to the floor in a heap.

"We need you, Shay, we need you strong. Do it for Serena, my dear."

As Faiay'aar spoke those words, something resonated inside Shaylee's mind, like a voice of reason. She closed her eyes and she could see Serena, begging for help, so she switched back into gear, strong, calmer, but with an overwhelming hatred in her heart that needed fulfillment. As she went to get up, she heard a commotion coming from the stairs on their side, and seeing who was making their way up, she suddenly felt even stronger.

Kalandrya, Van Coinan, and Darphanin had found them, and staying low they swiftly joined the rest of the group.

Kalandrya whispered, "We couldn't find her. Everything was leading us here." She paused as she saw her beloved friend without her wings, lying in a small pool of the remaining blood she had left after the attack. The others didn't speak. Shaylee was intent now on saving her sister. As the rage rose in Kalandrya, her jewels vibrated on her neck and the pale skin she'd once had was an off-red. Just as they were about to try to hold her back, the castle was filled with one final scream and then the sound of a newborn baby crying.

Pulling themselves back behind cover and out of sight, they waited.

"Bring the child, the mother, and those wings to the other side of the castle where my treasures are. Set the tables up and bring the witch to me now. The moon is nearing its apex."

Varzunnos' commands were assertive and fearful. As his demands were being fulfilled, the group realized that they were on the other side where the dark lord was sending his dark servants.

Fearing the worst, they hastily snuck into the first room they could find, hoping it wasn't occupied. As Marlifyn was the first to enter he was greeted by Glinoxx, who was also hiding from Viltzin. But before the loud goblin could open his screeching mouth, Marlifyn had his head on the floor, while lowering the rest of the goblin's body gently to the ground, taking in pints of squirting blood to his face as he tried to quietly fix the situation without making noise.

Van Coinan was the last to enter. He had a strange look on his face—he'd been holding everything in for far too long, and now he couldn't help but do something impetuously stupid. He was just about to jump on top of the goblin's head and kick it around, but Shaylee glimpsed his movements and intervened before he could do too much damage. The door quietly closed behind them, as Shaylee, still holding the pooka's arm, put her finger up to her lips, indicating silence.

Van Coinan wasn't stupid, not one bit, but he was a mystical creature with energy, and it was all getting too much for him seeing his beloved friends perish, one by one. Shaylee knew it and wouldn't chastise him. As the noise of traffic passed their doorway, they hoped no one needed any goblin clothes or tools from the small closet they were in.

≈

Viltzin, an evil Zeytar, had delivered Serena's son, something she would never forget as long as she lived. Being now a mage and once a scientist had come in handy, and he patched Serena up enough after the difficult birth to avoid blood loss by order of the dark lord himself.

Viltzin sensed his master wanted more with Serena afterward, but couldn't quite pinpoint what. It wasn't the time nor the place to concern himself at that late stage. He took the child, while two dark

Elvenfae lifted the unconscious Serena onto a long wooden trolley. They wheeled her out of the birthing room and into the halls, toward the newly modified sacrificial quarters where the Tuatha Dé Danann treasures were releasing their full power.

They had set up the altar, had the wings of an Elvenfae queen, of noble blood which Varzunnos thought would help, and he had his sword Severed Wing by his side, with three of the Tuatha Dé Danann treasure stones. The dark ones from the twisted hollows deep in the forest had been reluctantly persuaded to attend, and all that was needed was the apex of the blood moon, which was climbing ever higher as the bloody night went on.

The witch re-dressed Serena herself in a traditional dark purple and black gown of the old Tuatha Dé Danann, which had been found among old items by Viltzin and had been worn by the dark lord's low level witch mage long ago. Varzunnos wanted Serena to look the part for the ceremony, even though she didn't want any involvement in it.

The moon climbed higher, as the screams of battle could still be heard echoing from the dark of the night. Serena's body was now ready. Still out cold, she was unaware of what was about to happen. Her son lay on the altar with not one tear, as Viltzin checked the boy over for the prophecy markings, lifting his left eye, revealing brown, before looking at the right blue one. Once satisfied, he checked over the boy's hands, but there was no mark. So the twisted mage wiped the boy clean as best he could—but still no markings were visible.

Viltzin was getting nervous. He was not sure if the spell would work without all the markings of the prophecy being present. Too scared to tell Varzunnos, he gave his dark master the all clear as they waited just a little longer for the moon to reach its powerful apex.

A COSTLY NIGHT

SHAYLEE AND THE OTHERS HAD SETTLED on the best plan they could devise under such circumstances. They were running out of time and would need to act quickly if they were to stop any attempt on Serena or the child's life.

Kalandrya explained that the dark lord and his minion Viltzin'un'dandaar could see through any spells, but they had their goblin cloaks still with them. They needed a third dryad to fulfill the power of the sylphs and the treasure they had, but would try as best they could to stop them at all costs.

Using the element of surprise was the key strategy agreed on, since the dark lord and Viltzin were still very much unprotected—his creatures were still out fighting. Shaylee would be the one to rescue Serena and the baby, while the others would distract them long enough so Shaylee could fulfill the spell and destroy the dark ones.

They had one shot at it, and this was it. Shaylee looked all around the room at her close friends and fellow brave warriors. "It's time."

While moving quietly to the door, they jumped in fright at a sudden blast of blue and white light coming from behind them in the room. They turned to witness Van Coinan change from his pooka form to that of a full humanoid, still with whiskers and long ears, but now he had longer arms and legs. Standing quite tall, he wasn't covered very well by his overalls, which were now too small, revealing the grayish-white fur of his body. He reached down and found a goblin's cloak to put on.

One of his ears still pointed in the air and the other behind him, and his face looked the same, but he was able to move a lot more delicately and fight harder. Casting his eyes on the floor around him he saw a black-stained blade, so he picked it up. Then he looked at the rest of the group, who were still in shock, and whispered, "What? Are we going now, or standing around?"

Shaylee grinned slightly and shook her head. She just hoped that he could still use his mind-breaking dust as a backup.

Out into the dark of the halls they went. The light and noise was coming from far down the hallway to the right. They needed someone brave and quiet to creep down and see how many there were. Darphanin volunteered, but then they noticed two dark Elvenfae guards right at the entrance to the large room.

"Wait, Darph, it's too dangerous. Here, come behind this barrier out of the way and I will try something."

As they all took cover, Shaylee pulled out her crystal and began concentrating on Serena's position. She didn't want to appear to her, as she would be killed immediately, but her thinking was to at least get an understanding of where everyone was positioned. She closed her eyes and thought hard. She saw her sister lying at the rear of the room near the windows. Shaylee tried to look around but caught the eye of the dark lord who could see her shape in the room.

Shaylee broke her concentration immediately, turned to the others, and whispered, "They know we are here; we have to move. Serena is to the rear and the three dark mages, including Varzunnos, are in the center of the room, each near an active treasure. They are doing a sacrifice now so we must go, we have no choice."

As Shaylee finished, they could hear the two guards moving down the hall and diverting off down the stairs. Not more than a moment later, a loud horn reverberated out into the forest. "He's calling all his creatures. The guards have gone. Let's go now."

Varzunnos had his sword high above his head. Serena had just awoken and was screaming out for her son. She was being held by four goblins, while the moon was only minutes away from its perfect position. The other two, Viltzin and the witch of the Hollows, were focusing power from the treasures, awaiting the blood splash from the child and then the mother. The wings were being held by the last dark Elvenfae guard in the room, as the ending was about to begin.

All six ran as fast they could down the hall and into the room. Shaylee was first in and straightaway, as if he had been waiting for her, Varzunnos threw her against the wall, meters from Serena. She was stuck there, as if he had a permanent hold on her. Shaylee struggled but to no avail, and as the dark lord was about to thrust his sword down, Van Coinan, Darphanin, and Marlifyn started taking out the goblins that had let go of Serena. Meanwhile, Faiay'aar and Kalandrya were using as much force as they could on the three dark mages, who were jolted and stunned for a moment. The noise of the power was deafening. Faiay'aar let out a cry, "We need Felvora! It will not hold them!"

Different colored lights were swirling through the room as the dark lord overrode the two dryads, pushing their power back and forcing them against the wall. There were echoes coming from deep in the castle as the dark lord's minions were heading up to the top. Viltzin was out cold, the impact of being thrown knocking him straight out, but the witch turned and joined Varzunnos in spraying the dryads hard with blasts of elemental and personal power.

"I see you brought me a gift. Now I can take this world without a sacrifice—the last of the treasures is mine."

As the life force began draining from the two dryads, a green mist flew into the room screaming, "Did somebody call for me?"

Felvora smashed her staff filled with her power amulet at the witch, turning her to stone at once, as Grilif and Darf stormed in right behind her, along with Vaelenflixx Leafenvein, still with the tiny chain around his ankle. The twitchy sprite started pulling at a goblin's ear, doing his part, as a flurry of dark goblins began filling the room.

Felvora concentrated all her power onto the dark lord, giving the other two enough time to avoid the constant blast. Faiay'aar crawled toward Shaylee who had now been freed and was attending to Serena, when the whole castle shook and started rocking, and bricks fell from the sides and the roof. As the treasures had been focused on the dryads, the mist shield had lifted, allowing the outsiders to enter. Then the shaking stopped, and an enormous roar rang out over Xarkynan.

"Here, Serena, take your sword. Cut your child's hand now. We have little time."

Serena sparked enough maternal energy to do the task at hand. She trusted Shaylee to no end and would do as she asked. As soon as she lifted his tiny finger up to cut, though, she froze, as the three Alicorn marks appeared. She turned, hesitating a little, while Shaylee nodded, put the vial next to her, and whispered, "It's OK, Serena, just a few drops into this vial. I promise he will be fine." Serena turned back, made a small incision, and watched the blood flow freely into the vial.

As this was happening Varzunnos caught what they were up to out of the corner of his eye. He blasted Felvora back and lifted his sword to strike the altar as more and more creatures poured into the castle. Grilif, Darf, Vaelenflixx, Marlifyn, and Darphanin were working overtime to keep them away from Serena and Shaylee. Kalandrya had recovered somewhat, but as she stood, a goblin took Darphanin's head completely off in front of her, splashing her with his blood. As she watched the woodland elf fall, Marlifyn pushed her aside to avoid a blow from a dark Elvenfae, taking the full brunt of the force into his stomach. Bravely continuing, he took out the dark Elvenfae and moved on to a goblin, holding his stomach.

As the dark lord was just about to strike, a white light encompassed the room, stunning all the dark ones involved and giving Faiay'aar time to reach the sisters.

The dark creatures covered their eyes, all of them affected, even the dark lord, who dropped his sword to cover his horned head and face. Out of the light emerged a white figure floating above the altar.

Serena looked up. The light was not hurting her eyes at all. She noticed a black mark in the middle of the sweet-looking woman's forehead and was mesmerized for a moment.

The white woman spoke to Serena's mind, "My sweet, sweet child, you have endured so much. It's time now to end this. Now go, fulfill your destiny."

Serena knew instantly who it was. With her hand stretched out to the white woman and tears coming down her face, she whispered as the light kept stinging the dark, "Vyyuna, I miss you."

Shaylee too had tears in her eyes, knowing it was the last time she would ever appear to them. It had come at the right time as if she had seen a snippet of the potential future that was now taking place before them.

Serena gave the vial to Faiay'aar as the white light gave Felvora and Kalandrya enough time to take a Tuatha Dé Danann treasure each. The stones burned their hands, but they were the only ones who could wield them without the proper protection spell. With full force they cast the power from their staffs, red and green in one hand and a treasure each in the other, while reciting old powerful magic, all at the dark lord. At the same time the light faded and Shaylee yelled, "Now!"

Faiay'aar began reciting the old Tuatha Dé Danann spell she had remembered from the old book over and over as she poured the blood mixed with Alicorn over Serena's child. The boy was hysterical, but Serena could not touch him while the ritual of the prophecy was being conducted.

The blood moon had no bearing on this enchantment, but it helped with power. On the incantations went from all three dryads, working hard for two separate outcomes. As Felvora began shaking, Kalandrya noticed the dark lord moving off the wall and ambling toward them. Kalandrya screamed out, "Hurry, Fay, and finish it! He's getting loose."

Faiay'aar had another few moments to complete the spell. As the dark lord started breaking free, a massive burst of light hit the room. This time it wasn't from Vyyuna; it was coming from Serena's son. As he lifted his hand out, the light flowed like a wave of light blue mist, ceasing soon after as it took on a life of its own, turning everything of darkness to ash.

Kalandrya and Felvora could continue to hold the dark lord but without Faiay'aar's help they would lose their grip. She pushed away some goblins that were turning to dust at the same time as the blue light mutated and flowed, as if it were chasing the dark ones, growing, and changing from a light blue to light red and back again as it swallowed the darkness wherever it went.

Faiay'aar took up the post with a third Tuatha Dé Danann treasure, and while it burned her skin also, she could maintain enough power to hold the dark lord back with the others' full bursts of power. Shaylee helped Serena get her son and wrap him up, placing her sword Long Leaf inside the wrapping as Serena grew concerned about her motives, "What are you doing, Shay?"

But Shaylee continued, and then looked at her half-sister, and whispered, "I will love you, my sweet sister, until the end of time. Now go."

As Shaylee planted a kiss on her forehead, her tears fell onto Serena's son. She lifted her crystal out as Serena screamed "No!" over, and over. Soon a blue vortex opened and Shaylee whispered, "Go to your Eric in the woods. I love you."

Serena was falling deeper into the vortex in slow motion, when she saw Viltzin stand up, grab Shaylee's head as she watched Serena go, and push Howling Tooth into the right side of her back, poking the blade all the way through. Serena screamed out as she moved farther and farther away, while the long blade was retracted and entered Shaylee's body again, this time in the upper shoulder of her left side. The last thing Serena saw was Shaylee reaching out to her as she fell to the floor, with Viltzin staring at Serena with a horrific smile. Then she was gone.

Shaylee was out cold as Viltzin watched the vortex close, not realizing an outsider had barged through and witnessed the act. Rasarlin picked up the dark lord's blade with disgust and while Viltzin continued smiling his snarly smile, Rasarlin swung hard and took his head from his body.

He watched the hideous creature fall to the floor next to the dying Shaylee. The vile creature shook and vibrated, and his head was still letting out a horrendous screeching noise. Then the body lifted into the air along with the head as the Zeytar inside started rising out of its now useless host. Higher the lights of the Zeytar rose until Felvora turned, re-aimed her staff, taking it away from the dark lord for just a moment, and blasted the Zeytar essence into sparkles and embers, which fell to the floor and faded to ethereal dust before their eyes.

Faiay'aar and Kalandrya had not noticed this, as they were focused on watching the dark lord slowly age from their power. The castle was rocking very hard and the thunderstorms were in full violent force because of the energy that had been cutting the fibers of the realm all night. The spell had succeeded, as the castle started to crumble, but the work had not yet finished. Although the mist was growing and following the dark ones across the castle and out into the forest, it had still not reached the dark lord, as the Tuatha power was too strong.

The three dryads knew the treasures' potential, but they all wanted their piece of the monster, so he would never return. Faiay'aar stopped briefly and then took the fourth Tuatha treasure in her hands. Knowing the outcome, she turned and looked at the others. With a full blast from all four stones the dark lord let out a howling cry and was obliterated into microscopic dust.

But the force of having two treasures at once in concentrated form was far too much, and the blast forced Faiay'aar back hard against the wall, burning her so badly she was charred from head to toe. Felvora and Kalandrya had had no time to stop her as they screamed her name and raced over to help her.

"Here, Flora, take my pouch. It is healing dust and potions."

As Kalandrya handed Felvora the pouch, Faiay'aar lifted her severely burned arm, grabbed Felvora, and whispered with her final few strained breaths, "It's OK, I will be with my sylphs in the forest. I have loved you all and ..."

Both the dryads looked at each other in shock as they shed tears, all while the castle shook and the walls and bricks crashed down. They looked around the room but couldn't find Shaylee or Serena and her child, only Howling Tooth, all bloody and dusty. Van Coinan was lying still, along with a mess of black dust. The blue swirly mist had taken over much of the castle as the two dryads picked themselves up and started heading for the door to safety.

As Felvora turned for one last look, she noticed movement underneath one of the dark faeries' body. Returning quickly to see, she noticed Grilif trying to push it off him. She lowered her head down, and with a little smirk, though with watery eyes, she quipped, "Do you need a hand, my friend?"

Grilif let out an angry groan as bricks and shelves continued moving and falling around them. As she lifted the gnome up and out of the distress he was under, Kalandrya poked her head around the doorway and yelled, "Come on, Flora, let's go!"

At the same time Van Coinan, now back in pooka form, turned his head and tried to move. Felvora picked him up without saying anything, and ran for the door. As both dryads turned to mist, Vaelenflixx flew out of the doorway and followed them out into the darkness of the hall.

The spell had worked, destroying all the evil. As they made it out of the castle and onto land, they met up with some other survivors. They all witnessed the castle crumble from the air and onto the ground, while the surrounding forest started to spring to life.

Felvora smiled as she turned to Kalandrya. "We have sacrificed much this day for our people but look at what we have. There will never be darkness upon the lands again. We will start over and rebuild our peaceful world."

Kalandrya, emotional because of the many losses, looked behind her at the bourgeoning wildlife and colors, while thinking deeply about the sacrifices so many brave ones had made. She turned a little farther around and saw thousands of her kin, survivors of the war, standing among the vast foliage and trees, talking and comforting each other.

Pixies, gnomes, woodland elves, sprites, wisps, and all the wonderful creatures she called friends and companions, smiled and danced as they celebrated the fall of the darkness. It had been so long since they could breathe deeply.

Kalandrya turned back, wiping away a small tear as two merrow rose from the ocean and headed their way.

"We are so glad you are alive, Felvora. Where are the other three?"

Felvora pointed behind her to where Vaelenflixx hovered around Grilif and Darf, and all were laughing and smiling. How Darf escaped was still a mystery to her, but they were safe.

Telgran smiled and answered in his gurgled tone, "I wasn't sure if you survived. After we left you underneath the castle, we weren't sure if you made it. We had to leave because the storms were too much. We are sorry we couldn't do more."

Felvora moved forward, placed her hand on his soft, spiky shoulder, gently so as not to pierce her green skin, and whispered, "I will owe you forever. For saving us, then bringing us here in time for the war—I cannot thank you enough. Your part in this was just as important."

Telgran smiled, placed his webbed hand on Felvora's shoulder and whispered, "You have all saved us with your selfless actions. We can remember our loved ones and nurture those remaining."

Before long, without saying another word, he turned and placed his webbed hand behind Nelarvas' back. They slowly walked to the edge of the stairs of the grounded part of the castle and dove from the high cliff face into the water, heading back to their island.

Felvora turned to Kalandrya and said, "Well, I suppose we head home," as she sprinkled some green powder over Van Coinan's foot. He hadn't been injured, just stubbed his foot and fell over, then had a sleep in the middle of the battle. He hopped to his toes, and just as they were about to begin their journey home, they heard the same roar as before when they were inside the castle.

Looking up to the top of the remaining crumbling part of the castle, which was surrounded by some blue mist, they saw movement, and then another roar.

~

After hearing the horn, Rasarlin and Vaximardruusz moved toward the castle, knowing something was happening and innocents were in trouble. As they saw the devastation firsthand, they didn't want whatever was overrunning this land to take hold; besides, Rasarlin and his partner had been to a lot of worlds, seen a lot of darkness, and witnessed too many innocent lives fall. If they could help while they were there, they would, and anyway, they both had a thing for fighting.

Vax flew high and swiftly, following the noise, avoiding the lightning, and heading for the colors blasting from the castle. The wyvern landed on the roof of the castle which reminded them both of some dark lands from their world. Rasarlin slid off and found holes in the tower big enough to climb through, while Vaximardruusz roared to scare the evil inside. Rasarlin had three arrows left in his quiver, so went for his blade. He took it out and descended a level to where the commotion was coming from.

Immediately he faced grotesque creatures trying to kill him. He cut them down one by one, sometimes two at a time, with his swift and strong fighting style. Farther and farther he delved, slicing and cutting hard as he made it to the entrance of the room where it was all happening. That's when he saw a perfectly innocent being get cut down. With his anger rising, he worked out very quickly who the evil ones were and who were the innocents. Fully focused only on her, he entered the room, and as the sword was pulled out from the winged one the second time, he looked around, picked up a large sword from the ground, and quickly ended the dark creature's life.

As the green mist hit Viltzin's essence, Rasarlin leaned down to see if the beautiful-looking winged female was OK. He could hear her moaning as he checked her over, and tried to apply pressure, but couldn't stop the bleeding. He ripped some fabric from another strange winged creature lying next to him that was far uglier and twisted, before wrapping both wounds tight.

He had little time and if she stayed there, she would surely die. So he took her in his arms, and moved very quickly, trying to avoid goblins and other foul things, slicing them down with his new sword. He was out in the hallways before anyone knew he had even been there.

Rasarlin went the way he had come, trying not to trip over the mess he had left earlier, and witnessing mists surrounding the dark creatures and turning them to dust. Knowing he had to get to Vax as quickly as he could, he continued upward toward the tower. When he completed his final ascent, he was met by his friend, who whispered in his mind, *"That was quick. You only rescued one?"*

Rasarlin didn't bother responding to his comment. Instead, he reached into a large satchel tied to the left foot of Vax where he kept all his belongings, including his medicines. He hoped that if he could save this one, he could go back in and save some more, but there was something about this creature that resonated with him, a familiarity that he couldn't quite pinpoint. That's why he got so angry and homed in on her when he witnessed Viltzin's final blow.

Vax had his wing down where Rasarlin had laid her. She was still bleeding heavily so he needed to stop it as soon as he could. He reached in his pack, pulled out some green paste from a wooden box, opened the dressings, then spread it front to back over both wounds, watching it seep in.

He then found some soft powder and covered the dressings with it, before hitting them with a flint and lighting them on fire. Rasarlin then attached the burning garb to the end of his new sword. He waited a moment, took the burning garb off, and then fused all four wound openings with the burning hot sword. She let out a scream with each one, before passing out.

While this was happening, the castle was shaking and crumbling. They didn't have too much time before Vax would have to launch, but he couldn't move her yet.

Rasarlin opened the leftover dressing and split it, covering each wound with just enough material before he sat back and waited. He turned to his companion and whispered, *"I miss my magic. I could use the Marelarph shard, but it may thrust us out too early, so it's up to her now."*

They waited for as long as they could, witnessing the surrounding land change from a dark, horrific place to beautiful colorful scenery. As time moved forward, and the sun started climbing, the pair could not sustain their position any longer and had to take the chance and move the lady with wings.

Rasarlin placed Shaylee in between some rigid follicles on the middle part of Vaximardruusz's back, securing her with some rope from his pouch. The wyvern gave an almighty roar and started ascending high into the air.

≈

Felvora and Kalandrya, along with the rest of the Fae, looked high into the sky. Witnessing such a strange creature reminded them of similar beasts long forgotten and only existing in stories from an age past. The creature disappeared into the blue mist still floating through the land. In the next moment the castle exploded, throwing shards and debris for hundreds of miles. As the Fae took cover, the sky began exploding, opening up as if the skin of the world was shedding to reveal another sky.

As the swirls of lightning and thunder took hold, whatever it was kept unwrapping, closer and closer, until the morning was now night again and the trees disappeared all around them, revealing different landmarks. The mountain they were on seemed higher as the forest faded away, and they were now overlooking a green countryside with fences and strange metal machines.

Felvora turned to Kalandrya, took the arm she was shielding herself with away from her face, and as they lay where they had dropped to the ground to avoid the debris, she whispered, "I don't think we are in Faelynn anymore."

EPILOGUE

VAXIMARDRUUSZ CLIMBED HIGHER INTO THE AIR, trying to get some height so he could see a better place to land. As they moved up into the blue misty clouds, a great noise hit them and the mists faded, and they were met with not a morning but a dusk. Rasarlin fell from his ride as they entered the new strange place, thankful the mountain terrain now had some soft hay to break his fall with.

Thinking the time trap had sucked them back through far too quickly this time, he pulled out his sword, held it high into the air, and shouted, *"When will you send us home?"*

Rasarlin looked at the dull Marelarph shard on his chest while he lowered his sword, and then watched Vaximardruusz loop over and fly across the fields, roaring from the same frustration his friend had. As the beast turned back, he witnessed the last of the glow from the sun before it became completely dark and the moon turned to blood.

Rasarlin stood, awaiting his wyvern's return. Shaylee would not have come through if it was the shard that caused this. Vax landed with a thump and Rasarlin climbed swiftly onto the magnificent creature's back, with the ease of someone who knew every scale and every nook. He was, after all, the last of the Taarlin Knights from his world, so that skill set came with the territory.

He rushed over to where Shaylee had been but couldn't see her. Without panicking, he retraced their steps and deducted that in the heat of panic Vax had tightened his defenses and as a result buried her underneath his soft but firm follicles.

"Just relax, Vax. You're tightening too much. Loosen up your back a little."

Vax knew immediately what Rasarlin meant and opened the follicles on his back. In a way they had protected her from harm, so it wasn't a bad thing, but she was not in a good way at all.

Rasarlin, with the help of Vax, slipped her onto his wing. She was still unconscious and looked far too pale to be healthy. Meanwhile, there were more blasts in the sky and all around them. As Rasarlin looked across the countryside, he could see trees growing up, mountains crumbling away, and figures appearing from nowhere. It was something he had never seen before, ever. Dark magic was at play, he thought, as he heard some strange voices near him. When he looked over, he saw dozens of fresh arrivals, as more landmarks changed around them.

The talking become louder, but the language was still strange. Normally the Marelarph shard would manipulate his foreign speech to the new world's language so he could understand it, but it needed some time to gather source information. Looking behind him he saw the new arrivals coming closer to see the giant beast, but then suddenly Shaylee let out a scream, "Serena!" before fading out once more.

Some arrivals close by heard it and came running over. Felvora pushed Rasarlin aside as Kalandrya held a knife to his throat, which caught the attention of Vax who gave a loud snort and groan in response. Knowing they must have been friends and not wanting to get in the way, he put his arms up and stood back as Felvora took Shaylee's head into her hands and began checking her wounds. As barbaric as the dressings were to a healer, she nodded to him for his attempts and for saving her life. She then pulled out her potions and healing powders from her satchel, forgetting they were standing on a wyvern's wing.

Shaylee tossed and turned while Rasarlin observed the ever-changing landscape. Then Kalandrya whispered, "Flora, this is the old world where the humans dwell. I've seen it before. The air is heavy and gravity is dense, I can feel it in my bones."

Felvora replied straightaway, "But how can that be when the remains of the dark castle stairs are just there, and in the far distance I can see the Tuatha Dé Danann Monolith exactly where it should stand next to the Aurora Forest which is miles and miles away?"

They turned and looked back at each other as Felvora's color started to fade to a pale green instead of her usual glow. "What kind of dark magic did we unleash? We have combined the realms into a paradox, this is Faelynn, but it is also the human realm," she said.

Kalandrya looked up at the wyvern, over at the stranger, then back to Felvora, before whispering, "What have we done?"

GLOSSARY

Aethelwyne (*Ay-thel-wine*): The house name of the ruler of Faelynn.

Alicorn: The horn of a unicorn that holds power.

Alvantaar (*Al-vant-ar*): The merrow that washed up on shore and was taken by the shadow-clothed humans.

Alvina Whittleleaf (*Al-vine-ah*): A pixie from Maelenflitt.

Aurora Forest: The biggest forest in all Faelynn with an abundance of different life.

Baldaar (*Bald-ar*): A three-horned half tiger, half humanoid faery, husband to Faleesa.

basilisk dragons: Long extinct dragon snakes in the times of the Tuatha Dé Danann.

brownie: Mischievous faery who likes to steal trinkets.

Brumlemd (*Brum-lem-ed*): Grilif's father.

Chaxinn (*Chacks-in*): Young woodland elf boy.

Daarr: A dark Elvenfae guard from Xarkynan.

Darf: A gnome from Aurora.

dark elf/dark Elvenfae: Twisted and evil Elvenfae, turned by the dark lord to aid in his war against the Fae.

Darlygah Frostdrop: Former Elvenfae warrior guard/best friend to King Aethelwyne and current blacksmith for the palace.

Darphanin (*Darf-an-in*): The leader of the woodland elf warriors and prince of the woodland realm.

Draconian (*Drack-oh-nean*): Race of creatures from another planet fighting the Zeytars.

Dralixx (*Dral-icks*): A furious troll who killed Grilif's parents.

dread collectors: Dark witches send them out to find potions made from Fae.

dryad: A powerful nature mage, usually benevolent although protective of their people.

dullahan: A dark creature with no head, on a horse, that uses bones for its whip.

Edge Willows: Section of willows that line up in Aurora, creating a force field, protecting Vylass from evil.

Elvenfae: Full form of the sprites in the palace of Faelynn, extraordinarily strong but kind protectors of the land of the Fae.

Faelar Forest paths (*Fay-lar*): A path from Aurora meeting up with the city of Faelynn palace.

Faelondar (*Fay-lon-dar*): The head of the high council in the palace.

Faelynn (*Fay-lin*): The lands and realms of all the Fae/faery folk.

Faiay'aar (*Fay-i-ar*): Powerful dryad from Maelenflitt.

Faleesa (*Fa-lisa*): Wife of Baldaar and with child.

far darrig: A far darrig is a gnome-like creature, bent on tricking humans, who often wears a red cap with red clothing. They have very quick and spiteful tongues.

Fayetta Honeyleaf: A pixie from Aurora.

Feelik (*Fee-lick*): A trusted Elvenfae guard of the palace.

Felvora: Forest dryad mage living in the Aurora Forest who assisted in the dark war.

Fladinn: A dark Elvenfae guard from Xarkynan.

Flithiin: An Elvenfae guard of the palace.

flittinberry: A root from the flittinberry tree in Faelar, crushed as a spice and used as a sedative by mages.

Forland Rooms: A room where the council meetings are held in the southern halls of the palace.

full cycle: The moon as it passes all its phases. From full moon to full moon is a full cycle. It is used in reference to time.

Gaelenthark Quartermoon (*Gay-len-thark*): A benevolent Fae from the far darrig clan and human hater.

giants: Private folk from the far reaches of Toozookus.

Glabbish: A gnome near the under folk.

Glinoxx: Assistant goblin to the dark necro-mage.

gloffen: A large creature on Rasarlin's home world that wyverns like to eat.

gnome: Small, tough Fae that reside in the deep forests.

golloff elf: They are the size of gnomes but are far slenderer and are honest, hard workers.

gralik snails: A slimy, green-shelled slug, a little larger than normal snails.

Great Wisdom: A very ancient oak in Toozookus.

grilchin oil: A smelly oil made from the grilchin bug, alleged to help with muscular aches or other non-serious ailments.

Grilif: A strong and angry gnome from Aurora.

half cycle: The moon only halfway into completing its phase, it could be at full, half three-quarters or even a quarter, depending how the cycle is described and what time of transition it is in. It is used in reference to time.

hobgoblin: Mischievous creature and thief.

Howling Tooth: The name of Shaylee Aethelwyne's sword.

Japhony (*Jaff-oni*): A woodland elf and brother to Kapheeny.

Jestica Hornmyst (*Jess-tick-a Horn-mist*): Silk maiden to the queen of Faelynn.

Kalandrya (*Kal-anne-drea*): Dryad mage and queen of the far lands of Toozookus.

Kaldarik: A forest near Aurora where the trees grow fur and silk on the bark which is used to make clothes and some satchels.

Kapheeny (*Kaff-eeni*): A woodland elf and sister to Japhony.

leprechauns: Mischievous, selfish gnomes that live on the near islands of Toozookus. A very private clan that mostly dwell in the human realms, hiding their trinkets and gold.

Long Leaf: Serena O'Halloran's enchanted sword, which holds a very powerful secret.

Maalik Nightingstar (*Mar-lick*): A young Elvenfae guard of the palace.

Maelenflitt (*May-len-flit*): One of the main realms in Faelynn.

Malarviar: Woodland elf and sister to Darphanin.

Maliin: A rock troll in Xarkynan.

Maraenor (*Mar-ay-nor*): Shaylee's longest serving maiden and most trusted friend.

Marelarph (*Merrel-arf*): An extremely powerful dark purple crystal shard attached to Rasarlin.

Markendaar: A woodland elf warrior.

Marlifyn Strongholm (*Marly-finn*): Very tall Elvenfae
 warrior/guard and expert sword instructor.

Melex: A gnome with Darf and Grilif.

Mella: A sprite from Aurora.

merrow: A half man/woman and half fish.

Mileana (*Mill-ay-na*): One of many Fae servants in the palace of the
 Elvenfae.

Milfin Dugglebox: A sprite from Aurora.

milvaark: Tiny six-legged spider.

molar rock: Lava rocks that spew from the pits in Xarkynan's fire
 lake.

Moorelton the Wise (*Moore-el-ton*): A woodland elf mercenary
 from long ago paid to clean up the dark ones that leaked
 into the enchanted lands of Faelynn.

Moxxil (*Mock-sil*): Dark goblin in the dark lord's castle.

multhrai moth: An exceptionally large moth from Aurora and
 Maelenflitt, known for its ever-changing color and size.

muttlebark: A strong herb designed to relieve pain and put victim to
 sleep.

necro-mage: A powerful, twisted magister, master of the art of dark
 magic.

Neiphlax (*Ny-flax*): Dark Elvenfae warrior.

Nelarvas (*Nell-arv-ass*): Female merrow who saved Felvora and
 friends.

Nimaalah (*Nim-ah-la*): Woodland elf warrior.

Nixxin: King Aethelwyne's horse.

nochkz (*nocks*): Exceptionally large trees that protect the outer forests of Xarkynan.

the noorion marker: Truth detector used in the palace in extreme cases.

oaken nochkz: Benevolent oak trees from Maelenflitt that can move and fight if needed, not to be confused with the nochkz of Xarkynan.

Oakslarren: A small tavern at the edges of the town near the palace.

Paargus (*Par-juss*): Grilif's mother.

Palex (*Pay-lex*): Place in Aurora near the toadstool caverns.

pandaron: A large and dangerous pig with horns.

Pharnanin (*Far-nan-in*): A woodland elf elder.

pixie: A small male or female faery, around two and a half feet high, in all the light forests.

pooka: Large rabbit-like creature with a dangerous defense and abilities to talk and shape-shift.

quarter cycle: The moon is only in its first quarter of its phase. It could be at a quarter, half, three-quarters or full depending on where its phase is and how it's described. It is used in reference to time.

Rasarlin Ivelark (*Ras-ar-lin Iv-eh-lark*): A markyyn elf from another realm, tossed around the cosmos forever by the time trap of Seckpar.

saprock: A black tar-like sap that leaks from the weeping oaks attached to the castle of Xarkynan and used by goblins to make blade handles among other things.

Sarphonel (*Sarf-oh-nel*): Leader of the high woodland elf council.

Sasquatch: The beasts controlling the sprites once captured by the Zeytars.

scroot bats: Large four-winged bats that dwell in the dark woods of Xarkynan.

Seelie Court: The court of the good and peaceful faery folk of Faelynn.

selkies: Rare seal creatures who shed their skin when they come onto dry land.

Severed Wing: The name of Varzunnos' large broadsword.

Shaylee Aethelwyne: Elvenfae princess of Faelynn.

Sheeleymoon Lake (*Shee-lee*): Lake in Maelenflitt.

shrooms: Large mushrooms that glow in dark places.

Sidhe (*She*): Faery mounds where the Fae enter Earth realm.

Skaltzing path (*Scall-zing*): An old path close to Aurora.

sloop birds: When a Fae is born outside of Faelynn in the human realm, sloop birds are often seen flying in large groups.

spriggan: A dangerous and mischievous gnome-like creature bent on mayhem.

sprite: The small faery form of all winged faeries in Faelynn.

Stalixus Aethelwyne: Daughter of the king and half-sister to Shaylee and Serena.

Stella Rosegum: A sprite from the Aurora Forest and daughter to Queen Villara.

Stexinzar Crimsonmoon: Leader of the Elvenfae guards and number one warrior.

Stixx: A sprite from the Aurora Forest.

Swirling Splinter: Stexinzar's sword.

sylphs: Mystical faeries highly skilled in natural enchantment and protectors of the four Tuatha Dé Danann treasures.

Szelidus (*Zel-e-duss*): An evil sorcerer from another realm tossed around the cosmos by the time trap of Seckpar.

Taarlin Knights (*Tarlin*): A well-trained group of warriors and dragon keepers from Rasarlin's world, bound to a wyvern to protect the last dragons.

tarnaak (*tar-nack*): A creature born from the dark sap and wood of the oaks and elms in the dark forest.

Telgran: Male merrow who saved Felvora and her friends.

Tianna Aethelwyne (*Tee-ah-na*): Queen of all the realms of Faelynn.

Toozookus: One of the main realms in Faelynn.

Torc: A bracelet the dark lord Varzunnos wore with the emerald gem from Toozookus, used to control creatures.

Tuatha Dé Danann: The original people of Faelynn who escaped from the old lands and set up the four elemental treasure stones, giving enchantment to Faelynn.

unicorn: Mystical and powerful equine creature, only in Faelynn.

Unseelie Court: The court for the evil and vile throughout Xarkynan and hidden ones of Faelynn.

Vaargix Drop (*Var-gicks*): High point of the palace where sprites learn to fly, or for punishment.

Vaelenflixx Leafenvein (*Vay-len-flix*): A benevolent jittery sprite captured by goblins, who escapes, only to help Felvora.

Valixx: Dark goblin in the dark lord's castle.

vambraces: Wrist and arm armor.

Van Coinan (*Van-Coy-nan*): A cheeky pooka that has the form of a rabbit who can talk and shape-shift.

Varzunnos (*Var-zoo-noss*): The dark lord of Xarkynan.

Vaximardruusz (*Vax-ee-mar-drooz*): A wyvern from another realm, tossed around the cosmos forever by the time trap of Seckpar and accompanied by his rider Rasarlin Ivelark.

Viddiar Zill (*Vid-e-ar*): Pooka in Maelenflitt.

Villara: Queen of the sprites inside the magnificent tree of Aurora.

Viltherome Aethelwyne (*Vil-ther-rome*): The king of Faelynn.

Viltzin'un'dandaar (*Vilt-zin-un-dan-dar*): Dark necro-mage and assistant to the dark lord Varzunnos.

Vylass: Enormous tree in Aurora where the queen of the Aurora sprites dwells.

Vyyuna Majestixx (*Vi-yuna*): The last known unicorn in all Faelynn.

wisps: Tiny sprites who reside in the willows of Aurora and protect the unicorns.

witchin goblin: The most powerful of all the goblins, casting spells and illusions.

woodland elves: Race of peaceful warriors living in cities in the trees of Toozookus.

wraiths: Dark spirits of Xarkynan, usually work for dark witches.

Wyrm (*Worm*): The name of the Elvenfae spy.

Xack'Xax (*Zack-zax*): A very nasty hobgoblin from Aurora Forest.

Xarkynan (*Zark-in-an*): The dark lands, created by the dark lord Varzunnos after being banished and where all the evil resides in the Faelynn realm.

Zeexalin (*Zeek-zalin*): Woodland elf warrior.

Zeytar (*Zay-tar*): Race of insidious inter-dimensional gray aliens taking faeries for their evil purposes.

COMING SOON *FIRESTORM*

ABOUT THE AUTHOR

Troy M. Williams has researched and investigated all the different facets of the paranormal over many years, and is fascinated by deep folklore, sci-fi, fantasy, and horror. He writes about the fringes of all things strange, with elements of truth in some, and his stories have readers hooked from the very start.

Troy has many interests including comics, memorabilia, movie collectables, and coaching his kids in Taekwondo.

But it is writing, researching, and world building that keep his mind busy and have done so from an early age. His strong understanding of the paranormal and other subjects he is drawn to continues to feed his creative mind.

Fable is his second book, the sequel to his first book, *Shrill*, with many more to come.

www.ingramcontent.com/pod-product-compliance
Lightning Source LLC
Chambersburg PA
CBHW032233010726
47494CB00002B/476

9 780648 966432